I0576673

Randell Hunt, William Henry Hunt

Selected arguments, lectures and miscellaneous papers of Randell

Hunt

Randell Hunt, William Henry Hunt

Selected arguments, lectures and miscellaneous papers of Randell Hunt

ISBN/EAN: 9783337278540

Printed in Europe, USA, Canada, Australia, Japan

Cover: Foto ©Andreas Hilbeck / pixelio.de

More available books at **www.hansebooks.com**

SELECTED ARGUMENTS
LECTURES AND MISCELLANEOUS
PAPERS OF

RANDELL HUNT

EDITED BY HIS NEPHEW

WILLIAM HENRY HUNT

ASSOCIATE JUSTICE OF THE SUPREME COURT OF MONTANA

F. F. HANSELL & BROTHER
NEW ORLEANS, LA.
1896

CONTENTS.

BIOGRAPHICAL SKETCH.

For just half a century, from 1832 to 1882, the name of Randell Hunt was identified with many of the chief events in the history of the Southern States of this country.

He was conspicuous in the Unionist convention which considered the ordinance of nullification in South Carolina; he was a constitutional lawyer of reputation and of profound learning; he was a professor of law in the University of Louisiana for about forty years, and for a long time its president; he was a leader of the state senators in the legislature of his State; he took a prominent part in seeking to preserve the Union in gloomy days when secession was gaining ground in the South; he was an orator whose voice rose in eloquent and fearless appeals for the safety of the nation when civil war seemed imminent; he was for over twenty-five years, as Chief Justice Chase pronounced him, the "king of the bar of Louisiana:" yet, aside from mere newspaper accounts, no memoir of his life has been written. Certainly the influence of such a man has formed an important part of the history of the States in which he lived, and a brief account of his political and professional deeds, and of the virtues of a career which is so indelibly identified with the progress of his time, may be accepted as a well-meant contribution to the biographical records of our country.

Thomas Hunt, the father of Randell, was born at Nassau, in the West India Islands. His father, Robert Hunt, was a native of England, and was colonial governor of the Bahama Islands, and president of the King's Council at Nassau, in the island of New Providence. Thomas Hunt was a graduate of the University of Edinburgh, Scotland, and, when a young man of about twenty-one years, emigrated from the Bahamas. He was a scholar and a generous gentleman. He left the fortunes and prospects of an ancient English family to repair to Charleston, South Carolina, and settled there because he preferred the larger liberty established under the Constitution and laws of the United States to the monarchical institutions of Great Britain. He was of commanding presence, distinguished ancestry, and powerful moral character. There was a custom of his days in the South, following the aristocratic tendencies of ante-Revolution people, to acquire landed estates upon which the family home was established, and Mr. Hunt, like other gentlemen of the times, bought a plantation, Woodville, on the Wando River, a branch of the Cooper, about thirty miles from the city of Charleston. He soon renounced his allegiance to the king of England, and became an American planter and lawyer, having studied law in the office of Mr. John J. Pringle.

Randell Hunt's mother was the daughter of John Gaillard and Judith Peyre, both descendants of the Huguenots who went to Charleston about the year 1687. While visiting abroad, Louisa, their daughter, was born in the British Channel, close to the shores of France. Two of her brothers, John and Theodore Gaillard, were for a long time in the public service of South Carolina : the former as a United States senator for over twenty-one years, and president *pro tem.* for fourteen years ; the latter as an associate judge of the Court of Common Pleas up to his death in 1829.[1]

Louisa Gaillard and Thomas Hunt, having become acquainted in the then famous society of Charleston, were married January 1, 1805, and lived to have twelve children born to them, of whom Randell Hunt was the second, the date of his birth being December 31, 1806.

The schoolboy days of Randell were passed under the tuition of the best instructors in the city of Charleston until he became old enough to attend Bishop England's [2] academy in that city.

The family used to pass the Easter holiday season on the plantation, and the departure of Randell for a " big man's school " greatly impressed the slaves. The mode of travel between the plantation and Charleston was entirely by boat, manned by six stalwart negroes, who thought it no small honor to row the young man from his home to the city. The negroes generally sang as they rowed the boat, and the sweet refrain of an improvised melody, "Massa Randell is going to a ' big man's school,' " echoed in the forest as they moved along the picturesque shores of the Wando.

Randell is described as a clear-complexioned boy, with

[1] Benton, in his *Thirty Years' View*, has dwelt on the character of Mr. Gaillard as that of a wise and public-spirited senator. His brother, Judge Gaillard, was a scholar and a wit as well as a learned magistrate. Another kinsman, Dominick Augustin Hall, went to live in Louisiana, where he became the first district judge of the United States. It was by his order that General Jackson, then hero of the battle of New Orleans, was fined for invasion of the privilege of the writ of *habeas corpus*. Judge Martin, in his *History of Louisiana*, treats with deserved respect the character of Judge Hall. Judge Hall was appointed in 1813. He was not to be intimidated, and bore himself with stern judicial impartiality.

[2] Bishop England was Roman Catholic Bishop of Charleston, and, until the appointment of Cardinal McCloskey, perhaps the most distinguished of the prelates of his church in America.

expressive gray eyes, brown hair, a large mouth, and a head of noticeable height above the ears. He was not tall, nor was he at all handsome ; but his countenance was pleasing, his face intellectual, his expression thoughtful, and his manner particularly gentle. The teachers at Bishop England's school were surprised by his great industry, and impressed by his extraordinary love of reading. He devoured every book within his reach, and remembered what he read. This wonderful taste for reading, however, did not prevent a genuine love of sport in him. Indeed, he was very fond of fishing and hunting, being a keen and successful sportsman and a remarkably fine wing-shot. He would tramp miles and miles while looking for game, but when he rested it was his invariable habit to take from his pocket a book and intently read it.

In 1821 he graduated first in his class from Bishop England's academy, and entered the College of South Carolina, at Columbia, an institution then boasting a well - acquired reputation as a seat of learning. Dr. Thomas Cooper, the scholar, author, and political economist, was president of the college at that time.

The graduates of the class of 1825 included several men who attained national distinction. Among the first five of the class were Stephen Elliott and James A. Hammond. The former became professor of the evidences of Christianity and sacred literature in the College of South Carolina, a doctor of divinity, and a widely admired pulpit orator : he was made Protestant Episcopal Bishop of Georgia. Hammond, at the time when he appeared in college, was of surprising personal beauty. The exalted honor — for such it was accorded in his day — of being governor of the high-spirited and aspiring State of South Carolina, the haughty temper of which was like that of some independent republic, fell to him in the

period of early manhood.[1] After a subsequent retirement
of years he reappeared in the stormy period of the slavery
agitation as senator in Congress. To Hammond is properly to be ascribed the origin of the word "mudsills" as
applied to a portion of the people of the North whom he
likened to the slaves of the South. The speech using the
term was made upon the bill for the admission of Kansas
to the Union.

When the honors of college were distributed, Randell
Hunt received the first. Some action of the authorities
had changed the usual mode of assigning college honors.
Instead of giving the highest to the student of average
excellence in the general, it was determined to report the
standing and scholarship of graduates in each department separately. The result was that Randell Hunt was
awarded the first place in every one of his studies. A
letter from Dr. Cooper bore the intelligence to his father,
and filled his heart with purest happiness. To accomplish
such a feat, Randell had made it his devoted practice to
spend twelve hours out of every twenty-four in study.

As a student of the classics and history, his reading had
made him conspicuous for his knowledge and cultivation.
His memory had become a prodigious one, nor was he
without success already as a public speaker; and his professors sent him back to Charleston to do honor to his
Alma Mater in a career predicted to be full of promise.

The profession of the law very naturally attracted him,
and he entered the office of Mr. William Lance, a leader
of the bar of Charleston. With the close habits of study
which he pursued, and his superior education upon which
to found a legal education, Mr. Hunt was readily admitted to practice in the year 1828.[2]

---

[1] From 1842 to 1841.

[2] Mr. Boozee, the clerk of the Supreme Court of South Carolina,
writes that the roll upon which Mr. Hunt's name, together with the

Of his first appearance in presenting a case at the bar
of South Carolina little can be ascertained : but that he
soon became prominent is evidenced by the newspapers, in
1833, reporting in full, with editorial comment, his argument upon the right of a state court to require a sworn
allegiance to the State before admitting an alien to become a citizen of the United States. The speech of Mr.
Hunt (published among his other writings) might well
be quoted by any court, and is an exhaustive review of
the powers of the state courts under the federal laws of
naturalization. No lawyer of twenty-seven years of age
could have delivered so comprehensive and logical an
argument upon such a broad question unless possessed of
close reasoning powers, with a mind capable and trained
in methods of thought and study.

Wending his way homeward one night, about this
time, Mr. Thomas Hunt, attracted by the crowd which
thronged at a late hour of the night one of the city
court-houses of Charleston, made his way into it. The
scene was an animated one. The court was sitting.
The hall where the session was held was ablaze with
light. The multitude, and the judges themselves, hung
upon the glowing words of a young but eloquent speaker,
who held them entranced, and in whom Mr. Hunt soon
recognized his son Randell, already a man of distinction.
He paused, and then stood delighted. At last, overcome
by the emotions natural to such a situation, there, in the
presence of the spectators, he added to the triumph of
his son in the tears of a father's joy, a tribute which, according to the constitution of man's being, surpasses all
others that can be rendered.

But Mr. Hunt was destined to enter the political field,

exact date of his admission, appeared, was destroyed during the war.
The date is given by O'Neall's *Bench and Bar of South Carolina* as
1828.

and to fervently espouse the national cause, the insepara-
bility of the States of the Union from the Union itself.

South Carolina was agitated profoundly by the tariff
law of 1828, which was affecting the planting States so
visibly that the menacing doctrine of a nullification
movement was gaining ground. John C. Calhoun led the
opposition to the protective system of the law of 1828,
and kept alive the disposition to disregard the federal
laws of impost duties. Andrew Jackson, then President,
was not in opposition to a protective system. In 1831
Calhoun issued his famous " Address to the People of the
State of South Carolina," announcing the Constitution to
be a mere compact between sovereign States; that the general government is the mere agent between those sovereign
States; that whenever any one of the parties to the compact, any State, considers any law made by the general
government to be unconstitutional, it may " nullify " that
law, or declare and treat it as void. Calhoun again, in
1832, issued an address embodying the doctrine of state
rights, and advising issue to be taken on account of the
sufferings of the South.

The legislature of South Carolina was convened, and
by it a convention ordered to assemble on November 19,
1832, " to consider the character and extent of the usur-
pations of the general government."

Political excitement was general throughout the nation
and at fever heat in the State of South Carolina, where
the struggle of the Unionists, which had been a hard one
for several years, was about drawing to its close. The
nullifiers were in a large majority. They made inflamed
speeches, denounced the opposition in violent terms, and
organized defiantly. They wore palmetto cockades, like
the Southern secessionists just before the war of the
Rebellion. They looked forward to war, and measures
to precipitate it were set on foot. For a Union speech

made at this season at a meeting held in a church building, Randell Hunt was placarded and threatened to be hanged. But he and his brothers adhered unwaveringly to the cause of the country.

It is not material to recite the history of the passage of the ordinance of nullification, nor of the excitement prevalent generally during the year 1832. The student of the history of those times will find an abundant opportunity for research into a field full of the most interesting events, and he will be impressed with the powerful influence wielded by the orators and writers who were conspicuous in the movements of the times. But the Unionists were determined to express a last dissent from the action of the opposition, and a state convention, with representatives from all parts of South Carolina, met just after the nullification convention to record the sentiments of the Union party. Randell Hunt was a prominent figure in the assembly, and epitomized the views of the convention, and the questions it should consider, in three sentences : —

" That the Union party acknowledges no allegiance to any government except that of the United States."

" That in referring this resolution to the general committee, they be instructed to inquire whether it is not expedient to give a military organization to the Union party throughout the State."

" Whether it will not be necessary to call in the assistance of the general government for maintaining the laws of the United States against the arbitrary violence which is threatened by the late convention."

The work of the convention is well expressed by the following terse summary of its acts : [1] —

[1] From a paper by Mr. Gaillard Hunt entitled " South Carolina and Nullification," published in the *Political Science Quarterly* for June, 1891.

" The resolutions which were adopted declared that the ordinance of nullification violated the Constitution of the United States, and had virtually destroyed the Union, since, by preventing the general government from enforcing its laws within the boundaries of the State, it made the State a sovereignty paramount to the United States. They denounced the provisions of the ordinance as tyrannical and oppressive, and the test oath as especially incompatible with civil liberty, in that it disfranchised nearly half the citizens of the State. They pointed scornfully to the project of a standing army in the State. Such an army must necessarily be inadequate to protect the nullification party from the coercive power of the United States; its only object, therefore, must be to tyrannize over Carolina Unionists. They concluded by declaring the continued opposition of the signers to the tariff, and their determination to protect themselves against intolerable oppression. The resolutions were signed by all the members of the convention, about one hundred and eighty in number."

The difficulty was, however, that the sentiment of the people was adverse to the resolutions. Mr. Hunt was troubled by the dissensions dividing the people, and the future seemed dark.

To add to his dread, as a citizen, of the consequences destined to follow the Calhoun policies, there now came to him affliction and trouble in his home : but they only developed the same determination and honor within him towards his family that had been shown towards his State in the late preceding times of her adversity and misguided policy. His father died on December 25, 1830, leaving a widow and twelve children.

Just before Mr. Thomas Hunt's death some reverses in fortune befell him, so that when the lands were sold and the estate's debts paid there was little left for the support of the family.

Charleston did not grow. Political disturbances were likely to continue so long as Mr. Calhoun and his party retained their influence, and to a young man who abhorred the doctrines which were gaining ascendency in the State the prospect was by no means bright. Then, too, to maintain the fashionable style of life to which the family were accustomed, and in which other prominent households of the city of Charleston lived, was impossible. A change of residence was thought best. Theodore Gaillard, also a lawyer, and Thomas, a physician, brothers of Randell, concluded to go to New Orleans, Louisiana, — of all Southern cities, at that date, by far the most promising. The field was a broad one, and Louisiana was justly proud of numbers of professional men unexcelled in learning and reputation. Moreover, the Hunts [1] were

[1] Theodore Gaillard Hunt was a colonel in the Mexican war, and a member of Congress in 1853–51. He was district attorney, a judge of the criminal court in New Orleans, and a colonel in the Confederate army. He died in New Orleans, November 15, 1893.

Dr. Thomas Hunt was long the leading advocate of university education in the State, and was a scholar and an orator and a man of science, as well as a physician and surgeon of consummate skill and at the head of his profession. He was a surgeon of the Charity Hospital. He was the earliest and most active of the founders of the Medical College of Louisiana, and was professor of physiology and pathology and of special pathological anatomy in the medical department, and dean of the medical faculty. He received the appointment, just before his death, to be surgeon of the Marine Hospital, in the service of the United States. He was, when he died, president of the University of Louisiana, now the Tulane University of Louisiana. An heroic service in the interest of humanity, rendered in 1831 to the brig Amida, which was wrecked on Folly Island, the cholera raging among passengers and crew, earned for Dr. Hunt the thanks of the city of Charleston, as "the intrepid physician of Folly Island," and at twenty-four raised him to distinction. Hon. Carleton Hunt, an eminent lawyer of Louisiana, is a son of Dr. Thomas Hunt. Dr. Hunt died March 25, 1867.

One of the younger brothers was William H. He became one of

very willing to turn their backs on Calhoun's policies, and identify themselves with a growing community which would preserve the Union as Daniel Webster and Henry Clay would have it perpetuated.

New England invited those in search of education, and Mrs. Hunt concluded to move to New Haven, Connecticut. The family left Charleston later in the year 1832. Randell went on to New York, intending to practice in that city. The pecuniary circumstances of his mother and the education of the younger members of the family made his responsibilities great. He was unacquainted, and, being without means, the undertaking of establishing himself in the North seemed perilous. His brothers meanwhile urged him to make his home in New Orleans, where the prospects of immediate better circumstances invited him to go. Mr. Hunt was not in a position to run the risk of having to wait for professional success in New York, and a sense of responsibility not to be postponed caused him to adopt Louisiana as his home. From obvious present conditions it is to be regretted that he did not remain in New York, for had he done so his ability and learning would have found the broader scope they were entitled to.

But to New Orleans he went, content with his decision.

---

the leaders of the bar of New Orleans, and was distinguished as a very successful and eloquent advocate. In 1876 he was appointed attorney-general of Louisiana. In 1877 he was made an associate justice of the United States Court of Claims. In 1881 he was appointed Secretary of the Navy by President Garfield. In 1882 he was made minister to Russia by President Arthur. He died at St. Petersburg, Russia, February 28, 1884.

Copeland, another brother, went, a very young man, to California in 1849, and died of typhoid fever in San Francisco. He had served as captain of a company in the volunteer army of the United States in the Mexican war, and had already given proof of very uncommon abilities as a lawyer.

In 1833 New Orleans was a great commercial city, with advantages second only, it seemed, to New York, and with a future far ahead of any other city in the West or South. Its population was growing and enterprising, its society was distinguished for brilliant men and accomplished women, its climate was salubrious, and altogether, from a fair standpoint of the times, in its future it seemed to be certain of becoming to the South what New York was to the North. Surely the professional field was tempting. The names of Edward Livingston,[1] Etienne Mazureau, Francis Xavier Martin, Judah P. Benjamin, John R. Grymes, Pierre Soulé, Christian Roselius, George Eustis, and Alfred Hennen made the bar celebrated in Europe and America, and earned for it a reputation never surpassed by any State before or since.

Little did any of those distinguished men then know that there had come into their midst an ambitious young Carolinian, to whose powers and knowledge they would yet defer!

An occasional reference to the subject in after-years proved that his affectionate nature was also a strong motive for drawing Mr. Hunt to New Orleans, for there he knew he would have the associations and ambitions of his brothers to help him on. It is strange that he ever doubted his prompt success at the bar in New York, yet was willing to compete at once with such men as those named, in New Orleans.

Without further delay, in the year 1833 he entered upon the practice of his profession in his new home. Clients soon came to him, and with his indefatigable studiousness he mastered every legal question submitted to

---

[1] Mr. Livingston had been elected United States senator shortly before Mr. Hunt went to New Orleans. In 1833 he resigned as Secretary of State, and accepted the mission to France.

him. As he once wrote himself, " difficulties vanish before application and study." His habits of work were
peculiar and irregular. He often left his bed in the
middle of the night, after an hour's sleep, lit the lamp,
and resumed his labor. With unvarying patience he
searched for the foundation of all reason bearing upon
the points under investigation, and was not content until
he knew all there was to learn upon his topic. Of reading he never tired. Mr. Hunt's professional life is a
marked illustration of the truism that a lawyer's knowledge can be acquired only by labor, hard and untiring
mental work.

To enumerate his triumphs at the bar would be to review the most important lawsuits tried in the federal and
state courts of Louisiana for forty years, yet a few of the
causes célèbres may be mentioned, where his eloquence
and ability will long be remembered.

The first substantial fee he earned he put into a box
and shipped by sea to his mother in New Haven. Specie
coin being the principal money of those days, a box containing three thousand dollars must have been of some
weight, but railroads and drafts were not the possible
methods to remit money by, as they now are.

One of Mr. Hunt's first arguments before the Supreme
Court of the State was for the appellant in the cause of
Barelli *v.* Hagan, argued in 1839.[1]

He succeeded Edward Livingston in the celebrated
Batture litigation,[2] in which Livingston finally overthrew
Thomas Jefferson.

In the course of time he became counsel for the city
of New Orleans, and gave in that capacity an opinion

[1] 13 La. Rep. p. 581.
[2] This controversy arose in 1805, when Mr. Livingston instituted
a suit for John Gravier against New Orleans to quiet title to certain
lands on the banks of the Mississippi, adjacent to New Orleans.

that the city was liable for damages done by the mob which, on the occasion of the execution of the American filibusters,[1] broke into the houses of Spanish residents and destroyed their property. It will be remembered that Mr. Webster, as Secretary of State, took afterwards a like position for the government of the United States, and made reparation to Spain.

Mr. Hunt, towards the close of his career, was employed by the government of the United States as special counsel in the Wine cases, and prosecuted the wine merchants of New Orleans for violation of the revenue laws. And it was his argument at last, in the celebrated Slaughter-House cases, which, prevailing as it did in the Supreme Court of Louisiana, was accepted by the Supreme Court of the United States (16 Wall. p. 70), and gave to the fourteenth amendment of the Constitution the first authoritative interpretation. The court heard the case twice, and gave judgment at last, by the majority of a single vote, in favor of the contention Mr. Hunt had promoted below : that the first clause of the amendment in question was intended primarily to confer citizenship on the negro race, and that the second protects, from the hostile legislation of the States, the privileges and immunities of *citizens of the United States* as distinguished from the privileges and immunities of citizens of the States.

This memorable decision determined that the existence of the States, with powers for domestic purposes and local government, including the regulation of civil rights, the rights of person and of property, is essential to the perfect working of our complex form of government.

Curious to relate, the opposite view of the fourteenth amendment was contended for by Ex-Justice John A.

[1] 1851. Schouler's *History of the United States.*

Campbell,[1] a disciple of the Calhoun view of politics. Returning to New Orleans from Washington, Judge Campbell furnished a striking commentary on the relations of counsel to public affairs. He then called on Mr. Hunt and congratulated him. He went on to say that it was better for the country that the view of Mr. Hunt had prevailed over his own.

Before the *nisi prius* courts Mr. Hunt acquired a large practice because of his extraordinary success in jury trials. The strength and vigor of his understanding, the comprehensiveness of his studies as a scholar as well as a jurist, and the breadth and liberality of his views, the clearness and the elevation of his reflections, and the logic and accuracy with which he was able to array these, and then to express them, and the excellence of his declamation when brought to bear, as it habitually was with him, upon a perfect mastery of the particular case under discussion, enabled him to attain to a degree of true eloquence which is not often to be met with, and to command the admiration not only of the general public, but of the most critical listeners, practiced lawyers, and learned judges.

One of the leaders of the New Orleans bar writes of him in this manner : " In addition to profound studies he brought to advocacy in criminal cases the best powers I have ever seen in court. His examination of witnesses was very searching. His ability to lay down a principle and to show its application to the circumstances in hand was most striking. His whole action was splendid ; courage illuminated the entire man when he was aroused and enabled him to give every protection to his client. Nobody dared to assail him. Above all, he had pathos in speech such as is seldom found. He would wring the

[1] John A. Campbell, associate justice of the United State Supreme Court from 1853 to 1861, when he resigned, and practiced law in New Orleans.

hearts of his hearers, and move all their tender and compassionate feelings."

It is related that Etienne Mazureau, for years attorney-general of Louisiana, and the famous lawyer of his day, upon hearing one of Mr. Hunt's first arguments in New Orleans, said, "That is good;" and at a later period during the same argument he again said, "That is good;" but finally, when the argument was concluded, the distinguished advocate exclaimed, "That is indeed great!"

In the celebrated case of the State of Louisiana, State of Maryland intervening, *v.* The Executors of John McDonogh and the City of New Orleans, Mr. Hunt, as counsel for the city, was enabled to win one of the great triumphs of his professional career. The controversy in the Supreme Court of Louisiana, and afterwards in the Supreme Court of the United States on final appeal, was over the vast legacies established by the holographic last will and testament of McDonogh in favor of the cities of New Orleans and Baltimore. The bequest was of the residue of McDonogh's estate, wheresoever situate, unto the mayor, aldermen, and inhabitants of New Orleans, his adopted city, and the mayor, aldermen, and inhabitants of Baltimore, his native city, in equal proportions of one half each. The legacies to the two cities were for certain purposes of public utility, and especially for the establishment and support of free schools wherein the poor, and the poor only, of both sexes, of all classes and castes of color, should have admittance free of expense for the purpose of being instructed in the knowledge of the Lord, and in reading, writing, arithmetic, history, geography, and singing, etc., etc. The States of Louisiana and Maryland instituted suit against the cities of New Orleans and Baltimore, to avoid the legacies in favor of the latter. The collateral heirs of McDonogh also attacked the will, it being contended that the legacies in question were substitutions and *fidei commissa*, which are expressly forbidden by law, and that the legacies were made upon impossible conditions to corporations not having the capacity to receive, and were consequently null.

This case was argued in 1853 before the Supreme Court of Louisiana, where was filed in behalf of the legatees an elaborate opinion by French jurists of distinction, Delile, Delangle, Giraud, Duranton, and Marcadé. Mr. Hunt added to his reputation by an argument on the same side, distinguished by a profound knowledge of the civil law of France and of Louisiana, and of the Roman civil law which is the source of both.

The decision of the Supreme Court of Louisiana was in favor of McDonogh's will as a legacy to pious uses, of which the cities were recipients. According to the court, such legacies are an element in the polity of municipal administration in all countries which have preserved the features and jurisprudence of Roman civilization.

The decision applied the term " pious " to the encouragement and support not only of pious and charitable institutions, but of those in aid of education and the advancement of science and the arts. Under the benign doctrine thus established, and afterwards confirmed by the Supreme Court of the United States [1] as embodying the true rules of jurisprudence, great numbers of public schools, both in New Orleans and Baltimore, have been established, and will continue for all time to dispense the inestimable blessings of knowledge to those who stand most in need of them.

When McDonogh v. Murdock *et al.* was argued, Mr. Hunt had reached national reputation as a lawyer, but the court was, notwithstanding, hardly prepared for the practiced and masterly advocacy with which he urged his

[1] McDonogh v. Howard. The case is reported in 15 Howard, U. S. S. C. Reports, 369.

powerful argument, and by general admission overbore Reverdy Johnson, then the leader of the bar. Justice Campbell, who gave the opinion, always insisted that, of all the arguments he had ever heard, he liked this one best. It was his habit to return in memory to the occasion again and again, and to rehearse its incidents to others.

Another of the important suits in which he appeared was tried in 1865, and involved the genuineness of an asserted codicil to the will of John McDonogh, to whom reference has been made. A man by the name of Moses Fox, claiming to be McDonogh's nephew, sought to have probated the codicil wherein McDonogh bequeathed him three hundred thousand dollars. The cities of New Orleans and Baltimore set up that the codicil was a forgery. The trial was before the second district court of New Orleans, and attracted great attention. Mr. Hunt represented New Orleans; Christian Roselius, Baltimore : and Pierre Soulé, the petitioner Fox. The arguments were exhaustive, and upon appeal to the Supreme Court were characterized by Justice Howell, who read the opinion of the court, as of "singular ability." Mr. Roselius adopted the brief of Mr. Hunt as his own argument on behalf of the city of Baltimore, — a professional compliment which Mr. Hunt valued with the appreciation due the eminent lawyer who bestowed it. The forgery was proved against the claim of Fox, and the codicil rejected.[1]

Prominent members of the New Orleans bar, who have known of all the memorable civil trials for the last forty years, refer to the argument of Mr. Hunt in the case of the ship Russia as one of the most eloquent ever heard in

---

[1] The question of expert testimony as to handwritings was a most important feature of the case. Frenchmen were the leading witnesses on both sides, and the value of their knowledge was rigidly tested. The argument of Pierre Soulé is printed in full in the report of the case in the Louisiana Reports, but other briefs are recorded as "not found." The opinion of the court is reported in the 18th La. Annual Reports, p. 119.

the trial courts of the State. The Russia had foundered near the mouth of the Mississippi. Her owners sued the insurance companies for the amounts of their policies. They defended upon the ground that the loss of the ship was occasioned by the barratry of her master.

Sargent S. Prentiss,[1] Christian Roselius, and John Finney represented the owners, while Benjamin, Micou, Grymes, and Maybin appeared for the defense. During the progress of the suit Mr. Prentiss died, and it was upon the second trial below that Mr. Hunt first appeared in his stead. The trial attracted much attention on account of the issues and the many distinguished lawyers engaged.

Judge Mortimer M. Reynolds presided. Colonel John R. Grymes was the principal advocate for the defendants. He was then in his prime, and is described as "a model of manly grace, dressed like a dandy, with many eyes turned toward him." His speech was greatly admired.

Speaking of the conspirators, on whom he charged, Colonel Grymes reached a climax : "Gentlemen of the jury, since the sun and the moon and the stars shone in the heavens, there never stood three such rascals on a quarter-deck ! "

Mr. Hunt closed the plaintiff's case in an address which truly deserves to be remembered as splendid. He forged the links of his argument so as to make up a chain that could not be broken. He fell upon his adversaries with a power of sarcasm which made them writhe, and under which they could hardly sit. His argument lasted for hours, and resulted in a verdict for the owners.

A noteworthy case, in which it happened that Mr. Benjamin[2] and Mr. Hunt met, was that of the impeachment

---

[1] Sargent S. Prentiss was a native of Maine. He was known as a great orator and lawyer. His home was in Mississippi for years, but he moved to New Orleans about 1845.

[2] Judah P. Benjamin, United States senator from Louisiana from

proceedings in the state Senate of Louisiana of a judicial officer, Judge Benj. C. Elliott, charged in the year 1844 with wrongfully issuing naturalization papers to foreigners, and so prostituting to Democratic partisan purposes the powers of his high office. Pierre Soulé defended the judge, while Benjamin and Hunt appeared against him, as managers on behalf of the state House of Representatives, of which body Mr. Hunt was a leading member. Benjamin spoke first, and with great applause. Mr. Hunt followed. The speeches were contrasted by Alexander Bullitt, then editor of the " New Orleans Picayune." He greatly praised Mr. Benjamin, and likened his argument to a beautiful Corinthian column ; but the argument of Mr. Hunt, he proceeded to say, reminded him of a noble and complete edifice, in which the column was merely a single part.

The report recommending the removal of Judge Elliott from the office of judge of the city court of Lafayette was signed by Mr. Hunt as chairman. It was a most severe arraignment, and was prefaced in the following impressive language : —

" Our liberties depend upon the pure exercise of the right of suffrage. If we suffer that right to be abused and polluted, to be extended by fraud and corruption, or by carelessness and loose practices, to those not entitled to it by the Constitution and laws of our State, our government will at once degenerate from its high republican character and sink into a tyranny.

" Hence it becomes us to guard with the greatest vigilance against every encroachment on the right of suffrage, and to discountenance and reprobate, on the part of those in whom the administration of the naturalization laws is confined, any remissness or failure in the discharge of their duties.

1852 to 1861, when he withdrew. He became a leader at the bar of England after the war.

" The right of suffrage is the very life-blood of liberty. It is inseparable from the political equality and independence of man. It is essential to citizenship, and its honest exercise is alike the safety and glory of popular rule. It should, then, be maintained in its highest purity, and especially by its elected guardians, the officers of the law."

The Democratic members of the legislature presented a minority report ; and in April, 1844, the court of impeachment assembled in New Orleans. The arguments extended over several days, and the result of the impeachment was vividly described in the following language, quoted from the account of Henry C. Castellanos, Esq., a member of the New Orleans bar : —

" The dismissal of this disgraced and recreant functionary by the Senate of this State — a dismissal brought about by the concurrent action of Whigs and Democrats alike — awakened among all classes of citizens feelings of unmixed gratification. The sturdy independence of several Democratic senators was highly commended. Although it was nearly midnight when the result was first announced, still there were thousands on the *qui vive* awaiting the event. The news spread like wildfire. The St. Louis rotunda, Hewlett's Exchange, and Banks' Arcade disgorged their hundreds of *habitués*, who, all wending their course toward the State House, soon filled up that part of Canal Street. An impromptu demonstration was proposed, and at once got up. The cannon of the Washington Artillery were drawn from their armory, and a salute of twelve guns fired. Then forming into a procession, with blazing pine torches and a band of music at their head, the swelling crowd proceeded to serenade the House managers, — Messrs. Hunt, Benjamin, and Wadsworth, — as a compliment for their services in the cause of political honesty. And all this within the compass of one hour."

The Shepherd will case was another of the great cases wherein Mr. Hunt made an argument of such merit as to require some mention.

The dispute was over the distribution of a large estate left by James II. Shepherd, who died in 1837.

Mr. Hunt, Judge Campbell, and Mr. Roselius represented the heirs of a brother of J. II. Shepherd, who sued to recover shares of the property belonging to them by the will.

Mr. Hunt's brief, covering one hundred and fifty pages, shows research into the French, Roman, and English laws concerning wills, and in a style conspicuous for its purity and solidity presented the law and facts as they were upheld by the court, and resulted in a fortune for his grateful clients.

He must have been satisfied with his own argument, for he concluded it in these words : —

"This argument for the defense is here closed. It has been drawn from the purest fountains of justice and of law : the writings of the ancient sages and most learned doctors of the civil law, the decisions of courts of the highest character, and the comments and dissertations of the most illustrious jurists of the present day. It has not been confined to a mere exposition of the textual provisions of law, but has been extended, after the fashion of those by whose authority it is supported, into the investigations of principles, the search after the natural truths upon which the private relations of men, their contracts and rights of family and property repose, in the hopes to impart something of the charm of philosophy to that which otherwise would have been comparatively dry and contracted. For it is this association of philosophy and law that renders jurisprudence a science, and leads to the contemplation of the high and fixed rules of wisdom, justice, and beneficence, from which our dearest rights, the purest links of law's golden chain, are sustained.

" It is for you, judges, to pronounce upon the plaintiff's attempt, without legal proof and against moral evidence, to blast the memory of a good man who descended into the tomb with public veneration, to carry dishonor and shame into his daughter's family, and to despoil her of property held under a just judgment of court and sanctified by a possession of thirty years. From her distant home in Massachusetts, Ellen Brooks, the daughter of Rezin D. Shepherd, calls upon you to protect her from the speculations of cupidity, and her father, whose reputation is dearer to her than her own life, from the aspersions of calumny."

The great success which he had achieved in his profession was the reward of almost uninterrupted study. Politics did not disturb Mr. Hunt at all seriously, although his position at the bar placed him where he met the distinguished public men of the South. A Whig of a radical type, he had become well acquainted with Mr. Clay, who frequently visited New Orleans in the years preceding the campaign of 1844. Mr. Hunt ardently admired Mr. Clay, and belonged to the large number of old Whigs who never ceased to regret his defeat for the presidency. He spoke often for the Whig cause, and joined in the spontaneous enthusiasm which the name of Mr. Clay everywhere aroused. At Mr. Clay's request Mr. Hunt visited him at Ashland, and their relations became intimate. Mr. Clay urged at one time his appointment as Attorney-General of the United States.[1]

Not long after Clay's death, a snuff-box which had once belonged to Peter the Great was presented to Mr. Hunt by Dr. Mercer, of New Orleans, to whom Mr. Clay had bequeathed it. Dr. Mercer gave it to Mr. Hunt, " knowing," he wrote, " of the high regard that Mr. Clay bore for you always."

[1] Probably when Mr. Fillmore became President.

Louisiana was noted for the intensity of " Whiggism." In no other State were the leaders of that political party more active or sanguine. Even in 1851, when a total dissolution of the organization was inevitable, the Louisiana Whigs entered the fall campaign with vigor and confidence. Randell Hunt was on the stump, working earnestly for the Union and a new state Constitution. Pierre Soulé, then United States senator, had made a speech upon the admission of California into the Union, expressing opinions sustaining the right of a State to demand allegiance to it alone. The course of Senator Soulé gave Mr. Hunt full opportunity to reply to the senator's views, and at the same time to reiterate his own well-known Union sentiments. This he did at the close of a brilliant speech, devoted principally to the necessity for a new state Constitution. Among other things concerning the Union Mr. Hunt said : —

" Mr. Soulé declares that the right to secede was fully and most emphatically implied in the Articles of Confederation, and is not surrendered by the Constitution. The Articles of Confederation, upon their very face, declare that they are 'Articles of Confederation and *Perpetual* Union.' And in the preamble to the Constitution of the United States it is declared that 'the people of the United States, in order to form *a more perfect* Union, do ordain and establish the Constitution.'

" Mr. Soulé declares that a State, in seceding, would only ' exert her undoubted privilege as one of the sovereign confederates.' This declaration is based upon the notion that the Constitution of the United States is a mere league between sovereign States who have preserved their whole sovereignty. But the Constitution of the United States forms a government, and not a league. It operates directly upon the people, individually, and not upon the States. Each State has surrendered many essential portions of its sovereignty for the purpose of constituting, with the other States, a nation. To secede, then, is not to break a league, but, in the language of General Jackson, to destroy the unity of a nation.

"Mr. Soulé declares, substantially, that his allegiance is due to the State alone, and not to the United States. 'Does not each of us,' says he in his speech, 'possess — do we not exert whenever we please — the right of changing our allegiance by passing from one State to the other, or to a foreign state? Who denies it? Who doubts it?'

"Does Mr. Soulé suppose that his allegiance to the United States would be changed by his passing from Louisiana to South Carolina or to Massachusetts? Has he not taken an oath of allegiance to the United States? Has he not sworn to support the Constitution of the United States? Does not that Constitution provide that the Constitution and the laws of the United States shall be the supreme law of the land ; and does it not also provide that the members of the several state legislatures, and all executive and judicial officers both of the United States and of the several States, shall be bound by *oath* to support the Constitution? Does it not contain a clause expressly conveying a right to punish treason against the United States ; and is not treason the highest breach of allegiance?

"How can a citizen of the United States say, then, that he owes no allegiance to the United States: and how can he assert that his allegiance is changed by 'passing from one State to the other, or to a foreign state'?

"I can hardly imagine how even a native of a State who has not reflected seriously upon the true character and complicated structure of our government, and who has been educated with false feeling of state pride, and been taught the extreme doctrines of state rights in the school of abstractionists and metaphysicians, can so far lose sight of the operations of the national government as for a moment to believe that he owes allegiance to his native State alone, and that he owes no allegiance to the United States. But I confess myself entirely at a loss to understand how an adopted citizen, who may be naturalized in a Territory or in the District of Columbia; who may reside during his probationary term in one State and may be admitted in another; whose right of citizenship has been conferred upon him by the United States, and not by the State in which he may chance to live; and who, at the time of his application to be admitted, must have renounced and abjured all allegiance to the prince, state, or sovereignty whereof he was before a citizen or subject, and sworn to support the Constitution of the United States, — I confess myself entirely at a loss to understand how such a person can believe his allegiance is not due to the United States.

"These notions and these doctrines of Mr. Soulé, if carried into practice, would destroy our national character as Americans, and put an end to the Union.

"Mr. Soulé says 'he is not for breaking this confederacy; he is not for advising the State to join any secession movement which may be made by other States.' Oh no! He only argues the right in the abstract. He would have the people still *endure*. But this is a dangerous philosophy. Practically speaking, there is but one step from the conviction as to a right and its enforcement, from the suffering of a wrong to its manly redress. Ours is a government of sentiment and affection, and if the feelings of the people are once alienated from it, the government from that moment is at an end.

"What is it that the advocates of secession desire? What would they have who seek to destroy our Union, and to erect a State into an independent nation? . . .

"But what would be our condition if we were divided

into rival and hostile States? I turn with horror from the contemplation of the misery which would await us at home, and can see nothing but degradation abroad. Suppose Louisiana were to secede from the Union ; suppose one of her sons in a foreign land were to be threatened by the minions of a tyrannical government with wrong and injury, — what more ridiculous and insignificant an object can there be imagined than such a person claiming protection in the name of the sovereign nation of Louisiana, and pointing to a flag with a pelican on it as the emblem of his country ? "

When the old Whig party totally dissolved, Randell Hunt, like so many others in the South, united with the Americans or Know-Nothings. He was the American candidate for attorney-general of his State in 1855, and made a very active campaign. The yellow fever was violent in many towns that year, and traveling facilities were inadequate, so that between the two discomforts his tour of the State was not very pleasant. Politically speaking, however, it was a success, and he wrote of a large meeting he had addressed at Richmond in September, 1855, where great enthusiasm prevailed. Mr. Hunt's meetings were crowded at all points, and every form of compliment was showered upon him. He went into Mississippi, too, where the mayor of the city of Natchez and other dignitaries extended him what he termed "an ovation." The Democrats were equally active ; "the staple of their addresses," wrote Mr. Hunt, "being a vituperation and denunciation of the American party, mingled with praises of the Democracy and of the administration."

At Monroe, in Ouachita, he held a joint debate with Judge Richardson. He was heard with apparent rapture. Every patriotic sentiment was applauded to the echo, and even the dullest parts of his argument seemed to excite the intensest interest. Judge Richardson answered him, and Mr. Hunt rejoined. The judge was very uneasy during the rejoinder. He turned and twisted himself about in his chair, rubbed his face, stretched his legs, and at length rose and incontinently fled from the contest. The boys laughed at him as he retired, and a hearty and vociferous shout of victory, with three cheers for Hunt, made the welkin ring and ended the discussion. The American party, however, was defeated, and Mr. Hunt went down with it.

The question of a convention to revise the state Constitution of 1845 became a political issue during the campaign of 1851, — the Whigs favoring, the Democrats opposing revision.

Mr. Hunt argued for the Whigs that the Constitution, with its restrictions and prohibitions, had fettered the enterprise and industry of the people, and caused capital to seek a more natural and freer home elsewhere. He contended that railroads and other improvements needed stimulating by enabling legislation ; that the judicial system was defective, and the executive department too much restricted.

At the period in question Mr. Hunt was undoubtedly the most widely admired public speaker in the State of Louisiana. He prepared and delivered from the gallery of Stickney's Amphitheatre, in the city of New Orleans, an elaborate address in favor of a new Constitution, which carried conviction not only to his immediate listeners, but to the voting population throughout the State. His part in the discussion of the issues before the public had the effect of making an epoch in local history. He rolled up the Constitution of 1845, and put it aside like an old and useless parchment. That Constitution was now pronounced to be unsuited to the spirit of the times and to the growing requirements of a modern American commonwealth.

The Whigs carried the election. Mr. Hunt was elected a member of the convention, and readily became leader of the body, taking a chief part in its important deliberations, and moving, when it closed its session, the final adjournment.

He was the leading member of the Judiciary Committee. In the list of his colleagues were such men as Christian Roselius, Judah P. Benjamin, Ex-Governor Roman, Edward A. Bradford,[1] Duncan F. Kenner, and others, who contributed to the lasting honor and fame of Louisiana, and who helped to make up perhaps the ablest deliberative body that has ever assembled in the State. The Constitution adopted by the convention became the new law of the State, and remained so until 1864.

It being part of the history of the State that one of the causes leading to a change of Constitution was the popular wish to disembarrass legislation from some of the trammels of the Constitution of 1845, and to enable the State to grant aid to works of internal improvements,

---

[1] Mr. Bradford met with cruel disaster. He was, towards the close of the administration of President Fillmore, appointed associate justice of the Supreme Court of the United States, in the place which Justice Campbell was afterwards called to fill. On receiving the appointment Mr. Bradford left New Orleans and repaired to Washington, where Congress was in session. It happened that he was known (he was a graduate from Yale College) to gentlemen from the North. Some of these had seen his nomination with joy, and rose in the Senate to testify to the excellence of his character and of his attainments. This, happening in the height of the slavery agitation, ruined Mr. Bradford. An element from the South took alarm. They resented the praise that had been spoken. They suspected the sincerity of it, simply because of the quarter from which it came. They then appealed to party and to sectional passions, and the rejection of Mr. Bradford's name was the result. At a dinner-party given to Hon. Randall Gibson by Judah P. Benjamin, in Paris, Mr. Benjamin said to Senator Gibson that Mr. Bradford was the greatest lawyer he had ever known.

c

that subject naturally engrossed the legislative mind, and resulted in the adoption of the act of March 12, 1852, providing for the subscription, by the parishes and municipal corporations of the State of Louisiana, to the stock of corporations undertaking works of internal improvements, and for the payment and disposal of the stock so subscribed. As the conspicuous champion of the Constitution of 1852, as well as the most eminent constitutional jurist at the bar, for such undoubtedly had the position of Mr. Hunt become, he was employed, at large retainers, to defend the constitutionality of the act of March 12, just referred to. The judgment of the Supreme Court of Louisiana, following the views urged by him on argument, in police jury, for the use of the New Orleans, Opelousas, and Great Western R. R. Co. v. Succession of McDonogh, 8 La. An. 341, and in City of New Orleans v. Mrs. Graihle, 9 La. An. 561, proceeded to secure the building of the Great Western Railroad. Down to this time there were only eighty-one miles of railroad in the State of Louisiana. The adjudications here cited fixed the construction of two great lines of communication, one of which has grown to be part of the Southern Pacific Railway across the continent, and the other has become an important link in the Illinois Central Railroad. The territory of Louisiana was not only brought in this way into close intercourse with the other parts of the country, and a new commerce established for it, but it was also bound to the national destiny, and made irrevocably part of it.

Mr. Hunt was now at his best, and addressed himself to the discussion of his great cases with astonishing fullness of research, and with great breadth and liberality, as well as persuasive powers, in professional debate. It was on the occasion of the delivery of the argument for the railroad that Mr. Benjamin, then one of the leaders

of the bar of New Orleans, but afterwards the acknowledged head of the bar of London, paid Mr. Hunt's advocacy that tribute which is so often repeated in New
Orleans.   Mr. Benjamin returned from court in company with Thomas L. Bayne, Esq., a well-known member of the bar, who had studied law in Mr. Benjamin's
office.   The two gentlemen conversed as they walked.
Mr. Benjamin had just left the Supreme Court, where
Mr. Hunt had been speaking.   "Splendid!" he exclaimed.   "Did you hear Hunt?   Shall I ever be able
to make a speech like that?"   A measure of praise no
less than this was afterwards rendered Mr. Hunt by
Judge John A. Campbell, who, retired from his high office
of associate justice of the Supreme Court of the United
States, came himself in the course of time to stand at the
head of the legal profession in the city of New Orleans.
Judge Campbell, when Mr. Hunt was elected by the
legislature of the State of Louisiana to be senator in
Congress, declared that he was the strongest lawyer who
had ever argued before him.

Any sketch of Randell Hunt would fall short of rendering him justice which might leave it to be understood
that his professional engagements included only great
cases, such as have been mentioned.   As he advanced in
years his experience grew, and embraced many of the
complex and important relations of a civilized society.   It
became his practice to argue cases such as arose in the city
of New Orleans in exciting times of close party contests,
involving titles to offices of profit and emolument and
of influence, like those, for example, of district attorney
for the parish of Orleans, clerk of the great Commonwealth Court of the town, and commissioners of election.
His skill in the criminal practice and deep knowledge of
the criminal law, and his fearless character and eloquent
voice, attracted to him also numbers of criminal cases,

and enabled him to sustain the reputation of being first
at the criminal bar.   Life in New Orleans was full of
stirring incidents.   Parties were quite evenly divided.
Personal encounters were common, and led often to mortal consequences.   Mr. Hunt, whose standard of professional duty was the highest, at some personal risk defended Wadsworth, and had him acquitted.   Wadsworth
had been warned that one Carson would take his life.
Wadsworth met Carson and shot him dead in the great
rotunda of the St. Louis Hotel in New Orleans.   Mr.
Hunt also defended Pope Adams on a charge of murder,
making on his behalf an appeal for mercy such as only
the most consummate skill and oratory could produce.
Adams was convicted notwithstanding.   Sentenced to
death, he ended his life in prison by taking poison.

Mr. Hunt successfully defended Garland, city treasurer
of New Orleans, on a charge of robbing the city treasury.   He attacked the indictment and overthrew it.   He
also defended with success — Benjamin being appointed
with him — Kendall, postmaster at New Orleans, who was
charged with rifling the mails.   The signal forensic talents displayed by Kendall's counsel secured his acquittal,
and added fresh lustre to their high reputation.

The first candidacy of Mr. Hunt for the United States
Senate grew naturally out of the character which he had
earned by his service in public affairs, as well as out of
his eminence as a lawyer.   The contest was between
Duncan F. Kenner (who shortly afterwards became president of the Constitutional Convention of 1852), Mr. Benjamin, and Mr. Hunt.   The name of Mr. Hunt rallied to
his support an influential consanguinity of distinguished
merit and the best citizens, who saw in him the representative of sound constitutional opinions and of consistent
and devoted Unionism.   The choice of the legislature
fell at last upon Benjamin.   He was at the end of his

term reëlected, under circumstances not very gratifying to him, by a bare majority. It was not long before he left his place and plunged into the vortex of the Rebellion. It was reserved to Mr. Hunt to receive the honor of an election when the war which he had opposed was brought to a close.

We must turn from the narrative of his public life to his own affairs for a moment. Although he had now reached his forty-eighth year he was still a bachelor. Matters before the Supreme Court at Washington took him to that city in the spring of 1854. While there, Mr. Hunt became engaged to Miss Ruhamah Ludlow, a niece of Mrs. McLean, the wife of Justice McLean, of the Supreme Court of the United States. He telegraphed to New Orleans that he had "won two suits, — one in the Supreme Court and one in the Court of Love." Miss Ludlow was quite celebrated for her beauty and accomplishments. They were married at Cincinnati on the following July 12. Mrs. Hunt's grandfather was Colonel Israel Ludlow, one of the founders and proprietors of Cincinnati, and her ancestors were officers in the war of the American Revolution.[1] She was ever a devoted and loving wife. They had no children.

Resuming our glance at the political kaleidoscope, it would be out of place in this brief memoir to more than mention the downfall of the Know-Nothings. They never had any formidable strength, and the impending moral issue of slavery or no slavery was of so much more universal interest than any amendment of our natu-

[1] Benjamin Chambers was one of the early settlers (about 1726) in Cumberland County, Pennsylvania. His son was in the Revolutionary War.

Cornelius Ludlow was also an officer in the Revolution. Two of Mrs. Hunt's brothers, Israel and Benj. C., were gallant officers on the Union side during the war of 1861–65. Chief-Justice Salmon P. Chase married a sister of Mrs. Hunt.

ralization and immigration statutes that it is surprising
that Know-Nothingism had any substantial following.
The Southern Whigs seemed to have been considerably
tossed about between the years 1856 and 1860. Mr.
Lincoln, as the leader of the Republican party, was too
radical, they thought, in his abolition tendencies. On the
other hand, they could not tolerate Douglas, who represented all that was to them pernicious and dangerous.
They were violently opposed to Breckinridge, who was
purely the candidate of a section of the Union rather
than of the Union as a whole.

During the summer of 1860 a national convention of
delegates, largely comprised of old Whigs, Americans,
and Know-Nothings, in the North and South, met at
Baltimore, and, under the name of Constitutional Unionists, nominated John Bell, of Tennessee, for President, and
Edward Everett, of Massachusetts, for Vice-President.
The platform of the party may be summarized by its
adherence to the Union. An approved historian declares
that the new party were in favor of the Union, but just
how to execute a plan for its preservation was not clear
to them.

Blaine, in his "Twenty Years of Congress," thus puts
it: "Mr. Bell desired to avoid the one question that was
in the popular mind, and to lead the people away from
every issue except the abstract one of preserving the
Union. By what means the Union could be preserved
against the efforts of the Southern secessionists Mr.
Bell's party did not explain. The popular apprehension was that Mr. Bell would concede all they asked, and
insure the preservation of the Union by yielding to the
demands of the only body of men who threatened to
destroy it."

The leaders, as a rule, were opposed to total abolition,
and a "gradual emancipation" was discussed.

Bell and Everett were personally well-known patriots. They were statesmen of tried abilities, and could be trusted, old Whigs said, to preserve the Union and work out methods of emancipation by a more conservative process than the Republicans proposed.

The Southern Unionists, with Randell Hunt as a conspicuous leader, united in support of the new party, and entered the campaign with an ardor equaled only in the Clay-Polk times.

Mr. Hunt presided over the convention of the Constitutional Union party which assembled in the city of Baton Rouge July 4, 1860. The campaign opened early.

, Invitations to speak poured in upon him. They came from Pennsylvania, New Jersey, New York, Ohio, and by the score from the cities of every Southern State.

He was himself a candidate for state senator from his district in Louisiana, but his own election was a secondary thought. He was overwhelmed with professional matters, too, and decided to remain in the South. Some of the letters he received were couched in terms of the confidence and admiration the people entertained for him. A letter, for instance, signed by Wyatt C. Thomas, corresponding secretary of the Constitutional Club of Washington, Arkansas, pleads with him to visit that State, " to attend at a grand demonstration and barbecue in favor of Bell and Everett, which comes off in this place on the 20th of October. Preparations are on foot and in progress to make it the largest and most splendid meeting ever held in the State. From five to ten thousand persons will certainly be present, and upon that day, perhaps, will be decided the fate of this State. Will you allow us to appeal to you, then, under the circumstances, in vain ? One blast now upon your bugle-horn is worth a thousand men ! Come and be present with us, and the Union men of Arkansas and the whole nation will ever regard your

action with feelings of the most profound gratitude."
And another addressed to him by J. B. Jones, as president of the Constitutional Union Club of Burlington,
New Jersey, said that it would "afford our people great
gratification to hear you in behalf of the Union cause."
The pressure to have him go North was too great to
resist, so he went to Philadelphia. The substance of his
speech in Philadelphia, before the Continental Union
Club, is given elsewhere in this volume. One of his invitations, dated at Jackson, Mississippi, September 14, 1860,
contained the following sentence: " We expect a very
large assembly of the people from Mississippi, Louisiana,
Alabama, etc., and we do not intend to flatter when we
assure you that your voice will exercise a powerful and
beneficial influence on the result in each of the States
mentioned." The letter is signed by the following
names : F. Anderson, R. L. Buck, W. L. Sharkey, W. P.
Anderson, George L. Potter, Patrick Henry, C. L. Buck,
H. H. Miller, D. Shetlon, John Shetlon, and others.[1]

His tour was an ovation. Eulogistic introductions,
crowds of people, music, barbecues, receptions, serenades,
applause, and interruptions by occasional fights, — indeed, all the incidents and interest which marked a so-
called " red-hot" political campaign, before the war, in
the South and West, — were repeated wherever he appeared. The tenor of his speeches was for the Union. In
not one did he omit utterances of loyalty in a manner and
style which aroused throngs to the highest pitch of excitement. He always quoted from Webster and Clay, whose
conceptions of a united country conformed with his own,
and concluded with perorations of fervent hopes for the
safety of the country, no matter what adversities might
come. It is hard to say whether he believed Bell could

[1] Many of these persons were prominent in the State of Mississippi as lawyers and officials.

be elected, with the Republicans gaining such strength all over the North and West. He could not have believed so unless he was carried away by the expressions of others whose ill-founded hopes overcame sound judgment.

Bell was ingloriously defeated.

The sting of defeat made the Breckinridge men avow their sentiments of disunion, and secession was popular talk in the South. Conventions were being called throughout the States implicated in the movement, and civil war was fearfully close at hand.

South Carolina, Mississippi, Florida, Alabama, and Georgia had taken measures for secession. Louisiana was more tardy. There were very many Unionists in the State who dreaded the step, and prayed that it might be averted. The current was too strong, however. The governor issued his proclamation ordering the legislature to convene on December 10. A bill was introduced to call a convention to consider the adoption of an ordinance of secession. There were many expressions of a wish to hear from Mr. Hunt. His counsel was needed, and the more conservative men urged the state senators to hear him before they acted. But the steamboat upon which he had taken passage to Baton Rouge was delayed, and some impatience was shown. One prominent ultra-secessionist exclaimed : " What is the use of this legislature waiting to hear from Randell Hunt? We know what he will say." They did wait for him. however, and upon December 12, 1860, the eloquence of his voice rang out in favor of the Union. By those who heard the speech it was always regarded as the best he ever delivered. Baton Rouge was excited at the announcement that he would be heard, and hundreds of people were unable to gain admission into the senate hall. Stenographic reports, unfortunately, were not to be had, and no part of the speech was ever printed.

The movement to call a convention was too powerful: the measure was passed; and again Mr. Hunt found himself hopelessly fighting for the same high principle of a United States that he had struggled for in South Carolina nearly thirty years before.[1]

The way in which his remarkable oration was received can be gathered by the following editorial from a Baton Rouge newspaper: —

THE RIGHT KIND OF TALK IN THE RIGHT PLACE.

As announced the day before, the Hon. Randell Hunt, yesterday, soon after the opening of the Senate, stood up as the representative man of the day and generation passed away, and delivered the most forcible as well as eloquent address ever heard within the walls of the old Gothic building. His subject was the Convention Bill, which, the public is already advised, has passed both branches of the Assembly, and will presently have the force of law. The whisper about town that Mr. Hunt would speak drew a crowd of people to the Senate at an early hour, and hundreds went away unable to get within the compass of his voice. From the antecedents of the eloquent gentleman, and his well-known position on the great question which has absorbed all others, what he said was anticipated; but how he said it is only known to the fortunate few who listened to him. We cannot pretend to give his words, — no, not even the bright scintillations of his genius, as he clothed national and American sentiments in the most gorgeous drapery, and threw them about as gems, not only to dazzle, but to strike deeply into the very heart of his auditors.

Mr. Hunt denied the right of the legislature to call a convention of the people without first submitting the

---

[1] On January 26, 1861, Louisiana passed the ordinance of secession by a vote of 113 to 17.

question, according to time-honored precedent and Democratic usage. He dwelt on the madness of separate state action on a question involving the interest of others as well as our own vitality.

Is it too much to say that Mr. Hunt, who is a Louisianian by birth, education, and spirit, and is yet proud to call himself an " American citizen," had the heart of his audience, beating sweet music to that noble sentiment, " The Constitution and the Union, now and forever, one and inseparable " ? We think not, and gain fresh courage to battle in our own way along the dark path before us to this end.

The term of Mr. Hunt in the state Senate of Louisiana was not allowed, however untoward the circumstances, to pass without a renewal by him of his endeavor of a long time to reform and liberalize the law of evidence. In his character of professor of law, he had made the law of evidence a subject of especial study and reflection. He had prepared and delivered numerous philosophic essays in advocacy of the improvement of this branch of jurisprudence, and helped to train for the bar of the State many young men who, growing upward, were prepared to bring to his labors the support of their own best convictions. Mr. Hunt accordingly prepared the report of the Judiciary Committee of the Senate in support of the act by him introduced, relative to the law of evidence. It pronounced the exclusionary rules of evidence to be false and degrading. It condemned them as obstructing the inquiry after truth in courts of justice, as denying to innocence the proper and natural means of protection, and as securing immunity to fraud and crime. It was the contention of Mr. Hunt — and he supported it by an appeal to philosophy as well as to the experience of others — that the time had come when Louisiana should act on the subject, and, availing herself of the wisdom of others, admit the evidence of interested witnesses without exception, leaving the weight of evidence to be determined by the judging power.

The effort of Mr. Hunt failed, owing to the circumstance of its being made just as the civil war broke out. But the long and patient labors of his lifetime had not been thrown away. They had deeply impressed the minds of men, and he had the satisfaction of seeing them take form not long afterwards and develop into a law of the State.[1]

During the winter of 1861, after Mr. Seward had been chosen Secretary of State in the future Cabinet of Mr. Lincoln, he suggested to the President elect that it would be policy to appoint a Southern man to the new Cabinet, and he submitted for consideration the names of Randell Hunt, John A. Gilmer, Kenneth Raynor, and Colonel Fremont. It was doubtful whether any Southern man from a seceding State could be induced to enter the Cabinet, but Mr. Seward wrote him that he thought Randell Hunt would be well chosen. Mr. Lincoln, under date of January 12, 1861, said he preferred Mr. Gilmer, of North Carolina, over Mr. Hunt, "because," wrote the President elect, "he has a living position in the South, while they" (referring to Mr. Gentry and Mr. Hunt) "have not."[2] It is doubtful whether Mr. Hunt was ever communicated with directly in relation to this matter. His refusal to permit his name to be used for a high office[3] under Mr. Lincoln, at a later period, warrants the belief, moreover,

[1] Act of Louisiana Legislature, 1868. For the report upon the law of evidence, and for much else pertaining to the professional career of Mr. Hunt, grateful acknowledgment is made to Hon. Carleton Hunt, of New Orleans.

[2] Nicolay and Hays' *Life of Abraham Lincoln*. The words "living position" must refer to the fact that North Carolina had not yet passed an ordinance of secession, and a Unionist was therefore "living."

[3] Associate justice of United States Supreme Court.

that he would have declined to serve in the Cabinet. It will be remembered that not until after inauguration, upon March 4, 1861, did Mr. Lincoln complete the selection of his Cabinet ministers, and finally he compromised by making Montgomery Blair, of Maryland, Postmaster-General. Maryland, at the time, is described as having been balancing between loyalty and open secession, and the President thought that the recognition of Mr. Blair might stop the inroads of secession.

When the first States seceded, so violent an opponent of their course was Mr. Hunt that he would have brought them back into recognition of the Union by force. Never did he yield in any degree his unqualified disapproval of every initiatory movement of a secession which led up to the war between the States. Nor is it going too far to say that Mr. Hunt was bitterly disappointed at the attitude Louisiana and other Southern States were taking. But the mighty current of a popular movement, based upon conceived moral rights, was sweeping over the domain of eleven States. Political contagion often overtakes men with as little discrimination as do the treacherous fevers of a malarial country sicken their bodies. To turn his back upon six million of his fellow-countrymen was more than Mr. Hunt could do. Right or wrong, he wished to believe them right; his sense of duty told him not to forsake them; they needed his counsel. He never had withheld it in any prior emergency; he could not do so now. His fortunes lay with the South, and, secession having been undertaken, he then acquiesced in their plans of a confederacy.

Historians, in writing with perfect impartiality of the earlier days of the secession movement, will not detract from the sincerity of purpose or conviction of those Unionists, like Mr. Hunt, who permitted themselves to become identified with the new confederation. Southern men, of all others, loved their section and their States. Warm-hearted and brave, they sympathized with their fellow-citizens in ambition, sentiment, and hope.

Imbued with these natural traits to an unusual degree, Mr. Hunt thought that the government need not and should not use coercive force in opposition to the dissatisfaction that so many influential States finally expressed with the national administration, and he became unwilling to sanction what he announced to be an abrogation of all rights of self-government. This theory was based, of course, upon the view that so large a number of States of the Union represented a people rightfully entitled to self-government under the Federal Constitution. He did not advance any doctrine of inalienable "state rights" upon the Calhoun lines of independent sovereignty. Nor was the conduct of Randell Hunt, and hundreds of men who followed him in his radical opposition to secession, agreeable with the explanation of Alexander H. Stephens, who believed in the "reserved sovereignty of the States and the compact of the Union or Constitution of 1787," and therefore opposed the secession of Georgia "as a question of policy, and not one of right." [1]

Mr. Hunt contended there was no right of secession, but the policy having been adopted, allegiance was justifiable to the States who chose that policy; and that when so many States acted in concord, they were really a people, and that therefore a people's rights were involved and their liberties threatened by coercion of another part of the same people of the same country. This amounts to revolution, and is an inherent right. But it is from its nature perilous, and is to be exercised at the risk of those who invoke it. It is much to be regretted that in his papers his precise views cannot be found; but in stating

[1] Testimony of Mr. Stephens before the Congressional Committee April 16, 1866.

them as above, reference is had to such memoranda as are obtainable, and such recollections of his opinions as are given by those familiar with them. It is easy now to detect a flagrant inconsistency in the position above defined, but it was accepted in 1861, and acted upon by many men of lofty national patriotism.

Perhaps the most satisfactory explanation of the attitude of Union men in the South, who became passive when war was declared, may be found in the Virginia resolutions of 1798, where allegiance to the Constitution of the United States was expressed, but where it was declared that the Assembly of Virginia views " the powers of the federal government as resulting from the compact to which the States are parties as limited by the plain sense and intention of the instrument constituting that compact; and that in case of a deliberate, palpable, and dangerous exercise of other powers not granted by the said compact, the States who are parties thereto have the right, and are in duty bound, to interpose for arresting the progress of the evil, and for maintaining within their respective limits the authorities, rights, and liberties appertaining to them."

Mr. Hunt never adopted the resolutions of 1798 as expressive of his views. It is certain he never fully approved of them. His conduct, however, in countenancing the fact of secession, is not irreconcilable with the doctrines announced in them.

There was another motive which impelled him to countenance the civil war when once it had begun. Loyalty to blood and friends in affliction made him overlook the mistaken causes for their sufferings in his anxieties to share their burdens. This feeling is best expressed in the language of a letter written in 1861 by a friend who was solicitous of Mr. Hunt's attitude. " You know," said the correspondent, " Mr. Hunt's generous and chivalric nature, — the more afflicted a friend is, the firmer and kinder he is: so with this Confederacy, even if he were not entirely firm in his principle, he could never desert the South in her hour of adversity, — it would be contrary to his generous nature."

This much is beyond question: he never wrote a word or uttered a syllable savoring of disloyalty to the Union, or from which can be inferred a wish on his part at any time for its dissolution. No matter what results of the war were predicted by others, he had no ambition save a patriotic wish for the integrity of the United States as one nation. The peculiar principles upon which the Constitution of the Confederate States was established were never Mr. Hunt's political principles.

He saw his brother leading a Confederate regiment to the field. Three of his nephews, who were dear to him as sons to a father, left his house to join the army, and his heart was stricken with grief upon hearing of the gallant death of one of them, Captain Thomas Hunt Biscoe,[1] whom he had educated and loved with tender affection. Bowed down by daily sights of the horrors of such a war, disappointed, if not broken-hearted, that he should ever have lived to behold his country divided in itself, he patiently abided the future, in confidence that God would lead the nation unto conditions of common destiny and one harmonious whole.

He seems to have written nothing during the darkest days of the war: if he did, the memoranda are lost or destroyed.

Grateful for the peace which came in 1865, Mr. Hunt declared himself ready to accept the results of the war in a spirit of reconciliation, "which would allay pas-

---

[1] Captain T. H. Biscoe, Louisiana Volunteers, C. S. A., was killed at the battle of the Wilderness, May 5, 1864, while leading a charge of battle.

sions and heal the ghastly wounds inflicted in fraternal
strife."

Then came elaborate arguments upon the questions of
what was the exact status of the seceding States. In
these discussions every opinion he expressed was received
with respect. Mr. Hunt was opposed to negro suffrage,
and differed with Chief Justice Chase upon that question. When Mr. Chase visited New Orleans in 1865, he
and Mr. Hunt consulted often upon reconstruction matters. Judge Chase regretted that Mr. Hunt could not
favor universal suffrage, as he looked upon the question
as one of paramount importance in adjusting the relations
of the Southern States toward the Union.

Mr. Hunt thought, as did Andrew Johnson and many
other conservative Republicans, that negro suffrage could
not be made a condition precedent to a full restoration
of the Southern States to the Union ; that the States
were in the Union by virtue of their annulling their ordinances of secession and the abolition of slavery by constitutional amendment ; that the true object of the war
was to defend and preserve the Constitution against an
armed rebellion, and when that purpose was finally attained by the suppression of the rebellion, the authority
of the Constitution was thereby restored *ipso facto*, and
all its provisions resumed their original force and vigor ;
and that questions of suffrage belonged exclusively to the
legislatures of the States.

Mr. Hunt used to refer to a speech made by Ex-Governor Washington Hunt, of New York, on March 25,
1866,[1] as being a very fair presentation of the conservative views which he believed should obtain. Congress
took a different view, however, and again Mr. Hunt found

[1] The New York papers published the speech in full. It was
delivered at New Haven, Conn.

himself struggling on a losing side for a principle based
upon grave constitutional rights.

As soon as armed hostilities ceased, what the general
government was to do with Mr. Jefferson Davis and other
leaders of the secession movement was a subject of wide-
spread interest. A scrap written at the time by a listener
to an interview on June 3, 1865, between Mr. Hunt and
a gentleman now a distinguished citizen of Louisiana, is
given without alteration or amendment : —

"Well, Mr. ——," said Mr. Hunt, "this shuffling is
not answering my question. Do you think he ought to
be hung?"

"Well, Mr. Hunt, I think he is a great evil to the
country, a very bad element, and ought to be removed."

"How — you do not answer — how should he be removed? By imprisonment?"

"No : I disapprove of that."

"By banishment?"

"W-e-l-l, I have not made up my mind."

"Yes, Mr. ——, it is very evident you *have* made
up your mind, — you are in favor of hanging him : however, if you have *not* made up your mind, you will never
make it up. You must know what punishment you would
pronounce."

And so Mr. —— continued to shuffle, without expressing an opinion : it was evident that he was in favor
of the harshest measures, but was afraid to say so.

"Mr. Davis has always been dangerous to society and
to the Union," said Mr. Hunt, — "has always been ; and
Mr. Breckinridge, too, I consider a dangerous man. I
would remove him, too."

"But, Mr. Hunt, why would you not hang them?"

"Because, after having treated them as belligerents,
they have no right to call them traitors : that is contrary
to all the laws of nations. Because it becomes a great

nation like the United States to be generous and for-giving."

"Ah me," continued the listener, "I cannot remember the true and noble words of Mr. Hunt, but they made a great impression on me. He would be opposed to hang-ing from motives of state policy as well as the opinion of Europe (for a nation should ever look to that), and from motives of benevolence. He was not opposed to punishment entirely, — to banishment for a term of years, and then to be allowed to return on taking the oath and promising to be quiet citizens."

"Perhaps," Mr. Hunt added, "you may think I speak in this way because I am thinking of myself ; but I have no idea that I am in any danger."

The "reconstruction" of the South prolonged the un-rest of the people of Louisiana, and they found them-selves subject to severe military government.

During General Benjamin F. Butler's service at New Orleans there was no little friction between him and Mr. Hunt. He declared Butler's measures and means cruel and unwarranted by the conditions existing, and he always spoke of him as a man of coarse and brutal in-stincts, unworthy to be compared, as an officer and a man, with General Hancock, whose moderate methods and con-sideration of the people of Louisiana commended them-selves most highly to all men, radical and conservative.

Butler at one time issued an order requiring Mr. Hunt to leave New Orleans. When the latter was ready to leave, General Butler, being notified of his intended de-parture, canceled the order, with some statement in sub-stance that, although he regarded Randell Hunt as a very arrogant man, he knew as much as ten thousand men combined, and he might have need of him.

In the summer of 1865, for change, rest, and at the same time with the hope of aiding in the work of reconstruction, Mr. Hunt went to the North. Here again he was in company with Judge Chase, who introduced him to President Johnson in these written words : " A gentleman of great ability and perfect honor, and a devoted friend of the Union until the fact of secession, when he thought it his duty to submit and identify himself with the Confederacy; is now an earnest friend of restoration. He differs with me, I am sorry to say, on the question of universal suffrage, but neither you nor I will think him less entitled to confidence and respect on that account."

Mr. Hunt laid before the President, in burning words, the sufferings of the people in the South in the reconstruction time. President Johnson declared afterwards he did not believe any man had ever spoken more eloquently. The President thereupon actually prepared a proclamation for the establishment of a new government for Louisiana, and named Randell Hunt therein to be the military governor : but he afterwards destroyed this proclamation and discarded the policy in question, saying that his Cabinet advisers, as he considered, would not support him in it.

Since the resignation of Senators Slidell and Benjamin in 1861, Louisiana, as a seceding State, had had no representation in Congress. But the war being ended, a legislature met in 1866, and claimed the right to elect United States senators. There was some doubt expressed as to whether Congress would admit them until the exact status of the seceding States had been finally fixed by legislation. If the views of the President were to prevail, the cessation of the war and the expressed determination of the inhabitants of a seceding State to resume the powers of a State would require the admission of the new senators : but if the government was to take jurisdiction over the time and manner of the return of the rebellious States, as Mr. Samuel Shellabarger, of Ohio, argued in Congress, representation surely would be denied them.

To sustain the President, no ordinary man should be elected senator.

With unanimity the people turned to Randell Hunt, whose name was advanced by a leading newspaper in the following terms : " In the choice for senator all old prejudices [1] should be discarded, and those sterling qualities of mind which everywhere command attention and respect should, if possible, be secured. Entertaining these views, we have glanced among our men of worth and experience to ascertain who could best protect the interests and uphold the honor of this State in that august body, the national Senate, and our conclusion is that Randell Hunt, the jurist, the statesman, and the orator, should be one of the two on whom the choice should fall."

In joint assembly, and unanimously, he was duly elected for the term of six years, to commence March 4, 1865. In this way, as the people of Louisiana issued from a disastrous war, against which he had counseled, they made by necessary implication to him the greatest admission of error on their part that circumstances would allow, and then joined to render him the highest honor.

The day after he had been chosen the papers congratulated the State, referring to his " spotless character, his profound learning, large experience, unquestioned ability, and the unobjectionable nature of his political antecedents." " We think," said one editorial, " the legislature made a most admirable choice. The honor, interests, and dignity of Louisiana will be ably and faithfully sustained by Mr. Hunt, and when he takes his seat there will not be a State in the Union represented by a man of greater mark."

Reverdy Johnson, then a senator from Maryland, upon the 6th of January, 1866, offered the credentials of Mr. Hunt, " who appears by the certificate of the governor

[1] Opposition to secession must be meant.

of Louisiana to have been elected one of the senators from that State." " I move," said Senator Johnson, " that they lie upon the table, as that. I believe, has been, the course taken with the credentials from the Southern States." There being no objection, it was so ordered.[1]

It was during this period of his life that the University of Louisiana conferred upon him the degree of Doctor of Laws, it being the first time in its history that such a degree had been awarded by it. The diploma was sent to Mr. Hunt with the following loving and truly fraternal letter from the president : —

UNIVERSITY OF LOUISIANA.

MY DEAR BROTHER, — I have the honor to transmit herewith your diploma as Doctor of Laws from the University of Louisiana. Learned and scientific labors for the advancement of knowledge, the cultivation of letters, the moral and intellectual improvement of the citizens of the Commonwealth, the elucidation of legal science, the inculcation of principles of American patriotism and national liberty, have forever identified your fame with the foundation and history of the University of Louisiana. The distinction is the more honorable because it was liberally, spontaneously, and justly bestowed. I had the proud satisfaction, as President of the University, of conferring the degree before the public, and I felt and declared that, in discharging my official duty, I performed the most grateful act of my life.

May you be crowned with increasing honors, and achieve hereafter *all* that virtuous ambition can desire, is the heartfelt prayer of your affectionate and devoted brother.

THOMAS HUNT, *President.*

June 21, 1866,

To the Honorable RANDELL HUNT, LL. D.

[1] Upon March 1, 1866, Senator Johnson pursued the same course with reference to the credentials of Henry Boyce, who had been elected a colleague of Mr. Hunt for the term ending March 1, 1867.

Weeks and weeks after presentation of the senatorial credentials of Randell Hunt and his colleague, Congress deliberated the legitimate and proper relations between the Southern States and the general government, and not until this question could be settled forever was it probable Mr. Hunt would be seated. A general outline of his own views will be gathered by reading the notes given to the public in these pages.

Many senators were his personal friends and wished to see him seated. They were aware of his intense love of the Union, his character, and his standing as a lawyer. For these reasons they would have valued his services and his counsel. But the " iron-clad " oath of never having countenanced past opposition to the general government was no respecter of persons. Mr. Hunt declined to take it, and was placed upon the same footing with Mr. Graham of North Carolina, Mr. Stephens and Mr. Johnson of Georgia, Mr. Manning and Mr. Perry of South Carolina, and others who had been officials, legislators, and military men under the Confederate government, and from whose views he seriously dissented.

Louisiana was unrepresented. The policy of Congress was radically in opposition to the administration, and Mr. Hunt returned to New Orleans to resume his professional labors.

That he was personally disappointed was natural, but except to refer to what he believed was an injustice to his State he never evinced any individual regret.

It was not the first time that adherence to principle and truth had caused him sacrifice and sorrow.

In the highest development of his professional knowledge, for the fifteen years following his election as a senator he enjoyed a large and lucrative law practice. Political life had little temptation for him, except by way of interest in the general welfare of the whole country.

He was absorbed in legal and educational matters, and could scarcely be induced to go outside of them.

In Lizardi's Case, 20 La. An. 285, Mr. Hunt, who was deeply imbued with a knowledge of the commercial law, was enabled to expound before the Supreme Court of Louisiana the doctrine of partnership *in commendam*, or commendatory, or partnership with limited liability, and to apply those principles to the great issue before the court, whether or not Manuel J. de Lizardi, a foreign banker, was liable, as charged, for an immense sum, on the commercial paper of J. Y. de Egaña, a merchant of New Orleans. Partnership with a limited liability, as established by the legislatures of American States, affords but slender privileges, and presents, as a consequence, but a diminished theme, in comparison with the law of partnership, as the latter has developed in the countries of Europe and in the State of Louisiana, and adapted itself to the usages, the convenience, and the commerce of mankind. In Lizardi's case, as in the McDonogh case, Mr. Hunt and his distinguished colleagues had the support of the opinion of eminent French jurists, who, being consulted, offered their advice in the character of jurisconsults, and not as mere advocates. The counsel for Lizardi prevailed, notwithstanding powerful opposition, marshaled under the leadership of John A. Campbell. Listening to the argument of Mr. Hunt in the Supreme Court, Judge P. H. Morgan, long time an associate justice on the Supreme Bench of Louisiana, considered he gave it highest praise when he said he doubted whether Mr. Hunt had ever done anything better.

In Zunts *v.* Stackhouse, 23 La. An. 481, an injunction suit to prevent the enforcement of a mortgage on a plantation, on the ground that the consideration of the notes given by plaintiff to defendant, and amounting to one hundred thousand dollars, was for the price of the sale of persons, *i. e.*, slaves, Mr. Hunt was able to achieve one of the signal triumphs of his life. The Supreme Court had rendered judgment to prevent the enforcement of the mortgage in question, which was held by his client. Plaintiff was represented by Christian Roselius, perhaps the ablest of the civilians of Louisiana since the time of the founders of her jurisprudence. The bench of the Supreme Court consisted entirely of Republicans, and their precedent decision in Wainwright *v.* Bridges, 19 La. An. 234, had ruled that the abrogation of the law which gave sanction to the condition of slavery had left the courts without authority to enforce contracts relating thereto : but the circumstances seemed only to nerve Mr. Hunt to unusual exertion. He found in the plaintiff's offer to prove that the consideration of the notes in controversy was slaves a just opportunity in behalf of his client to establish what the consideration truly was, in order to avoid suppression of the truth. Recalled from original error by the address of Mr. Hunt, the court proceeded, on principles of law, resting on the best and surest foundation, to overrule their own judgment, and to remand the case for proper trial. The victory which Mr. Roselius had achieved was wrested from his grasp. The argument of Mr. Hunt, which effected the result, is described by those who listened as having been a forensic effort of the very highest order. It is probably the last of the elaborate efforts made by him in the Supreme Court of the State.

In the controversy which arose over the great franchises of the New Orleans Gaslight Company, Judge John A. Campbell was aroused to admiration by the resources exhibited by Mr. Hunt's argument.[1] He went on to express his estimate of Mr. Hunt as a jurist. Judge

[1] Crescent City Gaslight Co. *v.* New Orleans Gaslight Co., 27 La. An. Reports, p. 138.

Campbell was himself of counsel. It was his opinion, expressed in argument in trial court, before the public, that in this broad land the number of Mr. Hunt's equals at the bar was so limited that they could be counted on the fingers of the speaker's hands.

The proceedings in the Circuit Court of the United States, Judge Edward H. Durell presiding, by favor of which William Pitt Kellogg was made governor of Louisiana, and the machinery of a state government set on foot in 1872, were condemned as odious and usurpatory by Mr. Hunt.[1] He gave his services as counsel for the defense. He considered it was a flagrant abuse to employ a bill in equity to perpetuate testimony, for the purpose of substituting the compilations of the Returning Board, to stand for titles to officers elected by the people. The issuance of the writ of injunction by Judge Durell, prohibiting the meeting of those who claimed to be members of the Senate and House of Representatives of the State of Louisiana, was, as Mr. Hunt believed, an act of judicial malfeasance amounting to outrage on the public liberties. Such, it will be remembered, became the judgment of the bar and of the country. The state government, of which Mr. Kellogg was chief executive, thus brought into existence, encountered tumult, and almost brought on civil war. Judge Durell, overcome by the force of public opinion aroused against him by the transactions here referred to, and by the profligate distribution of patronage in his court, was compelled to resign. He retired after the House of Representatives of the United States had instituted inquiry into his conduct, and the shocking particulars thereof had been spread before the American public.

Meanwhile, with gathering years, Mr. Hunt separated himself more and more from public affairs. As one

Kellogg v. Warmouth et. al., 14 Federal Cases, p. 257.

embraces a friend with whom he has long traveled, before the time of parting arrives, so he drew closer and closer to his cherished studies of the law. He had begun life in New Orleans by lecturing on commercial law. On the organization of the law department of the University in 1847 he became professor of commercial law and the law of evidence. He now added to his professional duties instruction in constitutional law. He clung to the opportunity, even in his old age, of imparting to the young the principles of American constitutional jurisprudence, as they are to be derived from " The Federalist," and from Marshall and Story and Kent, and, justly speaking, did more in his time than all others in Louisiana to hand down to those who were to succeed him the construction of the Constitution of our common country. While professional rewards poured in on him in a copious stream, he grew poor instead of rich. The distresses of the time just after the war brought him many appeals for help. These he answered with a generosity so complete that he actually despoiled himself to go to the assistance of others. The tenderness of his heart made him really suffer when those he loved happened to be in distress, and he could not hear the call of charity without going to the rescue of the afflicted.

General Hancock, while in command at New Orleans, in 1868, sought Mr. Hunt's counsel upon all questions affecting the government of the States where any construction of rights was involved. It is pleasant to note the cordial intercourse between General Hancock and Mr. Hunt. " I desire to consult with you upon matters of public welfare," wrote the general to him, soliciting his advice. Letters defining his interpretation of the acts of Congress, over General Hancock's signature, were submitted to Mr. Hunt's inspection ; so were orders issued. A note dated February 22. 1868. from Hancock, upon state finances, among

other things, says : " I have, unfortunately, lost the power
of expression of your matured views. My order is crude,
borrowed in part from yours : but being a patchwork, it
has lost much that was valuable." And repeatedly the
general thanked him for his kindness and valuable aid.

His friends were opposed to his giving up public life,
and we find him forced into some prominence again about
1870. Louisiana was confronted with political misfortunes. Northern men were holding office by appointment
throughout the State. The so-called " Carpet Bag Rule "
was at its height, and distasteful to the large majority of
the whites of the South. Business depression, political
difficulties, and general internal disorder were common.
The Republican party was in power nationally and in
Louisiana. General Grant, as President, believing that
it was necessary to enforce the amendments to the Constitution of the United States rigidly, pursued a course
unsatisfactory to nearly all of the white persons in the
State. Committees were formed in New Orleans to set
forth the grievances of the people, and again we find the
leading men of Louisiana appealing to Mr. Hunt to help
secure a political prosperity which could not come with
strangers governing the State. He responded to their invitations by letters of advice, but took no very active part.

In 1873 he was appointed a member of the committee
selected by the People's Convention of Louisiana to visit
Washington in the interests of the State, but was obliged
to decline.

A single speech during the presidential campaign of
1876 virtually closed his participation in politics. His
sympathies were with Mr. Tilden, because he thought the
whole country, and the progress of the South as a part
of the country, would be more advanced by Democratic
success than it would be under the Republicans. The
announcement that Mr. Hunt would express his views

drew a large audience, and his remarks were most favorably received. "The power, the cogency, and the earnestness with which he spoke last evening gave proof that he still retained his wonted powers," was the criticism of the press. It was his last public oral expression upon purely political issues, and by a fatalism, almost a destiny in his career, he lived to again behold the policies he contended for rejected and cast aside.

His health was somewhat impaired. A paralytic stroke severely shocked his physical system, and he was not as strong after recovery as he had been before. Retirement from public affairs was welcome to him, and he preferred his profession.

During the excitement which followed the elections of November, 1876, he became interested in the electoral commission bill, and, yielding to requests, wrote an article denouncing the measure as an invalid makeshift. The portions of the essay which have been found are given to the public. Many of the ablest constitutional lawyers took similar views, and many yet regard the commission as but an expediency created at the time to avert possible bloodshed.

Educational affairs always had his close attention. The University of Louisiana was a source of much pride to him, and he regarded its growth as an honor to the State. With the Law School he was especially identified, having been elected one of the professors in 1847, when it was founded. He lectured upon the law of evidence, commercial and criminal law, for forty consecutive years. The students looked up to him in admiration of his erudition and eloquence. Of a cultivated ease of style, of grace of diction, of felicitous expression, of varied learning, — historical, political, and classical, — his lectures are in themselves beautiful monuments to his knowledge of the law, and to the liberal expansion of his mind. He was a

student of the science of the law.   With industry he devoted his life to his profession, and to such literary pursuits
as would tend to perfect him as a counselor and an in-
structor.   The range of his reading was almost without
bounds, and in the lecture-room he displayed a wealth of
talent and scholastic accomplishments that placed him on
an equality with the greatest lecturers of the law known
by the profession in America.   No student who ever attended his lectures can forget him when he extolled the
Constitution.   Defining in eloquent words the composition
of the political organization of our land, often throwing
aside his lecture-book, and moved by the inspiriting mention of the liberties handed down to us by the Revolutionary heroes, his apostrophes to freedom made him seem
an orator of the times of Webster, or a commentator of
the days of Story and Adams.

In 1867 he succeeded his distinguished brother. Dr.
Thomas Hunt, as president of the University, continuing
as a professor in the Law School until 1888.

His vigorous constitution had been yielding to the infirmities of advanced age for several years.   His hearing
became seriously impaired, and his mind seemed less
active.   His disposition was to work as hard as he ever
had, and he did little else besides read and study : but he
complained of his eyes, and said he had to read slowly in
order to follow the thoughts of his text.

He had passed his eighty-fourth birthday when he
wrote his commentary upon the Louisiana State Lottery.
It was the labor of many weeks, written very slowly and
in a somewhat detached manner.   The manuscript shows
that, in resuming from time to time, he often wrote what
he had covered before.   Pages were skipped, and occasionally the tremulousness of the handwriting makes his
letters difficult to read.   The method by which he treated
the subject, commencing with a review of the origin of

contracts of hazard, illustrates the thoroughness with which his mind investigated whatever it dwelt upon.

He retired as a professor in the Law School in 1888, having previously been elected Emeritus Rector. The Board voted him an annual sum, to continue during his life, and unanimously passed the following resolution : —

" The Board desires to tender to Mr. Hunt its thanks for his eminent services as a professor from the establishment of the University, more than forty years ago, and as president for nearly twenty years of its existence, and its congratulations to him that in a green old age, while removed from the heat and burden of the day, he can still employ the leisure of his clear and vigorous intellect in literary tasks, for which his profound learning and great ability fit him ; and, finally, it begs leave to express the hope that peace and happiness may crown his labors, and his presence with us may long shed honor on the University and State."

Although aged and infirm, a last duty to his State made him vote against the lottery candidates at the state election in 1890.[1] In conversing upon the perniciousness of a legalized lottery he displayed the deepest feeling. It was, perhaps, the subject of all others of a public nature which, in the last years of his life, most aroused him. He spoke with sincere regret of his inability to go forth and battle against the candidates of the company, for he would regard their success as a disgrace to Louisiana.

The alumni of the Law School, at their last banquet before his death, as was their custom, cordially asked him to join them in their festivities. His response, written in a faltering hand to Judge W. T. Houston, closed in these words : —

[1] An issue in the Louisiana elections of 1890 was whether the lottery company should or should not have its charter extended. The anti-lottery candidates were elected.

"'The law which you have chosen for your profession. gentlemen, is the only safeguard of the rights of man, — of his life, liberty, property, and character, and whatever else is dear to a rational being. He who, by diligent study, acquires a profound knowledge of its principles and engages in its practice faithfully, necessarily contributes largely to the peace and happiness of society. There is no higher office on earth — none that more strongly commends itself to the esteem, confidence, and grateful respect of man — than that of the wise and upright judge administering the law. Lawyers have been, throughout time, as history attests, the fearless and powerful champions of popular liberty against tyranny and oppression. The noble sentiments of the Roman and Grecian orators, of Cicero and Demosthenes, and others, still resound in our republican ears, in delightful unison with those of the grand host of our Revolutionary fathers in favor of our American liberty.

"'I trust, gentlemen, you will pardon this encomium of our profession, as naturally evoked by your friendly invitation."

Loving relations, friends, and admirers made the last few months of his life as peaceful as he could have wished. Several times he seemed so close to death that physicians were astonished at the vitality of a system which enabled him to recover and move about again. But the rally was temporary. He died on the 22d of March, 1892.

Throughout Louisiana unusual marks of respect were paid his memory. The faculty of the Law School adopted these resolutions : —

"Whereas, RANDELL HUNT, whose death we mourn, was for many years connected prominently with the University of Louisiana, afterwards and now the Tulane University of Louisiana, and his long and distinguished services as president of the University, as professor of constitutional law, commercial law, and the law of evidence, and as dean of the law department, render it proper that this faculty should mark their respect for his memory :

" *Resolved*, That this faculty attest the great learning as a jurist and the talent of the highest order displayed by the deceased as a professor, and the very large number in this and in other States, prepared for the highest positions at the bar and on the bench by the legal education received at his hands, are deeply impressed with the obligation they owe to him, and will ever hold his memory in grateful veneration.

" *Resolved*, That this faculty recognize the great and deserved professional eminence attained by the deceased ; they recall that this distinction was won in litigation extending over half a century, conducted before courts of uncommon ability, and that his triumphs were achieved in competition with adversaries of the highest character as jurists and advocates ; and in view of the long career of the deceased at the bar, prolonged beyond the usual limit, this faculty affirm the appreciation of the bench and bar that the deceased, in the period of his vigor and usefulness, held his place in the foremost rank of the profession.

" *Resolved*, That the deceased was conspicuous for public spirit and responsiveness to all the duties of citizenship, and illustrated in his life and conduct the virtues incident to the domestic relations.

" *Resolved*, That the dean record these resolutions, and transmit a copy to the family of the deceased.

" THOMAS J. SEMMES.
" HENRY DENIS.
" HARRY H. HALL.
" HENRY C. MILLER.
" F. A. MONROE."

The administrators of the University of Louisiana passed the following resolutions : —

" *Resolved*, That in receiving the announcement of the death of Randell Hunt, LL. D., we recall with grateful recollection the valuable services rendered by him during his long and conspicuous life in this city. For many years he was the distinguished chancellor of the University of Louisiana, a professor in the law department, the active and influential exponent and defender of its interests, guiding and protecting it through trying and eventful periods of its history. His profound learning and varied accomplishments, his liberal and comprehensive views on all important questions, the weight and influence of his personal character, his earnest, persistent, and zealous advocacy of the cause of education through all phases of its development, from the common school to the university, have combined to give him a place among the most illustrious names of the Commonwealth. He has left the impress of a noble personality, of the highest professional eminence, of splendid intellectual attainments, consecrated to patriotic and unselfish ends, upon the State of Louisiana, which he loved so well and served so faithfully, and upon the destinies of the University to which he gave so large a share of the best efforts of his manhood. Forced, during the last few years of his life, by the increasing burdens of age and declining health, into comparative seclusion and retirement, there has been for those who knew and honored him always the remembrance of a past filled with the full measure of a distinguished and an honorable citizenship. Now that death has removed forever the form that was once familiar in the University, and hushed the voice that once could thrill the multitude with its eloquence, the historic record of his eminent services, his loyal fidelity to sound learning, his patriotic zeal and devotion, will serve as an inspiration to others, and remain as an ineffaceable page in the annals of the State."

Many other complimentary tributes were paid by the press and bar of the State.

It is thought proper to preserve the solemn and kindly words of the Rev. Dr. Percival, of the Episcopal Free Church of the Annunciation in New Orleans, who said : —

"It is but once in a lifetime, if at all, that occasion is offered us of assisting at a solemnity of so notable a type. The character of the large assembly now gathered here bears witness to this ; testifies to the fact that an illustrious member of this community has departed from us, that the earth has opened to receive the ashes of one of God's noblest sons. The wonderful energies of the master intellect. the throbbing of the great heart, the rich activities of the splendid manhood. have now at length finished their earthly appointed service ; and while we gaze pensively and in sadness yet once more on the mortal past, so restfully sleeping before us, which endured so much and so long. we are reminded of the personality which it typifies, that towered so high when in our presence. that stood ever so conspicuous among us. — of him who now is viewing. let us believe it, with rapture and amazement, his radiant heavenly and earthly crown.

" Time will only permit here of a hasty and most imperfect review of the earthly career of one of whom it may be truly said, ' Though dead, he yet speaks.' . . .

" We must not, however, close this poor tribute to him whose record is so full of all that is elevated and illustrious without at least a brief allusion to those many qualities of heart and soul which lent to the whole fabric of his lofty character that peculiar beauty and sweetness which won all who came within the circle of their gracious influences.

"Generous even to a fault, all he had he gave to others. Tender even to weakness, his ear never closed to any appeal. The sacrifices he made for others cannot be exaggerated, and his many good deeds, though unknown to the world, will yet come to view, for they shall live and shine forever. Farewell, brother beloved, son of eternal principle, exemplar of noble conduct, brave, courageous heart, ever decided, ever true to conviction.

"For the last time thy trembling footsteps have sought the table of the Lord; for the last time thou hast invited the angel guardian to bring the much-coveted message, setting thee free from those bodily infirmities, those mental troubles, which have been for so long a period thy weary, thy wearing, thy heavy cross. A husband's, a brother's, a friend's greeting thou hast given for the last time; and thy strong faith has now carried thee into the presence of that God whom thou hast always loved so well, whose sovereign will thou hast ever revered, and to whose mysterious dispensations thou hast ever meekly bowed."

Followed by the most distinguished men in the State, including the members of the bar, the president, faculty, and students of Tulane University, Mr. Hunt was buried at the Metairie Cemetery, on the outskirts of New Orleans. Shading his grave grows a mighty moss-covered oak, to mark the spot by a natural and appropriate monument of power and strength.

Upon the opening of the Supreme Court at its April, 1892, term, Edwin T. Merrick, the venerable ex-chief justice of Louisiana, presented to the court resolutions concerning the death of Mr. Hunt. Judge Merrick's review of Mr. Hunt's career was accurate and clothed in most graceful terms. After speaking of the many learned men who practiced in the early days of Louisiana, he referred to Mr. Hunt in the following language: —

"In the city the bar was adorned by such conspicuous names as Mazureau, Grymes, Preston, Pierre Soulé, Roselius, Micou, Bradford, Legardeur, and Benjamin. It was among such men and orators as these that a place of distinction was assigned to Mr. Hunt by them, and he was classed as a leader. I think I may say that the consensus of all placed Mr. Hunt, in those days, as the most finished orator we had at the bar in the State.

"Of course there was a vast difference in conducting arguments by these distinguished men : some could win by the masterly array of the facts of a case, some by the mere force of dry logic, others by a power to awaken interest and sympathy and carry the juries by adorned reason.

"In this last category Mr. Hunt could well be placed. His oratory so ornate and polished, his periods so full and flowing, filled with sentiments elevated and noble, seemed to be formed upon the great models of Cicero, which had charmed us all in our earlier studies as it had done each preceding age.

"Without knowing Mr. Hunt's habits, I never heard him without thinking the excellency of his orations was the result of much study ; but then they were worthy of that study.

"As a statesman Mr. Hunt was controlled by an ardent and exalted patriotism.

"As dean of the legal department of the University he was honored and admired by the graduates."

The resolutions recited the distinguished services of Mr. Hunt as a lawyer and an advocate and a professor.

Chief Justice Bermudez, in speaking for the court, used the following words : —

"Upon the Hon. Randell Hunt Providence had lavished munificently choice favors.

"He was exceptionally endowed, physically and mentally.

" His deportment was such that it attracted attention wherever he went, and provoked inquiry. The eye was pleased to dwell upon him and observe his movements and ways.

" He was blessed with a broad, scanning, searching, penetrating, analytical mind, which, after possessing itself of a subject, made him master it in its entirety and in its important details.

" It was a prompt and ready mind, essentially logical and judicious, which at once realized the strong and the weak points of the subject under its survey and scrutiny.

" He was a scholar, having received a thorough classical education, which enabled him to furnish his intellect plentifully from all the fields of learning and knowledge.

" He could read and speak, with marked correctness, languages not his own, which permitted him to enrich his mind abundantly from stores not entered by the many.

" The study of the law had a special and irresistible attraction for him.

" His classical education, his knowledge of the Latin, French, and Spanish languages, enabled him to explore the immense regions of the Roman, French, and Spanish systems, so as to imbue himself fully with a scientific appreciation of the laws of Louisiana, which are mainly derived from those different sources.

" He belonged to a bar composed of men of acknowledged eminence, such as Livingston, Eustis, Slidell, Hennen, Grymes, Soulé, Mazureau, Benjamin, Bonford, Grailhe, Roselius, Janin, Bradford, and others, whose equal he was, and with whom he coped frequently and successfully.

" He was a splendid orator, learned, impressive, and eloquent, fascinating judges and jurors at his pleasure.

" He was an admitted leader in his profession, and quite often was employed in the most complicated and important controversies. He was a jurist, and a man of great talent and genius.

" It would take too long to enumerate and describe the celebrated instances in which he was thus engaged. The State and Federal Reports which mention them show what difficulties they presented, and he controlled them successfully. The Girard, McDonogh, Shepard will cases, the Slaughter-House, Lizardi, Wine cases, figure conspicuously among them.

" He was for some forty years a distinguished professor of law, commercial, constitutional, criminal, and other, at the University; at times, its dean; retiring finally, on account of ill health, as emeritus professor, with the previously received degree of doctor of laws.

" Very many are those who have studied under him during this long period, and to whom he has imparted liberally his varied and extensive acquirements. Many of them have reached to superiority, and even to eminence in their department, and cherish the recollection of their invariably pleasant intercourse with him, officially and personally.

" He was a faithful citizen and a devoted patriot, serving his country in legislative halls, and was always found among the leaders in political conservative movements.

" He would sway popular assemblies, invariably championing the good and rightful cause, most promotive of public weal and happiness. He was a statesman.

" He might, on several occasions, have filled important federal positions, had he chosen, such as attorney-general, justice on the Supreme Bench, and others: and had he done so he would surely have signalized himself in any of them. He was eminently qualified for all.

" The country has sustained a heavy blow in losing him, but he has gone from among his fellow-men after an honorable, well-filled, and glorious life, regretted and loved, never to be forgotten."

Intellectual greatness alone is often known by the eminence of a position which may demonstrate the talents, but which too often shrouds from general view the inner nature of a man who holds exalted station.

Respect and reputation are sometimes gained and bestowed when no greater intimacy exists than the semi-official relation between pastor and parishioner, or conference between counsel and client, or the consultation with the visiting physician.

But the nobleness of a man's nature, his qualities of heart, his generosity, his benevolence, his consideration of others, his charity of thought, his kindness, his patience, his gentle ways, his affections, his secret ambitions, his pride of family, his wit, temper, unselfishness, habits, — all are best observed and well known only by those who live under the same roof, who sit at the same table, who see him in good and ill health, who watch him when gratified by success or disappointed by defeat, who study his moods in the morning and by night, who learn his motives, who feel his sympathies, listen to his conversation, know his sacrifices, sound the depths of his convictions and the sincerity of his tones, share the happiness of his fortunes and help bear the trials of his adversities.

Of Mr. Hunt it must be said that in his private life his virtues rounded off the measure of his greatness.

No unkind word, no inconsiderate expression which could hurt the feelings of those about him, ever escaped his lips. His nature was very simple, and in the gentleness of his disposition he associated and conversed with the humblest pleasantly and kindly. He never advanced any idea for his own pleasure until he had considered the comfort of others. If there were two motives to be attributed to the conduct of men or women, he preferred that which was founded upon charity to that begotten of malice. His clients always respected him, and though he himself often forgot the labor he had devoted to their interests, they never did, and he was constantly receiving handsome presents from those who expressed themselves as glad to be grateful for services he had rendered.

In their home life very few men have been more truly beloved. His temper was so even and his nature so patient, and withal he was so hospitable and kind. His sense of loyalty to blood was strong. He relied upon the counsel of his brothers, and was happiest when his sisters and other members of his family were immediately about him. To his wife his devotion was beautiful and constant. He addressed her in words of almost poetic endearment, and when writing to his family he often told of his love for her companionship and his pride in her character in language most fit for a lover to use in describing his sweetheart.

The sympathies of his heart and the fellow-feeling within him are well described by the following extract from an argument he once made himself where he touched upon the obligations of nature and morality : —

" The domestic relations of consanguinity, especially in regard to those of the same household, have always been worthy of respect and cherishing. The relation of brothers is the natural source of permanent friendships and intimacies, which soften the cares and contribute to the success and usefulness of life. Their recollections are a bond, in all after-life, of sympathy, interest, and affection. The endearments of childhood : the ruder sports and adventures of the school ; their common interest in events and persons : their common blessings and bereavements: the noble and manly counsels of a father, the wise and tender lessons of a mother, which each can recall to the other's memory ; with interests involving their mutual happiness : protected during life by one roof, and whose dust is to be mingled in the sepulchre of a common soil, — these ties of blood and affection, of kind and tender memories and associations, of habitual sympathies enduring beyond life, give a charm and a dignity to human nature alike pleasing to God and man, and reflecting honor upon those who faithfully observe them, and upon those to whom filial love and reverence are due by divine commandment.

"Who that has a brother can fail to know the large resources that he has in a brother's attachment? The honor or shame of the one must concern the other. A brother can enter fully into a brother's feelings, and his sympathy and confidence be more than those of other friends.

"The members of a man's own family, those who usually live in the same house with him, are naturally the objects of his warmest affections. He is more habituated to sympathize with them. What is called affection is said by a moral philosopher to be in reality nothing but habitual sympathy."

Children were dear to him and attracted his attention. Upon one occasion, Dr. Hawks,[1] the distinguished Episcopalian clergyman, saw him playing marbles with a crowd of little boys. "I see," said the doctor, coming up to Mr. Hunt on the street, upon discovering the distinguished lawyer about to shoot a marble, "the sports of the children amuse the child."

Like most great men, Mr. Hunt knew his power and valued it, but he was free from personal vanity. Notwithstanding the repeated requests of relations and friends, he never sat for a photograph in his life.

With a benevolent and strong face, he was a striking-looking man. He wore a full beard, had a large mouth,

---

[1] Francis Lister Hawks, Doctor of Divinity and Doctor of Laws, long time a celebrated pulpit orator in the United States. He was a native of North Carolina. He was for some time rector of Christ Church, New Orleans, and first president of the University of Louisiana.

with a deep, broad forehead, rather large nose, and partially bald head.

In conversation his voice was soft and his speech slow, but in court or in public it was stern, sonorous, and of tremendous power.

His love of reading prevented his being remembered as a great talker; yet by no means was he a silent man. But he generally had a book before him, even at the times when his family were engaged in general conversation. When he became interested in his reading it absorbed his mind, but when he joined in the discussion, from his richly stocked mind came "treasures of greatest value," which he let fall with unassumed and charming modesty. He had a free and elevated mind. He loved the truth, and had the courage to pronounce for it. Mr. Hunt revered the character of General Washington, and at one time wrote a short life of him, but dropped or mislaid the manuscript, and never heard of it again.

He especially admired oratory. Cicero and Demosthenes, the Earl of Chatham, Daniel Webster, Edward Everett, and Rufus Choate were the examples he generally held up to young men as eloquent, fervent champions of the rights of the others.

Literature was his recreation. Shakespeare, Goldsmith, Coleridge, Bulwer, Pope, and Scott were authors he frequently quoted. Dr. Johnson especially delighted him. But his reading embraced the widest extent, and made him familiar with most writers worthy of study.

The classics, as he thought, were the highest types of pure style. To him the Latin and Greek statesmen and philosophers were the broadest in their schools. Quotations from Horace, Juvenal, Virgil, Socrates, Homer, and Plato adorned his lectures, his arguments, and his conversation.

For years he was a communicant of the Episcopal

Church, and a fairly regular attendant. The Bible was one of his many studies, and was often referred to in his essays. In his opinion men could not live without religion, nor could a nation prosper without reliance upon a superhuman Providence.

He was a deep student of Christian philosophy, and occupied himself early and late with its sublime reflections.

The life of Randell Hunt was within eventful periods of American history. The journey from the gateways of disunion, in 1832, unto the threshold of a celebration of the peace of 1892 was long and tiresome.

In the glory of professional fame his name will live always as an American lawyer, seldom equaled in learning and forensic powers.

If as a statesman his career seems at first to involve disappointment in its immediate results, in the light of events it deserves to be recorded as that of a wise and strong citizen, constantly contributing to the improvement of his State, even where he failed to control her action, and a patriot, whose devotion to the Union was the only foundation of his hopes and desires.

Though that foundation was once shaken, the base was unimpaired by the vibration.

He lived to happily behold his country and his State in the mutual and dependent relations which sixty years before he had contended must exist between the federal and state governments.

As a citizen and a man, he was high-minded, full of courage, and just.

The sorrows of his time, the regrets suffered in his heart, the griefs of repeated failures, never visibly affected his uniformly patient character.

SELECTED ARGUMENTS, LECTURES, AND MISCELLANEOUS PAPERS.

A COURT, A TEMPLE OF JUSTICE.

[The following extract from an argument appeared in "The New Orleans Book," published in 1850 by Robert G. Barnwell. It contained essays by the most distinguished men of Louisiana. In the same publication were articles by François Xavier Martin, Edward Livingston, Etienne Mazureau, Judah P. Benjamin, S. S. Prentiss, and others.]

EDUCATED under the wise and liberal institutions of a republic of laws, I look upon the place in which I stand as a Temple of Justice, not as a theatre for a vain display of powers of disputation in personal rivalry. I regard this Court, not as a weak assembly of individuals, who can be easily operated upon and misled by the dictatorial spirit and arrogant airs of certain orators, who, forgetting that they are mere advocates, foolishly imagine themselves to be, and would make others believe them to be, the true and only oracles of the law, but as an august tribunal, composed of men of good sense, firmness, integrity, and learning: who, uninfluenced by any passion or prejudice, examine the questions properly submitted to them, in a calm and patient spirit of investigation, and, after a full and impartial consideration, decide upon them agreeably to the principles of law and justice.

True liberty is a practical and substantial blessing.

Its existence and its enjoyment depend upon principles which are equally important, and should be equally dear to every man. These principles are founded in the laws, and are recognized, protected, and enforced under every social condition and civilized form of government. They are the safeguards and guarantees of the most invaluable personal rights, of personal security, personal liberty, and the right of private property. In the case now about to be submitted, the last only of these rights is assailed. But this does not diminish the magnitude or interest of the cause itself : for it would be vain to speak of any other right, if it be once authoritatively proclaimed that the acquisitions of labor shall no longer stimulate, cheer, comfort, and enrich industry, but shall be the prize, or rather the prey of unprincipled, reckless, and rapacious power. Such a proclamation would be a declaration of war against humanity and civilization, — against those principles which the very savages hold sacred, as essential to the peace, safety, and harmony of society, and even to the support of individual existence.

The secure enjoyment of property, under the supremacy of the laws, while it incites to industry and promotes enterprise in all the departments of labor, maintains and strengthens in the bosom of the citizen a sense of personal independence which is the foundation of human happiness, and enables him at once to discharge his obligations to his family and to the community of which he is a member. This truth is so simple, so self-evident, that it is universally acknowledged, and even forms a part of the most despotic code. Napoleon himself, in the zenith of his power and glory, would not have dared to lay violent and sacrilegious hands upon the property of the humblest subject of the empire. And what is the spectacle that is now presented? What could not be done under the despotism of a tyrant is audaciously attempted in this com-try of republican equality. A rich, unscrupulous, and greedy corporation has insolently appeared before this Court, and calls upon it to strip private individuals of their hard-earned property, the title to which is not only established and confirmed by every principle of justice and by the special provisions of our own code, but by the uniform opinion and practice of the whole community, and the solemn decisions of our highest Courts under the Spanish laws.

To such a call this Court will not fail to give the stern rebuke of insulted justice. The jurisprudence of the State, so long settled, will remain, under your action, as fixed and stable as the eternal principles of truth and equity which form its basis, and the faith of the Court solemnly pledged in its judgments will continue to be the surest guarantee for the secure enjoyment of property purchased upon it. No licentious or disorganizing doctrine will be suffered to disturb or in any manner to affect the sacredness of a just title ; and the poorest citizen, while he betakes himself to repose under his humble shed, will reflect with pleasure and confidence that the fruits of his honest labors, under the protection of the laws of his country, are beyond the reach of the most unprincipled rapacity, though backed by wealth and acting under the high-sounding name of a CORPORATION.

AN HISTORICAL DISCOURSE UPON THE UNITED STATES.

[The MS. discovered in the papers of Mr. Hunt leaves this essay incomplete, but as far as it goes it is so beautifully written that it has been thought best to publish it. It was composed in the later years of his life, and if he ever finished it the notes were mislaid.]

IT was a common opinion with ancient writers that emigration and the emission of colonies were undertaken in religious obedience to the commands of oracles; but it is probable that on these occasions the oracles did not speak a language dissonant from the views and purposes of the state. But of the motives which led the first settlers of New England to a voluntary exile, induced them to relinquish their native country and to seek an asylum in the then unexplored wilderness of America, the first and principal, no doubt, were connected with religion. They sought to enjoy a higher degree of religious freedom, and what they esteemed a purer form of religious worship, than was allowed to their choice or presented to their imitation in the Old World.

Men have never existed without some religion, "whether," as is said, "it be in the form of the grossest fetish religion, adoring bodies which do not even represent real or imagined animal beings, or polytheism, or monotheism." The consciousness of our dependence and the great limitation of our power, fear or hope, the desire of superior aid or a longing for support and comfort in adversity, which every man feels that he himself or his fellow-men cannot afford, has invariably led man to acknowledge a superior agency of some sort or other. Man has always adored, — the savage and the sage.

Pope expresses and illustrates this with philosophy and with instructive simplicity : —

> Lo, the poor Indian ! whose untutored mind
> Sees God in clouds, or hears him in the wind ;
> His soul proud science never taught to stray
> Far as the solar walk or milky way ;
> Yet simple nature to his hope has given,
> Behind the cloud-topped hill, an humbler heaven ;
> Some safer world in depth of woods embraced,
> Some happier island in the watery waste,
> Where slaves once more their native land behold,
> No fiends torment, no Christians thirst for gold.
> To be content 's his natural desire ;
> He asks no angel's wing, no seraph's fire ;
> But thinks, admitted to that equal sky,
> His faithful dog shall bear him company.

Religion considers and occupies itself with the relation of man to his supreme Ruler. God willed the state and the relation of justice among men. Society is interested, deeply interested, in religion. It affords two powerful agents of morality, namely : mental communion with a Being who is absolutely pure and omniscient, searches the motives in the deep recesses of our heart, and affords support to those who seek it in purity with him ; and, on the other hand, the belief in the immortality of the soul. The love of religious liberty, the freedom which the conscience demands in the cause of religion and the worship of the Deity, and which men feel bound by their hope of salvation to contend for, prepares the mind to act and to suffer almost beyond all other causes. It sometimes gives an impetus so irresistible that no fetters of power or of opinion can withstand it. . . . and is able, with means apparently most inadequate, to shake principalities and powers.

It is certain, said Mr. Webster, that although many of our New England ancestors were republicans in principle, we have no evidence that they would have emigrated, as they did, from their own native country, would have become wanderers in Europe, and finally would have undertaken the establishment of a colony here, merely from their dislike of the political systems of Europe.

They fled not so much from the civil government as from the hierarchy and the laws which enforced conformity to the church establishment. This was not the flight of guilt: it was religion flying from causeless oppression, it was conscience attempting to escape from arbitrary rule.

The Mayflower sought our shores under no high-wrought spirit of commercial adventure, no love of gold, no mixed purpose, warlike or hostile to any human being. Solemn supplications had invoked for her the blessings of Providence. Civil and religious liberty were her guides : her deck was the altar of the living God. Fervent prayers on bended knees mingled, morning and evening, with the voices of ocean and the sighing of the wind in her shrouds. Every prosperous breeze awoke new anthems of praise, and when the elements were wrought into fury, neither the tempest nor the darkness and howling of the midnight storm ever disturbed, in man or woman, the settled purpose of their souls to undergo all, and to do all that patience, resolution, and the highest trust in God could enable human beings to suffer or to perform.

When Columbus, after landing on this continent, returned to Europe and revealed the discovery of America, it at once commanded the attention of all the maritime and commercial states of Europe. Stimulated by love of glory and hope of gain and dominion, ambition and greed uniting, many of them early embarked in adventurous enterprises to found colonies, or to search for the precious metals, or to exchange products of the Old World for whatever was valuable or attractive in the New. The master minds of Europe and America have been directed to this portion of worldly annals, — the history and progress of the European colonies from their establishment in America to the time when they instituted governments of their own, the advance of knowledge and civilization in the Old World during that period of nearly three hundred years, the political and religious events which then took place, the advance of commerce and the love of human liberty, — and have drawn therefrom wise principles of government, law, religion, politics. The present discourse will not examine in detail the events of the period of nearly three centuries. Undoubtedly the religious controversies of the period affected society as well as religion. They changed man himself in his modes of thought, his consciousness of his own powers, and his desire of intellectual attainments, and in the habits of abstraction and reflection and the consequent attachment to principles and laws. The spirit of commercial and foreign adventure, therefore, on the one hand, and on the other the assertion and maintenance of religious liberty, strengthened by divisions among the reformers themselves, and this love of religious liberty bringing with it, as it always does, an ardent devotion to the principle of civil liberty also, were the powerful influences under which character was formed, and men were trained for the great work of introducing English civilization, English law, and, what is more than all, Anglo-Saxon blood into the wilderness of North America. Raleigh and his companions may be considered the creatures of one of the causes that introduced better education, greater knowledge, juster notions of government, and sentiments favorable to civil liberty. High-spirited, full of the love of personal adventure, excited too, in some degree, by the hopes of sudden riches from the discovery of mines of the precious metals, and not unwilling to diversify the labors of settling a colony with occasionally cruising against the Spaniards in the West Indian seas, they crossed and re-crossed the ocean with a frequency which surprises us when we consider the state of navigation, and which evinces a most daring spirit. The other cause peopled New England.

There was a marked difference of principles on which the colonization of the tropical region and of the whole of South America by Spain and Portugal was conducted, and the principles on which the colonies in the northern part of the continent were founded and governed. Long before the first permanent English settlement had been accomplished in what became the United States, Spain pushed her settlements in America with vigor and eager-ness; conquered Mexico, Peru, and Chili, and extended her power over other territory. The precious metals were her object; and the subjugated natives were set to work for their conquerors in the mines of silver and gold. Spain is described descending on the New World in mili-tary garb, with military commanders and rude soldiers, robbing and destroying the native race by authority of her king for the aggrandizement of his power and the ex-tension of his prerogative. She swooped on South Amer-ica like a vulture on its prey. Her colonies, from their origin to their end, were subject to the sovereign authority of the mother country. Their government, as their com-merce, was a strict Spanish monopoly; and the important posts in the administration of the colonies were filled ex-clusively by natives of old Spain. Wise, benignant prin-ciples of government may be found in the fundamental laws of the colonies. But the kings of Spain delegated their powers to the "Council of the Indies:" wise laws were left unexecuted, and oppression and extortion reigned. Advance in a colony absolutely guided by the mother country, notwithstanding the great assistance the latter may afford to the former, is small and tardy compared to the advance of a community allowed to manage its own concerns unaided, and even checked at times by a distant administration. This is signally illustrated in the difference of principles on which the colonization in South America by Spain and Portugal was conducted, and the principles on which the colonies on the northern part of the continent were founded and governed. Martin, in his history of Louisiana, said, "Judge Marshall has shown this;" adding somewhat quaintly, "Sequar, sequar: sed haud passibus æquis."

Leaving South America and Mexico to Spain and Portugal, this discourse proceeds to France and England struggling for the possession of North America. There was something different, perhaps characteristic, in the settlement and colonization by these states. The English, disposed to maritime adventure, settled, when they first set foot on America, on the seacoast, in a rocky strand and a sterile soil; cleared it by the efforts of persevering industry; and, after the lapse of a century and a half, surmounted the ridge of the Alleghanies and spread themselves over the alluvial plains of the Ohio and the Mississippi. The French followed from the first the course of the great rivers, and established stations which, Alison declares, if adequately supported, would beyond all question have given them the empire of the New World. Their American colonies, planned and planted with extraordinary and prophetic sagacity, rose up with great rapidity, and early assumed a formidable aspect; but the French, though amply endowed with the genius which conceives, had not the perseverance which matures colonies. They thought to snatch greatness as by military conquest : they could not submit to win it by the toil of pacific exertion. They did not spread into the woods and subdue nature by the enduring labor of free men. So wrote the British historian.

The English colonists settled in thirteen colonies, distinct and separate, contiguously situated along the margin of the shore of North America, but chartered by adventurers of various characters, including sectarians, religious and political, which for the two preceding centuries had agitated and divided the people of the British islands, and with them were intermingled the descendants of Hollanders, Swedes, Germans, and French fugitives from the Revocation of the Edict of Nantes. Enterprise, stubborn endurance of privation, unflinching intrepidity in facing danger, and inflexible adherence to conscientious principle had steeled to energetic and unyielding hardihood the characters of the primitive settlers of all these colonies.

Since that time two or three generations of men had passed away, but they had increased and multiplied with unexampled rapidity, and the land itself had been the recent theatre of a ferocious seven-years' war between the two most powerful and most civilized nations of Europe, contending for the possession of this continent. The victorious combatant had been Britain. She had conquered the provinces of France : she had expelled her rival totally from the continent, over which, bounding herself by the Mississippi, she was to hold divided empire only with Spain : she had acquired undisputed control over the Indian tribes, still tenanting the forests unexplored by the European man : she had established an uncontested monopoly of the commerce of all her colonies, who had loyally and valiantly played their part. The colonial history of the United States is now amply written.

In the bosoms of this people there was burning, kin-

dled at different furnaces of affliction, one liberty, says
Adams. The quality, the leading feature in the character of the American colonial people in the age of the
Revolution was what Edmund Burke, the profound and
eloquent British statesman and orator, declared in Parliament was their "fierce spirit of liberty." "The love
of liberty is stronger in them than in any other people
on the face of the earth." "It is the united voice of
America," wrote gallant and glorious Warren, little more
than six months before he fell on the heights of Charlestown, "to preserve their freedom, or lose their lives in
defense of it." Rufus Choate of Massachusetts properly
estimated and prized this trait in the character of the
people. The people of New England, at the beginning
of the Revolutionary War, to describe them in a word,
were the Puritans of Old England as they existed in that
country in the first half of the seventeenth century, but
changed, — somewhat improved. The original stock was
the Puritan character of the age of Elizabeth, of James
I., and of Charles I. For a hundred years they were
the sole depositaries of the sacred fire of liberty in England, after it had gone out in every other bosom. When
they first took their seats in the House of Commons,
they found it the cringing and ready tool of the throne ;
they reanimated it, remodeled it, reasserted its privileges,
restored it to its original rank, drew back to it the old
power of making laws and imposing taxes, abridged the
tremendous power of the crown and defined it. And
when at last Charles Stuart resorted to arms to restore
the despotism they had partially overthrown, they met
him on a hundred fields of battle, and, after a sharp and
long struggle, buried crown, despotism, and the headless
trunk of the king himself beneath the foundations of a
civil and religious commonwealth. It was just when Pu-
ritanism had attained in England its highest point, and

the love of liberty had grown to be the master passion that guided all the rest, — just then our portion of its disciples came hither. The Puritan character has been justly described as "an extraordinary mental and moral phenomenon, developed, disciplined, and perfected for a particular day and duty." The influences which combined to form it from the general mind of England; which set this sect apart from all the rest of the community, and stamped upon it a system of manners, a style of dress and salutation and phraseology, a distinct. entire scheme of opinions upon religion, government, morality, and human life, marking it off from the crowds about it, — these things are matters of popular history, and need not be enumerated. . . . But the whole history of the Puritans, — not only of those who remained in England, but also of those who came out from it, and nobly aided in founding our free American republican commonwealth, — their religious and active character, their theological doctrines, their notions of the divine government and economy and of the place they filled in it. everything about them was out of the ordinary course of life.

Wonderful cases of popular delusion, which, infecting every class of society and gaining strength from its very extravagance, triumphing over human reason and cruelly sporting with human life, should teach man never to countenance a departure from that moderation and those safe and sure principles of moral rectitude which have stood the test of time, and received the approbation of the wise and good in all ages. In Great Britain as well as in America, the opinion had long prevailed that, by the aid of malignant spirits, certain persons possessed supernatural powers which were usually exercised in the mischievous employment of tormenting others. and the criminal code of both countries was

disgraced with laws for the punishment of witchcraft.
Some instances had occurred in New England of putting
this sanguinary law in force; but in 1692 this weakness was
converted into frenzy, and its destructive, baneful activity
was extended to persons in every situation of life. . . .
Never, says Mr. Hutchinson, was there given a more
melancholy proof of the degree of depravity of which man
is capable when the public passions countenance crime.
It hath been said, "The persecutions of the Quakers,
the controversies with Roger Williams and Mrs. Hutchinson, the perpetual synods and ecclesiastical surveillance
of the old times, — a great deal of this is too tedious to
be read, or it offends and alienates you. It is truth, fact,
but it is just what you do not want to know, and are none
the wiser for knowing." Yet the author said, more truly
and justly, "History is full of instruction, and written for
instruction. Especially may we say so of our own. Its
moral lessons are the most valuable."

From this painful notice our discourse turns to the
circumstances by which the spirit of liberty which brought
these colonists hither was strengthened and reinforced,
until it burst forth and wrought the Revolution. Let it
be remembered that the colonists came to settle in America,
to seek a home for themselves and their posterity, — a
new home, to become dearer and dearer as time should
wear away; not a mere sojourn or place of temporary
residence for the acquisition of means to return and live
in a better society and better place of enjoyment, but a
home of permanent abode, a shelter from persecution
and the storms of life, a place of final earthly rest and
burial for themselves, and of refuge, comfort, and enjoyment for their children. Local attachments and sympathies would spring up, the ground which was to cover
them in death would be hallowed, like the consciousness
that they would sleep, dust to dust, with the objects of

their affections. Before they reached the shore, they had, on board the Mayflower, established the elements of a social system. At the moment of their landing, therefore, they possessed institutions of religion. The morning that beamed on the first night of their repose saw them already at home in their country. From the first there was a repugnance to an entire submission to the control of British legislation. The colonies stood upon their charters, which, as they contended, exempted them from the ordinary power of the British Parliament, and authorized them to conduct their own concerns by their own counsels. The more distinguished of them refused to come to America, unless they could bring charters providing for the administration of their affairs in this country. They saw from the first the evils of being governed in the New World by a power in the Old. While they acknowledged the proper general power of the crown, they insisted on the right of passing local laws and of local administration. They utterly resisted the notion that they were to be ruled by the mere authority of the government on the other side of the Atlantic, and would not even endure that their own charter should be established there. They had freedom enough to teach them its value from the contentions and trials of England, and to love it: but their liberty was still incomplete, and it was constantly in danger from England. " From the day that the Pilgrims on board the Mayflower at Plymouth, before they landed, drew up that simple but pregnant form of democracy, and subscribed their names, and came out a colony of republicans, to the battle of Lexington, there were not ten years together — I hardly exempt the Protectorate of Cromwell — in which some right, some great and sacred right, as the colonists regarded it, was not assailed or menaced by the government of England, in one form or another." From the first, the

mother country complained that the colonists had brought
from England, or had found here, too much liberty, —
liberty inconsistent with prerogatives of the crown, inconsistent with supremacy of Parliament, inconsistent
with the immemorial relations of all colonies to the country they sprang from, — and she set herself to abridge it.
They answered, with great submission, that they did not
honestly think they had brought or had found much
more than half liberty enough, and they braced themselves to keep what they had, and obtain more when they
could ; and so, with one kind of weapon or another, on
one field or another, on one class of questions or another,
a struggle was kept up, from the landing at Plymouth to
the surrender at Yorktown.   It was all one single struggle from beginning to end, — parties, objects, principles,
the same, — one long, glorious, triumphant struggle for
liberty.   The topics, the heads of dispute, varied from
reign to reign ; but the question was one, — Shall the
colonists be free, or shall they be slaves ?   Encroachments
of the British ministry upon their chartered rights, the
tyranny of the mother country and the evils under which
the colonies labored, the attempt to tax the people of the
colonies without their consent, and the claim of a right
to do so without limitation, and to bind them by her statutes in all cases whatsoever, plainly manifested a determination to reduce the colonies to a condition of slavery
too grievous to be endured, — utterly intolerable to such
men as our Fathers, and destructive of their right to
property.   No man has a right to that which another has
a right to take from him.

From the commencement, at every step or increase of
encroachment, the colonists, in their fierce love of liberty
and with jealous vigilance, detected the movement and
approach of tyranny, and resisted its advance.   They
augured misgovernment at a distance, and snuffed tyranny

in every tainted gale. A philosophic statesman, H. S. Legaré, declares: I think it may be truly said that the first settlers were, of all men, the most sensitive and the best informed upon their rights and liberties. They were heterogeneously composed: Huguenots who, having extorted by their valor a short interval of repose from persecution, at length abjured forever their beautiful native land: not to search for gold and silver, not to overrun vast regions with lust of ambitious dominion, but to plunge into the depths of an untrodden wilderness, because in its dreary solitude they could commune with God, and pour out their feelings of adoration, which they could not utter in the land of their birth without being hunted down like wild beasts. They were the austere and gloomy Puritans of England, the stern and fanatic followers of Pym and Hollis and Hampden, who had been republicans even in Europe, and had quitted Europe because it was unworthy of a republic, — those men to whom England is altogether indebted for the democratic part of her constitution. It was these heroes and tried champions of religious liberty, who looked upon the riches and honors of this world as dust and ashes, in comparison with the principles upon which they built their steadfast faith, who not only loved liberty as something desirable in itself and essential to the dignity of human nature, but regarded it as a solemn duty to free themselves from every species of restraint that was incompatible with the fullest rights of conscience: who, possessing all that devotedness and elevation of character so natural to minds nursed in the habitual contemplation of such subjects, and penetrated with their majesty and importance, had learned " to fear God and to know no other fear," — it was such men as these, together with the unfortunate, the persecuted, the adventurous, the bold, the aspiring of all climes and conditions, congregated and confounded in one vast asylum, and exercised, by the hardships incident to the colonization of a new country, with a sort of Spartan discipline that laid the foundation of our flourishing commonwealths.

Differences were traced between the descendants of the early colonists of Virginia and those of New England, owing to the different influences and different circumstances under which the respective settlements were made : but the habits, sentiments, and objects of both soon became modified by their condition in the New World ; and as both adopted the same general principles of English jurisprudence, and became accustomed to the authority of representative bodies, these differences gradually diminished by the progress of time and the influence of intercourse, and the necessity of some degree of union and coöperation to defend themselves against the savage tribes, — tending to inspire mutual respect and regard, thus creating among these colonies a pleasing variety, in the midst of a general family resemblance, frequently and classically likened, —

Facies, non omnibus una,
Nec diversa tamen, quatem decet esse sororum.

Let us here pause. The situation of the colonies at such an immense distance from the centre of the British empire must, in those days of navigation, have weakened the allurement and attraction that drew to it ; and the peculiar character of the first settlers produced an interest and a feeling in the colonies different from those of mere Englishmen. They were in a new country, in a new world, a new home, with established social system, institutions of government and of religion, endeared to them as a place of refuge. They were not to return and abide again in England. Local attachments and sympathies sprang up in their breasts, friends and families in relation of love and affection ; property rewarded their

2

industry and enterprise. Children were born, and the hopes of future generations arose in their new habitation. The second generation found this the land of their nativity, and saw they were bound to its fortunes. Their fathers' graves were around them : they read the memorials of their toils and labors, and rejoiced in the inheritance which they found bequeathed to them. The soil answered genially to its culture and the sea presented its way to commerce, without a barrier. Neither they nor their children were again to till the soil of England nor again to traverse the seas which surround her. But here was a new sea now open to their enterprise, and a new soil which had not failed to respond gratefully to their laborious industry. Hardly had they provided shelter for the living ere they were summoned to erect sepulchres for the dead. The ground had become sacred by inclosing the remains of some companions and connections. Where the heart has laid down what it loves most, there it is desirous of laying itself down. A new circle of engagements, interests, and affections occupied the heart, till an undivided sentiment prevailed that " this was their country, and patriotism became local to America." A government of their own, and existing immediately within their limits, was absolutely necessary to gratify the wishes and secure the rights and liberty of the colonies. They brought with them English liberties, — the trial by jury, the Habeas Corpus and Magna Charta, the principle that if any power can tax the people without their consent there is an end of liberty. They brought the general principles of the common law of England, and adopted only that portion applicable to their condition. " I deride," wrote Jefferson, " the ordinary doctrine that we brought with us from England the common law rights. . . . The truth is, we brought with us the rights of men, expatriated men. We adopted that system with which we are familiar, to be altered by us occasionally and adapted to our new situation. Political institutions were to be framed anew, and our fathers, acting boldly, put in force principles of philosophy and freedom which had nowhere else been fully admitted in practice."

The limits of this discourse do not allow any detailed examination and history of the bloody Indian wars which harassed the colonists, nor of the discouragements inherently belonging to all forms of colonial governments, nor of the violations by the mother country of the rights granted to the colonists in express charter, nor of the numerous encroachments, illegal threats and illegal attempts to tax and monopolize the trade of her colonies, and a continued effort of the colonies to resist or evade that monopoly. The character of the primitive English settlers has been sufficiently described. Since that time two or three generations had passed away, but the colonists had increased and multiplied with unexampled rapidity; and the land itself had been the recent theatre of a seven-years' war between France and Britain contending for the possession of this continent.

        .   .   .   .

Here we pause. From our discourse we have looked back to the settlement of the English colonies in North America: to the origin of their union; to the conflict of war, by which the severance from the mother country and the release from the thralldom of a transatlantic monarch were effected : to the undaunted and steadfast maintenance of independence through that fiery ordeal, and the conclusion of peace with the same monarch whose sovereignty over them they had abjured, " in obedience to the laws of nature and of nature's God."

The Continental Congress constituted, in fact, the national government and conducted the national affairs until near the close of the Revolution, and extended only to the

maintenance of the public liberties of all the States during the contest with Great Britain.   It would naturally
terminate with the return of peace and the accomplishment of the ends of the revolutionary contest.   How
great would be the danger of the separation of the confederated States into independent communities, acknowledging no common head and acting upon no common
system, presented itself to the consideration of Congress.
What rivalries, jealousies, real or imaginary wrongs, di-
versities of local interests and institutions, would soon
sever the ties of a common attachment, and bring on a
state of hostile operations, dangerous to the peace and
subversive of their permanent interests!   These and other
considerations of the immediate public safety, the pressing urgent condition of affairs, had led finally to the
unanimous approval and adoption of Articles of Confederation in March, 1781, which thenceforth became the
government.

　　.　　.　　.　　.　　.　　.　　.　　.　　.

Our discourse will now pass, by an easy and natural
transition, from emigration and allegiance to the subject
of " Colonization and Colonists," but will first state anew
what hath been briefly said of obedience and the power of
the State.

Commanding and obeying are the first two foundations
of all human society.   Society without laws would lose its
moral character, and man would forfeit his destiny as a
social being ; and therefore man's destiny requires obedience to laws.   Absolute obedience is impossible, and, if it
were possible, immoral ; for man cannot divest himself of
his moral individuality and responsibility.   It is a maxim,
Ad impossibilia nemo obligatur ; and further it is a
maxim, *Ad turpia nemo obligatur,* — No man is bound to
do what is iniquitous.   Lieber writes : When Charles IX.
of France, or his mother, issued orders to slaughter the

Protestants in the provinces, as they had been murdered
in Paris on the eve of St. Bartholomew, several governors
and other officers — Sully mentions seven — declined obedience. Viscount Orthes, or Ortes, commandant at Bayonne, wrote back: " Sire, I have found in Bayonne honest
citizens and brave soldiers only, but not one executioner.
They and myself supplicate your Majesty to use our arms
and lives in possible things." He was right to call this
commanded murder an impossible, an unfeasible thing for
man, an honest man, to do. Obedience is necessary in
general; disobeying or non-compliance is the exception.

The efficiency of the land and naval forces of a nation
depends essentially upon unity, quickness, and energy of
action. At all times, therefore, stricter obedience has been
exacted in the army and navy than in any other branch.
Armies without discipline are positive evils to their country, and discipline consists mainly in a universal habit of
obedience throughout the whole body; not that discipline
can become a substitute for patriotism. It was said: One
Spartan, who glories in falling for his country, is worth
twenty Medes, who, as Herodotus tells us, were whipped
into the fight by their officers against the Grecian band at
Thermopylæ. Patriotism in an army, however, will become efficient only in the same degree as it is coupled
with discipline. Yet even in the army and navy absolute
obedience is not and cannot be demanded. Disobedience
to commands of superiors may take place, because the
command may be unlawful, contrary to the established
law of the land. It is settled in the United States that
an officer of the forces who executes the unlawful order
remains personally answerable. Before he disobeys, he
ought to be thoroughly convinced that the command is
clearly unlawful. He must decide it at his own peril or
responsibility. This is also the law in England. The
British and American articles of war demand obedience

to all lawful commands. All obedience, even the military oath of obedience, is conditional. The military man does not become an unfeeling, unthinking, absolute instrument. If the orders of his superiors are palpably at variance with the essential objects of the State and traitorous to his country, he is bound to disobey.

According to the British law, the monarch is commander-in-chief of all the forces, and disposer of peace and war. Admiral Pennington had been sent by Charles I., amid the acclamations of England, to give effect to a generous treaty with the oppressed and besieged Huguenots at Rochelle : but he had no sooner arrived at the place of his destination than he found himself under secret orders to give up his vessels to French command under a " murderous warfare against British honor and the Protestant religion." Here was a flagrant conspiracy of Charles and Buckingham against the State, an outrageous abuse of power, with criminal deception : and Pennington was right not to obey, and to draw up his high-minded protest. The sailors were right who wrote what is called " a round robin " against the service, and laid it under the Bible of their admiral, whose sentiments accorded with their own.

The State must have power and authority for its government. Justice requires that every man shall have his due. The State, through its government, must protect every citizen against the violation of his rights by wrong-doers and enemies, and must maintain its jural moral character as a society of right. The State has, it is one of the main objects of the State, to obtain jointly that which is necessary for society and cannot be obtained by individual exertion, to obtain publicly what cannot be obtained privately, as we have seen. Public power is founded upon confidence. However circumscribed, definite, and carefully limited the power granted, confidence must be reposed in him who is finally to carry out that law, — the confidence of common sense and moral sense. But this confidence may be abused. Why? Republicans complain of the abuse of power practiced by monarchs, their ministers, commanders; and yet each complainant carries within himself the germ of a despot, and abuses power proportionately within his sphere as much as the others in theirs. Each party that is out complains of the abuse of power in that which is in. These complaints are not all mere declamation.

Where power, energy, or any faculty for action or activity has been given, there likewise exists an intense desire to exercise, to practice and apply it. It is its very nature, and without it the world would be at a stand. Whatever we may undertake originally by way of interest, the love of activity, the desire to leave some memorial of one's self, to produce and effect something, soon supersedes it. Thus Lieber in his book on political ethics contends : " What impels every votary of science to pursue his toilsome paths? Is it interest? Is it utility alone, or chiefly? Or is it the delight which the human mind feels in the consciousness of activity? *Omnis enim scientia et admiratio (quæ est semen scientiæ) per se jucunda est,* says Bacon. And what is this *admiratio* but the delight of intense activity and consciousness of the power and penetrating or combining action of our mind?" All absence of activity pains us.

Few who have power are willing to give it up, whether in the people or the monarch. All power, however lawful, being resisted, the first feeling in those intrusted with it is, not that of regret at this resistance on account of the object they had in view, but of offense at the opposition itself. This is not peculiar to one set of men or class of society, but without exception true of all. Monarchic power is not more offended at resistance than democratic or parental power. Few men indeed are ever opposed without at the first moment having the feeling of being wronged ; and this extends even to the most atrocious criminal. Whoever wields the public power feels irritated by opposition, be it ever so peaceful or loyal. Power, therefore, would overcome everything in its way, if not modified, or if not generated in a manner which insures the least possible danger. Power imposes, misleads, receives everywhere respect by its own character. However illegally acquired, the great action of power obtains homage, and may find aids and abettors. This shows the importance, the necessity to limit and prevent the executive, the depositary of this vast acting and imposing power, from luxuriant rank growth, and the independence of the judiciary.

This portion of our discourse will close with the following remarks on the eloquent and noble epigram, the inscription decreed by the national council of the Amphictyons, having a special reference to the Spartans who fell at Thermopylæ with their king in obedience to their laws. The epigram has been often translated. The English version of it by Bowles —

      "Go tell the Spartans, thou that passest by,
      That here, obedient to their laws, we lie" —

has been pronounced perfect. "The epigram is but two lines, and all Greece for centuries had them by heart. She forgot them, and Greece was living Greece no more."

[During the political difficulties which followed the presidential election of November, 1876, Mr. Hunt was begged to express his views upon the law governing the action of the Louisiana Returning Board. He took no active part in the trial of Thomas C. Anderson for having uttered and published certain alleged forged and counterfeited public records or statements of votes in the parish of Vernon, but wrote a history of the case, together with his own views upon the law governing the facts brought out upon the trial. A statement of the facts is found in the article itself.]

THOMAS C. ANDERSON was tried and found guilty by the verdict of a jury upon the charge of having falsely and feloniously uttered and published as true a certain altered, forged, and counterfeited public record, to wit, the consolidated statement of votes in the parish of Vernon for presidential electors on the 7th November, 1876, knowing the same to be false, altered, forged, and counterfeited, with intent to injure and defraud.

The information was based on the following section of the Revised Statutes of Louisiana : —

" Sect. 833. Whoever shall publish as true any false, altered, forged, or counterfeited public record, knowing the same to be false, altered, forged, or counterfeited, with intent to injure or defraud any person or any body politic or corporate, shall, on conviction, be punished by imprisonment at hard labor, not less than two nor more than fourteen years."

Anderson, having been convicted and recommended to

the mercy of the court, was, after unsuccessful motions
for a new trial and in arrest of judgment, sentenced to
two years at hard labor in the penitentiary of the State.
The sentence was the least punishment the law allows.
It was pronounced 25th February, 1878, and on the same
day he was granted an appeal to the Supreme Court of
Louisiana, returnable within ten days, under a statute of
the 19th of that month.

When the jurors were impaneled upon Anderson's
trial, they were to try not only the fact whether he uttered
the false and altered writing, but also whether he uttered
and published it, knowing it to be false and altered, with
a fraudulent design, the intent to deceive and defraud.
The information sets forth not only the particular act
committed, but also the motive to which it owed its origin
and received its complexion, and thus specifies the crime:
It charges that the uttering was done feloniously, falsely,
with intent to injure and defraud. The design is interwoven with the transaction. Both depend upon a collected
view of particular circumstances from the testimony, from
the character of the witnesses, the parties, the occasion.
This was the issue. The intention constituted the crime.
It was a proper subject of inquiry by the jury. It is a
mental fact: it exists in the mind of the man who conceives it. He may conceal it from others, but often declares it by words or reveals it by some act. When the
jury, after receiving the advice and assistance of the
judge as to the law, determined, upon the circumstances of
the case, that Anderson was guilty, they declared upon oath
the entire charge against him to be true and proved beyond a doubt, namely: first, that he uttered and published
as true the false, altered, forged, and counterfeited public
record or statement, knowing the same to be false and
altered and forged; and second, that he committed the
act willfully and feloniously, with the intent to defraud.

The verdict and the sentence of the criminal court settled forever the fact that Anderson premeditatedly, deliberately, and corruptly uttered as true a statement which he knew to be false and altered of the votes of a large portion of the people of Louisiana, with the felonious intent to defraud the people of the State, and so of the whole United States, of the right to choose their own chief executive magistrate, the President of this mighty republic!

It would be absurd and contrary to every criminal prosecution to say that a jury cannot judge from the evidence of the motive and intention of the accused. Suppose a jury impaneled to try one accused of murder. They may find him guilty of the fact of having killed the deceased, but not of having killed him maliciously, and may find him guilty of manslaughter only, or even of excusable or justifiable homicide, and by their verdict decide upon the law and fact. Again, suppose a jury impaneled on the trial of one charged with publishing a false and malicious libel : would a judge be allowed to charge the jury that the only question for them to consider was whether the writing in the information was published by the accused, but that the question whether the writing was a libel or not was a question of law for the judge to determine, that libel or no libel was a question of law exclusively for the court to decide, and not for the jury?

The true and just rule and the invariable course is first to give a legal definition of the offense, and then to leave it to the jury to say whether the circumstances and facts necessary to constitute the offense have been proved to their satisfaction. If the judge's opinion must rule, the trial by jury would be useless. He might by a too latitudinarian construction bring the fact within the severity of the law, or by a too strict and confined construction he might exclude it, though clearly within the spirit of the law, and in either case do manifest wrong. A mistake of judgment in an impartial jury, after receiving the advice and assistance of a judge upon the law, is less to be apprehended than the possible error of judgment or will in the judge, who, whatever may be his knowledge or probity, is but a man; and therefore the State of Louisiana hath wisely ordained that her judges shall aid the jury in criminal cases in obtaining knowledge of the law applicable to them, but shall abstain from stating the evidence or giving any opinion on it to influence their decision.

Numerous cases have been decided by the Supreme Court of the State in conformity with this law. We cite a single one to show how strictly it has been interpreted and enforced. It is the case of Cammeyer et al., in 8th A. 312–315. "The defendants were indicted and convicted of the crime of larceny. On the trial of the cause in the district court, their counsel requested the court to charge the jury that the facts, as sworn to, did not amount in law to larceny. The judge refused the charge, but gave the following as the law to the jury: 'It is necessary, in order to constitute larceny, that there should be a felonious taking, and that may be properly thus defined: the taking and carrying away are felonious when the goods are taken against the will of the owner, either in his absence or in a clandestine manner, or where possession is obtained by force or surprise, or by any trick, device, or fraudulent expedient, the owner not parting voluntarily with his interest in the goods, and where the taker intends fraudulently to deprive the owner of his entire interest in the property against his will. Whether in this case there has been such felonious taking the jury must determine from the facts proved.' The defendants rest their hope of reversing the finding of the jury upon the distinction between obtaining the mere possession of the thing by artifice and deceit, and the case where the owner is induced by fraudulent representations to part both with the property and the possession of the thing. The jurisdiction of this (the Supreme) Court extends to criminal cases on law alone; and if we were to examine the facts on which the jury found the verdict, in order to determine whether the court below erred in refusing to charge them that those facts did not constitute larceny, we would certainly be exceeding our jurisdiction, and deciding on the facts as well as the law. We have attentively considered the charge which the judge did give the jury, and are of opinion that it is a clear and correct exposition of the law."

The 7th November, 1876, was an important day in the history of our common country and of the State of Louisiana. It was the day fixed for the appointment of presidential electors by the several States of the Union. It was also the day set apart by the people of Louisiana for choosing their own state officers; and elections were accordingly held. There was a majority of popular voters throughout the entire Union in favor of Democratic presidential electors, and there was a majority in Louisiana — large and decisive — not only for Democratic electors of President, but also for Democratic state officers. The Republican party had conducted their election campaign with unscrupulous activity. They used the entire power, patronage, and influence of the general government, with its host of officers, employees, and agents, its countless jobs and vast expenditure of public money, to corrupt, control, and debauch the virtue and action of the people. None were deemed too high to be tempted, none too low to be purchased. A member of the Cabinet at the seat of government was placed at the head of their central committee. Agents were stationed at the door of pay offices to exact contributions from subordinate officials. The whole class were made to exert and exhaust their power. Even the army of the republic was moved about for electioneering purposes. All ordinary means of success were applied in vain, some remarkably bad, and perhaps even criminal, — promises, menaces, intrigue, bribery! What, then, was to be done? To preserve the party from ruin, the administration of the government, its offices, power, patronage, must be retained, and this could only be effected by stifling the voice and defeating the will of the people, and by substituting in their place a false and altered return of votes cast at the presidential election. This called for contrivance, secrecy, concerted action, and boldness, surmounting all sense of danger and of shame. It was a last resort.

Flectere si nequeo Superos, Acheronta movebo.

Then, in Washington, the capital of the country, honored with the name dear to every true American, was devised in Republican conclave the scheme to procure, from "state officers and canvassers of election" for presidential electors, false and fraudulent certificates, framed to serve as a pretext for a false count of the electoral votes, to enable the president of the Senate, by an usurpation of power, to determine all questions in controversy, and to threaten the enforcement of his pretended authority by the army and navy of the United States: the falsification of the records and returns of election to be made, prepared, and furnished by local officers and agents, and the fraud to be consummated in Washington.

Pudet et hæc opprobria nobis
Et potuisse dici, et non potuisse refelli.

Among the victims doomed to be sacrificed to this fraud, the State of Louisiana and her good people were conspicuous. More than any other State of the Union had she suffered from the oppression and spoliation of the dominant faction, after the baleful attempt at secession, from the overthrow of her government and the military

establishment of corrupt rulers over her. Long, too long
and too patiently, had she endured the dark reign of
terror, of usurpation and depravity, whereof the gloom
had occasionally — for a moment, and only for a moment
— been relieved by a popular display of valor and regard
for constitutional rights. Time, however, was bringing
healing on its wings. The citizens of the State were
gradually, steadily acquiring — yea, had acquired, to the
dismay of their profligate oppressors and despoilers —
power to check their career and to defeat the faction.
But tyranny was cunning grown. Forewarned, fore-
armed. It noted from afar that the political atmosphere
was troublous and a storm was brewing, and foresaw the
necessity of guarding and perpetuating itself by strong
and artful means, which would control and command the
return of votes necessary in popular elections, and vest in
subservient officials the power and duty of appointing to
public trust and office none but its own tools and favorites, regardless of the people's will. It invented, devised,
and constructed, in 1870, the infernal machine ycleped
the " Returning Board," created and used originally
for state elections, and afterwards altered and employed
in the presidential election by the Washington conspiracy.

The invention, the description of its component parts,
powers, action, etc., is set forth in an act of the General
Assembly of the State, composed of seventy-one sections,
and designated, " An act to maintain the freedom and
purity of elections, and to enforce Article 103 of the Constitution, which ordains that the right of free suffrage in
elections shall be supported by laws prohibiting all undue
influence thereon from favor, bribery, tumult, or other
improper practice." (Rev. Statutes La.) The act created a board of five persons, constituted them a close
corporation, and gave them perpetual succession. At

first one Democrat was appointed on the Board, but he was soon got rid of, and the other four members, belonging to the Republican faction, desiring to work in secret, refused to fill his place.   It gave the Board power to canvass and compile all statements of votes and election returns in the State, and to pronounce who were lawfully elected : to examine and determine charges and questions of fraud, violence, or other improper practice to influence the election, and, in case there was any such thing, to exclude all the votes of the parish, etc., and thus to condemn and punish by disfranchisement thousands of voters, without a hearing, for the offense, real or supposed, of others, over whom they had no control, and to make a mockery of the people's will.

Judge Black, in a masterly essay on the Electoral Conspiracy, declared the Returning Board " a machine entirely new, with powers never before given to any tribunal in any State.   Its object was, not to return, but to suppress the votes of the qualified electors, or change them to suit the occasion."   It was no sooner called into existence than it entered upon its nefarious and infamous work. No delay, no hesitation, no faltering.   On and on it proceeded in its ruthless and wicked task !   The people of the State at every election expressed their condemnation, strong and indignant, against the odious and corrupt faction that oppressed and ruled over them.   The Board intercepted the election returns, kept them in strict and close custody, and so altered them as to make a majority the other way.   Kellogg was a candidate for governor. He was defeated.   The Board certified him elected. " The certificate was so glaringly false that carpetbaggers themselves would not help to install him.   The outraged people rose in revolutionary wrath, and inaugurated McEnery, the man who had been really elected.   But General Grant placed and retained Kellogg in office by a shameful military usurpation. The Democrats regularly elected a majority of the legislature; as regularly the Returning Board certified a majority of their seats to carpetbaggers or scalawags, or negroes not chosen; and when the true members met to organize for business, the army was punctually in hand to tumble them out of their hall." [1]

Nothing could be more unjust, unconstitutional, oppressive, and intolerable to freemen than the condition of Louisiana. The government was a usurpation and despotism. It exercised, through the Returning Board, exclusive control over elections; in disregard of truth, justice, and popular action, it abolished existing courts, and substituted others, with election provisions, and judges appointed by the governor; it enacted criminal punishment of all persons attempting to fill official positions, unless returned by the Returning Board; it created unjust, mischievous, grievous, and odious monopolies and corporations, offices, and employments: involved the State, already overburdened with debts, in heavier and further obligations; oppressed the people with ruinous taxes and exactions; converted the police of New Orleans into an armed brigade, subject to the command of the governor; and vested in the governor of the State a degree of power scarcely exercised by any sovereign in the world.

This was the condition of Louisiana on the 7th November, 1876, the day on which her people were to choose a governor, members of her legislature, and other state officers, and to vote for a President and Vice-President of the United States. The election was duly held on the appointed day. All the offices and officers of election, the registration of citizens entitled to vote in the several parishes, every poll and voting precinct, the reception or rejection of ballots and their counting, the returns and

---

[1] *North American Review*, No. 257.

result of the election, — all, everything, from the beginning to the close, and the promulgation of the result, to be performed, supervised, and controlled by party men, creatures of the Republican faction, commissioners, superintendents, deputy-marshals, and attendant soldiers and police.

The elections were peaceable, quiet, undisturbed. The vote was regularly taken and properly counted, and a true record made of it. Returns from every Democratic parish were sent to the Returning Board without a single charge or protest of fraud, violence, or intimidation. The vote was large, free, unrestrained, a true expression of the people's judgment and choice. If the state government was a constitutional Democratic - Republican government, if the people had the appointing power, the (Tilden) Democratic presidential electors were appointed. Not only would the people have had a governor, legislature, and state officers of their own election, but, united with the people of the other States of the Union, a President and Vice-President elected by the free voices of this great nation. The people of Louisiana gave a majority of 7,639 for the Tilden electors : the people of the whole United States gave a majority of upwards of 250,000. From every quarter of the national domain electric messengers conveyed the news to the conspirators in Washington. The crisis had arrived. The people had condemned the party in power, and had chosen Democratic electors to cast their votes for the Democratic candidates for President and Vice-President of the United States. But it remained for the officers, ministers, and tribunals of the election system to carry into effect and practical operation the action of the people. And these officers in several States, and especially in Louisiana, were all of the condemned political faction. Success or defeat of the right of self-government in the people — of the right to choose and change their officers and rulers, to dismiss the faithless and corrupt, and to put in their place the honest, capable, and patriotic — was made to depend upon the right, true, and honest count of the electoral vote in this election. To ascertain this the Louisiana vote was essential, and the action of the Returning Board in regard to it called for strict and searching investigation. It was well known to the whole country, soon after the election, that the Tilden electors had received a majority of nearly eight thousand votes at the presidential election in this State. But the character of the Board, its action on previous elections, its present unjustifiable delays and protracted meetings, its secret sessions and consultations, its violent and partisan conduct, unjust and unlawful rulings, whispered rumors of bribery and corrupt offers, etc., apprehensions of perjury and falsified returns, filled the public mind with distrust and gloomy foreboding. Expert of wiles, the hypocritical offspring of dissembling fraud, shameless, audacious, stimulated by former successful villainy and supposed favor of General Grant, the Returning Board in this State, after a venal attempt to obtain money from the Democratic party,[1] consummated the "false return" deemed essential to the election of Hayes and the defeat of the people.

How was this nefarious return, this false count, fabricated? The Board received, in conformity with the statutory provisions of the State, returns from every election poll and parish in the State, which they were ordered to canvass and compile, to ascertain the result of the election, and to publish and proclaim the same. They set to work, not truly and honestly to ascertain the result,

[1] Witness the conversation of Madison J. Wells, president of the Board, with Mr. D. F. Kenner; and the statement of Mr. Tilden of his refusal to ransom from the Board conclusive documentary evidence of the false count.

but, as heretofore stated, in violation of sworn official duty, by a resort to manipulation, destruction, change, and falsification, to bring out a result absolutely false and fraudulent. Some returns were mutilated and essential parts cut off; some were entirely suppressed: some were altered by a double process, throwing out good votes actually cast, and putting in and counting spurious votes known not to have been actually polled. The statute conferred upon them certain authority in regard to "returns, accompanied by a statement, charge, or protest, attached thereto by an election officer, of fraud, violence, riot, etc., having prevented a fair election, and corroborated under oath by three respectable electors of the parish." There was no such charge, protest, or statement, and, of course, no such corroboration by affidavits to any return from a Democratic parish. How then could the authority be exercised? The Board met the emergency! They made a protest. They procured affidavits, fabricated, it is said, in the New Orleans customhouse, and used them with a full knowledge that they were counterfeits. It was proved, as we state anew, that the election was peaceable, quiet, undisturbed, free from violence. What of it? The Board declared, "There must have been intimidation, from the comparative smallness of the voters." The truth is, it was the largest vote ever given in Louisiana, and larger, in proportion to the whole population, than the average of all the States in the Union.

Judge Black truly said: "It is unnecessary to mention with particularity all the infractions of law, frauds, crimes, and felonies committed by the Board and the individuals that coöperated with it, perjury, subornation of perjury, falsification and spoliation of documents, and forgery, to cheat the people of the right to elect their own ruler. There is hardly any species of the *crimen falsi* which was not made a part of the great fraud when the defeated electors and state officers of Louisiana were falsely certified as chosen by the people."

It was the object of the fathers of our country to secure for themselves and their posterity a government of laws, of reason, and of justice. All our governments, state and federal, are popular governments on the basis of representation, as nearly equal as circumstances allow. The will of the majority fairly expressed has the force of law. Written constitutions founded on the immediate authority of the people, regulating and restraining all the powers of government, — legislative, executive, judicial, — form the supreme sovereign rule. And these governments and these principles must be supported by general education and a wide diffusion of pure morality, public and individual. Without virtue in the people a just republican government cannot subsist. The people, then, being the source of all political power, to be exercised through representatives elected by suffrage, every man by voting shares in the sovereign power, and performs his duty in organizing and maintaining the government and guiding its policy.

Of all the offices in the United States, the office of President is the most important. Kent was of opinion that the election of a President of the United States affects so many interests, addresses itself so strongly to popular passions, and holds out such powerful temptations to ambition that it becomes a trial to public virtue and hazardous to public liberty, and that if we continued to elect the chief magistrate of the Union with integrity we would stamp the highest value on our national character and republican institutions. Another American patriot, statesman, and jurist says: " Liberty is more precious than gold. In the judgment of the virtuous and wise men who won the independence and built up

the institutions of this country, the privilege of choosing
our own rulers was the richest part of the great inheritance they left us. With a full price in blood and
treasure they bought this freedom for their children, and
I do not know one tolerably decent American who would
sell his single right on any terms. The successful scheme
to cheat the people of Louisiana out of their votes for
state officers and presidential electors is a crime of the
greatest magnitude, worse even than a conspiracy to steal
any amount of public money."

With these remarks we proceed to a fuller examination
of the case of Anderson, a chief actor and leader in the
fraud perpetrated in Louisiana. On the 27th June, 1877,
the grand inquest of the State, in a special report, recommended that Thomas C. Anderson be prosecuted for
forgery and altering the election returns of the parish
of Vernon and other parishes of the State. On the 5th
July following, the district attorney filed an information
against him in the superior criminal court, and the
court issued a *capias*, or order for his arrest. He fled
from the jurisdiction of the state court, sought refuge
within the walls of the United States custom-house, and
called upon the United States authorities and forces to
support him in resisting and defying the authority of the
State that he had wronged. He was at that time United
States collector of customs at the port of New Orleans,
where he was finally arrested in his office by the sheriff,
and brought before the state tribunal on the 28th day
of January, 1878. Thereupon he moved through his
counsel to transfer the case to a court of the United
States. The motion was refused, and the trial of the
case was left to the state court. He then applied for a
change of venue to have the case removed from New
Orleans to another parish in the State. The application
was rejected. He next objected that the prosecution was

by an "information filed by the State's attorney, and not
by an indictment found by a grand jury."   The objection
was overruled: the proceeding by information was regular, sanctioned by express statute and settled practice.
He next "objected to being tried alone, and insisted that
he could only be tried jointly with Wells, Casanave, and
Kenner, the other members of the Returning Board."
He was again overruled. He then "excepted to the *venire*
and the jury summoned to try the case," and this in its
turn was overruled.   A bill of exceptions to these rulings
was reserved by the lawyers of Anderson, and the court
ordered the trial to proceed. . . .

CITIZENSHIP AND ALLEGIANCE.

[In 1833, a judge of an inferior court in the State of South Carolina declined to admit to citizenship one George Granstein, upon the ground that the said Granstein declined to take the oath of allegiance to South Carolina. Judge Bay certified his action to the last court of appeals of the State of South Carolina, and justified his refusal to admit the petitioner because he would not take " the usual and customary oath of allegiance to the State of South Carolina," as well as " that of fidelity to the United States." The case attracted much attention at the time. The editorial of the Charleston " Courier " of July 20, 1833, contained the following reference to the speech of Mr. Hunt. The speech is also given in full.]

WE take pleasure in gratifying our readers, and at the same time enriching our columns this morning, with the able and eloquent argument of Randell Hunt, Esq., before the last court of appeals, on the subject of citizenship and allegiance. We feel constrained, however, to dissent from some of his views on the latter topic. Allegiance, even in the strictest meaning of the term, is not, in our opinion, exclusively due to the United States. If there is any one point clear in our political history, it is that our government was intended to be an admixture of the federal national forms, and that it was adopted with that understanding by the people of the several States, the general government or political association of the United States acquiring sovereignty by grant within specified limits, and the States retaining the residue. Wherever sovereignty resides, allegiance is due as a matter of course, and it belongs as properly to the residuary sovereignty of the States as to the delegated sovereignty of the United States, each having an exclusive right to it within its legitimate sphere. It is very certain that the government of the United States is a limited one, that the political association of the United States is a limited one, — in the language of Mr. Jefferson, "a nation for certain purposes only." It therefore does not possess entire sovereignty, and cannot claim entire allegiance. The States, then, retaining residuary sovereignty, have of course a rightful claim to residuary allegiance. The old feudal notions of allegiance and fealty have no application to our free institutions. The allegiance due to the States, within the reserved powers, is not a fealty subordinate to, but wholly independent of that due to the United States within the granted powers. The state and federal governments are wholly independent of each other, within their appropriate spheres, and there is no relation between them analogous to that between the lords paramount and the mesne lords of the feudal system. In fact, allegiance, in this free country, simply means obedience to lawful authority. Allegiance to the United States consists in fidelity to the Constitution and Constitutional laws of the United States ; allegiance to the several States consists in fidelity to their several constitutions and constitutional laws, provided they do not conflict with the Constitution or Constitutional laws of the United States. This proviso, however, does not impair our position, for the fact that a provision of a state constitution or a state law in conflict with the federal constitutions or laws is void no more impairs our allegiance to the State within the reserved powers than the nullity of an unconstitutional federal law impairs our allegiance to the United States within the granted powers. All of the States have acted on these principles, and required of their citizens oaths of fidelity, directly to themselves or to their constitutions and laws.

Mr. Hunt said: In availing myself of the opportunity, politely offered me by my friend, of laying before the Court the grounds on which the petitioner in this case moves that the decision of the judge below should be reversed, I cannot but regret that I have not had time for as ample a preparation as I desired, from a sense of justice to myself as well as from the high respect which I entertain for the Court. I ask, therefore, an indulgent hearing from your honors, while I submit to you the views which have presented themselves to my mind, and which appear to me conclusive on the subject.

And here, said Mr. Hunt, on the very threshold of the argument, I must declare myself embarrassed by the simplicity of the case. If there were anything in it obscure or involved, I might endeavor to illustrate and explain it; if anything doubtful, I might perhaps prove it by argument. But the case is so clear, so simple, so self-evident, that to state it is to argue it; or rather I should say, to state it is to prove it. What is the case?

The Constitution of the United States declares, art. 2, sec. 8, p. 4: "The Congress shall have power to establish a uniform rule of naturalization, and uniform laws on the subject of bankruptcies, throughout the United States." In the exercise of this power, Congress, on the 14th day of April, 1802, passed an act, entitled "an act to establish a uniform rule of naturalization," etc. The act, or that portion of it applicable to this case, is in the following words: [1] —

"Sec. 1. Any alien, being a free white person, may be admitted to become a citizen of the United States, or any of them, on the following conditions, and not otherwise:

Bacon, 175. Ingersoll's Digest, tit. Aliens, p. 21, 2 Story's Laws U. S.

" *First*, That he shall have declared on oath or affirmation, before the supreme, superior, district, or circuit court of some one of the States or of the territorial districts of the United States, or a circuit or district court of the United States, three years at least before his admission, that it was *bona fide* his intention to become a citizen of the United States, etc. . . .

" *Secondly*, That he shall at the time of his application to be admitted declare on oath or affirmation, before some one of the courts aforesaid, that he will support the Constitution of the United States, and that he doth absolutely and entirely renounce and abjure all allegiance and fidelity to every foreign prince, potentate, state, or sovereignty, and particularly by name the prince, potentate, state, or sovereignty whereof he was before a citizen or subject, which proceedings shall be recorded by the clerk of the court."

The petitioner, George Graustein, according to the judge's report, "appeared to be entitled to be admitted," and offered to take the oath prescribed by the act of Congress. But the clerk of the court tendered to him an additional oath, an oath of allegiance to South Carolina. This he declined to take. "Whereupon," says Judge Bay, "I refused to admit him, unless he took the usual and customary oath of allegiance to the State of South Carolina as well as that of fidelity to the United States!"

The case then comes to this : Congress, exercising a constitutional power, declares that any alien, being a free white person, may be admitted a citizen of the United States, or any of them, on certain conditions and according to a prescribed rule. Has a clerk of the court of sessions and common pleas for Charleston district a right to prescribe other conditions and establish another rule? Has he a right to interpolate into the law whatever his fancy may suggest? Or has a district judge of

the State of South Carolina power to legislate for the
Union? Did the people of the United States ever dele-
gate to him power to make laws on the subject of naturalization? It is a wise remark that Lord Bacon made,
when writing of judicature : "Judges ought to remember
that their office is *jus dicere*, and not *jus dare*, — to interpret law, and not to make law or give law ; else will they
not stick to add and alter, and to pronounce that which
they do not find, and by show of antiquity to introduce
novelty."

The act of Congress of 1802, establishing an uniform
rule of naturalization, is drawn with great clearness and
precision. It repeals all previous laws on that subject.
It not only expresses the conditions on which an alien
may be admitted to become a citizen, but it says "he
may be admitted on those conditions, and not otherwise."
What of this? argues the judge. The usage of the sovereign State of South Carolina has been otherwise. To
require aliens on being admitted citizens to take an oath
of allegiance to her is "one of the highest prerogatives
of the State, and the longest in use. I could not therefore permit it to be called in question!" Upon this
point I will content myself for the present with remark-
ing, that the usage, if it ever prevailed, is illegal. The
Constitution of the United States, and the laws made in
pursuance thereof, are supreme over state laws and state
constitutions.

I could, may it please the Court, rest content with this
statement, and leave the case without further comment to
the decision of your honors. But the judge below has
based his opinion on the most untenable ground. He has
assumed positions wholly unsupported by law, and advanced doctrines directly at war with the Constitution of
the United States. It becomes necessary, therefore, to
examine these doctrines, lest, having the sanction of ju-

dicial authority, they may produce a baleful influence on the public mind.

The judge, in his report, having stated that he refused to admit the petitioner, proceeds thus : —

" The grounds upon which I refused to admit him were, briefly, the following : —

" *First*, That South Carolina was a sovereign and independent State, and had an unquestionable right to prescribe the terms and conditions upon which she would admit aliens to the rights and privileges of citizenship, from the day she assumed her sovereignty to the present time, by the law of nations and the rights of all civilized States.

" *Secondly*, That she had uniformly exercised this right and power from the earliest period of her independence [even before the independence of the United States was declared] ; for in the constitution of 1776 the form of the oath is prescribed and directed.

" And in the constitution of 19th March, 1778, the same form was laid down and directed, after the independence of the United States was declared.

" Also, in the act of March, 1786, to confer the right of citizenship, the oath is prescribed to be administered to aliens on being admitted.

" *Thirdly*, Because it was one of the highest prerogatives of the State, and the longest in use. I could not therefore permit it to be called in question, and dismissed the petition.

E. H. BAY."

Now, I deny, in the first place, that the State of South Carolina has, either in her constitution or laws, any provision requiring an alien, before he can be admitted to become a citizen, to take an oath of allegiance to the State of South Carolina. I have carefully examined the constitutions of 1776 and 1778, and compared them with the present state constitution. The only oaths to be found in them are oaths of office,[1] and are superseded by art. 4, Con. of South Carolina. There is not a word that ingenuity can torture into a support of the judge's assertion.

I proceed, therefore, to an examination of the laws or statutes of South Carolina, in which we are told, "the oath is prescribed to be administered to aliens on being admitted." The first act on this subject is an act of 1696. It required an oath of allegiance to King William. This was altered by act of 1704 to an oath of allegiance to Queen Anne. These acts are to be found in Trott's Laws.[2] It is unnecessary to dwell upon them: they were evidently repealed by the Declaration of Independence. The act of 1704 was afterwards expressly repealed by the act of 20th March, 1784,[3] entitled "an act to confer the rights of citizenship on aliens;" and this act of 1784 was declared to be repealed, as well as that of 1704, by the act of 22d March, 1786.[4] This act denies to every alien the rights of citizenship in voting, etc., "until he shall have been naturalized by a special act of the General Assembly." On the 27th February, 1778,[5] an act was passed, prescribing the manner in which records should be kept, and certificates granted, of the admission of aliens to the rights of citizenship. There is no other act among the laws of South Carolina on the subject of naturalization.

On the 23d day of May, 1788, the people of South Carolina ratified the Constitution of the United States, by which they transferred to the general government

[1] Constitutions of So. Ca., 1776 and 1778.
[2] Trott's Laws, pp. 63, and 108, 109.
[3] Grimke's Pub. L., pp. 339, 340.
[4] Grimke's Pub. L., p. 112.   [5] Grimke's Pub. L., p. 113.

power to establish a uniform rule of naturalization. From that time, South Carolina has never interfered with the naturalization of aliens, but has looked for her guide to the rule established by Congress.

Then, may it please the Court, neither the constitutions nor the laws cited by the judge support his position. The truth is, South Carolina considered the power of naturalization vested in Congress alone. No State in this Union can pass laws for naturalizing aliens. The only power she possesses of conferring rights on aliens is by means of denization.

Two acts of South Carolina conferring rights on aliens, passed since the adoption of the Constitution, remain to be examined: I mean the act of 18th December, 1799,[1] and that of December, 1807.[2] They relate wholly to denizens. The first secures to them the same protection that citizens are entitled to, but prohibits them from voting or holding any office of profit or trust in this State. The second looks to the law of Congress, and pays it a proper deference. It requires every " alien, previously to being entitled to avail him or herself of the benefits of that act. to declare his or her intention to become a citizen of the United States, agreeably to the act of Congress in such case made and provided." Such has been the legislation of South Carolina.

It appears, therefore, that there is no state law requiring an alien, upon being admitted to the rights of citizenship, to take an oath of allegiance to South Carolina.

The distinction which I have made between the power to make citizens and the power to make denizens is an old-established and well-recognized real distinction. In Great Britain, the king can grant letters patent to make a denizen. But Parliament alone can naturalize an

---

[1] 1 Faust's Laws, 273.

[2] Acts of Assembly, 1807. Pamphlet, pp. 59, 60.

alien.   Blackstone says,[1] " A denizen is an alien born, but who has obtained *ex donatione regis* letters patent to make him an English subject, a high and incommunicable branch of the royal prerogative." He then enumerates the privileges and disabilities of a denizen, and comes to the subject of naturalization.[2] "Naturalization," says he, " cannot be performed but by act of Parliament ; for by this an alien is put in exactly the same state as if he had been born in the king's liegeance ; except only," etc. Judge Tucker also supports the distinction.[3] " The common law has affixed such distinct and appropriate ideas to the terms denization and naturalization that they cannot be confounded together or mistaken for each other in any legal transaction whatever. They are so absolutely distinct in their natures that in England they cannot both be given by the same power. The Federal Constitution declares that Congress shall have power to establish an uniform rule of naturalization throughout the United States, but it also further declares that the powers not delegated by the Constitution to the United States, nor prohibited by it to the States, are reserved to the States respectively or to the people. The power of naturalization, and not that of denization, being delegated to Congress, and the power of denization not being prohibited to the States by the Constitution, that power ought not to be considered as given to Congress, but, on the contrary, as being reserved to the States. And as the right of denization did not make a citizen of an alien, but only placed him in a middle state between the two, giving him local privileges only, which he was so far from being entitled to carry with him into another State that he lost them by removing from the State giving them, the inconveniences which might result from the indirect communi-

---

[1] 1 Black. Com. ch. x. 374.   [2] 1 Black. Com. 375.

[3] 1 Black. Com. 178, 257, 365.

cation of the rights of naturalized citizens, by different modes of naturalization prevailing in the several States, could not be apprehended. It might, therefore, have been extremely impolitic in the States to have surrendered the right of denization as well as that of naturalization." [1] Naturalization in Great Britain, we have seen, can be performed only by Parliament. This it does by virtue of its omnipotence; Parliament, according to the theory of the British Constitution, having the sole and uncontrollable power. [2]

The power of naturalization is evidently a sovereign power. Every nation is bound to look to its own safety. It has a right to determine whether it will admit a stranger into its society. It has a right to prescribe the terms on which he shall be permitted to enjoy the benefit of that society. Vattel says: [3] " A nation, or the sovereign who represents it, may grant to a stranger the quality of citizen, by admitting him into the body of the political society. This is called naturalization." When the Constitution of the United States was framed, which made the people of the several States, to a certain extent, one people or nation, and clothed the general government with the attributes of sovereignty, it seems, then, from the nature of the thing itself, that the power of granting to a stranger the quality of citizen, by admitting him into the body of the political society, should have been transferred to the national legislature. And this was done, as the Court perceives, in the clause of the Constitution now under consideration.

Before I proceed more fully to argue that the power of naturalization is vested exclusively in Congress, I beg leave to call the attention of the Court to the inference

[1] 1 Black. 257.
[2] 4 Coke's Inst. 36.   1 Black. Com. 162.
[3] Vattel, Book I. ch. xix. sec. 214.

4

drawn from the rights and character of South Carolina as a sovereign State, and to the argument which will probably be based thereon. It will be contended that no man can be a citizen of the United States before he is a citizen of a single State; that every citizen of a State, *ex rei necessitate*, owes to her allegiance; that therefore an alien is bound to take an oath of allegiance to a State before he can be admitted to the rights of citizenship in the United States; and that George Granstein, having refused to take the oath, was properly rejected.

Now, what I maintain to be the true doctrine is this: No State in the Union has a right to require an oath of allegiance to her, because, in strictness of speech, allegiance is not due to her.

What is allegiance? The term is derived from *alligo* (*ad* and *ligo*), to tie, or bind to. Blackstone defines it to be [1] "the tie or *ligamen* which binds the subject to the king, in return for that protection which the king affords the subject." It is, as Lord Coke describes it, the highest and greatest obligation of duty that can be. It is the obligation that every citizen owes to support, in all its power and dignity, the government which protects him in the enjoyment of his rights. And this protection must be of a national character. According to the general understanding of mankind, allegiance can be predicated only of a government clothed with the attributes of sovereignty, and recognized at home and abroad as having an equal and proper station among the nations of the earth. It is evident that in this sense our allegiance is due immediately and directly to the United States.

An attempt has been made to separate the government and the people. It is said that all sovereignty resides in the people, and that there is no sovereignty in the government, and hence no allegiance is due to it. We must

---

[1] 1 Black. Com. 366.

not suffer ourselves to be misled by subtle distinctions. How can we bear true allegiance to the people, except by preserving, protecting, and defending their government and obeying its laws? For most practical purposes the people are the government, and the government is the people. There is nothing magical in government. It is with us, as it should be everywhere, a popular institution, deriving its strength and influence from the affections and support of those by whom and for whom it was made.

The late metaphysical disquisitions on the nature of sovereignty are not calculated to produce any useful results, and are not entitled to the least respect. No government in this country has unlimited absolute sovereignty; all power resides in the people, who have restrained their governments by written laws. And this is a broad distinction between our governments and those of Europe. It is a mistake, however, to suppose that all European governments possess absolute sovereignty. In fact, absolute sovereignty, or the right of governing the State without any fixed laws, is, by the experience of all ages, proved to be unfitted for human happiness.[1] Hence, most, and those the wisest nations, have set bounds to the powers of their sovereigns. Indeed, it is argued by writers on politic law that a people cannot divest themselves of this sovereignty, and give it to any individual, or body of individuals, without renouncing their own lives and duty, so that all sovereignty, how absolute soever it may be supposed, hath its limits.

Sovereignty is frequently trusted to agents by the people, who may, by regulating the government by a fundamental law, commit the exercise of the different parts of the supreme power or sovereignty to different persons and bodies.[2] The only just foundation of the acquisition of

---

[1] Burl. Pol. Law, Part I. ch. vii. sec. 27.
[2] Burl. p. 50, and Book II. ch. iii. Part II.

sovereignty is the consent or the will of the people.
Vattel says: " Sovereignty is that public authority which
commands in civil society, and orders and directs what
each is to perform, to obtain the end of its institution.
This authority belonged originally and essentially to the
body of the society, who trust it frequently to a senate
or to a single person." [1] This public authority, thus denominated " sovereignty," is called by Judge Tucker
" the government " or " administrative authority of the
State," which he defines to be " that portion only of the
sovereignty which is by the Constitution entrusted to the
public functionaries : " these, he adds, " are the agents and
servants of the people." According to these authorities,
then, and without authority it is sufficiently manifest, a
government may possess the attributes of sovereignty.

What is the great end of sovereignty ? It is the tranquillity and happiness of the State as well within itself
as with respect to its interests abroad, and these are the
essential parts of sovereignty : [2] (1.) A legislative power.
(2.) An executive power. (3.) A judicial power. (4.) The
power to make war and peace, and raise troops. (5.) The
power to make treaties and alliances. (6.) The power to
appoint ambassadors and other ministers. (7.) The power
to tax. Burlamaqui and other political writers add
another power, that of determining what doctrines shall
be publicly taught. But in our country the right of free
decision is almost universally acknowledged. These essential parts of sovereignty are sometimes called immanent
and transeunt rights, and all these must concentre and
unite in a government to make it sovereign. No one will
pretend that the several States in this Union have these
powers. The people have transferred them to the general government, to which our national sovereignty is

---

[1] Vattel, Book I. ch. iv.
[2] Heinec. Book II. sec. 133, 134, 135.   Burl. ch. viii.

entrusted, and to which we must look for national protection. That government has power over the purse and
power over the sword. It has power to declare war and
make peace, to levy taxes and raise troops, to form
treaties and appoint ambassadors and other ministers. It
has, under certain wise and salutary checks, power to
make laws, to expound them and enforce them. The
general government is, then, clothed with the attributes
of sovereignty. True, the States have power to legislate
concerning matters of an internal or local nature ; but
this does not interfere with the power of the general government. Nor does it affect the question of allegiance.
Allegiance is due to the paramount, and not to the subordinate authority, — to the United States, whose Constitution and whose laws made in pursuance thereof are
declared superior to all state laws and state constitutions.[1] I repeat, then, that our allegiance is due immediately and directly to the United States ; it is single
and undivided, and of paramount obligation. There is
and there can be no such thing as a double or contradictory allegiance. And it is only by a looseness of speech,
calculated to produce in times of excitement the most
dangerous consequences, that it has ever been applied to
matters of a merely local or domestic nature.

Under the feudal system, allegiance was used only to
express the obligation due to the sovereign ; the inferior
duty that a vassal owed his lord was known by the appropriate term fealty.

Chancellor Kent speaks, in the second volume of his
Commentaries, of primary or paramount allegiance and
of secondary allegiance. The expression is inelegant and
unphilosophical ; allegiance is of itself of paramount obligation.

In this view, it is evident that, in strictness of speech,

[1] Cons. U. S. art. 6, sec. 2.

our allegiance is due to the United States only. I allow that there is an inferior or subordinate fealty due to the State, but this cannot interfere with our primary and paramount obligations to the United States.

I now beg leave to bring to the attention of the Court a brief reference to our civil and political history, in order to illustrate and strengthen the view of allegiance here presented. Previous to the adoption of the Articles of Confederation, Congress was a mere advisory body. The colonies were engaged in a common cause, and were practically one people or nation. They were represented by a common body, or Congress. That Congress, having passed the resolution declaring the Americans absolved from all allegiance to the British government, very properly deemed an adherence to the king of Great Britain, or other enemy of the colonies, an attack on the common cause. They, therefore, on the 24th of June, declared that [1] "all persons, members of, or owing allegiance to, any of the United Colonies, who should levy war against any of the said colonies, within the same, were guilty of treason against such colony," and recommended to the legislatures of the several colonies to pass laws for the punishment of such treasons. In pursuance of this recommendation, the States passed the laws requisite for self-protection, and inflicted the punishment of death on such as were found guilty of treason.

Under the Articles of Confederation, the laws on the subject of treason were undisturbed. Treason was still a common offense as defined by Congress, but yet punishable by the several States, in consequence of the non-existence of a government acting directly upon individuals. During all this time, however, we continued practically one people or nation, engaged in a common cause, having one regular body of troops, governed by united counsels,

[1] 1 Pitkin's Civ. and Pol. Hist. of the U. S. 371, 372.

and assisted by quotas paid for the common purpose of common defense.

The Articles of Confederation were found inadequate to national purposes, and our present Constitution was built upon their ruins. By this the whole frame of our government was remodeled. It is a constitution of government, with powers to execute itself. The government has power to tax individuals, and to demand from them military services. It has power to punish them for crimes committed against itself. It is entrusted, we have seen, with sovereign power. Its laws operate immediately and directly upon the citizen, and thus create an immediate and direct connection between the citizen and the general government.

Under these circumstances, it was found necessary by the framers of the Constitution to make some new provision on the subject of treason. Accordingly, they declared that " treason against the United States shall consist only in levying war against them, or in adhering to their enemies, giving them aid and comfort," and gave Congress power to declare the punishment of treason. Now, it must be borne in mind that treason is the highest breach of allegiance. Whether we regard, then, the nature of allegiance, the sense in which it is understood by all civilized nations, the civil and political history of our country as explanatory of the Constitution, or the Constitution as speaking distinctly for itself, we are forced to the conclusion that our allegiance is due immediately and directly to the United States.

And this conclusion is strengthened by the eighth section, art. 1, Cons. U. S., which conferred on Congress the " power to establish an uniform rule of naturalization throughout the United States." This power is exclusive. Its purpose [1] was to deprive the States individually of

_____
[1] 1 Kent's Com. sec. 19.

the power of naturalizing aliens according to their own will and pleasure, and thereby giving them the rights and privileges of citizens in every other State. If each State can naturalize upon one year's residence, when the act of Congress requires five, of what use is the act of Congress, and how does it become an uniform rule?

In the case of Collet v. Collet,[1] tried in the Circuit Court, Pennsylvania District, it was held that the power of naturalization was concurrent. "The true reason," says the Court, "for investing Congress with the power has been assigned at the bar: it was to guard against too narrow instead of too liberal a mode of conferring the rights of citizenship. Thus, the individual States cannot exclude those citizens who have been adopted by the United States; but they can adopt citizens upon easier terms than those which Congress may deem it expedient to impose." But this decision and the reason on which it is founded are alike erroneous. Mr. Madison, in the forty-second number of "The Federalist," addresses himself to this point. He says, "The dissimilarity in the rules of naturalization has long been remarked as a fault in our system, and as laying a foundation for intricate and delicate questions." He then comments on the defects in the Articles of Confederation, in the clause intended to give the citizens of each State the privileges of citizens in the several States, and in concluding says: "The very improper power was retained by each State of naturalizing aliens in every other State. In one State, residence for a short time confers all the rights of citizenship; in another, qualifications of greater importance are required. An alien, therefore, legally incapacitated for certain rights in the latter, may by previous residence only in the former remove his incapacity, and thus the law of one State be preposterously rendered paramount to the law of another,

[1] 2 Dallas, 296.

within the jurisdiction of the other. . . . By the laws of several States, certain descriptions of aliens, who have rendered themselves obnoxious, were laid under interdicts inconsistent not only with the rights of citizenship, but with the privileges of residence. What would have been the consequence if such persons, by residence or otherwise, had acquired the character of citizens under the laws of another State, and then asserted their rights as such both to residence and citizenship within the State proscribing them?" The new Constitution has with great propriety, he therefore urges, given the power of naturalization to Congress. In the thirty-second number of "The Federalist," Alexander Hamilton says exclusive power is delegated to the United States in three cases only : (1.) Where the Constitution in express terms grants an exclusive authority to the Union. (2.) Where it grants an authority to the Union, and prohibits the State from exercising the like authority. (3.) Where it grants an authority to the Union to which a similar authority in the States would be absolutely and totally contradictory and repugnant. He gives examples of these cases from the Constitution. The third will be found, he says, in that clause which declares that Congress shall have power "to establish an uniform rule of naturalization throughout the United States." This must necessarily be exclusive ; because if each State had power to prescribe a distinct rule, there could be no uniform rule.

Indeed, the decision in the case of Collet v. Collet may be considered as in effect overruled. In the same Circuit Court, in 1797, Judge Iredell, in the case of the United States v. Villato.[1] declared that if the case had not previously occurred. he should be disposed to think that the power of naturalization operated exclusively, as soon as it was exercised by Congress. And in the Circuit

[1] 2 Dallas, 370.

Court of Pennsylvania, in 1814,[1] Judge Washington gave it as his opinion that the power to naturalize was exclusively vested in Congress. In Chirac v. Chirac,[2] the first point made was that the estate of which John Baptiste Chirac died seized was, in his lifetime, escheatable, because it was acquired before he became a citizen of the United States; the law of the State of Maryland, according to which he took the oaths of citizenship, being virtually repealed by the Constitution of the United States and the act of naturalization enacted by Congress. It was contended by Mr. Harper, for the plaintiff,[3] that he acquired no capacity to hold by his naturalization under the local law, since by the Constitution Congress alone has the power of prescribing uniform rules of naturalization; and the act of Maryland is a general naturalization law, not a special act authorizing citizens to hold lands, or conferring other particular privileges. If the States could make such a law, the Constitution of the United States would be completely evaded, as the citizens of one State are entitled to all the privileges and immunities of citizens in every other State. It was contended on the other side, by Mr. Martin and his colleague, that the Constitution of the United States, and the laws made under it, do not *ipso jure*, repeal a state law relative to the same matter, but only annul such parts of the latter as are inconsistent with the former. The respective States still preserve the right of making naturalization laws, giving certain civil rights to foreigners without conferring universal political citizenship. Chief Justice Marshall, who delivered the opinion of the Court, observed that " it certainly ought not to be controverted that the power of naturalization is exclusively in Congress."[4] In Sturges

[1] Golden v. Prince, Wharton's Digest, tit. Const. Law, 26.
[2] 2 Wheaton's Rep. 259.   [3] 1 Wheaton's Rep. 193.
[4] 3 Dallas Rep. 386.

v. Crowninshield, the chief justice laid this down as a correct general principle, that whenever the terms in which a power was granted to Congress, or the nature of the power, required that it should be exercised exclusively by Congress, the subject was as completely taken from the state legislatures as if they had been expressly forbidden to act on it. In Houston *v.* Moore,[1] Judge Washington, in delivering the opinion of the Court, said that when Congress exercised their powers upon any given subject, the States could not enter upon the same ground and provide for the same objects; for if the laws of the State, argued he, agree in every respect with the laws of Congress, they are useless. If they differ, they must, in the nature of things, oppose each other so far as they do differ, and the laws of the State must be void. Judge Story mentioned in the same case the power in Congress to establish an uniform rule of naturalization as one which was exclusive, on the ground of there being a direct repugnancy or incompatibility in the exercise of it by the States. So that, as Chancellor Kent says,[2] "the weight of authority as well as of reason may be considered as clearly in favor of this construction."

This power, which I have thus shown to be exclusively vested in Congress, relates wholly to the allegiance of all adopted citizens : and yet, in spite of this, in the face of the express provisions of the Constitution, with a total disregard to the civil and political history of our country and the true nature of allegiance, it has been said that we owe no allegiance to the United States ! And the citizen of this republic, when called on to designate his national banner, must point to the palmetto-tree, and not to the stars and stripes of that flag which has floated in glory and in triumph over the lakes and at New Orleans ! All our oldest and most cherished associations must be broken

[1] 5 Wheaton's Rep. 1.   [2] 1 Kent's Com. 398.

up; the ties which bind us to our brethren of the North and the East and the West must be cut asunder; our common labors and common sufferings in the cause of liberty must be forgotten; the American history must be blurred and blotted out; the Union is no longer to be regarded with patriotic pride; all our duties, all our aspirations, must be hemmed in by state lines; we are to be taught that there is no such thing as a citizen of the United States, and that, instead of looking for the emblem of our country to the bird of Liberty, soaring aloft, we must cast our eyes on a venomous reptile, with "*A noli me tangere*" inscribed on the ground that supports it.

These things cannot be right: the questions of citizenship and naturalization are of an international nature. We must extend our views beyond the narrow limits of our own State, and even beyond the United States, and look abroad among the nations of the world. What more ridiculous and contemptible object can be imagined than an individual in a foreign land standing in need of protection and claiming it in the name of the sovereign people of South Carolina? On the other hand, what more delightful spectacle can the American patriot contemplate than the citizen of this Union unfurling for his protection our well known and universally respected national banner, and recounting to an attentive and admiring auditory the history of his country? When I think of these things my heart beats high with pleasurable emotions, and I thank God that I am a citizen of the United States. I confess I cannot envy the feelings or judgment of the man who thinks there is no such thing as a citizen of the United States.

"No such thing as a citizen of the United States!" I take up the Constitution; I open it; I find in the very first article, second section, that "no person shall be a Representative who shall not have . . . been seven years a citizen of the United States." I turn to the next section : I find, " No person shall be a Senator who shall not have . . . been nine years a citizen of the United States." The expression "citizen of the United States" is again and again inscribed on the very face of the instrument. I cannot believe that the framers of the Constitution were so ignorant or inattentive as not to know or not to regard the import of the phrase.

" No such thing as a citizen of the United States! " The wildest theorist in his most extravagant dreams has never denied that there is a government of the United States. Who ever heard of a government without citizens?

I have brought to the view of the Court the constitutional provision concerning treason against the United States. Can there be treason where there are no citizens?

These remarks, may it please the Court, appear to me to furnish a satisfactory reply to the argument that no alien can become a citizen of the United States until he first becomes a citizen of a single State. We have seen that the power of naturalization is vested exclusively in Congress. It is undoubtedly true that the state courts admit aliens to the right of citizenship. But they do this as agents of Congress, by virtue of the power entrusted to them by Congress, and according to the rule prescribed by Congress. The right of citizenship is conferred by the United States, not by the State. An alien may be naturalized in a Territory, he may be naturalized in the District of Columbia, he may reside during his probationary term in one State and may be admitted in another. The certificate which he receives from court declares him " a citizen of the United States." When naturalized, then, he becomes immediately a citizen of the United States; and it is in that character alone that he

can become a citizen of a single State. The Union forms
the bond of connection between him and the State. Before
he can be admitted he is required to swear that he will
support the Constitution of the United States, thus pledg-
ing his allegiance to the United States; for allegiance, as
I have shown, is a paramount obligation and is due to the
supreme authority, and the Constitution declares itself,
and the laws of the United States passed in pursuance
thereof, the supreme law of the land.   I have now shown:
(1.) That the petitioner, George Granstein, who has complied with all the other conditions of the act of Congress,
and offered to take the oath prescribed by it, was entitled
to be admitted a citizen of the United States.   (2.) That
if the State have a concurrent power with Congress in the
subject of naturalization, she certainly has not exercised
it since the adoption of the Constitution of the United
States, no provision being found in the Constitution or
laws on this subject.   (3.) That the State has no such
power, but that she retains the power of denization.   (4.)
That the power of naturalization is necessarily exclusively
vested in Congress, as appears from the nature of the
power itself, from the contemporaneous exposition, and
from judicial opinions.   (5.) That in strictness of speech
our allegiance is due to the United States only, but that
there is a fealty (or "secondary allegiance") due to the
State, and that the inference drawn by his honor from
the alleged rights and character of South Carolina as a
sovereign State is clearly erroneous.   (6.) That when an
alien is naturalized in our country he becomes immediately a citizen of the United States, and it is in that character alone that he can become a citizen of a single State.[1]
These propositions are in strict accordance with the Constitution and the laws, and appear to me perfectly clear
and undeniable.   I should not have dwelt upon them so

---

[1] Laws of Congress.

long were it not that directly repugnant doctrines have been industriously circulated throughout our State, and are said to have received the sanction of some popular assemblies, and appear now to have received the sanction of the judge below. But I am sure they will never receive the sanction of this Court.

Isocrates, in one of his orations to the sophists, speaking of the ease with which a false proposition may be supported to the satisfaction of a common auditory, says the reason is that when men find that something can be said in favor of what on its very face appeared indefensible, they grow distrustful of their own reason, and are easily hurried on by the orator to whom they abandon themselves. But your honors are not to be hurried on in this manner, nor to be deceived by the gloss that sophistry confers on ingenious falsehoods. It is our pride, a matter of just pride and gratulation, that we have in this judiciary a tribunal that will not be swayed by popular error or momentary excitement, — a tribunal that will hear patiently and gravely, deliberate carefully and calmly, and decide according to the well-settled principles of law and the Constitution of our country. To this tribunal I now submit the case of the appellant.

N. B. The opinion of Judge Bay was reversed by the court of appeals. *Ex parte* Granstein, 1 Hill, South Carolina Reports, 141.

ARGUMENT IN THE SLAUGHTER-HOUSE CASES.

BEFORE THE SUPREME COURT OF LOUISIANA.

[The construction of the amendments to the Constitution of the United States was involved in the so-called slaughter-house cases. The legislature of Louisiana, by an act passed in March, 1869, had granted to a certain corporation an exclusive right for twenty-five years to have and maintain slaughter-houses and yards for inclosing cattle intended for sale or slaughter within several parishes in that State, which included the city of New Orleans, and prohibiting all other persons from building or keeping cattle-yards or slaughter-houses within those limits, and requiring that all cattle and other animals intended for sale or slaughter in that district should be brought to the yards of the corporation, where certain fees might be charged. The act of the legislature was assailed upon the ground that it was unconstitutional and in conflict with the provisions of the thirteenth and fourteenth articles of amendment to the Constitution of the United States. The Supreme Court of Louisiana held the act of the legislature valid, and afterwards, upon appeal to the Supreme Court of the United States, the judgment of the Supreme Court of the State was affirmed, Justice Miller being the organ of the Court. *Vide* 16 Wallace, United States Supreme Court Reports, p. 37. Mr. Hunt's argument before the Supreme Court of the State is given.]

MAY it please your honors, I had hoped not to trouble you in this case. The arrangement made was that it should be discussed by my colleague (Mr. Roselius), who opened the case with such ability, and should be closed by my brother (Mr. William H. Hunt), but circumstances rendered him incapable of addressing the Court, and I therefore take his place.

The argument presented to you against my clients has been of the most extraordinary character. Whether I consider the unfounded, illegal, and unconstitutional doctrines of the first counsel (Mr. J. B. Cotton), and the manner in which he presented them, his fine voice, his action and declamation, or the solemn, slow, labored, and heavy humor with which the counsel who followed him (Mr. J. Q. A. Fellows) was pleased to liken my eloquent colleague to Rip Van Winkle, a witticism which delighted nobody except the counsel who succeeded him ; or whether I consider the grave, serious, vituperative, and lengthy address delivered before you this day, abusive of the character and standing of seventeen citizens against whom there is no evidence in the record, and illegally and acrimoniously denunciatory of a coördinate branch of the government, I am pained that such a scene should have been displayed and such things heard in an American court ; shocked especially that he who last addressed you (Judge Campbell)[1] should have resorted to such a system of attack.

Judges, you have heard him declare that all the defendants in this case ought to be in the penitentiary, and that they are all guilty of fraud ! I should like to know if he ever brings a suit against any one who is not charged by him with fraud : if fraud is not his monomania ; if it is not upon that that he speaks whenever he addresses a court of justice, and seeks to uphold the wrong against the laws of the land.

I will not follow him through his entire argument at present. Time does not allow it. I shall only select

[1] John A. Campbell, formerly an associate justice of the U. S. Supreme Court.

5

those points which I think deserve notice. It will not
"amaze" you, with your judicial experience, — although
it may "amaze" some of the interested persons in court
who have heard his speech, — to know that there is
nothing in this case but a simple question of law, which
ought to have been presented without declamation, denunciation, or mystification.

What *is* the case? The legislature of this State, in
the exercise of its police power, has thought proper to
designate and fix a place for the slaughter of animals
whose meat is intended for sale in the city of New
Orleans. I need not tell you how important health is to
the individual or to the community at large, and I shall
take it for granted, in the commencement of my argument, that it is within the police power of the State to
pass regulations concerning the health of the people of
the State. What are the circumstances, then, that
induced the legislature to exercise the power upon this
occasion?

When this city was under the government of the
Cabildo, and afterwards under the government of the
charter of 1804, the population of New Orleans was comparatively very small, — a few thousand inhabitants. Yet
they found it necessary, even at that time, to regulate the
slaughtering of animals whose meat was to be sold in the
market of the city, and a place was assigned for the purpose, at or below the point where the slaughter-house is
established at this time by the act of the legislature.
What was the object of the regulation? Simply this:
that the blood and the offals, and those things which were
noisome and offensive and dangerous to public health,
should, after the animals were slain, be thrown into the
Mississippi, where they would be taken up and carried
along its rapid current until they reached the waters of
the Gulf of Mexico, where they would be innocuous, or

serve as food for the fishes and monsters of the deep. Things continued under this regulation for a long time; but our population increased, and, as the Americans came in, more vigor was exhibited in the government of the State and city. The population at first chiefly settled and concentrated in what is now the lower part of the city. Above the line of Canal Street there were few, if any inhabitants. But as the Americans increased in numbers, they established themselves beyond it and moved upward for the purpose of meeting the commerce coming down the Mississippi. The butchers, who had been carrying on their business quite conveniently from the opposite side of the river, below the city, began to find the situation inconvenient. They had been in the habit of bringing over to New Orleans, in pirogues, the meat of the animals killed at the slaughter-house on the opposite bank of the river, below the city, and selling it in the markets of New Orleans. But with the increase of population there came, of course, an increased demand for food and meat. The butchers' business was more extended and enlarged. They had more employment and more gain, and gradually acquired more power. They determined to move to the upper part of the city, and to slaughter there the animals whose meats they sold; and this they did to the annoyance and injury of the public.

After the lapse of some time a series of municipal ordinances was passed upon this subject. They were entitled " Ordinances for the protection of the health of the city, and to guard against public nuisances." They provided that no establishment for the burning of bones, no establishment in which any business deleterious to the public health was intended to be carried on, nothing noisome, nothing that emitted a poisonous vapor, etc., should be permitted within the corporate limits of the city of New Orleans; and they particularly provided that no beef should be slaughtered except in "slaughter-houses," and that the heads and entrails, the offals, and other refuse parts of the animals, etc., should be taken away and thrown into the river at a point below the city.

Things remained in this condition until the city of Lafayette was incorporated. But there existed a constant desire and continued exertion to remove from the limits of New Orleans all slaughter-houses. But this did not prove successful until the butchers themselves saw that their own convenience and interests would be advanced by erecting cattle-pens and slaughter-houses above Jackson Street, where there was a tavern called the " Bull's Head," at which the butchers used to meet and converse, and carry on their business, except the actual slaughtering of animals. Population and business continued to extend and move upwards, higher and higher; and the butchers again found it convenient and advantageous to move up. They went, as the enactments show, to the city of Jefferson, where they have landed their cattle on the bank of the river, put and kept up pens, slaughtered animals, throwing the offal, etc., into the river, and established and kept up a constant source of nuisance and annoyance to the community, injurious and dangerous to the health, the limbs and lives of the citizens, and obstructing and stopping the prosperity and growth of the city.

I ask your honors to reflect for a moment upon the actual condition and situation of persons and things, under this evidence: two or three hundred beeves arriving every day for the purpose of being slaughtered for the New Orleans market, landed directly at the foot of Louisiana Avenue; persons who pass along the levee and the streets adjoining the landing, in a densely populated part of a town, watching invariably with fear or anxiety, and continually inconvenienced by these untamed animals, sometimes breaking loose and rushing wildly and madly through the streets, endangering the limbs and the lives of men, women, and children. Is it not palpable to any man who will look at things as they are, instead of indulging in wild ideas of liberty for every man to do whatever he pleases, regardless of others' rights, that the public welfare and the protection of the lives and limbs of the citizens require that a stop should be put to this? Of all the places in New Orleans, there is none, at certain seasons of the year, more pleasant than the bank of the river Mississippi; the people come to it for pleasure and for enjoyment, and they use it also for their business purposes. The whole portion of the city upon which the cattle were landed and slaughter-houses were built was cut off from the use of the inhabitants. Grand jury after grand jury reported against it as a public nuisance, and called upon the municipal council of New Orleans to exercise the police power vested in it by the State and pass ordinances to correct the evil, and the councils did so. They called upon the city council of Lafayette to pass ordinances, and they too did so. They reported it to the district courts of the State, in order that it might be known to all the State. It was a matter of grievous public complaint, day after day, week after week, month after month, and year after year. At length, in 1862, the city of Jefferson passed an ordinance for the express purpose of removing the slaughter-houses.

It was similar to the law that is now before you, and conferred upon Messrs. Rochereau and Hepp, two citizens of great wealth and respectability, rights and powers of the same kind with those conferred here upon the corporation. It fell through. I need not dwell upon the reason. The Court is aware of the late history of the country: that the Southern States, supposing themselves strong enough to effect their purpose, determined to separate from the Union, made an unsuccessful and baleful attempt at secession. Messrs. Rochereau and Hepp, though rich men, were unable to make any use of the authority which was given to them. The city of New Orleans was cut off from trade and commerce, and from intercourse and communication with other parts of the Union. General Butler was here; a large number of citizens were expelled: the city was walled in by military rule. Is it a wonder, then, that Hepp and Rochereau could not use the powers and privileges conferred upon them by the ordinance?

In 1866, peace having been reëstablished, and the power of the Union once more acknowledged, matters began to resume their regular course. The grand jury of this city once more presented to the district court this important subject, and earnestly invoked the action of the State to remove "the greatest of all nuisances." They stated that, in consequence of the impurity of the water of the Mississippi by the throwing of offals and filth (especially from slaughtered animals by butchers) into it, above the city, more contagion and disease had been produced than by any other cause: and they complained in strong and direct terms that it was impossible to preserve the public health so long as the abattoirs or slaughterhouses in Jefferson were kept up above the city.

In the year 1867 the State felt it necessary to relieve the suffering people, and an act was passed by the legislature for the object. It was entitled "An act to prevent offal and nuisances from being thrown in the Mississippi River within the limits of the cities of New Orleans and Jefferson." The first section provided: "That the city council of the city of New Orleans, and the city council of the city of Jefferson, be, and they are hereby required, before the first day of May, eighteen hundred and sixty-seven, to pass ordinances prohibiting any offal or nuisance from slaughter-houses, and feculent matters from privies, from being thrown into the Mississippi River anywhere above Slaughter-House Point,"— Slaughter-House Point, the very point now occupied by the company. To enforce obedience to this command, the act declared that no ordinance of either council should have force until that ordered by this act should be passed.

It then further provided : " That after the said first day of May, eighteen hundred and sixty-seven, it shall be unlawful for any person whatever to throw any offal, carrion, or dead animals, or feculent matters from privies, into the Mississippi River at any point in front of the corporate limits of the said cities of New Orleans or Jefferson, under a penalty of fifty dollars for each offense, to be recoverable before any court of competent jurisdiction, for the use of the State, one half to go to the informer. the said penalties to be in addition to any fines and penalties which may be imposed by the ordinances of the said cities of New Orleans and Jefferson."

This act was passed March 23, 1867. Its object was to compel the municipal powers to do their duty, in spite of the butchers' opposition, which had become so formidable as to control the town councils. The legislature used the plainest words, and adopted the simplest means. Nothing can be clearer and more positive than the order which it gave to the town councils. Why did not they obey it? Because they were overawed or circumvented and deluded ; because the butchers, represented here by the counsel who last addressed you, were suddenly converted into champions of liberty for themselves, regardless of all others, and boldly declared that no police regulation, however necessary to the happiness or even the existence of the community, could interfere constitutionally with that liberty and their free use of their own property. They knew that the use which they were making of that property was against public health, prevented, or at least checked the growth of the city, and was incompatible with the welfare of this community and the general good of the commonwealth. But what of that? They would join themselves together and form a corporation of six, ycleped the "Benevolent Association of Butchers." The *Benevolent* Association of Butchers, and champions of the right to use their own property as they please, without regard to law or the liberty of others! There is their act of incorporation, dated immediately after the law of 1867. It sets forth that the six persons therein named had become " benevolent butchers " to one another, and for the purpose of trading in cattle, and of importing and selling cattle in the market of New Orleans ; and, sirs, — it is strange, yet true, — they exercised sufficient influence to prevent the councils from obeying the order of the State.

Time rolled on : the nuisance increased : the voice of the people was louder ; public opinion could no longer be stayed. When the legislature of this State met again, the people presented new petitions, numerous and largely signed, praying for further and direct state action. They urged : "You have sent us to the councils : we cannot induce them to do their duty. Look at our situation! You are here to legislate, not merely for one particular spot or parish, but for the entire State. You, sir, come from Caddo, in the extreme northwestern part of Louisiana. You come from Plaquemines, at the mouth of the river. You, legislators, are all assembled here, representing every interest and every parish of this State. This is a matter of common concern and interest. Our commerce is with each and all of you. On you New Orleans depends : it is a great and noble city, of which we are proud. Make those regulations which are essential to the health and comfort of the city, to its growth and pros-

perity, to the security of the lives and limbs of its inhabitants, and to the best and freest use of the banks of our
river for business and pleasure, and you will confer a
benefit and a blessing on the State. We call upon you
to act as citizens of Louisiana. It is your duty to protect life and health, and to promote the comfort and
prosperity of the entire people. You cannot discharge
the duty with regard to New Orleans without doing good
to every other part of the State. Deprive New Orleans
of your proper protection and guardianship, and the whole
commonwealth suffers. We are bound together inseparably, one in heart, one in feeling, one in interest, and we
call upon you to exercise the power that is vested in you
for the good of all." Was that constitutional, right, and
patriotic, judges?

Suppose, instead of being here, you had been members
of the legislature. Suppose an appeal of that kind had
come to you from good and true men. What, I ask,
would you have done? What would you do if called on
now to act under such circumstances? Refer it to a committee to take full evidence on the subject, and to report;
and when that report should be fairly before you, then
you would do that under the Constitution which the public
good might demand. That is the part of wisdom; that is
the part of honor; that is the part of American patriotism; that is the duty of the legislator true to liberty and
law. I am not talking now of wild, abstract notions of
liberty, — that a man has by nature the right or liberty
to do whatever he desires, irrespective of the rights and
liberties of other men; such impracticable notions, pushed
to excess, lead only to crime and ruin, — but I am speaking this day for liberty regulated by law. I love liberty
everywhere, and at all times, — such as she is depicted in
the classic pages of Rome and Greece, as she has been
exhibited in England and in other lands; but the liberty

I love and advocate above all is American liberty, supported by constitutions and laws. Lawless liberty is mere licentiousness; where law ends tyranny begins.

Then, sirs, when you are called upon to consider the action of the legislature on this matter, it is just to look into the documents of which I have spoken in a general way: and, first, I will read from the report of the grand jury, August 14, 1866. It states: "In consideration of the prevalence of cholera and other diseases in our midst, the grand jury makes a special report upon the impurity of the water taken from the river and supplied by pipes to the city, caused by throwing offal, refuse from slaughter-houses, etc., into the river above the works of the water-works company, at the foot of Richard Street. The superintendent of the water-works states that the suction pipes of the river occasionally become clogged by such water being drawn into them, requiring constant attention to keep their orifices clear. Two large vessels lie at the wharves immediately above and in front of the suction pipes, and act as fenders to guide the floating offal, etc., out into the current. When they have been loaded and gone, the collection of effete matter will naturally increase as in an eddy. How many slaughter-houses exist above the works I cannot say; but their entire removal to the lower part of the city would be a public benefit.

"A petition signed by more than five hundred of our most prominent citizens for such removal of slaughter-houses was addressed to the council last spring, and reported upon favorably by the committee on police and health of the lower board June 12, 1866; but the resolution submitted by them failed to become a law, and the city passed, on the 31st July, 1866, an ordinance, No. 233, N. S., authorizing the erection of slaughter-houses in the Fourth District, although under the health ordinance (sec. 26), approved August 2, 1866, they are expressly forbidden. Every diligence is exercised now to keep the suction pipes clear from all effete substances, and after the water is pumped into the reservoirs a laborer is engaged throughout the day in skimming the scum which forms upon the surface."

The grand jury continue: "Many persons of this city (especially the poorer classes, amongst whom most of the deaths of cholera have lately taken place) use the hydrant water for drinking and other purposes. We believe that the water must be impure and unhealthy, and liable, if not to create disease, at least to increase that which may exist. We recommend that the city authorities should take this matter into immediate consideration, and that, besides adopting requisite ordinances, they should petition the legislature to pass an act that there should not be allowed to exist any slaughter-houses, or similar places, above the city within a specified number of miles. We consider such an act of the legislature necessary, because, should the city authorities cause the removal of such establishments from the upper portions of the city, they could be reëstablished barely above the city limits, and would be as great nuisances then as now."

I read from the journal of the House: "Under a suspension of the rules the following bill was brought in: 'An act to protect the health of the city of New Orleans and of the town of Algiers, on the right bank of the Mississippi River, parish of Orleans.'"

This bill is very like the act of 1869. It was read and referred to a committee. That committee reported, "from personal and careful observation," as also "from the opinions and personal experience of persons thoroughly competent to judge on the question;" as well, too, as from "a petition signed by eleven hundred respectable property-holders of New Orleans, urging the removal of this foul nuisance."

"The first question which arises on this important matter is, what becomes of the immense quantity of filth and offal which is accumulated at and in the vicinity of the stock landing? The result of our investigations is that it all goes into the Mississippi River, which, if not prejudicial to health, is certainly very revolting. The immense suction pipe of the New Orleans water-works is immediately below, and sucks in objects floating on the water at a distance of fifty or sixty feet. When the river is low, it is not uncommon to see intestines and portions of putrefied animal matter lodged immediately around the pipes. The liquid portion of this putrefied matter is sucked into the reservoir. Vessels arriving here with cattle, especially those that have been in a storm, invariably throw the dead cattle — of which they often have many — into the river at the stock landing. These are again taken from the river and subjected to the process of skinning, after which the carcass is again thrown into the river. It is not unusual, during the sultry heat of the summer months, to see these floating objects about the shipping, no doubt causing disease among the sailors on board these vessels. There is not the slightest doubt in the mind of your committee that this must be extremely prejudicial to the health of New Orleans. To recapitulate, we would state that the two subjects which deserve the most important consideration are: first, the water we drink is contaminated with macerated and decomposed animal matter, and is a constant source of disease and injury, occasionally acute, but generally slow and certain; second, the air we breathe at times is contaminated and poisoned by the filth from different slaughter-houses, — blood, urine, and other refuse matter, all in a state of decomposition, thrown into the water, floating down the shore, an abominable nuisance."

I refrain from reading the rest of this report. It is all

to the same effect. There is appended to the report a document entitled to the highest respect, from the character and learning of the persons who signed it. It is a certificate from the president of the Board of Health, J. S. Smith, from Dr. Choppin, and from J. T. Pennington, and it corroborates the conclusions of the committee. With this evidence before us, I need not add a word to refute the reckless and groundless assertion by the counsel on the other side, that there is nothing in this question that concerns the health of the city of New Orleans; that the legislature, when they acted on this information, and passed the act of 1869, entitling it " An act to protect the health of the city of New Orleans," etc., were guilty of falsehood, and acted in bad faith and corruptly.

But let me go further, and refer more fully to the title and to the body of this act of 1869, which is bitterly denounced. The title commences, " An act to protect the health of the city of New Orleans," etc. Is that a proper subject of legislation? Does it fall within the police power of a sovereign State to adopt measures for the protection of public health? The title continues, "To locate the stock landing and slaughter-house." I have shown that, in point of fact and in the opinion of the legislature, the location of the stock landing and slaughter-houses, immediately above the water-works and above the city, was injurious to the health, comfort, safety, and prosperity of its inhabitants, and imperiously demanded legislative action. Does the act of 1869 cease, then, to be an act to protect the health of the city of New Orleans, because it goes further and wisely locates a stock landing and slaughter-house elsewhere? To carry into effect these objects, the legislature deemed it prudent to charter a company, and therefore added to and concluded the title with the words " and to incorporate the Crescent Live Stock Landing and Slaughter-House Company." That is the title of the act. Is there anything in it that is unconstitutional and destructive of rational liberty? I am speaking of the practical operation of a free constitutional government, to you who are to judge of the action of public functionaries. Is there any impropriety, any ground for charging legislators with frauds, in the mere passage of the act under the circumstances which have been detailed?

It is said, there is no doubt that the legislature could have erected slaughter-houses; could have exacted fees and tolls, and made persons pay for the use of facilities afforded them by the State, in the exercise of its power to protect the general health and advance the comfort and welfare of the people of New Orleans. What! do you admit that? And will you yet undertake to say that if the position of public affairs is such that it is not convenient for the State to use a million of dollars or more for such a purpose, the State cannot create a corporation, with limited franchises and restrictions, under constitutional authority, for the purpose of doing that which, while it advances the private interests of the corporators, subserves the public good?

The power of creating a corporation may be properly used for the purpose of attaining a public and useful end. When the end is legitimate and within the scope of the Constitution, the means which are appropriate and plainly adapted to this end, and which are not prohibited, are lawful. Private corporations have been deemed, in certain cases and in certain respects, public agents. There is no doubt of the constitutional doctrine on this subject, or of the policy adopted by this State. Was the lighting of the streets in New Orleans deemed of public importance and use? A gaslight company was incorporated. Was wholesome water a public necessity? The waterworks company was incorporated. Is a railroad — through

the streets of a city, or between different parts of the
State, or between Louisiana and other States — wanted for
public convenience and commerce? A corporation is
established. Who in this country doubts the power of
the legislature in these cases? I speak not of visionary
theorists wandering in the fogs of metaphysical abstractions
of absolute liberty, but of practical American statesmen
and judges. In our country, when a large and consolidated capital is necessary to accomplish works important
to the public good, it is quite customary for the States
to grant charters of incorporation to private individuals,
with special and often exclusive privileges, to effect that
end. And this has been a means of making the gigantic
improvements which private enterprise, directed by prudence and aided by scientific and mechanical knowledge
and skill, has successfully and beneficially made throughout the Union. Will it be said, Massachusetts can do
this, New York can do this, the young and giant State
of Illinois can do this, and, with proper limitations and
restrictions of the privileges and the profits and emoluments of the corporations, can do this to the promotion of
the people's comfort and weal? But liberty is destroyed
and the Constitution is violated when in Louisiana her legislature, exercising police power, incorporates a company
to erect, in aid of the health, comfort, and prosperity of her
citizens, an abattoir, and confers upon the company the
right to charge those who use it a reasonable fee or remuneration, limited by the charter, for the advantages and
facilities furnished them by the outlay of the company's
capital in lands, buildings, machinery, etc.

I need not refer to the judicial decisions cited by my
colleague on this subject, nor to the numerous legislative
precedents in our statutes. The current of authority is
strong and unbroken against the assertion and against the
doctrine that no exclusive right can be conferred upon a

corporation. I will notice a single case that has not yet been commented on. The Pontchartrain Railroad Company was incorporated in 1830 with " the exclusive right and privilege of constructing and using a railroad or railway to and from the city of New Orleans and to and from Lake Pontchartrain for and during twenty-five years." Some years after this time the New Orleans and Carrollton Railroad Company was incorporated to construct a railroad between the city of New Orleans and a point at Carrollton on the Mississippi River; and still subsequently, in 1840, the legislature incorporated the Jefferson and Lake Pontchartrain Railway Company for the construction of a railway from Carrollton to Lake Pontchartrain. These two companies united to transport freight and passengers between New Orleans and the lake. In June, 1853, the Pontchartrain Company instituted suit to restrain the two companies from transporting freight and passengers to and from the lake, and to recover damages for their violation of its exclusive right ; and this Court decided that the legislature had granted an exclusive right or monopoly to the plaintiffs for twenty-five years, that the grant was valid, and that the plaintiffs therefore were entitled to the injunction and to recover the damages they had sustained, and gave judgment accordingly.[1]

My colleague, in opening this case, analyzed the act of 1869, and placed its leading provisions so clearly before the Court as to render futile the erroneous construction and statements that have since been urged against it. He showed that the law provided for the establishment of one place for an abattoir, where alone, "solely and exclusively," cattle intended for the New Orleans market should be slaughtered : that it conferred no exclusive privilege on the company to slaughter such cattle, but compelled it to furnish whatever is essential to the convenience and

[1] La. An. Reports, 256.

accommodation of the butchers for killing their cattle,
cleaning and taking them away, to dress and prepare
their meat for food. When, then, it is said that the act
drives one thousand butchers from their business and deprives them of the right to follow their ordinary occupation,
the assertion is plainly and palpably untrue. Undoubtedly,
as the effect of machinery is to become a substitute for
manual labor, the introduction of machines must for a season throw some persons out of employment, but experience teaches that it tends eventually to the good of all.
One man at the slaughter-house, by the aid of its machinery, may do as much as it would have required ten men to
perform without that aid ; and thus labor may be saved,
or performed more cheaply and more accurately. But
this is no argument against the improvement. If it were,
all improvement would stop. However, in the present instance no butchers are thrown out of employment. They
are facilitated in their work, and carry on their trade
and art as heretofore after the slaughter-house company
has afforded them aid in killing their cattle, a work which
they may perform themselves or employ any other to perform for them. But it has been vehemently asserted that
the act of 1869 conferred upon seventeen individuals, unworthy and unknown, an odious, oppressive, and arbitrary
power to exact fees and perquisites from the butchers
without furnishing any consideration for the same, and
that every one of the seventeen was guilty of bribery in
procuring the passage of the act, and ought now to be in
the penitentiary. Counsel after counsel has reiterated
these charges before you, judges, and persisted in declaring that nothing has been done to entitle the company to
any remuneration. Is this true? No. False ! False !
False ! Is it nothing to have purchased land, to have
erected on it buildings, slaughter-houses, sheds, pens, etc.,
to have furnished machinery sufficient for all the pur-

6

poses of the abattoir, and to have employed faithful and skillful persons to keep everything in order and to furnish the butchers with every facility? Is it nothing to have done this promptly and faithfully, at the expense of an immense outlay of money and in strict conformity with the law? The company is entitled to no fees. It demands and receives no remuneration except from those who use the facilities which it affords, and who are bound in law and justice to pay according to the rate established by legislative judgment. The charge of bribery against every member of the company is indignantly denied and denounced as a calumny.

It has been argued that the act is unconstitutional in prescribing that the cattle, etc., shall be landed at a particular part of the bank of the Mississippi, and that the owners shall pay for the facilities afforded them in the wharves, etc., erected there, and that the act of Congress of 1812 and our own civil code make the river free, and give every one a right to land and unload his vessels on its banks without charge. This matter has been settled by custom, by good sense, and by the judgments of the highest tribunals. Do you not, judges, in walking along the levee, see one place used for the landing of small vessels, another for large sea-going vessels; one place for river steamers, another for ocean steamers; flatboats discharging their coal and other freight in different designated places? It necessarily follows that in the exercise of police power there must be a regulation of these things in order that business may be carried on conveniently and without constant disputes. The Supreme Court of the United States has said, " Regulations of this kind are necessary and indispensable for the convenience and safety of commerce, and local authorities have a right to prescribe at what wharf a vessel may lie and unload and take on board particular cargoes." The Supreme Court of the

State held that the municipalities of New Orleans might charge for the facilities afforded commerce in the shape of wharves, laying it down as a fundamental rule that if the State had erected them there could be no doubt of its right to impose the wharfage. Similar doctrines and views were recognized in the Navigation Company case, and the reports of the Supreme Courts of the United States abound in authorities on the point, and establish that such a regulation is a matter of police, and not of commerce, and is not only consistent with, but essential to, the enjoyment of rational liberty in the matter.

But it has been contended that the act of 1869 interferes with the liberty of labor and the liberty of property. The butchers have exercised their art and business for many long years in Jefferson, and have there slaughterhouses and pens. They have a right to continue to use their property as they hitherto have done. Their right of property is absolute, and so is their right of labor. The State cannot interfere with them. The act deprives them of the power to support themselves and their families by an unconstitutional interference with their liberty, — liberty to work and carry on their business where they please, liberty to use their property as they please. There is a law higher even than the written constitution, a law recognizing the right of every man to labor, to receive the reward of his industry, to use the property he has acquired, and every infringement of that law is a violation of vested rights. This is a mere repetition of every argument that has been made against the exercise of the police power in our State. The reports are full of cases in which the very question has been examined and decided in regard to nuisances in this city, and the constitutional and legal power has been invariably sustained.

There is one case of a very striking character in which the argument was like that used in the present suit. An oysterman had pursued his business in New Orleans, and had been in the habit of selling his oysters in his own private house. The municipal council passed an ordinance forbidding the sale of oysters in the city except at particular places, but the oysterman continued to sell at his own house, regardless of the ordinance. The city instituted a suit against him for the violation of its regulation, and Judge Preston defended him. I need not tell this Court that he was a man of genius, of singular simplicity and largeness of mind, a profound thinker, of great purity in private life, but an enthusiast, inclined to that species of republican radicalism which carries to an extreme general doctrines of liberty. The district court decided against his client, and to the question, "What! Shall I not open and sell my oysters in my own house that I have used for that purpose for so many years?" answered, "No, because they who are to regulate this matter declare it a nuisance." The case came before the Supreme Court. It was contended for the oysterman that the trade was useful to all those engaged in it, — it was necessary for the support of their families; that the defendant had been in the habit of selling oysters in his house for twenty years; that the ordinance interfered with the freedom of property and of labor in an honest pursuit, that of fishermen ; and why not, it was asked, in shell-fish as with fish with scales ? The ordinance created a monopoly in the business. An appeal was made to the highest principles, to the right of every man to labor for himself, to use his own property, and to receive the fruits of his labor and use of that without interference from the council. The court decided that it was a proper matter to be entrusted to the common council of the city, who had the right to say where oysters should be sold and where they should not, and they gave judgment against the defendant.

The counsel for the butchers have read with emphasis,

as applicable to this case, a passage from Cooley's Constitutional Limitations : " The man or the class forbidden the acquisition or enjoyment of property in the manner permitted to the community at large would be deprived of liberty in matters of primary importance to his or her pursuit of happiness." It is difficult to see the applicability of this quotation to the present case, but if the counsel had only read the next paragraph he would have found the following passage : " There are unquestionably cases in which the State may grant privileges to specified individuals without violating any constitutional principle, because from the nature of the case it is impossible they should be possessed and enjoyed by all ; and if it is important that they should exist, the proper state authorities must be left to select the guarantees. Of this class are grants of the franchise to be a corporation."

If this Court desired authority upon so plain a matter, I do not know where it can be found more fully and better explained than in the following extract from the ablest judges and constitutional jurists of the land : " The police power affects the use and enjoyment of property. It is much easier to perceive and realize the existence and sources of this power than to mark its boundaries or prescribe limits to its exercise. It extends to the protection of the lives, limbs, health, comfort, and quiet of all persons and the protection of all property within the State. According to the maxim, ' *Sic utere tuo ut alienum non ladas,*' etc. By this general police power of the State, persons and property are subjected to all kinds of restraints and burdens in order to secure the general comfort, health, and prosperity of the State, of the perfect right in the legislature to do which no question ever was, or upon acknowledged general principles ever can be made, so far as natural persons are concerned. But though property be protected, it is still to be understood that the lawgiver has a right to prescribe the mode and manner of using it, so far as may be necessary to prevent the abuse of the right to the injury or annoyance of others or of the public. The government may, by general regulations, interdict such uses of property as would create nuisances, and become dangerous to the lives or health or peace or comfort of the citizens. Unwholesome trades, slaughter-houses, operations offensive to the senses, the deposit of powder, the application of steam power to propel cars, the building with combustible materials, and the burial of the dead may all be interdicted by law in the midst of dense masses of population, on the general and rational principle that every person ought so to use his property as not to injure his neighbors, and that private interests must be made subservient to the general interests of the community." [1]

The time allotted to me for a reply to the opposite counsel is drawing to a close, and I am reminded by my colleague who sits beside me that it is important to notice another point. The counsel for the butchers have, with great boldness and effrontery, undertaken to say here, over and over again, that they had charged and offered to prove that members of the legislature that passed this act had been bribed to vote for it, and that if the slaughter-house company had not shrunk from it those members of the legislature and the seventeen corporators mentioned in the act would have been in the penitentiary. I deny it. There has never been any legal charge made in a form susceptible of legal proof. There has never been any proposal of proof, except in such vague and indefinite terms as amounted to a vain parade or mockery. They pretend that my clients shrank in fear from the investigation. You shrink and you skulk. You skulk behind a general railing and informal accusation. You say mem-

[1] 2 Kent, 432.

bers of the legislature were bribed. Tell us who they
are. Name them. Name any one. You say you have
witnesses to prove it. Who are the witnesses? Let us
have their names. It will not do to come in here and say,
" We are ready to prove the whole body was bribed." It
is the height of injustice thus to indulge in indistinct,
general, and malignant accusations. You say you know
the individuals who are guilty. Are you men? Have
you the courage of men? Go to the criminal court; give
information against them. You say these men ought to
be in the penitentiary. Why not do your duty and have
them put there? If you are prepared with proof for conviction, patriots and friends of public justice, why do you
not use the law against these high offenders? The courts
of criminal jurisdiction are open for their prosecution and
punishment. Do you want an illustrious precedent for
the course? You will find it in the life of Cato, the
censor, a man of wisdom and of severe public and private
virtue; a man of truth, justice, and public spirit. Imitate him, and the community will believe there is something worthy of consideration in your charges, and that
they are not a shallow pretext for slander and the support
of an unjust case. This is the patriotic and practical
course. The proposition for disregarding the legislative
department, and putting it under the feet of the judiciary,
betrays a spirit alien to law and kindred to the worst
radicalism.

Has this Court power to inquire into the motives and
conduct of the legislature in passing the act? Under the
theory of free government, the powers of government are
distributed into three departments, which should be kept
as separate from and independent of each other as the
nature of such governments will admit. In the former
constitutions of this State, this distribution of powers was
distinctly and expressly made. In the present constitu-

tion there is no article expressly making such a distribution, but the distribution is practically and substantially
made into the legislative, executive, and judicial departments. There would be no reliance upon the stability of
the law, if its vitality and force were to be suspended and
hindered by railing accusations against the members of
the legislature who passed it, not contemplating penal
justice, but having only in view the private interests of a
suitor acting under the influence of motives of whatever
nature may be supposed. The legislature, under such a
theory, would cease to be independent, and the judiciary,
ceasing to be mere interpreters of the law, would practically become the makers of it. All security for liberty
and property would be disturbed or destroyed, and confusion and distrust lead the way to general demoralization.
Our government is founded upon the theory of confidence
in the virtue of man and the power of public sentiment.
We have been asked, If the legislature should prove base
enough to pass a law under the influence of bribes, and
the judiciary cannot inquire, upon a general accusation,
into the motives of the legislature, what is left to the citizen? We answer, Nothing but an appeal to public sentiment. Change the members; purify the temple of
legislation: repeal what ought to be repealed: correct
injustice; indemnify loss through public wrong.

No human institution is perfect. The system of American government has its defects, but it would be madness,
on account of temporary evil, to throw off established government and remove the ancient landmarks of liberty.
We have been told there are a great many decisions to
show that the Court has power to enter upon the inquiry.
I ask for one decision: name it, produce it. I say such a
thing has never been done. You are bound to suppose
members of the legislature honest. You are bound to
suppose they act from patriotic motives. You cannot

listen to a charge against them preferred in this way. What! are you a separate department of the government? Are you, whose judicial function it is to interpret the laws, — are you to undertake to say the legislature passed such a law, but they were very foolish? The legislature passed such another law, but they did not know what they were about, and therefore we will declare it is not the law.

I do not deny the power and the duty of the Court to declare an unconstitutional law void. On the contrary, I hold it to be the distinguishing mark and glory of American liberty that the power and the duty exist. But I hold that the Court cannot impute to the legislature any other but public motives for their acts. In the very authority quoted by our opponents it is said : "And although it has sometimes been urged at the bar that the courts ought to inquire into the motives of the legislature where fraud and corruption were alleged, and annul their action if the allegation were established, the argument has in no case been acceded to by the judiciary, and they have never allowed the inquiry to be entered upon." It is said : "The powers of the three departments are not merely equal ; they are exclusive in respect to the duties assigned to each. They are absolutely independent of each other. It is now proposed that one of the three powers shall institute an inquiry into the conduct of another department and form an issue to try by what motives the legislature were governed in the enactment of a law. If this may be done, we may also inquire by what motives the executive is induced to approve a bill or withhold his approval, and in case of withholding it corruptly, by our mandate compel its approval. To institute the proposed inquiry would be a direct attack upon the independence of the legislature, and a usurpation of power subversive of the Constitution." The opposing counsel have referred to the history of Georgia, where a corrupt act was passed by a corrupt legislature. Granted. Was it not, however, decided by the Supreme Court of the United States, in the case of Fletcher *v.* Peck,[1] which grew out of the act, that it was impossible to look into the charge of corruption preferred against the members of the legislature of the State in that case? Chief Justice Marshall said: "It would be indecent in the extreme, upon a private contract between two individuals, to enter into an inquiry respecting the corruption of the sovereign power of a State. If the title be plainly deduced from a legislative act, which the legislature might constitutionally pass, if the act be clothed with all the requisite forms of a law, a court, sitting as a court of law, cannot sustain a suit brought by one individual against another, founded on the allegation that the act is a nullity, in consequence of the impure motives which influenced certain members of the legislature which passed the law." Mr. Justice Johnson delivered a separate opinion in the case. He said: "As to the idea that the grants of a legislature may be void because the legislature are corrupt, it appears to me to be subject to insuperable difficulties. The acts of the supreme power must be considered pure, for the same reason that all sovereign acts must be considered just, because there is no power that can declare them otherwise. The absurdity in this case would have been strikingly perceived could the party who passed the act of cession have got again into power and declared themselves pure, and the intermediate legislature corrupt. The security of a people against the misconduct of their rulers must lie in the frequent recurrence to first principles and the imposition of adequate constitutional restrictions."

In a case decided in Indiana in November, 1858, the Court said: "It is averred that the bill was passed by

[1] 6 Cranch, 87.

the fraud, corruption, and bribery of several members of the legislature. In Wright v. Defrees, 8 Ind. R. 298, it was held that this Court cannot inquire by what motives the members of the legislature were governed in the enactment of a law. That, however, was a case between citizens, and the Court, in the opinion delivered, use this language: 'We say nothing as to what rights the State may have in a case of this kind. The State is no party in these proceedings.' Thus the Court withholds an opinion in regard to the question whether, on the complaint of the State, a law can be impeached for the fraud, etc., of members voting for it. In the present case the State is the plaintiff. But is there any reason why she, as a party litigant, should be allowed more than an individual citizen to put in issue the conduct and motives of the legislature or any of its members? We know of no principle or authority upon which an issue of that character can, in any case, be tried before a judicial tribunal. To institute such an inquiry, as said in Wright v. Defrees, would be a direct attack upon the independence of the legislature, and an usurpation of power subversive of the Constitution." The Sunbury and Erie Railroad Co. v. Cooper, 7 Am. Law Reg. 158.

A great deal has been said about monopoly. No one is more strongly opposed to monopoly in general than I am. It leads to inequality and injustice, interferes with the freedom of labor and the true spirit of the common law. Undoubtedly the courts in England decided against monopolies in the cases cited. I have not time to examine them severally. They fall within two classes: first, monopolies granted by the crown in the exercise of its pretended royal prerogative; and second, monopolies granted without authority, and in violation of general rights, by corporations. The struggle for liberty was on the part of the people, who contended that they alone could judge and determine when and where and to whom to grant peculiar privileges, and that the power could be properly exercised only through Parliament, either directly or indirectly; and the people were victorious in the courts and in Parliament. In the long list of cases produced by the opposite counsel, there is not one in which a monopoly created by act of Parliament was decided to be void. The power of the people to grant them is fully recognized and established. We have been told that our ancestors brought with them from England their common law rights and constitutional principles. This is true; but while bringing with them the valuable principles of English law for the protection of life, liberty, and property, they left behind whatever they considered worthless and bad. They brought with them no allegiance to crowned heads; no royal prerogative to suspend laws and grant monopolies to favorites. The whole American system of government is popular. The people underlie and control every department of it. And it is in support of the power of the people and for the preservation of American liberty that I raise my voice against the dangerous doctrine advanced here to-day. I have lived to see these doctrines pushed to an extreme and threatening the stability of our government, when the people were urged to nullify the tariff laws of Congress, because it was pretended that those laws tended to create a monopoly.

But I have not time to pursue this subject. I feel it, however, a duty, before dismissing it, to warn you, judges, of the attempt in this case to make you, the sworn ministers of the law, lend your authority to overturn the laws. It is said that this act is void because it was approved by the governor after the legislature adjourned. This objection has been briefly and sufficiently answered by my colleague, who has referred to a case of highest authority,

and decisive upon the point, in 21 N. Y. R. 517.[1] The
legislature adjourned on the 4th March, and fifty acts
of the session of 1869 were signed on or before that
day. Eighty-nine acts were signed after the adjournment; among them were the revenue bill for the support
of the government, the appropriation bill, the education
bill, and other acts necessary to the existence of the government and the welfare of the people. You are asked
by the architects of ruin to break down all this legislation.

It has been argued that the Court must treat the act of
1869 as a private statute. But it is a statute passed by
the State, in the exercise of her police power as a sovereign, to protect the public health, to prevent public nuisances, and to advance the comfort and prosperity and
business of this city and of this State. It contains provisions giving penalties to the State. Such a statute is
clearly a public statute. The latest writers upon statutes
in our own country declare that the disposition has been,
in the United States, to enlarge the limits of the class of
public acts, and to bring within it all acts that affect the
community at large and are of a public character.

[Mr. Hunt was here informed by the Court that the
time allowed him had expired.]

---

[1] People v. Bowen.

POLITICAL AFFAIRS IN LOUISIANA.

[In 1851, Mr. Hunt delivered the following speech at a Whig mass meeting held at the Poydras Market in the city of New Orleans.]

FELLOW-CITIZENS, — It is a long time since I have had the pleasure of meeting and communing with you in a body. During that time many questions of great importance and delicacy, touching the peace and harmony of the Union and the very existence of our national government, have arisen, been discussed, and finally settled to the satisfaction of the great body of the American people, by the constitutional, honorable, and expedient measures embraced in the Compromise, adopted under the lead of Clay and Webster, Cass and Foote, and other distinguished statesmen and patriots, who, whatever may be their differences on matters of mere party politics, have, by their magnanimous conduct on this occasion, entitled themselves to the gratitude of every true-hearted American. And I should not be true to myself, to liberty, and to the duty which I owe the country, if I refrained from rendering them the humble tribute of my applause. During that time, too, the State of Louisiana and the city of New Orleans have remained under the regular and peaceable operation of the present Constitution of the State; but I regret to say, fellow-citizens, that we have failed to keep pace with our sister States in the great march of progress. In spite of the natural advantages which the city of New Orleans has enjoyed, she has been outstripped in the race of improvement by New

York, and Boston, and Baltimore, and Philadelphia, and other cities of the Union. Situated not far from the mouth of the Mississippi, with nearly half of the States of the Union at one time tributary to her, New Orleans has, within the last five years, seen a large portion of the rich commerce of the Northwest gradually taken away from her. Though she has increased in population and wealth, the increase has been small in comparison with that of other cities, and her commerce, if it has not declined, has at least been stationary.

What is the cause of this? Why is it that New Orleans has been thus arrested in her progress? Why is it that the State of Louisiana, with her fertile soil and great natural resources, has not kept pace with her sister States? The cause may be found in the mal-government of the State. The Constitution of the State is a failure. The Constitution is bad, and the legislation under the Constitution has been bad. For the last five years the government of Louisiana has been a failure. I do not say this upon the spur of the moment, nor do I speak for rhetorical effect. I have carefully watched the operations of our state government, and long weighed and studied these things; and the result of my best judgment upon them is, that we have been retarded in our progress and paralyzed in our action by the Constitution and legislation of the State. The Constitution has indeed sat like a nightmare on the bosom of Louisiana and prevented her from breathing healthfully. With its restrictions and prohibitions, it has fettered the enterprise and industry of the people, and caused capital to seek a more natural and freer home elsewhere. It has failed entirely in answering the purposes for which it was framed; and the proper remedy for the people is to alter it or to abolish it, and to substitute a new Constitution in its place. I propose to say something on these subjects.

The Constitution divides the powers of the government into three departments, — legislative, executive, and judicial. The legislative department is defective, the executive department is defective, and the judicial department is defective. The whole government is defective. It has had little effect for good, and great effect for evil. The Constitution provides that "representation in the House of Representatives shall be equal and uniform, and shall be regulated and ascertained by the number of qualified electors." This is fair and equitable. It means that if three hundred qualified electors in Opelousas or in Jefferson are entitled to a representative, three hundred of the qualified electors in New Orleans are also entitled to a representative. This is republican equality. But when the Constitution lays down the rule in relation to representation in the Senate, it declares that the senators "shall be apportioned among the senatorial districts according to the total population contained in the several districts." The change in the basis of representation here made was intended to give greater proportionate weight to the country in the Senate of the State. In the House, the number of qualified electors forms the basis. In the Senate the total population, colored and white, slave and free, constitutes the basis. The proportion of slaves to the white population in the country is much larger than the proportion in the city. The senatorial basis therefore gives an evident advantage to the white population of the country over the white population of the city. Without stopping to dwell upon this, and admitting it for argument's sake only to be republican and just, I call your attention, fellow-citizens, to the manner in which the Constitution proceeds to apply the rule.

After declaring that senators shall be apportioned according to the total population contained in the several senatorial districts, the Constitution provides, "that no parish shall be entitled to more than one eighth of the whole number of senators." The number of senators being thirty-two, no parish or district can ever be entitled to more than four senators. This is evidently aimed at New Orleans. Her population entitled her to a representation of at least one fourth of the number of the senators. In order to carry out this injustice, the Constitution especially provides that, in apportioning representation in the Senate, "the population of New Orleans shall be deducted from the population of the whole State, and the remainder divided by twenty-eight, and the result produced thereby shall be the senatorial ratio entitling a district to a senator." Thus, one man in any other parish of the State was made politically equal to two men in New Orleans. Is this republicanism, equality, justice? The city of New Orleans is divided from the city of Lafayette by Felicity Road. By what reason, by what principle of justice, is a man on the other side of this division line made equal to two men on this side? Why is the resident of Ouachita or Jefferson given a representation in the Senate double that of a resident of New Orleans? It has been said by Mr. Taylor and others that the Constitution extended the right of suffrage. Doubtless this is true. But it is evident that in extending the right of suffrage the Constitution deprived the electors in New Orleans of the object of that right, — an equal and fair representation in the legislature. And yet Mr. Taylor and Mr. Dunbar think this Constitution good enough, and seek to obtain the votes of the citizens of New Orleans, while at the same time they are endeavoring to uphold a Constitution which stigmatizes those citizens as unworthy of equality with the other citizens of this State. The framers of the Constitution were not satisfied with putting this stigma alone on the citizens of New Orleans. They went still further, and ordained

7

that the city of New Orleans should stand accursed and proscribed, — that the very soil on which she rests shall be considered as infamous and polluting, and that the corrupt and pestilent atmosphere that envelops her shall be held to embrace and poison the surrounding portions of country within a circle of sixty miles. They provided that the General Assembly should, within a month of the first session under the Constitution, designate and fix the seat of government at some place not less than sixty miles from New Orleans; and that, when so fixed, it should not be removed without the consent of four fifths of the members of both Houses of the General Assembly.

I wish, fellow-citizens, that every one of you would read the arguments urged in the convention in favor of this provision. "New Orleans," it was said, "was immoral and corrupt; the country members would be bribed by dinners and parties and moneyed influences, so as to be controlled by city factions, and would sacrifice the interests of their immediate constituents." Miserable pretext for a mean injustice! Why, the very argument is a calumny against the constituents of the members who used it. Those constituents never dreamed of this foul wrong. They never contemplated any injustice or inequality in the political rights of the citizens of the different parts of the State. Their main object, in common with the entire people of the State, was to extend the right of suffrage and to effect a reform in the judiciary of the State. The people of the country parishes are an intelligent, honest, high-minded, and republican people: and when these matters shall be brought properly before them, they will stamp with reprobation the conduct of those who have misrepresented them. I do not say that they will remove the seat of government; but I do say that they will remove the stigma which is now fixed on New Orleans, and that they will put her citizens on a footing with the citizens of other parts of the State. For my own part, I must frankly declare, with respect to the best seat for the government, that the city of New Orleans presents many advantages. It is the emporium and mart of the commercial business of the West. From its situation, it receives the first information and news from other parts of the Union and from abroad. It is the centre of the arts and sciences and literature of our State, and it abounds in libraries and other sources of information, necessary or important to the business of enlightened legislation.

The evil effects of the unjust provisions of the Constitution in the apportionment of representation in the Senate have been seen and felt. In the spring of 1849 a crevasse occurred beyond the limits of the city of New Orleans. The river broke through the levee at Mr. Sauvé's plantation, some six miles above Carrollton, in the parish of Jefferson. The rear of our city was overflowed. I do not remember that I have ever looked upon so melancholy a spectacle. The city of New Orleans, after repeated efforts and a great expenditure of money, succeeded in closing the crevasse. It was deemed necessary for the future protection of the city to make a protection levee : and the best informed and most experienced engineers in the State prepared a plan, and presented a report to the legislature upon this subject. A bill was introduced into the House of Representatives, making an appropriation for such a levee. It passed the House, where the people of New Orleans were fairly represented. In the Senate, however, where we had but one half of our just quota of members, it was defeated or lost by a single vote. If there had been a just republican equality in the apportionment of senators, if we had had the four or six additional members in the Senate to which we were entitled, even upon the basis of the population of the State the bill would have passed, and the spectacle would not have been witnessed of the State voting thousands for internal improvements in other parts of the State, but refusing a cent to New Orleans (in which was centred more than one fourth of the taxable property of the State) to save her from the danger of inundation.

Fellow-citizens, if we examine the laws that have been passed by our legislature since the adoption of the present Constitution, we will find them characterized by injustice and a narrow and illiberal policy. Never has such legislation been seen. Many laws passed on the most important subjects have been pronounced by the courts to be unconstitutional, while others have been drawn up in such a bungling manner as to be utterly unintelligible, contradictory, and incapable of being executed. Without going beyond the last session of the legislature, our statute book unfortunately furnishes convincing proof of this. Two acts only need be mentioned. The act creating a board of liquidators for the consolidation of the debts of the municipalities had scarcely gone into operation when it was pronounced by the courts to be unconstitutional. The act establishing the mayor's and recorder's court in the city of New Orleans is so clumsily and inartificially drawn up that it has never been put, and cannot be put, into useful operation. The only effect of these acts has been to give Messrs. Benjamin and Micon, as attorneys of the board of liquidators, some fees which were doubtless well earned, but with no benefit to the public, and to give Mr. Reese the office of second district attorney, a sinecure of $1500 per annum. These are fair specimens of the legislation of the last legislature of Louisiana. The legislation was bad : the theory upon which the legislation was based is bad. The present party in power has been substantially in power since 1845, and might have done some good, but it has not done any. Nothing whatever has been done for New Orleans. She is in a condition of atrophy. She looked to the legislature for bread, and received a stone. Perhaps, under the present Constitution, it would be difficult to pass laws giving New Orleans the benefits adequate to her wants. That instrument prohibits the legislature from subscribing to the stock of any corporation or joint-stock company. It prohibits the creation, renewal, or extension of any corporate body with banking or discounting privileges; it prohibits the creation of corporations by special laws, except for municipal purposes; it directs the legislature to provide by general laws for the organization of all other corporations, except corporations with banking or discounting privileges, the creation of which it again specially prohibits.

New Orleans is in rivalry with the other great cities of the Union, with Boston, New York, Philadelphia, and Baltimore. She is in want of banking capital, of capital for commerce and business purposes. The whole circulation of bank issues of the State does not exceed three and a half millions. Look along the levee, and consider the vast quantities of produce under which it annually groans! You will see at a glance that our bank issues are utterly inadequate to our commercial wants. In all the other great cities in the country, in Boston, in New York, in Philadelphia, and in Baltimore, they have proportionally ten times the amount of bank facilities that we possess. How is it possible, under such circumstances, for New Orleans to compete with them? We want capital. We want the benefit of a large capital for business of every kind, and especially for banking. Under this condition of things, the framers of the Constitution have thought proper to prohibit the creation of any banking corporation in this State. It is true, the banking system has been a subject of great abuse, and thousands have been involved in ruin by that abuse.

But are we never to learn by experience? Can other commercial cities enjoy the benefits of banking corporations with safety and advantage to themselves, and is New Orleans alone incapable of managing such institutions? What commercial country in the world prospers without them? The Whigs, in a paper called their platform, have declared themselves the advocates of "a well-regulated system of free banks," and Mr. Miles Taylor is reported to have said that we have free banking now among us. This assertion of Mr. Taylor may be true in one sense, but it is unfounded in another sense, and in the sense in which free banking is understood by the people. It is true that every citizen who chooses, and who has the means of banking, is free to bank upon those means. There are no laws in this State to restrain him from doing so. Mr. Robb, we all know, is a banker, and Mr. Jacob Barker is also a banker, and issues his notes for circulation. In this sense Mr. Taylor may be right in saying that we have free banking now. But this is using the terms in a sense peculiar to himself, and different from the general understanding of the community. At all events, this is not the system of free banking which the Whigs refer to in their platform.

In the State of New York restraints upon private banking were adopted by the legislature at an early day. In 1781 Congress incorporated the Bank of North America, and recommended to the States to prohibit any other bank or bankers within those States during the war. The legislature of New York in 1782 followed the recommendation. After the treaty of 1783 there was no law restraining banking in New York until 1804, when an act, generally called the Restraining Act, was passed to restrain unincorporated banking companies. In 1838 a law was passed authorizing free banking associations in New York, and the system of free banking was established.

Mr. Dunbar, in a letter to the editors of the " Delta," says that there is no need of any change in our Constitution to establish free banking here, because in New York and in England it has been decided that joint-stock companies or associations may be created, in which the shares may be made transferable, the responsibility of the shareholders may be limited, and the company or association may be declared not dissolved by the death of a member, and suits may be prosecuted by and against the president of the association or company, and all this without making such associations corporations. And in support of this view Mr. Dunbar refers to a case in 23 Wendell's Rep. 100.[1] The decision to which Mr. Dunbar refers supports the doctrine for which he contends. The distinction between such associations and corporations is nice and shadowy, and has, I admit, been recognized by the courts. But the transferability of shares, the limited responsibility of shareholders, the non-dissolution or continued existence notwithstanding the death of a member, and the prosecution of suits in a name other than the names of the members of an association are usual elements of corporations as described in the books. Attorney-General Bronson gave his opinion on the 6th January, 1835, to the Senate of New York, that such associations would enjoy corporate privileges, and in 1837 Attorney-General Beardsley expressed the same opinion. And in the Constitution of the State of New York of 1846 it was expressly declared that " the term corporations shall be construed to include all associations and joint-stock companies having any of the powers and privileges of corporations not possessed by individuals or partnership." Two of the judges of our Supreme Court, Chief Justice Eustis and Judge Preston, were members of our convention. They had signalized themselves as opponents of the

---

[1] Lincoln vs. Crandell et al.

banking system,— of any credit system. They both
voted for the clauses in the Constitution prohibiting
banks to which I have referred. Judge Eustis has
recently declared in substance that, in reflecting on his
votes in the convention, he was fully satisfied with those
he had given upon the subject of banks. With this bias,
then, upon the minds of Judge Preston and Chief Justice
Eustis, with the dissenting opinions of two attorney-
generals of New York as to the nature of free banking associations, and with the provision in the Constitution of New York, adopted in 1846, declaring such
associations corporations, can it reasonably be expected
that capitalists and the holders of securities will be
induced to vest their stocks and money in institutions
created under the present Constitution of the State?
With such doubts, whether well founded or ill founded, as
to the constitutionality of such institutions, or rather as to
the probable decision of our Supreme Court, would capital
come here and engage in the business of free banking?

What is this free banking? It is not, as I have already
said, what Mr. Taylor defines it to be, a mere right of
every man to bank on his own money or capital. That is
not the system of banking which the people of Louisiana
want. They want the system as advocated by the Whig
platform. They want a well-regulated system of free
banks, so guarded that while it will diffuse the benefits of
capital, it shall at the same time afford a safe circulation
convertible into specie at all times and under all circumstances. They want a system which may produce a beneficial influence upon our embarrassed affairs and depressed
community. They wish a system such as exists in New
York or Massachusetts. By such a system, individuals
and associations formed for the purpose of banking may,
upon a transfer of public stock of the United States or
such other stock or securities as the State may designate,

obtain from the auditor of public accounts, the treasurer of the State, or any other officer who may be appointed for the purpose, such quantity of circulating notes, to be countersigned and registered by the officer, as the State may deem it expedient to issue upon the stock or securities pledged. These notes after having been executed and signed as required by law may be circulated as money. If not paid on demand, they must be redeemed by the state officer with the stock or securities thus transferred; for this purpose, the officer is authorized, after ten days' notice, to sell the same at public auction. The system then is to give to individuals the right to associate, and to enable them to obtain upon a pledge of good securities countersigned bills proportioned to the amount of stocks or securities pledged. It will be the duty of the State to take care that the stock or securities offered shall be good and sufficient. By a provision of law the amount of bills issued may be limited so as to prevent those who receive the bills from all danger of loss. For instance, individuals or associations holding United States stock to the amount of ten thousand dollars may, upon the pledge of that stock, be furnished with notes for circulation to the amount of five thousand dollars. If the notes should not be redeemed or paid in specie when called for, the stock pledged will be sold and the bill-holders paid out of the proceeds. Where too large an amount of notes is not issued on stock there cannot ultimately be any loss to the note-holders.

What I have said is only by way of illustration. It will be for the State to determine the proportion between the stocks or other securities and the notes. What has been said of ten thousand dollars is equally applicable to one hundred thousand dollars, or five hundred thousand dollars, or any other amount. Make the notes payable at the proper point, at the point most convenient to the note-

holder, and with prudence and care, and the adoption of
such guards as experience has pointed out in New York
and Massachusetts to be necessary and effectual, the system cannot fail to be highly beneficial to our struggling
commerce, to the workingman in New Orleans, and to
the people of the State at large.

And what are the inducements which this system holds
out to capitalists to use their stocks and securities as proposed? Why, in the first place, they would have the interest upon their stock, which would remain safe in the
hands of the state officer; and, in the second place, they
would have the profits of their banking business. This,
then, is a safe and a profitable system for the capitalist,
and it will be a safe and a proper system for the community at large. The circulating medium will be perfectly
safe, and the community will be accommodated with bank
facilities. This is the system of free banking proposed
by the Whigs: the free banking by which capital is to be
invited and induced to come here; the free banking by
which every class in the community is to be alike benefited, money made plenty, confidence established, commerce and industry stimulated, and the value of labor
raised.

It is said that the Democrats are in favor of this system.
I am glad of it. I believe the great body of the people
— Democrats as well as Whigs — are in favor of the system. But I advise you, fellow-citizens, to distrust the
professions of those who have been so long in power, but
who have never taken a step towards the introduction of
the system. Turn from them, and give your support to
those who stand publicly pledged and are ready to create
and give legal efficacy to the system at the earliest possible moment in the best and safest form.

However beneficial, fellow-citizens, a well-regulated system of free banking might prove to New Orleans, it would

yet be inadequate to regain the commerce which she has lost, to open new sources of wealth, and to restore her to prosperity, unless a wise and liberal system of railroads and other improvements should at the same time be adopted for the encouragement of the labor and the development of the resources of the State. New Orleans may be considered at present, for all practical commercial purposes, as cut off from communication with the rest of this State, and (if we exclude Mobile) with other parts of the Union except by means of the Mississippi. Content with the natural advantages which the river affords and with having so long received tribute from the great valley of the Mississippi, she has remained supine and inactive, while other commercial cities of the Union, by their superior enterprise in making railroads and other internal improvements, have opened artificial communications with almost every portion of our country, and by the facilities which they have afforded have diverted from New Orleans a considerable portion of the produce which heretofore came to her market and constituted a great source of her prosperity. New York and Boston have been taking away the commerce of the rich and growing States of the Northwest. Philadelphia, Baltimore, Charleston, and Savannah are rapidly drawing from us a portion of the trade of the valley, and Mobile is endeavoring by means of the Mobile and Ohio road to turn from its accustomed channels a large portion of the trade of Mississippi and Tennessee. During the present season of the year, when the rivers are low, a person can come from Louisville to New Orleans by the way of New York sooner than by the way of the Ohio and the Mississippi. All this is owing chiefly to the advantages arising from a system of railroads. Louisiana has but eighty-one miles of railroad within her limits.

We must arouse ourselves, fellow-citizens, and enter at once upon the work of improvement. We, too, must

build up railroads if we wish to prosper. New Orleans
must stretch her iron arms into the interior of the State
and extend them even beyond the limits of Louisiana.
She must carry her improvements to the doors of her
neighboring States and connect her roads with their roads.
The efforts made by her rivals to draw her trade from her
will then prove unavailing. Large quantities of land of
great fertility within our own limits will be brought into
cultivation. Along the whole line of her railroads land
will increase in value, while the property, and especially
the real estate of New Orleans, will also be enhanced.
The benefits arising from railroads may be seen in the
progress of other cities and other States in the Union,
and have been clearly shown by the writers on the subject.
The advantages attending improved means of transport
are evident. The products of agricultural labor have in
general great bulk with proportionally small value. It is
important, therefore, to the agriculturist that such improvements should be made as will enable him to carry
his goods at the cheapest rate and in the shortest time to
market. The expenses incidental to transport frequently
amount to a large portion of the price of the article. For
instance, if a person should buy ten thousand dollars'
worth of cotton on the banks of the Cumberland River
for the purpose of shipping it from New Orleans to Liverpool, the price that would be paid by the consumer would
be not only the price paid to the farmer on the Cumberland, but also the price paid for its transport from that
place to the consumer. This would consist of the freight
paid for conveying the cotton, the interest on the price
paid to the producer from the time of purchase till it
reaches the consumer, and the insurance. There are many
articles, indeed, which are of little or no value except in
consequence of transportation. For instance, ice in the
middle of the winter in Long Pond, near Boston, has no

value, but when transmitted to New Orleans or to Havana it becomes of considerable value. Guano is of no value in the place where it is found, but when transported to the field of the agriculturist it becomes eminently useful and valuable.

Dr. Lardner states that when the Houses of Parliament were occupied with the Railway Acts, a great mass of evidence was produced illustrating the advantages which both producer and consumer would obtain by the increased cheapness and expedition of transport which railways would supply. Extensive graziers declared that animals of every species, driven to market on the common roads, suffered so much that when they arrived at market their flesh was not in a wholesome state, and they were frequently obliged to be sold for what they would fetch. The butchers declared that the value of cattle receiving such injury was considerably less, in consequence of the inferior quality of the meat. It was shown, further, that steam vessels did not altogether remove the objection; and all parties agreed that a speedy transportation, even though it cost double the price, would be a benefit. The evidence was still stronger respecting the produce of the dairy and the garden. Milk, cream, fresh butter, vegetables of every description, and every kind of fruit were usually supplied from a narrow strip of soil about the outskirts of great cities. The milk was of a very inferior quality. The animals that yielded it were fed on grain and other similar articles, in a great degree, and not upon wholesome and natural pasturage. But since the introduction of railroads, numerous wagons are brought from pasturages at great distances from the cities where it is used. It is evident that these advantages from railroads accrue equally to the inhabitants of the city and the inhabitants of the town. The milk, the cream, the vegetables, the fresh butter, the fruit, which are of little or no value in St. Landry, St. Mary, and other parishes, would, if the Algiers and Opelousas Railroad were established, become articles of considerable value; because, by being transported immediately to New Orleans, they would furnish a supply to the inhabitants of that city. The inhabitants of the city would not only have the pleasure of enjoying these things, which are now wasted, but, inasmuch as they would obtain them at a less price than they pay for similar articles at present, they would have some surplus money which they might expend for other purposes.

We may form some idea of the increase in the value of property along railroads and at their termini by looking, as I have suggested, to the progress of other cities and States in the Union. Massachusetts commenced making railroads in 1835. In 1839 Boston had 167 miles of railroad, radiating thence in various directions. In 1850 she was connected with 3000 miles, one third of which is within Massachusetts, 1350 within the other New England States, and 650 in the State of New York. And we all remember the celebration lately of the opening of the railroad between Boston and Canada. These great works, it is said, have enlarged the area of country which contributes to her commerce probably tenfold, and the effect is unprecedented. In 1834 the value of all the property of Boston was $21,590,300: in 1849 it was $102,827,500: and on the first of January, 1851, it was $238,000,000. The increase of the value of property was not confined to Boston. The State felt the benefit of the railroads. In 1840 the total value of the property in the State was $299,878,329, in 1850 it was $590,531,881; making an increase in ten years of $290,653,552.

The population and the valuation of property in the counties of New York traversed by the Erie Canal were : —

	Population.	Real and Personal Estate.
In 1830	460,562	$43,484,580
In 1850	564,685	84,000,350
Increase in ten years	104,123	$40,515,770

Colonel Gadsden, of South Carolina, states that land all along the road to Hamburg and Columbia, for five miles each side of the South Carolina Railroad, has appreciated in value since its construction, in some cases 5000 per cent, and where there was not $20,000 of trade there is now upwards of $250,000. In Georgia, lands that in 1846 could readily be bought for 25 and 50 cents per acre can now command $10, $12, and $15 per acre. I might refer to the increase in the value of real estate in the counties bordering on the Vicksburg and Jackson Railroad, and in the counties bordering on the Nashville and Chattanooga road, to the increase in Charleston, in Baltimore, and in Savannah; but I shall content myself with saying generally that while population, production, and wealth have been produced by railroads, real estate has felt most directly and powerfully the influence of those improvements.

The railroad system seems, indeed, to have a creative power. In estimating the advantages of a road, we are correctly told, therefore, not to confine ourselves to a consideration whether the production at the time of construction will be sufficient to reimburse the cost of a road. "We must estimate the increased production caused by the improvement itself: the opening of new channels of trade, the development of the resources of the country, the expansion of commerce, the growth of population, and the increase of traveling." Time is money. We are all of us, fellow-citizens, laboring men, and cannot afford to waste our time. Hence, increased speed in the transport of persons is a matter of importance. A person in Louisville, who has commercial business to transact, can now go to New York, make his purchases, and return home in less time than it would take him to come from Louisville to New Orleans. If the speed at which persons can be transported from place to place is doubled by means of railroads, the distance is diminished one half. The man, therefore, who can be carried to his place of business five hundred miles in thirty hours is practically nearer that place than another man would be who lived two hundred and fifty miles from that place, and who had no other mode of conveyance than by a horse. If we would induce travelers to come among us ; if we would attract to New Orleans men engaged in trade and commerce and the general business of life ; if we would retain the trade which we are now in danger of losing, through the exertions of rival cities ; if we would keep the tide of commerce within its accustomed channels : if we would bring back to us any portion of that produce now drawn aside from our market by the railroads and improvements of other cities : if we would take advantage of our proximity to Texas and to the Western States, and of our position as a great commercial depot and an emporium of trade, where those engaged in mercantile business in the interior can most conveniently purchase what is required for their customers ; if we would invite to us the trade of the East Indies through California : if we would give new value to the real estate of New Orleans and of Louisiana : if we would expedite the transmission of news and general intelligence, and facilitate the diffusion of knowledge by cheap and speedy conveyance ; if, wisely looking forward to the happening of a war, we would provide for the quick transportation of a sufficient body of troops from various parts with a view to the defense of this State and of the country at large : if we would give encouragement to labor, raise the wages of industry, restore our credit, and advance the general prosperity of the

State, we must, fellow-citizens, at once adopt the wise and liberal system of railroads recommended by the Whig candidates before you. To effect this scheme of improvement, it is your duty to bestow your confidence upon men who have never deceived you, and who are capable of performing the work they undertake.

Under the present legislation of the State, no scheme of internal improvement can be carried on. The Constitution, we have seen, declares that the legislature shall provide by general laws for the organization of all corporations except banking corporations. In 1848 a law was passed to provide for the organization of corporations in this State, and it has been well said that looking to its minute provisions relative to formalities, and its restrictions on the companies to be formed under it, the act should have been entitled an " Act to prohibit the organization of corporations." The time and place of opening books of subscription, and the names of the commissioner to superintend them, must, according to the act, be specified in the agreement of the parties who propose to form a company. The act of incorporation is required to be published for thirty days, together with the names of the corporators, etc., before the corporation shall commence business. The act of incorporation must be passed before a notary public, and a certified copy of it must be presented to a district judge to be by him examined. A copy also must be served on the district attorney, who is allowed ten days to file his written opposition to it. Thirty days' previous notice of the application to the judge must be published, and any citizen of the State may make opposition. If opposition be made by any one individual, Mr. Benjamin thinks that it is impossible to say that a corporation can act in less than eighteen months or two years. The expropriation of property by railroad companies is prohibited without the express

8

authority of the legislature previously obtained, and the company is prohibited from entering into the limits of a city or any incorporated town without the sanction of the authorities who are given the right of determining the rates of tolls and fees. A single proprietor, therefore, on the line, or any municipal corporation, may cause the work to be stopped. Twenty per cent must be paid by each subscriber at the time of subscription, although one sixth of that amount would be sufficient for all preliminary purposes. And the legislature retains to itself the power at all times to alter and amend the law. It is evident that no adequate subscription for any useful purpose can be obtained under such conditions.

The projectors of the New Orleans, Jackson, and Northern Railroad have not been deterred by these provisions from making some preliminary organization, and raising by voluntary subscription an amount sufficient for the necessary preliminary expenses of survey, location, etc. Under this arrangement the stock taken amounts to $400,000. This is evidence, under the law and under the circumstances of the case, of the zeal, enterprise, and good faith with which the road has been projected. It is insisted, however, that this road is a work eminently public in its character, and calculated to promote the general prosperity of the State, and especially to enhance the value of the entire property situated on the line of the route and at its termini, and that justice therefore requires that means for its construction be provided at the expense of all those who are to share its benefits. This seems equitable. Experience, as I have heretofore observed, has shown that real estate is the first to feel, and to feel most directly, the beneficial influence of internal improvements. It is proposed, accordingly, to obtain the passage of a law vesting in the parishes of the State, with the concurrence of a majority of their legal voters, the right to levy a special tax upon real estate for the promotion of railroads. Individual subscriptions have generally proved insufficient for such works, and it is not just to suffer those who will participate in their advantages to throw the whole burden upon a few. There are always to be found in every community some rich men who acquire real estate, and who, knowing that such estate will be enhanced in value by whatever adds to the value of real estate generally, and especially by works of internal improvement, will refuse to aid in such works because not at first profitable in themselves, however advantageous in their general results to the community. They say, " Why should we subscribe? If others subscribe, and the community benefits thereby, we will share in the common benefit without paying or risking anything." Such a man was the late John McDonough, and I know half a dozen such at this time in New Orleans. The object of the proposed law is to compel such persons to contribute a fair quota for the benefit they will receive from the establishment of the railroad. And the question of determining whether the tax shall be imposed or not is to be submitted to the people themselves, in the city and in the parishes through which the road is to run. They are all interested in the general rise or depreciation of real estate, and if not proprietors, at least expect or desire to be so.[1] The tax proposed will be very light. Upon real estate one half per cent would give five dollars on a thousand. At the end of four years it would amount to twenty dollars. But the tax is not without some equivalent in addition to the benefit conferred upon real estate by the road; for the amount of the tax is to be represented by stock, to be parceled out to the property-holders, who may dispose of the same if they think proper, and thus diminish the amount of their

[1] Report of Mr. Robb.

assessment. I trust, fellow-citizens, that you will give your support to a law so equitable and just, so well calculated to advance the interests of every portion of our city and of our State. I know no other way in which any great work of improvement can be carried on with a probability of success under the present Constitution of the State.

With a system of free banking and with a system of railroads such as are proposed in the Whig platform, the people of New Orleans will enjoy the benefits of capital and of a sound circulation, convertible into specie at all times and under all circumstances, while a new spirit of enterprise will be infused into commerce, and will develop the resources of the State, and give new encouragement to labor.

If we turn to the judiciary department of the government, we will find its structure equally defective. The Constitution provides that "the Supreme Court shall be composed of four judges, viz., of one chief justice and of three associate justices," and that "in all cases in which the judges shall be equally divided in opinion the judgment appealed from shall stand affirmed." The act of 1846 divides the State into seventeen judicial districts. For each district one judge has been appointed, except in the first judicial district, composed of the parish and city of New Orleans, in which there are five district judges. Now in the district courts of New Orleans we have five judges of very different characters and very different minds. A question may be brought before Judge Buchanan in the fifth district court, which he may decide in favor of the plaintiff. A precisely similar case may be brought before Judge Kennedy in the third district court, and he may decide it in favor of the defendant, and in direct opposition to the opinion of Judge Buchanan. Suppose an appeal should be taken from each of these decisions, and that both cases should be argued before the Supreme Court at the same term, and, it may be, on the same day. If the judges of the Supreme Court should be equally divided in opinion, the judgment of Judge Buchanan would be affirmed in one case, and the judgment of Judge Kennedy would be affirmed in the other. The consequence is that, under the operation of the Constitution, we may have, in cases of appeal, directly contradictory decisions upon the same point by the Supreme Court.

The same thing may occur in cases of appeal from any other district courts of the State. And it has been held that one decision of the Supreme Court on a point in one case is not conclusive or binding upon the same court in another case. The truth is, the court may decide cases, but it cannot settle principles, and the people of Louisiana are in that condition which has been described by enlightened jurists as wretched slavery, where the law is vague and uncertain. There is scarcely a difficult and important question presented to the court upon which there is not some division of opinion among the judges. It is not uncommon to see some of the junior members of the bar going to the Supreme Court on Monday morning, smiling at the anticipation of hearing that which fills the elder and graver members of the bar with deep regret and mortification, the dissenting opinion of Judge Preston, or of Judge Rost, or of Judge Slidell, or of Chief Justice Eustis. It is, indeed, lamentable to reflect that the frequent contrariety of opinions has greatly impaired the moral power of the court over the sentiments of the people, and shaken the public confidence in the wisdom of that tribunal.

The Supreme Court themselves have, under an extraordinary interpretation, decided that the Constitution has not given them adequate power to protect the rights of the citizen in criminal cases. The Constitution, therefore, I submit to your consideration, fellow-citizens, has in this respect also failed to answer one of the main objects for which it was established.

Under the Constitution of 1812, and the legislation of this State prior to 1843, no appeal was allowed in any criminal case. The judge of the first instance heard, and finally determined the matter. In this state of things, there was no fixed principle to govern the judges alike, but each judge of necessity laid down the rule in the court over which he presided. Hence, it not unfrequently happened that what was adjudged law in one district was declared not to be law in another. In 1843 a remedy was applied to this evil. It was urged that a man acquitted in one district of an offense could be condemned under the same circumstance for a similar offense in another district as a felon, and that law, to be just and entitled to the respect and obedience of the people, must be fixed and certain, — an invariable rule operating in the same way through every part of the State. It was insisted, also, that if a party is entitled to an appeal whenever the matter in dispute exceeded three hundred dollars in a civil case, he ought certainly to be entitled to an appeal in a case involving his life, his liberty, or his reputation. The legislature yielded to the force of this reasoning, and in 1843 established a " Court of Errors and Appeals in Criminal Cases," and gave it "only appellate jurisdiction with power to review questions of law." Our present Constitution has given to the Supreme Court " appellate jurisdiction only," and " in criminal cases on questions of law alone." The appellate jurisdiction, then, in criminal cases under the act of 1843, and the appellate jurisdiction in criminal cases under the present Constitution, are alike confined to questions of law, and conveyed in terms tantamount and equivalent.

Under the act of 1843, it was contended that the court, being confined in its jurisdiction to questions of law alone, had no power to revise the decisions of inferior tribunals in criminal cases on questions of continuance and new trial, which were said to be questions of discretion merely. But the court declared that as much injury might be inflicted on an accused by an improper exercise of discretion as by the erroneous decision of any point of law during the trial ; that this discretion meant a sound legal discretion, which must be exercised in such a manner as not to deprive the party accused of any right guaranteed to him by the law : and that when such discretion was improperly exercised the acts of the inferior court must be reviewed. This is the doctrine of the courts of England when properly understood, the doctrine of the courts of New York, of Virginia, New Jersey, Indiana, Massachusetts, and Connecticut ; and it was invariably maintained by the late Court of Errors and Appeals in this State. It was reasonable, therefore, to suppose that the framers of our Constitution, by inserting in it the provisions of the act of 1843, and copying substantially the words of the act, were aware of the construction they had uniformly received, and intended that in the Constitution they should have the same meaning. But each citizen is not at liberty to construe the Constitution for himself. He must take it as it is judicially interpreted, and our present Supreme Court have decided that in criminal cases questions of continuance and new trial are purely questions of discretion, which they have not the power to review.

In the case of a man who was prosecuted for murder, where it appeared, on the affidavit of Mr. B. B. Lee, that the accused had been forced into trial without an opportunity of summoning his witnesses or preparing his defense, and where the jury — after Judge McHenry, eager for a conviction, had compelled them by a species of duress to render a verdict — "recommended him to the mercy of the court on the ground of the prisoner not being prepared for trial," the Supreme Court refused to interfere, and adhered to its iron rule. That man, whether innocent or guilty, is now a convict in the state penitentiary, without having had an opportunity of defending himself. The judiciary department, therefore, fellow-citizens, has failed from a defect in its structure : it is incapable of settling principles and of establishing the law in cases within its acknowledged jurisdiction ; and it has been denied, by the construction of the court, the exercise of the power absolutely necessary for the protection of the life, the liberty, the reputation, and the property of the citizen. I speak with the freedom of history, and I hope without offense. But I speak regardless of the consequences of offense, determined as a free man to give free utterance to my opinions and judgment, when speaking to you on matters of high public importance. The judiciary department, then, of our government, like the legislative department of the government, has proved an entire failure. The only remedy is in the overthrow of the Constitution. The Constitution must be abolished.

Fellow-citizens, I have already detained you so long that I will trouble you with only a few remarks on the executive department of our government. The structure of that department is less defective than that of either of the other departments. The principal objection to it, as it at present exists, is the immense patronage attached to it through the power of appointing to office. This defect it has been and still is in the power of the legislature in some measure to correct, by exercising their constitutional right to prescribe the mode of appointment to offices established by law. But the legislature have failed in this part as in other parts of their duty. I need not speak to you, fellow-citizens, of the manner in which the appointing power has been exercised under the present Constitution. [Several persons here called out, " Go on ! go on ! Let us hear. Let us hear how it has been exercised." The speaker resumed.] Look, fellow-citizens, at your judiciary. See the persons that have been appointed judges in the city of New Orleans, — the four judges of your Supreme Court, the judges of your district courts. Extend your view further, and see the other district judges throughout the entire State! Have they not been appointed in the main on party grounds and by way of rewarding party services? Is this right? The office of a judge is of a pure and sacred nature. It ought to be the reward of learning, virtue, and ability, and not the prize of partisan labors. Look next to the appointment of notaries in this city. Is it not well known that men were appointed who were utterly incompetent to discharge their duties, — men, some of whom could not draw the most common act, had never read a book of law, and were actually incapable of even undertaking the business of the offices to which they were appointed? This was surely a gross abuse of the executive power, and all candid men who reflect upon the subject must admit that the executive department of the government has been badly administered.

I have endeavored, fellow-citizens, to point out clearly and distinctly some of the leading defects in the Constitution of the State, and in the legislation under it. And I declare that, in my best judgment, that Constitution and that legislation have been injurious to the best interests of the State and of the city, and that those interests will be still further injured, and the prosperity of New Orleans altogether sacrificed, unless " the people shall come to the rescue." I can see no means of effecting a change from our present condition except by a change of men and a change of the Constitution. You must select for your

representatives in the state legislature and in the national
legislature men of enlarged and enlightened views, who
are not behind the times, who are attached to the Union,
and who will promote internal improvement.   In selecting your representatives in Congress, you should be particularly careful to choose those who will endeavor to obtain
from Congress appropriations to aid internal improvement for the benefit of this State and of the other States.
The United States are large owners of public lands, of
nearly twenty-eight millions of acres in Louisiana alone.
As these public lands are benefited by the construction
of roads, Congress has pursued a wise and liberal system
of donating portions of them in aid of works of internal
improvement.   There is no reason why Louisiana should
not, in common with other States, participate in the benefit of the system.

And now, fellow-citizens, while the Whigs are advocat-
ing this system of reform and progress, — of reform in the
Constitution and laws, remedying injustice, removing unwise and illiberal restrictions and prohibitions upon the
legislature, remodeling and rendering efficient the judiciary department, diminishing the power of the executive
by depriving it of a patronage corrupting and debasing in
its tendencies, protecting and advancing the interests of
commerce, calling forth and putting into useful action the
now dormant energies and resources of the State, reviving
credit and inviting capital among us, stimulating, cheer-
ing, and rewarding labor, protecting the homestead of the
poor man from the hand of oppression, and providing a
more perfect system of public education, — Mr. Taylor,
a leading member of the Democratic party, sneers at them
as being conservative, because they are attached to the
fundamental principles of American liberty, and can recognize no action as truly progressive which is opposed to
those principles : and he vauntingly proclaims that he and

his party are the only progressive party of this State. Impudent assertion! Progressive? In what? In removing the restrictions and injustice of the present Constitution? No. Stand fast. The Constitution is good enough for him. In introducing the benefits of a free banking system? No. Stand fast. In promoting the cause of public education? No. Stand fast. He is satisfied with what has been already done. In advancing the cause of internal improvements? Alas! the Whigs recommend it. Progressive in what, then? In that only which leads to ruin. I do not believe that the great body of the Democratic party favors such progress as Mr. Taylor seems to contemplate. Ambitious men, anxious to display a zeal which may recommend them to the favor of party, and burning with the desire to become prominent leaders, frequently lose sight of the safe ground on which they should intrench themselves, and running ahead, or, more properly speaking, running away from the people, assume positions untenable and ruinous.

Mr. Soulé,[1] in his speech delivered last month in Opelousas, declared that "there cannot be two opinions among sensible men as to the absolute right of a State to secede from the Union if she chooses," and he quotes General Jackson as sustaining, in what he (Mr. Soulé) calls "his counter proclamation," the right of secession. But you all know, fellow-citizens, that General Jackson in his proclamation expressly denied the right of a State to secede, and declared that "to call it a constitutional right can only be done through gross error, or to deceive those who are willing to assert a right, but would pause before they make a revolution or incur the penalties consequent on a failure." The speech of the senator at Opelousas and his speech on the admission of California into the Union are certainly extraordinary productions, and contain opin-

---

[1] Pierre Soulé, U. S. Senator from Louisiana from 1845 to 1853.

ions and doctrines directly at war with the great principles of the Democratic party. In his speech upon the admission of California into the Union he declared that if the people of the South quietly submitted to the measure, "then truly would those masters of slaves deserve to be slaves themselves, that they could be reconciled to a condition where to submit to disgrace were prudence, and to be contemptible a necessity." In his speech in Opelousas, after denouncing in strong terms all the measures of the compromise, he exclaimed, "What! submit to evident and undeniable wrong! Upon my heart and soul, never, never!" Oh no, fellow-citizens, he will not submit. But he will "endure." Still, while he lives he shall with all the energies of his lungs protest against it. Mr. Soulé declares that the right to secede was fully and most emphatically implied in the Articles of Confederation, and is not surrendered by the Constitution. The Articles of Confederation, upon their very face, declare that they are "Articles of Confederation and perpetual union." And in the preamble to the Constitution of the United States it is declared that the people of the United States, in order to form a more perfect union, do ordain and establish the Constitution.

Mr. Soulé declares that a State in seceding would only "exert her undoubted privilege as one of the sovereign confederates." This declaration is based upon the notion that the Constitution of the United States is a mere league between sovereign States who have preserved their whole sovereignty. But the Constitution of the United States forms a government, and not a league. It operates directly upon the people individually, and not upon the States. Each State has surrendered many essential portions of its sovereignty for the purpose of constituting with the other States a nation. To secede, then, is not to break a league, but, in the language of General Jackson, to destroy the unity of a nation. Mr. Soulé declares, substantially, that his allegiance is due to the State alone, and not to the United States. "Does not each of us," says he in his speech, "possess, do we not exert whenever we please, the right of changing our allegiance by passing from one State to the other, or to a foreign state? Who denies it? Who doubts it?"

Does Mr. Soulé suppose that his allegiance to the United States would be changed by his passing from Louisiana to South Carolina or to Massachusetts? Has he not taken an oath of allegiance to the United States? Has he not sworn to support the Constitution of the United States? Does not that Constitution provide that the Constitution and the laws of the United States shall be the supreme law of the land, and does it not also provide that the members of the several state legislatures, and all executive and judicial officers, both of the United States and of the several States, shall be bound by oath to support the Constitution? Does it not contain a clause expressly conveying a right to punish treason against the United States? and is not treason the highest breach of allegiance? How can a citizen of the United States say, then, that he owes no allegiance to the United States, and how can he assert that his allegiance is changed by " passing from one State to the other, or to a foreign state"?

I can scarcely imagine how even a native of a State, who has not reflected seriously upon the true character and complicated structure of our government, and who has been educated with false feelings of state pride and been taught the extreme doctrines of state rights in the school of abstractionists and metaphysicians, can so far lose sight of the operations of the national government as for a moment to believe that he owes allegiance to his native State alone, and that he owes no allegiance to the

United States. But I confess myself entirely at a loss to understand how an adopted citizen, who may be naturalized in a Territory or in the District of Columbia, who may reside during his probationary term in one State and may be admitted in another, whose right of citizenship has been conferred upon him by the United States and not by the State in which he may chance to live, and who at the time of his application to be admitted must have renounced and abjured all allegiance to the prince, state, or sovereignty whereof he was before a citizen or subject, and sworn to support the Constitution of the United States, — I confess myself entirely at a loss to understand how such a person can believe his allegiance is not due to the United States. These notions and these doctrines of Mr. Soulé, if carried out into practice, would destroy our national character as Americans and put an end to the Union.

Mr. Soulé says " he is not for breaking this confederacy; he is not for advising the State to join any secession movement which may be made by other States." Oh no! He only argues the right in the abstract. He would have the people still endure. But this is a dangerous philosophy. Practically speaking, there is but one step from the conviction as to a right and its enforcement, from the suffering of a wrong to its manly redress. Ours is a government of sentiment and affection, and if the feelings of the people are once alienated from it, the government from that moment is at an end.

What is it that the advocates of secession desire? What would they have who seek to destroy our Union, and to erect a State into an independent nation? Who is not proud that he is an American? The sun never shone upon a happier and more prosperous people. We have increased in wealth, in population, and in power with a rapidity which has astonished mankind. Our territory now reaches from ocean to ocean. The power and prowess of the nation have been illustrated by sea and by land. Star after star has been added to our national flag. The freedom of our institutions excites the attention and commands the admiration of the world. Our country continues to be the asylum of the oppressed of all nations. Free, happy, and powerful, we are known and respected in every quarter of the globe. Such are the results of our Union. But what would be our condition if we were divided into rival and hostile States? I turn with horror from the contemplation of the misery which would await us at home, and can see nothing but degradation abroad. Suppose Louisiana were to secede from the Union; suppose one of her sons in a foreign land were to be threatened by the minions of a tyrannical government with wrong and injury: what more ridiculous and insignificant object can be imagined than such a person claiming protection in the name of the sovereign nation of Louisiana, and pointing to a flag with a pelican on it as the emblem of his country? Suppose the Union to continue: what more sublime spectacle on earth could there be exhibited than the American in a foreign land unfurling the glorious banner of the stars and stripes, proudly pointing to the bird of liberty as the emblem of his country, and, in the name of the United States of America, demanding justice even from the tyrant on his throne? [The speaker was here interrupted by applause; after a moment or two he resumed.]

Fellow-citizens, your applause shows that it is unnecessary to pursue the theme. I have spoken of high matters, and I trust not unworthily. I shall detain you no longer. Let your votes at the polls show that you are the friends of true progress and reform, of liberty and the Union.

LECTURE ON THE LAW.

[For many years Mr. Hunt delivered an opening address to the law students of the University of Louisiana. The manuscripts left by him show that he revised, each and every year, the definitions of the law. The selected lecture given below was probably the last delivered by him, although the total absence of any dates upon his books renders it impossible to accurately fix the time of the delivery of the particular lecture here given.]

WELCOME, gentlemen, to the Tulane University of Louisiana! Welcome to this temple of Science, dedicated for a place of instruction and study, for the communication of knowledge and the circulation of thought! And specially welcome to this hall set apart for the science of Law!

Gentlemen, the chief end of all government is to secure to the governed the blessings of liberty. And this end can only be attained by the education of the people. It is accordingly the paramount duty of a good government to foster and promote public education. A people that thoroughly understand their rights will appreciate and maintain them. The foundation of despotism is ignorance; of popular rule or republicanism, knowledge. Knowledge is the parent of Liberty, and her natural and only safe guardian.

Impressed with these truths, Louisiana ordained by her Constitution in 1845 the establishment of free public schools throughout the State, of a seminary of learning, and of a university in the city of New Orleans. Under this authority, and as a part of the university, the legislature established a department of law, and founded the college of which you are matriculated sons. To the study of law you are about to devote yourselves; and of that science it is my province now to speak.

Law, in its most general and comprehensive sense, signifies a rule of action, and applies indiscriminately to every kind of action, whether animate or inanimate, rational or irrational. Thus we say the laws of motion, of gravitation, or of mechanics, as well as the laws of nature and of nations, and the like. The Supreme Being, the Creator of all, when he formed the universe, and created matter and various classes of beings, animate or inanimate, in his infinite wisdom, allotted to every class its condition and appropriate functions. Order, proportion, and fitness pervade the whole. The whole world around us and the whole world within us are ruled by law. We see, we feel, we regard with wonder and admiration the rule. Our very spirits, which yet seem so spiritual, so subtle, so free, are subject to it. The material world, the heavenly bodies, the earth, and the different elements of the universe have their laws; beasts have their laws; man has his laws. The celestial as well as the terrestrial world knows, and, without swerving, observes and obeys its prescribed course. And the Creator, the preserver and ruler of all things, acts not without an eternal decree, never violating or disregarding laws, but adjusting, combining, and so adapting them to the accomplishment of his purpose.

This truth is illustrated in the grandest and most sublime of the works in nature, and in the least and lowliest, — in the laws which regulate the planetary motions, the range of planets, suns, and adamantine spheres wheeling unshaken through the void immense, and in those which form a drop of water. The vastness and multi-

9

tude of the celestial bodies, the laws which astronomy in
its higher branches discloses and applies, the distances
which it spans, the periods which it estimates, impart a
sublimity which lifts the soul to the heavens. The law
of gravitation is the most universal law known to us. It
prevails apparently through all space. But it does not
prevail alone. Its function is to balance other forces, of
which we only know that these again are needed to
balance the force of gravitation. Each force, if left to
itself, would be destructive of the universe. Were it not
for the force of gravitation, the centrifugal forces which
impel the planets would fling off into space. Were it
not for these centrifugal forces, the force of gravitation
would dash them against the sun. The orbits, therefore.
of the planets, with all that depends upon them, are determined by the adjustment between the law of gravitation
and other laws which are less known, so as to produce
and maintain the existing solar system. This grand
example of the principle of adjustment gives no idea of
the extent to which the principle is required and is
adopted in the works of nature. The revolution of the
seasons, seed-time and harvest, depend on the law of
gravitation in this sense, that if that law were disturbed,
or if it were inconstant, they would be disturbed and inconstant also. But the seasons equally depend on a multitude of other laws, — laws of heat, laws of light, laws
relating to fluids, to solids, and to gases, and to mag-
netic attractions and repulsions. — each of which laws is
invariable in itself, but each of which would produce
utter confusion if it were allowed to operate alone, or if
it were not balanced against others in the right proportion. The seasons depend not only on the facts and laws
which astronomy reveals, but on other sets of facts and
other sets of laws revealed by other sciences, such as
chemistry, electricity, and geology.

Chemistry abounds with illustrations of the law of forces in mutual adjustment. The forces which determine chemical combinations all work under sharp and definite rules. Some of the laws which regulate this combination are wonderful and beautiful, of great exactness, having invariable relations to numbers and proportion. Each elementary substance has its own combining proportions with other elements, so that, except in these proportions, no chemical union can take place at all. And when chemical union does take place, the compounds which result have different and even opposite powers according to the different proportions employed. The same elements combined in one proportion are sometimes a nutritious food or a grateful stimulant soothing and sustaining the powers of life; whilst, combining in another proportion, they may be a deadly poison, paralyzing the heart and carrying agony along every nerve and fibre of the animal frame.

The whole progress of plants from the seed to the root, and thence from the root to the seed again, the method of animal nutrition, digestion, and all other branches of vital economy, are not left to chance, but are performed in a wondrous manner, and guided by unerring rules laid down by the great Creator. Thus it is through the whole of nature: laws everywhere, — laws in themselves invariable, but so worked and so adjusted as to produce effects of inexhaustible variety, by being pitched against each other and made to hold each other in restraint. Not a tree, not a flower, not a blade of grass, not even a drop of water, not one of the countless varieties of form in clouds, but is ruled by law, by forces which are free only within the bounds of law : —

" All are but parts of one stupendous whole.
Whose body Nature is, and God the soul :

That changed through all, and yet in all the same,
Great in the earth as in the ethereal frame,
Warms in the sun, refreshes in the breeze,
Glows in the stars, and blossoms in the trees ;
Lives through all life, extends through all extent,
Spreads undivided, operates unspent ;

. . . .

To him no high, no low, no great, no small :
He fills, he bounds, connects, and equals all ! "

Such is law in its general and most comprehensive
sense.   Hooker describes it in terms often cited, but never
stale or vapid.   Of Law there can be no less acknowledged than that her seat is the bosom of God, her voice
the harmony of the world ; all things in heaven and earth
do her homage, the very least as feeling her care, and the
greatest as not exempted from her power, — both angels
and men, and creatures of what condition soever, thought,
and manner, yet all admiring her as the mother of their
peace and joy.   There are no phenomena visible to man
of which it is true to say that they are governed by one
invariable force.   That which does govern them is always
some variable combination of invariable forces.   No law
of nature — that is, no elementary force of nature — is
liable to change.   But every law of nature is liable to
counteraction ; and the rule is that laws are made
habitually to counteract each other in precisely the manner and degree that some definite result requires.   No
man can have any difficulty in believing that there are
natural laws of which he is ignorant ; nor in conceiving
that there may be beings who do know them and can use
them, even as he himself now uses the few laws with
which he is acquainted.   The relation in which God
stands to those rules of his government which are called
laws is of course a mystery to us.   But the very idea of
a Creator involves the idea not merely of a being by

whom the properties of matter are employed, but of a being from whose will the properties are derived. Our own experience shows that the universal reign of law is perfectly consistent with a power of making those laws subservient to design, even when the knowledge of them is but slight, and the power even slighter. How much more easy, how much more natural, to conceive that the same universality is compatible with the exercise of that supreme will, before which all are known, and to which all are servants! There is nothing in religion incompatible with the belief that all exercises of God's power, whether ordinary or extraordinary, are effected through the instrumentality of means; that is to say, by the instrumentality of natural laws brought out, as it were, and used for a divine purpose. Advancing knowledge of physical law has been constantly accompanied with advancing power over the physical world, and has enabled us to do a thousand things which a few centuries ago would have been considered supernatural. The man of real science recognizes more than the superficial observer the concord between physical and moral laws, between science and religion. Both come from one great source; and every step that we make in the investigation of the physical laws and of their principles ought to lead us to a nearer and better acquaintance with those of the moral universe, and with the majesty and grandeur of him who has wished to grant us the growing evidence of himself and of his attributes, by allowing his works, perfect from the beginning, to be unveiled and explained to our researches.

Law, universal, constant in its influence, uniform in its operation, supreme in its obligation, its power to command and enforce obedience, must emanate from a lawgiver infinitely wise and transcendently powerful. "I had rather," said Bacon, "believe all the fables in the

Legend and the Talmud and the Alcoran than that this universal frame is without a mind. And therefore God never wrought miracle to convince atheism, because his ordinary works convince it." Our address, by an easy and a natural transition, here brings before us the rights and duties of man for consideration ; in a word, jurisprudence.

Law in a restricted sense denotes the rules by which man is commanded to regulate his conduct. Its precepts are for the guidance of man alone as a moral, intellectual, and accountable being. In this sense they form the subject of jurisprudence. When law is applied to any other object than man, it ceases to contain two of those essential ingredients, disobedience and punishment. Commanding and obeying are the two foundations of all human society. They are relatives ; they mutually respect, engender, and conserve one the other. We are told, a wise man being once asked why the commonwealth of Sparta was so flourishing, whether it was because its kings commanded well, replied, Nay, rather because the citizens obey well ; for if the subjects once refuse to obey, and shake off the yoke, the state must necessarily fall to the ground.

Man is a social being. His inclinations and wants, physical and moral, irresistibly compel him to associate with his kind : and he has accordingly never been found, in any age or country, in any state other than the social. In no other could he exist ; and in no other, indeed, were it possible for him to exist, could he attain to a full development of his moral and intellectual faculties, or raise himself in the scale of beings much above the brute creation. This necessary social state cannot exist without government.

What then is that constitution of human nature which renders it impossible for society to exist without government ? Physiology shows the structure of man : the superiority of the human organization, its various functions, and all that is connected with the animal life of man, over those of the rest of the animate creation. Man is endowed with sympathy or fellow-feeling; that is, a feeling for the pains and pleasures of others, though unconnected with any interest of his own or standing in no direct connection with him. This feeling is of a peculiarly expansive character, and constitutes an "essential attribute of the ethic character of man." It can only be proved by our consciousness of it, and its effects being observable everywhere. Some writers would reduce it to self-interest, to egotism. But this, says Lieber, would nearly destroy the basis of all that is good or worth living for. " It may be decided in a practical way only by asking, are you a brother, or a son, or a friend? Have you ever seen a venerable old man insulted by a wanton youth? Have you never read a satisfactory vindication of a person against whom grave and plausible charges had been brought? And had you heard of these things without feeling joy or pain? Has the perseverance of Columbus never reached your ears? Who learns without emotion his tumultuous and intense thoughts and feelings when he found that, in spite of every difficulty and danger, he had accomplished his object, revealed the great mystery of the ocean, triumphantly established his theory which had been the scoff of sages, and secured to himself a glory durable as the world itself, and, landing on the New World, threw himself on the earth, and returned thanks to God with tears of joy? Has no drama ever touched you? On what indeed is nearly the whole literature of *belles-lettres* founded, if not on sympathy, — sympathy even with fictitious beings?" The existence of the family, love of country, friendship, public spirit, and whatever is noblest or best in man are, in whole or in part, founded on this great element of the human soul.

The constitution of man's nature makes us feel more intensely what affects us directly than what affects us indirectly through others; in other words, our direct or individual feelings are stronger than our sympathetic or social feelings. This necessarily leads to conflict between individuals. Each, in consequence, has greater regard for his own safety and happiness than for the happiness or safety of others, and where these come in opposition is ready to sacrifice the interest of others to his own: and hence the tendency to a universal state of conflict between individual and individual, accompanied by the passions of suspicion, jealousy, anger, and revenge, followed by insolence, fraud, and cruelty, and, if not prevented by some controlling power, ending in a state of universal discord and confusion, destructive of the social state and of the ends for which it is ordained. This controlling power, wherever vested or by whomsoever exercised, is government.

Society and government, then, are intimately connected. Both are necessary to the existence of our race, and equally of divine ordination; rules and laws are a mode of God's government of the world, and rules and laws are a necessary mode of human government.

The constitution of our nature, which renders government in some form or other necessary, deserves a further and more searching examination. Man is endowed with intellect, the faculty of reflection. He analyzes, compares, combines, abstracts, concludes, and judges, and elevates himself above the sensible world. In forming notions of his nature, a comparison is often made between men and animals, the only creatures endowed with thought that fall under our senses. There are writers who maintain that the mental powers of the highest animal approach so closely to those of the lowest man that it may be said there is no essential difference.

but merely a gradual transition, and no ethic conclusion can be drawn therefrom. But certainly the comparison is favorable to mankind. On the one hand, we see a creature whose thoughts are not limited by any narrow bounds either of place or time; who carries his researches into the most distant regions of this globe and beyond this globe, to the planets and heavenly bodies; looks backward to consider the first origin, at least the history of the human race; casts his eye forward to see the influence of his actions upon posterity, and the judgments which will be formed of his character a thousand years hence, — a creature who traces causes and effects to a great length and intricacy, extracts general principles from particular appearances, improves upon his discoveries, corrects his mistakes, and makes his very errors profitable. On the other hand, we are presented with a creature the very reverse of this: limited in its observations and reasonings to a few sensible objects which surround it, without curiosity, without foresight, blindly conducted by instinct, and attaining in a short time its utmost perfection, beyond which it is never able to advance a single step. What a wide difference between these creatures!

Among the other excellencies of man, this is one, that he can form an idea of perfections much beyond what he has experience of in himself, and is not limited in his own conception of wisdom and virtue. All the world is agreed that human understanding falls infinitely short of perfect wisdom.

Undoubtedly there is mental action in the brute animal: the animal thinks, but man reflects. "A mule," said Frederick the Great, "though it might have made ten campaigns under Prince Eugene, would not become for all that a better tactician." The animal is, with rare conceptions, confined within its own sensuality, — the sphere and influence of its senses alone : they direct its actions ; it lives and moves within the sensible world alone. But man, belonging in part to the sensible world, and subject according to his sensuality and its laws, in which everything is determined, has, on the other hand, the great privilege to determine himself. He can guide and determine himself by reason within certain limits given him by the material world ; he can choose. According to his sensuality man is bound ; if he feels pain, he cannot help being prevented by it from freely thinking. According to his rationality he is free ; he reflects and chooses, — he enjoys freedom. His will is free, because he can determine himself with regard to willing an object of which he is conscious. The proof is, our consciousness of being able to will something which is repugnant to our sensuality, or which may cost us the sacrifice of our warmest affections.

Now, a motive is that which moves or tends to move the mind in a particular direction. Man is exposed to certain motives in common with the lower animals. But there are other motives, motives which operate upon him which can never operate upon them. Among the motives which operate upon him, man has a selecting power. He can bring them to the test of conscience. He can reason on his own character, and when he knows that a given motive will be too strong for him, if he will allow himself to think of it, he can shut it out of his mind by "keeping the door of his thoughts." Motives of all kinds, the highest and the lowest, rise in the mind unbidden. It is by an act of will that we summon different motives to the presence of the deliberative faculties, that we cherish one and dismiss another, or determine to spend our thought and time in making choice between motives which are conflicting. " *Potentia libera est, quæ, positis omnibus requisitis, ad agendum potest agere et non agere.*" (Power is free, which, all the requisites for action being presented, is able to act and not to act.)   If man acts, he may be impelled by instinct or prompted by his sensuality, — for instance, when he drinks, being thirsty, or struggles to save himself from drowning ; or he may determine his own will, in which case he may be actuated either by motives of expediency, when he simply judges whether his action will lead to the object he has in view, — for example, when he grinds his sickle to reap his wheat, — or by moral motives, which make an action good or bad, praiseworthy or hateful, deserving of applause or condemnation.

The subtlest intellect, the most vigorous mind, unaided by anything else, cannot arrive at any other idea with regard to an action than that of obedience, fitness, correctness, respecting the choice of means for the object in view.   Yet we find with all men a feeling entirely independent of the expediency or judiciousness of our action, — the moral element in the human soul, the consciousness of right and wrong.   This original consciousness of right and wrong is called conscience, from the Latin word *conscientia*, from *con* and *scire*, to know, because " it is the most important of the different species of consciousness."   Some philosophers have maintained and others have denied what conscience is, and its very existence.   Locke calls conscience " our own opinion or judgment of the moral rectitude or pravity of our own actions," and proceeds to show that it cannot be inborn.   The very term " opinion " involves the idea that it is something arrived at by reflection, which is an act of the mind : how then can it be inborn ? A faculty may be inborn, an action cannot.   According to Locke, the mind is a blank paper on which our senses write impressions, which the intellect analyzes and combines.   According to some others, it analyzes and combines the perception of things, but it does not infuse new elements of thought or feeling.

Conscience is then an original consciousness of right and wrong, good and bad. Like every species of consciousness it begins with an indistinct feeling, and becomes clearer the more effectually the matured mind acts upon it. So it is with all ideas we receive through the senses. The sense of sight is first but dim. The mind must act upon the impression received, and the sense itself must be practiced before it becomes clear. Astonishing instances of the keenness which can be acquired by the human eye, and of the rapidity with which it can observe distinctive marks, are on record. Yet the sense of sight is innate, or the idea of color could not possibly have been arrived at. So man feels, at doing certain things, that he ought to have done them or not, and by the operation of the mind constantly analyzing and generalizing he arrives gradually at more distinct ethic notions. Conscience is developed, cultivated, made delicate in connection with reflection, the development of our feelings in general, and experience: but the consciousness of right and wrong is primordial and general.

The writers who deny that conscience is universal and innate urge the difference of moral opinion, and the fact that some tribes actually consider laudable what others punish as the vilest crime. The fact is admitted that people have burned and racked their fellow-creatures, — Catholics Protestants, and Protestants Catholics; that some of them, at least, believed they did right while they perpetrated their acts, every one knows. All these persecutors said that they relied for the rectitude of their actions on the Bible.

The Spaniards who conquered the southern continent of America committed every species of cruelty and oppression. We read of Indians being slowly worn down by excessive labor to satisfy the diabolical lust for gold. We find the names of mastiffs, bloodhounds, handed down to posterity, because they distinguished themselves in hunting and tearing the Indians, for which their masters received the regular share of booty allotted to an armed man! "Leoncico" was the name of the bloodhound belonging to Nuñez. And all this, it is urged, "in return for genuine kindness and humanity; for Las Casas testified, the Indians always did more by way of hospitality than they were bid to do. Refined torments were paid back in return for unsuspicious and kind reception. Those Spanish adventurers, cruel almost without parallel, from the meanest of motives, the yearning for riches, were most chivalrous, urbane, and charitable toward each other, ready to make any sacrifice. Those that were vindictive, bloodthirsty, and without any faith toward the Indian were magnanimous and full of honor toward each other." [1] The principle of morality, therefore, had not been plucked out of their hearts, but bigotry and avarice had perverted their judgment and moral feeling. The fact that bands of criminals always form a certain moral code among themselves shows the inalienably moral character of man, however perverted his judgment and feeling may be by passions. A robber or thief might feel indignant at theft or cheat within the band.

The moral codes of all nations are more uniform than discordant. There is a natural or innate horror at certain specific crimes, which cannot be denied. "We know," says Dr. F. Lieber, "that man can be reconciled to the worst by custom: yet, on the other hand, it takes time to denaturalize him as to some actions; for instance, murder. The moral principle, it is contended, is absolute

---

[1] Irving, *Voyages of the Companions of Columbus.*

and universal.   Individuals, nations, may rest in very different ways, — sitting, reclining in hammocks, or lying on
couches : but all must acknowledge the principle that rest
is requisite after exertion."   In regard to the uniformity
even of laws, M. Michelet, in a work on the origin of
French law, says : "We have studied the juridical sym-
bol under the two points of view of its age and nationality, which diversify it infinitely : nevertheless, whatever
variety may be discovered, unity predominates.   It is an
imposing spectacle to find the principal legal symbols
common to all countries throughout all ages.   In truth,
to one who considers not the human race as the great
family of God, there is in these multitudinous voices, out
of hearing of each other, and which nevertheless respond
each to each, from the Indies to the Thames, in recipro-
cating sounds, something wherewithal to dismay the
intelligence, to strike the heart and spirit of man with
consternation.

"Transporting was the emotion which I myself experienced, when, for the first time, I heard this universal
acclaim.   Unlike the skeptic Montaigne, who so curiously
ferreted out the customs of different nations to detect
their moral discordancies, I have found a consentaneous
harmony among them all.   A sensible miracle has arisen
before me, — my little existence of the moment has seen
and touched the eternal communion of the human race."

Far more striking, however, is the uniformity, or at
least agreement of the moral views, when we observe the
daily intercourse of individuals and nations.   There are
many exceptions, undoubtedly, but they attract more
attention because they are exceptions.   That man is a
social being, and cannot exist and develop fully his
moral and intellectual faculties in any other state than
the social, has been sufficiently considered for the present.
Our discourse makes it necessary to consider his individ-

uality also, his separate and distinct existence, his inalienable ethic attributes.

Superior intellect, sympathy, freedom of will, rationality, and conscience constitute man's ethic character, his moral dignity, and make us at once conscious of the law, " Do unto others as you wish others may do unto you." This is a fundamental law, a supreme law of practical use, the law of virtue. It comes home to a greater number of persons than any other law that can be devised. Christ, in his sermon on the mount, taught the lesson : " All things whatsoever ye would that men should do to you, do ye even so to them : for this is the law and the prophets." And Paul the Apostle wrote to the Romans : " When the Gentiles, which have not the law, do by nature the things contained in the law, these, having not the law, are a law unto themselves : which shew the work of the law written in their hearts, their conscience also bearing witness, and their thoughts the mean while accusing or else excusing one another." Man's senses, perceptions, thoughts, emotions, his reasoning and actions, are individually his own. Man's responsibility is therefore his own. Fault, crime, virtue, goodness, or immorality is his own. Responsibility involves the idea that the individual might, and if he has acted wrong ought to have acted differently, which presupposes free will and individuality. God " will render to every man according to his deeds." What man is in mind and body first of all, he is as individual, yet not made to be purely selfish. The Creator connected him with his kind by a thousand ties, — by sympathy, love, friendship, and by the mysterious attachment growing out of the difference of sexes.

We can only reason from what we know. Every science has to start from some axioms, — truths universally acknowledged or self-evident in their nature. The most elaborate and sublime reasonings in mathematics are founded upon them. Natural law shows the rights which man has according to his inalienable ethic nature. It treats of his rights, and of his obligations and duties, flowing from the fact of each man's being possessed of the same rights. The only axiom necessary to establish the science of natural law is this: "I exist as a human being; therefore I have a right to exist as a human being." Spinoza, never willing to admit unwarranted truths, remarks: "*Quomodo autem id sciam — si roges — respondebo — eo modo, ac tu scis, tres angulos trianguli, æquales esse duobus rectis: et hoc sufficere, negabit nemo, cui sanum et cerebrum, nec spiritus immundos somniat, qui nobis ideas falsas inspirant veris similes.*" (If you ask how I know this, I will answer. In the same way as you know that the three angles of a triangle are equal to two right angles; and no one will deny this whose brain is sound and does not dream of unclean spirits that inspire us with false ideas seemingly true.)

Undoubtedly there are certain laws of good and evil, of right and wrong, which man is enabled by his moral sense and his reason to discover, and which are inseparably connected with human happiness. They are the result of the natural feelings, the impartial judgment, and the experience of mankind. They are founded on the paternal precept that man should pursue his own true and substantial happiness. They constitute the law of nature, which treats of man's rights, and of his obligations or duties flowing from the fact of each man being possessed of the same rights, as already stated. Justinian reduces the whole doctrine of law to these three general precepts, *honeste vivere, alterum non lædere, suum cuique tribuere* (to live honestly and honorably, to wrong no one, to give every one his due).

Of the law of nature Cicero speaks with the comprehension of philosophy and the copiousness of eloquence.

" It is," says he, " true law, right reason, conformable to nature, diffused among all men, unchangeable, eternal. It cannot be impaired, it cannot be altered, it cannot be abolished. The senate and the people are unable to dissolve its obligation. It requires no interpreter, no commentator. It is not one law at Rome, another at Athens; one law now, another hereafter. It is the same, — eternal and immutable, at all times and for all nations! The precepts of moral and natural law are generally obligatory on man. But natural law and revealed law operate only upon the reason and the conscience, and are insufficient to restrain the violence and prejudices of men inflamed by passion, and the tendency to a state of conflict between individual and individual, ending in a state of universal discord and confusion, destructive of the social state, if not controlled. To establish public order, to maintain peace, and to execute justice, it becomes necessary to establish government and laws; to point out the decrees of equity; to institute offices and other means to punish transgressors, correct fraud and violence; and to oblige men to live peaceably and to respect the rights of others, under the pain and penalty to every offending member of the community of having the entire power of the society directed against him by public authority." And that law which each people, or men formed into a separate society or government, establish for themselves is called civil law or municipal law. " *Jus civile est quod quisque sibi populus constituerit.*"

Men cannot enjoy the protection of government without submitting to the restraints which a just government imposes. Laws are dead letters unless they operate and are enforced to oblige men, however reluctant, to consult their own real and permanent interests. Obedience becomes a duty to support the duty of justice; and the ties of equity must be corroborated by those of allegiance.

10

The division of law into natural law and municipal law is not merely scholastic and doctrinal, but is philosophical and based upon the essence of things. The precepts of natural law are not in every instance enforced by the government, but the rules of municipal law are expressly declared and enforced by it.

The origin of governments has been variously and fancifully suggested. How they began, on what principles they were originally formed, what share in their formation should be ascribed to stratagem, what to convenience, what to force, were said by a learned statesman to be so obscured by the mists of time as to be merely chimerical. But the history of the progress of government is curious and useful. The various stages through which it passed, from savage independence, which implies every man's power of injuring his neighbor, to legal liberty, which consists in every man's security against wrong, — the manner in which a family expands into a tribe, and a tribe into a nation, in which public justice is gradually engrafted on private revenge, and temporary submission is ripened into habitual obedience, — form a most important and extensive object of inquiry, comprehending, as Sir James Mackintosh observes, all the improvements of mankind in police, in judicature, and in legislation. As civil governments were established, and men became divided into many great societies, and formed themselves into separate states, commonwealths, and nations, independent of each other, and yet liable to mutual intercourse, there naturally and necessarily arose another kind of law to regulate their intercourse, called the law of nations. Nations are equal in respect to each other, and entertain and claim equal consideration for their rights. They acknowledge no common superior. The law of nations, therefore, cannot be dictated by any state. It depends upon the rules of natural law, or upon compacts.

agreements, treaties, and leagues, to be construed according to that law. The same rules of morality which hold men together in families, and form families into states, link together these states as members of the great family of mankind. Nations as well as private men may be injured or benefited by each other. It is therefore their interest as well as their duty to practice and enforce these rules of justice, which control and restrain injury, regulate and augment benefit, and which, if generally obeyed, would establish and maintain the well-being of the universal commonwealth. Hence it is that states are considered as moral persons, under the same obligations mutually to practice honesty and humanity as would have been individuals; and hence the science which teaches the duties of states and individuals, and enforces national and individual morality, has been with propriety termed the law of nature and of nations. " *Quod naturalis ratio inter omnes homines constituit, vocatur Jus gentium.*" It is received as the code of the great legislator of the universe for the guidance of man to happiness, guarded and enforced, as experience has shown, by the penal sanctions of shame and remorse, of infamy and of misery, and still further enforced by the dread of penalties in a future state of existence.

The law of nations, then, civil or municipal law, and the law of nature, upon which human laws are founded, are embraced in the science of law. Man, happier and more content in civil society than in any kind of solitary living, is not satisfied with this. We covet to have a kind of society and fellowship even with all mankind, which Socrates signified when he declared himself a citizen, not of this or that commonwealth, but of the world, and which is apparent in the natural desire and delight men have to visit foreign countries, to know the customs. the affairs and dealings of other people. and to be in league of amity with them.

Judge Story wrote to Dr. Lieber, in 1837, that he had read with great satisfaction the manuscript of the second book of his work on ethics, entitled " The State," which he declared " the fullest and most correct development of what constitutes a state that he [the judge] had ever seen, and which put the state upon its true foundation : a society for the establishment and administration of general justice, justice to all, equal and fixed, recognizing individual rights, and not impairing them. The aims and ends of the work are practical."

This discourse now passes to the consideration of the state. Every man should know his duty, and his duties as a citizen are among the most important, especially in countries which enjoy civil liberty and have a free government. The state is so intimately connected with nearly everything which concerns man, all our interests are so interwoven with the public weal, that it cannot prosper or remain harmless without a faithful and correct discharge of duties on the part of every citizen. To be a good citizen one must be a good man, and should entertain sound principles of public morality. This knowledge and these principles can be durably and with certain effect impressed in our youth.

The state and politics disclaim immorality. Rare exceptions indeed exist, but in them is always found a desire to gloss them over with the appearance of justice. Marat and Robespierre, Renbel and St. Just, had the name of virtue always on their lips. Witness, for instance, the massacre of St. Bartholomew, August 24, 1572, " one of the most atrocious crimes recorded in history." When the massacre had been perpetrated with unexampled treachery, cruelty, and disgusting vice and villainy by Catherine de Medici and Charles IX., the king, after a long and cold-blooded consultation between him, his wicked mother, and Anjou as to the invention of the best means of justifying themselves, proceeded on August 26 to Parliament, and there added to this stupendous wrong the solemn lie, after having heard high mass, that all had been done to save themselves from a vast yet timely discovered conspiracy of the Huguenots. Their bodies were weltering in blood, and could not gainsay the falsehood. But on August 24, the day of the carnage itself, the king and queen sent a declaration into all the provinces that the whole had been done by the Guises; nay, though Philip II. of Spain celebrated this event by the performance of a drama representing the triumph of the Church Militant, and Pope Gregory XIII. ordered a solemn Te Deum to be performed in the church of St. Louis, Charles IX., or his wily mother, found it necessary to order, even two months after the bloody deed, the torturing and execution of an old nobleman, Briguemant, and one of the royal counselors, Cavannes, as having been accessories, so that the appearance of truth as to a Huguenot conspiracy might be kept up.[1]

It is the destiny, the glorious destiny of man to be always progressive; so it is his duty to press on towards things before him. In the order of Providence, the progress of society towards protection resembles that of an individual. Hitherto it hath been slow, and has often been interrupted by unpropitious events; but there have been, and there always are, some steps gained which are never lost. No man can look back on the history of modern civilization without seeing that it presents the phenomena of development and growth. Whatever may be the decline of particular communities, the progress of mankind on the whole is a progress to higher and better things. Man's conduct will in the main be guided by his moral and intellectual convictions.

---

[1] Lieber, *Political Ethics.*

Civilization cannot be conceived of without society; that is, without men congregated in large masses, and closely united by a variety of important relations and strongly affecting each other's welfare. Without society, no fellow-feeling and sympathy, no intellectual progress from generation to generation, no common stock of science and moral experience, no fine arts, no expanded idea of justice and mutual rights, no public spirit with its elevating qualities, no division of labor, no extensive exchange of produce, no works to benefit the many, — without society, no humanity in man!

Civilization, then, is man's truly natural state, adapted to and affected by his nature. Hooker, carefully observing and sagacious, said: "Men, if we view them in their spring, are at the first without understanding or knowledge at all. Nevertheless, from this utter vacuity they grow by degrees, till at length they become even as the angels themselves are. Man was essentially made for progressive civilization, and this, therefore, is his natural state." A tree in blossom or with the ripe fruit is in no less a natural state than in winter deprived of all foliage; nor is the plant in an unnatural state when in the germ.

Men, at a very early time, were led to imagine a period when plenty rendered labor unnecessary, and universal content prevented contest and clashing of interest, — a golden age of happiness, a dream which gave to the fancy at least that for which the heart yearned and to which reality offered a decided contrast. Man is destined by nature to labor, to gain by exertion, to conquer all that is necessary for him. There is no "ready-made happiness," not even comfort for him. Instead of the many physical specific instincts with which the brute creation has been endowed he has received superior intellect; but this intellect itself has first to be developed gradually from generation to generation.

We are told the golden dream of original happiness was coupled with another equally erroneous view. Rousseau, in the opening sentences of "Emile," his work on education, says: "All is good as it comes out of the hands of the Author of things; everything degenerates in the hands of man, who wishes nothing to be such as nature has made it, not even man."

This erroneous view has been fully exposed and its error pointed out by philosophic writers, by no one more satisfactorily than by Dr. Lieber. It is man who improves upon unaided nature everywhere; makes the soil bear hundred fold, enlarges the fruits, ennobles the stock, saves from destruction, unites what was severed, carries the blessings and pleasures of one climate to another, and renders palatable what was repulsive, harmless what was poisonous, etc.

What is, philosophically speaking, the true state of nature of any being or thing? Doubtless that in which it fulfills most completely that end and object for which it is made, according to its organization. This discourse has clearly shown that "man was essentially made for progressive civilization, and this therefore is his natural state."

Law, we have seen, is a rule of action. The world was not made for the indolent; the active rule. We have to work, to labor, to learn honestly and gather industriously, that we may learn to do right. We must not minister to one of the worst dispositions by telling the idle that they have to learn nothing, that the cultivation of the mind is useless, that common sense is sufficient for everything.

Man's ethic character is founded on his individuality and sociality. He is first and essentially individual; his acts are his own, his responsibility is his own; for his reasoning and acting are his own; he has an inalienably

moral character, and cannot, by his own consent or the
force of others, become a non-moral being. He has a
natural aversion to being absorbed in an undefined
generality, and each man is anxious to be a distinct
individual. But he cannot be and never was without
property, which is nothing else than the application of
man's individuality to external things, effecting a relation, a relation between man and things without him,
involving a power over them, of disposing of them, growing out of the very nature of man : and consequently we
find him at no stage without property.

Kent says, the sense of property is graciously bestowed
upon mankind for the purpose of rousing from sloth and
stimulating them to action. It leads to the cultivation
of the earth, the institution of government, the establishment of justice, the acquisition of the comforts of life, the
growth of the useful arts, the spirit of commerce, the productions of taste, the erections of charity, and the display
of the benevolent affections.

Whatever is absolutely necessary for man's existence,
physical or intellectual, Providence has accompanied with
pleasure. It is a pleasure to eat when hungry, to drink
when thirsty, to sleep when tired, to awake after a long
sleep, to love and care for one's children, to commune
with others after a long, long solitude. It is a pleasure
to meditate, to analyze, to produce, to work with effect,
to assist others, to accumulate property.

In considering the nature and character of man, our
discourse has viewed his individuality, his distinct existence, and his sociality, the necessity imposed upon him to
associate.

The protracted state of the child's dependence upon
the parents produces habits of obedience, respect, and
love for a more advanced period, a consciousness of mutual
dependence. The members of a family soon discover how

much benefit they derive from reciprocal assistance and from a division of occupation among them. Men were induced to live in society, and, in a social state, were led to further improvement and gradual progress to civilization. With every progress in society and civilization the family continues and increases its importance and value. It is in the family, between parents and children and brothers and sisters, that those strong sympathies and deep-rooted affections grow up, which become the vital spark of so many good actions, which are the medium through which we view other and vaster spheres with purer and intenser feelings, and which survive blasts of later life that would chill most hearts into cold egotism. With them is mingled, and a thousand fold entwined, all that attachment which expands into patriotism; that warm devotion to our country which dwells in every noble heart, and without which no free state can long exist. To " fight for our hearths, for our country," goes through all countries and centuries, and appeals to every soul. " *Cari sunt parentes, cari liberi, cari propinqui, cari familiares; omnes omnium caritates patria una complexa est; pro quâ quis bonus dubitet mortem appetere, si ei sit profiturus.*" (Dear to us, beloved, are our parents, children, friends, and intimate associates; but the love of our country embraces all other loves whatsoever, for which no good man would hesitate to sacrifice his life, if by his death he could render it any necessary service.)

The mutual attachment between members of the family, depending on personal relations, first induced by ties of consanguinity, on kindness and forbearance, on a degree of disregard of one's own personal considerations, that which renders the family so admirable, is love and continued forgetfulness of a separate individual interest.

The relation between man and man, leading to further consideration, naturally conducts us to the relation between man and things without him, to which allusion was made in Kent's remark on the idea or sense of property. We have seen that labor must be divided : that men stand in constant need of each other ; that this division does not prevent men from associating for a common purpose, but carries with it what is indispensably connected with it, union of labor or association of energy, leading to and in fact constituting exchange, a peculiar and characteristic tic of man. Lieber declares that there exists, as far as he knows, no solitary instance of exchange among animals, no case of any exchange of labor or produce, of which a certain degree exists among all men, the lowest Hottentot or the most barbarous South Sea islander not excepted. There is no human tribe known which has not risen to this incipient state of all civilization. Even the most brutish Pelew Islander willingly parts with the fish which he has caught for a bar of iron. So common an act of man is the exchange of articles and of labor.

Beside consanguinity and exchange, there exist between man and man the relation of social intercourse and intellectual relations, embracing ties which grow out of the constant exchange of thoughts, feelings, taste, common literature, arts, sciences, and national custom, and the relation of right, upon which the state is founded.

What is right ?

Man has been shown to be a moral individual, yet bound to live in society. He is a being with free agency, freedom of action ; but as all his fellow-men with whom he lives in contact are equally beings with free agency, each making the same claim of freedom of action, there results from it the law that the use of freedom by one rational being must not contradict or counteract the use of liberty by another rational being. This demand of what is just, made by each upon each, is the relation of right.

Right, then, being that which I claim as just, because necessary to me as man, and granted by me to others, is the condition of union, that by which man's individuality and personality and his sociality can coexist. It applies to the society of comity as well as to the state.

What then in particular are the rights on which the state is built? A state is a society of individuals united for a common purpose, and having common interests; thus the inhabitants of a state constitute a society. In a more enlarged sense, the whole family of man is the human society.

The state is founded on those rights which are essential to all members and which can be enforced. It is then that society which has to protect the free action of every one, as its first basis; and as other relations between man and man imply action, each of these becomes likewise a relation of right, either claiming to be enforced or to be protected against infringement. The state speaks through laws, laws which command and must be obeyed. The idea of the just, and the action founded upon this idea, called justice, form the foundation and great object of the state. "*Quid enim est civitas, nisi juris societas?*"

The state is called a "jural society," denoting that it has reference to the doctrine of rights and obligations. The individual demands of the state that his right, his jural relation to others, be maintained inviolate, and the state demands that the individual shall not interfere with the right of others; in other words, shall not disturb their jural relations. The individual being unable to obtain the ends for which he was made, in a state of insulation, but bound from his very nature to live in society, it is matter of right that he obtain through and conjointly with society what he cannot obtain singly, and what nevertheless is essential to his well-being as man. The state, therefore, has the right and the duty to obtain

all these ends by the combined energy of society for each
individual, and has a moral character and must maintain it.

It is thus seen that protection is the aim and object of
the state, and is but another word for justice, and includes: (1) individual security; (2) social security, the
protection of society as such; (3) the protection of each
member as a being who cannot obtain otherwise his great
ends of humanity. " *Salus populi suprema lex.*" The
state exists to procure or maintain the weal, welfare, happiness, and prosperity of the people, and affords a means
to each individual to be truly man, all that he ought to
be. It is a form and faculty to lead mankind toward
perfection; it is the glory of man.

The state speaks through laws, and laws must be
obeyed. The state exists by necessity, as effect and
consequence of our physical and intellectual nature. The
right of society to legislate — that is, the right existing
somewhere of prescribing general and imperative rules —
has, it is believed, never been doubted, any more than the
right of breathing in the individual; both flow from the
same source, necessity, according to our nature. They
are conditions of our existence as human beings. We
might live as brutes, without the institution of the state;
but, for our existence as human beings, the state is an
absolute condition, a condition *sine qua non;* and this
absolute necessity constitutes the ground on which is
founded what is called sovereignty, — that is, the self-suffi-
cient power which derives its vital energy from no other,
is founded by no superior authority, but imparts it and
extends over everything that is requisite in order to obtain the object of the state, which man has to obtain in
and by society, in as far as it is founded on jural relations: that is, on right, on terms of justice or mutual
obligations.

The character of the state becomes more powerful with every advanced stage of civilization. Its members do not stand as mere individuals, brought together for the sole purpose of protecting one another from bodily harm, or for any selfish and temporary purpose. There are yet more important objects to be obtained in the course of civilization. Ignorance and barbarity, for instance, are likewise to be warded off, because if not they will produce insecurity, and because knowledge and education are necessary for man's civilization, and must be obtained by society jointly if they cannot be obtained by individual energy or voluntary association.

This leads to the following, perhaps a more formal statement: "The state, according to its jural relations, has for its legitimate objects all those things necessary or highly important for man, which he nevertheless (1) cannot obtain singly, (2) ought not to obtain singly (because he exposes himself or his fellow-citizens to great danger by doing so; for instance, by redressing privately interferences with his rights), and (3) will not do singly (because burthensome, disagreeable; for example, to keep roads in good order, establish common schools, pay what we owe)."

The state and the individual stand in jural relations to each other; reciprocity exists between them, and right, all right is, in its very meaning, founded on reciprocity. The moment that any particular state is actually to treat me as merely existing for it, demanding only, and giving nothing, or demanding without giving the equivalent, the bond is dissolved, and the state does not any longer exist for me, — it is not my state.

Rights imply that he who has them can insist upon them: he ought to have the power to preserve and enforce. His jural relations to the state — obligations, rights, and penalties — must be judged of by laws: they cannot depend upon personal views and feelings and affections, and lie in the indefinite in the breast of some one. Each member of a state has a right to be judged by laws through the courts. Frederick the Great, who was very anxious to remove a windmill close before the " centre window of his favorite palace at Potsdam," could not induce the miller to sell it. The king, irritated, threatened the owner to force him to consent. " There is a supreme court in Berlin," answered the miller. The king was silent, and the mill stands to this day, an annoyance to the palace, but one of the best monuments which an absolute monarch ever erected to himself, as an ambassador wrote home from Potsdam.

The rights of persons in private life are either absolute or relative. The absolute rights may be resolved into the right of personal security, the right of personal liberty, and the right to acquire and enjoy property. These rights are natural, inherent, and inalienable, primordial. The state, therefore, cannot take the life of the individual for the benefit of others, because that would violate the first of his rights, the right of living, without being able to give him an equivalent, unless the state have acquired a right over his life on the specific ground of his having forfeited it. There can be no doubt as to the right in the state to punish capitally for certain crimes.

Closely connected with the right of living and essential to personal security is the claim of protection for the body, limbs, and health. Many considerations of high importance must give way if clashing with sanitary interests, the life and health of members of the community ; every other right is to give way if under absolute necessity to save one's own life. " *Necessitas non habet legem, jus necessitatis.*" (Necessity does not establish a right, but annihilates responsibility.)

The United States of America, in their Declaration of

Independence, set forth as self-evident truths the rights of individual man, by the laws of nature and of nature's God, to life, to liberty, to the pursuit of happiness; that all men are created equal; that governments are instituted among men to secure these rights, and derive their just powers from the consent of the governed.

Assuming this, there is no theoretical difficulty respecting the subjects which require the action of the state or not, and those which the state ought never to touch. But in practice there is much difficulty.

Life is absolutely necessary for man, and if he cannot possibly obtain medical assistance society is bound to furnish it. Public hospitals are not a mere matter of charity; they are a matter of right. That they may be abused, and easily abused, we know.

Again, if society be convinced that institutions of deep learning, universities, are of absorbing importance to society, because science must always be far in advance of practice, and because the cultivation of the sciences for their own sake, and not with a confined view of immediate practical application, raises the standard of knowledge in general, and is a great blessing to a community; and if the state be convinced that private means must ever be insufficient for the erection of a university, and the collection of large libraries, museums, etc., then the state has the same right and the same obligation to found and aid such institutions as it has to aid in the foundation of common schools or courts, hospitals or armies. So it hath been held. If the Greeks thought that the development of "taste" was essential to the whole development of man, and that individual means were insufficient to effect the necessary cultivation of the fine arts, the state was right in promoting them by public means.

Personal liberty is a condition of man's free agency as a member of society; as a being who has to obtain

certain objects in society with others, he must be personally free. There is no right more essential to him than
the right of property and the means wherewith he acquires
it; that is, labor, skill, and exchange. It is his duty to
maintain himself and his family; he has a fair share in
the means of support offered by nature and the various
ways of acquisition belonging to his nature. He has a
primordial right to use his labor as he chooses, if he do
not thereby transgress the right of others, and the state
must neither disturb him in this lawful pursuit nor allow
others to disturb him. Exchange is one of the most
necessary and natural means of acquisition, founded in
the variety of soil, clime, genius of people, agents of nature, etc., and one of the most effective means of civilization, as already stated. It lies in the great order of
things.

The sense of property is inherent in the human breast.
Man was fitted and intended by the Author of his being
for society and government, and for the acquisition and
enjoyment of property. This is the law of his nature.

No right calls for more modification and regulation by
the state than that of acquisition of property; it relates
more than any other right to the material world, and more
affects in its enjoyment the jural relations of others.
The legislation, therefore, of every country has necessarily
acted upon the subject. Nor has property been considered a right which could on no consideration be abolished
or remodeled. Other means of acquisition than by labor,
though not absolutely furnished by nature, have been
found excellent for the welfare of society, entirely dependent on legislation: for instance, the law of inheritance.

Everything in the state must be founded on justice,
and justice rests on generality and equality. The state,
therefore, has no right to promote the interest of one and

not of the other. It promotes my interest if it assists in
getting my debts paid, but it is ready to do so for everybody. It promotes private interest if it gives a pension to
the widow of a soldier, but it is on the ground that society owes her a debt, or that it is good for society thus
to encourage soldiers. So if a state gives money to a
traveler into distant regions, or to study the fine and
useful arts and usages in foreign cities and lands, it gives
it because the public is believed to benefit by it, directly
or indirectly; but the money is not given to the private
individual as such. Public gifts of this nature, pensions
and the like, have frequently been bestowed in a shameless manner, under a pretense of rewarding services for
some public good. Witness Somerset and Buckingham.

It is not easy to decide what is of sufficient general importance to call for public action. The general principle
is, interfere as little as possible with the private affairs
of the individual.

The intermeddling of the state with private affairs
frequently springs from other motives than a wish to
serve the affairs of those intermeddled with. Individuals and private associations should be left to private exercise of their industry as much as the public weal, comfort,
and morality will allow: but the state, through its public
authorities, has frequently means of obtaining more correct
and wider views, fuller and more detailed knowledge, in
short, official information, unattainable by the individual,
and can command the aid of better qualified persons: so
that interference becomes just, because demanded by public interest. Lieber, after this statement, says: " I do
not know that what is lawful for the state to do, and how
it ought to be done, has ever been more lucidly expressed
than in the following passage : ' *Erit lex honesta, justa,
possibilis, secundum naturam, secundum consuetudinem
patriæ, loco temporique conveniens, necessaria, utilis,*

11

*manifesta quoque, ne aliquid per obscuritatem in capti-
one contineat, nullo privato commodo, sed pro communi
utilitate civium scripta.'"*

Man cannot be man without communion, utterance, be
this by sound or sign, and be this sign transitory (as the
sign made by the deaf and dumb) or enduring (by writing); our whole existence as human beings depends upon
it. We cannot imagine a human society consisting of
beings deaf, dumb, and blind.

Mankind could never have advanced had not members
of the existing generations held free converse among
themselves, and had not, in the course of time, one
generation learned to commune with the next, or people
separated by space to exchange their ideas. The more
the earth became peopled, the more the stage of action,
knowledge, and intercourse became extended; and the
more the collection of facts and reasoning required
communications too extensive for mere oral converse, the
more writing became necessary, and the knowledge of
what has been written became indispensable. Writing is
nothing but utterance and converse. Without it, man
would never have shaken off the thralldom of distort-
ing tradition: knowledge could not have accumulated
in any high degree: it could not have descended by way
of inheritance from one to the other. Interference with
writing is, therefore, interfering with thought. No authority, man, or body has a right to disturb a man's communion with his fellow-men by whatever means of utterance he chooses, if no right of others is infringed.

But though the right of utterance is primordial, indis-
putable, it yet may be regulated or suspended. Military
circumstances may justify or give a right to a commander
of troops to declare that a single word uttered should be
instantly punished with death. It is done not unfrequently.

The Dutch Colonel Haraugière, in 1590, hid himself with his seventy men on board the peat vessel, to be dragged into the fortress of Breda, occupied by the Spaniards, and exercised the right to make the order. The same order, it is said, was given by General Wayne when he marched to capture Stony Point in 1779. So may utterance by writing be suspended or limited. But these are exceptions.

Nothing is more certain than that we are not intended solely for ourselves. Our happiness, nay, our whole existence as human beings, as already stated, depends upon communion, converse, social intercourse.

Cicero, who knew so well how to illustrate law by philosophy, says: " If we could suppose ourselves transported by some divinity into a solitude replete with all the delicacies which the heart of man could desire, but excluded at the same time from every possible intercourse with our kind, there is not a person in the world of so unsocial and savage a temper as to be capable, in those forlorn circumstances, of any enjoyment." Nothing, he continues, is more true than what the philosopher Archytas is reported to have said. If a man were to be carried up into heaven and see the beauties of universal nature displayed before him, he would receive but little pleasure from the wonderful scenes, unless there were some person to whom he could relate the glories which he had viewed. Man, like those plants which are formed to embrace others, is led by an instinctive impulse to recline on those of his own kind. Pope, our philosophic poet, thus briefly says : —

> " Man, like the gen'rous vine, supported lives ;
> The strength he gains is from the embrace he gives."

Man, the individual, has the right to move where he pleases. The right of personal liberty, as well as of exchange, would already sufficiently warrant this right, the right of emigration, of expatriation. "Next to my life is the place where I live, where I exchange my labor, — the most important to me of all my rights which touch the physical world." Special circumstances may limit this right, as that of utterance, but it can only be by way of exception, notwithstanding all that has been said to the contrary on the ground of natural allegiance. It must be one of the first of all rights of a free being to choose that place and that society where he thinks he may best obtain his individual objects.

Man, it is repeated, has far nobler objects than merely good living; before all, he must obtain the common comforts of life for himself and family, as the basis of higher things. If over-population or over-taxation grind down a man so that he can hardly obtain food for his family, still less elevate them morally and intellectually, and he has an opportunity to remove to an unoccupied virgin soil, which, like a kindly friend, renders readily to every exertion with ungrudging abundance: should such a man linger out a life of wretchedness and bring up his children in sloth and ignorance, — that is, prepare and fit them for vice, perhaps for crime, — merely because some suppose it unpoetical to leave the native soil for a better one, and to toil hard to become independent, a worthy, noble object to every man? "There is poetry in the emigrant who goes, with nothing but a willing arm and his plough, a conqueror, to the West."

It is the order of things to emigrate. No nation was more given to emigration than the ancient Greeks, who thereby conferred incalculable advantages upon mankind. Yet who loved their country more?

If a man has a right to emigrate, he has likewise the right of expatriation; for man ought to be a citizen according to his destiny. It is plain, says Mr. Locke, by the law of right reason, that a child is born a subject of no country or government. He is under his father's tuition and authority until he comes to the age of discretion, and then he is a freeman, at liberty to choose what government he will put himself under, what body politic he will unite himself to.

"O glorious regulations! originally established by our ancestors of Roman name," said Tully, " that no one of us should be obliged to more than one society : that no one, contrary to his inclination, should be deprived of his right of citizenship : and that no one, contrary to his inclination, should be obliged to continue in that relation. The power of retaining and of renouncing our rights of citizenship is the most stable foundation of our liberties."

In civil society previously to the institution of civil government, all men are equal. From one source the whole human race has sprung.

When it is said, "all men are equal," it is not meant to apply this equality to their virtues, their talents, their dispositions, or their acquirements. In all these respects there is, and it is fit for the great purposes of society that there should be, great inequality among men. In the moral and political as well as in the natural world, diversity forms a part, an important part, of beauty and utility. How spiritless, how dull, would man, would human life and manners be without the beautiful variety of colors reflected upon them by different tastes, different tempers, and different characters!

Men are formed mutually to afford and to stand in need of service and assistance. The social happiness arising from the intercourse of good offices could not otherwise be enjoyed. Hence the necessity of great variety and of great inequality in the talents of men, bodily as mental.[1]

---

[1] " Had it been the intention of Providence that some men should govern the rest without their consent, we should have seen as indis-

Observe the varieties of human genius, human dispositions, and human characters! One man has a turn for
mechanics, another for architecture: one paints, another
writes poems: this excels in the arts of a military, the
other in those of a civil life. It is difficult, perhaps
impossible, to account for these varieties of taste and
character. But their final course, the intention of Providence, we can see and admire. They induce different
persons to choose different professions and employments
in life. These render mankind equally beneficial to each
other, and prevent too violent oppositions in the same
pursuit. Hence we enjoy a variety of conveniences: the
numerous arts and sciences have been invented and improved, the sources of commerce and intercourse between
different nations have been opened, the circulation of
truth has been quickened and promoted, and the operations of social virtues have been multiplied and enlarged.

Pope, in his "Essay on Man," philosophically observes : —

> "Heaven forming each on other to depend
> Bids each on other for assistance call,
> Till one man's weakness grows the strength of all.
> Wants, frailties, passions, closer still ally
> The common interest, or endear the tie ;
> To these we owe true friendship, love sincere,
> Each home-felt joy that life inherits here."

But, however great the variety and inequality of men
may be with regard to virtue, talents, taste, and acquire-

putable marks distinguishing these superiors from those placed
under them as those which distinguish men from the brutes. The
remark of Rumbald, in the non-resistance time of Charles II.,
evinced propriety as well as wit. He could not conceive that
the Almighty intended that the greatest part of mankind should
come into the world with saddles on their backs and bridles in their
mouths, and that a few should come ready booted and spurred to
ride the rest to death." — *Wilson's Works*, vol. i.

ments, there is still one aspect in which all men in society, previous to civil governments, are equal. With regard to all, there is an equality in rights and in obligations, there is that *jus æquum*, that equal law in which the Romans placed true freedom. The natural rights and duties of man belong equally to all. Each forms a part of that great system whose greatest interest and happiness are intended by all the laws of God and nature. He has, therefore, a right to exercise his powers in such a manner and upon such objects as his inclination and judgment shall direct, provided he does no injury to others and more public interests do not demand his labors.

This right is natural liberty, suggested to us by the selfish part of our constitution, by our generous affections, and by our moral sense. States which manage best their affairs will offer the strongest inducements to their own citizens to remain, and to others to incorporate among them. It is both inhuman and unjust to convert the state into a prison for its citizens by preventing them from leaving it on a prospect of advantages to themselves.

The important question is then to be considered : Has a citizen a right to dissolve the connection, the tie between him and his country, and renounce his allegiance?

The notion of natural, perpetual, and unalienable allegiance from the citizen to the society, to the state, or to the king or head of the society of which he was born a member, has been frequently and gravely discussed by philosophic writers. Kent declares: " In American jurisprudence, the better opinion would seem to be that a citizen cannot renounce his allegiance to the United States without the permission of government to be declared by law, and that, as there is no existing legislation on the case, the rule of the English common law remains unaltered."

The old English jurists speak of a law of nature above Parliament, according to which the indissoluble tie between subject and liege lord or lady exists, so that outlawry could not even affect the tie. A man cannot abjure his native country nor the allegiance which he owes his sovereign.

Every citizen, it is said, as soon as he is born, is under the protection of the state, and is entitled to all the advantages arising from that protection. He therefore owes obedience to that power from which the protection that he enjoys is derived. While he continues in infancy and nonage he cannot perform the full duties of obedience. The performance of them must be respited till he arrives at the years of discretion and maturity. When he arrives at those years, he owes obedience not only for the protection which he then enjoys, but also for that which from his birth he has enjoyed. Obedience now becomes a duty founded on principles of gratitude as well as of interest; it now becomes a debt which nothing but the performance of the duties of citizenship during a whole life will discharge.

Blackstone says: "Natural allegiance is therefore a debt of gratitude which cannot be forfeited, canceled, or altered by any change of time, place, or circumstance, nor by anything but the united concurrence of the legislature."

Refraining from unnecessary criticism, it is just to state that Blackstone finally acknowledges (vol. i. p. 24): "It is found by experience that whenever the unconstitutional oppressions, even of the sovereign, advance with gigantic strides and threaten desolation to a state, mankind will not be reasoned out of the feelings of humanity, nor will sacrifice their liberty by a scrupulous adherence to those political maxims which were originally established to preserve it. . . . Law and history leave it to future generations whenever necessity and the safety of the whole shall require it, the exertion of these inherent though latent powers of society, which no climate, no constitution, no time, no contract, can ever destroy or diminish."

How then can allegiance be a natural, perpetual, unalienable tie and duty from the citizen to the state? We are told, " It became a debt of gratitude." A debt of gratitude ! What for ? " That protection which the country or sovereign affords him." Protection! Suppose the sovereign strives to undermine the laws made for his protection : refuses to enforce those which are essential to the enjoyment of his personal rights to liberty, the acqui- sition and possession of property, the equal right to free- dom of labor, to security and the pursuit of happiness, and to just and free government. Suppose the sovereign assumes power absolute and direct, and strives by unequal taxation and grinding exactions, by harsh monopolies and other grants of privileges, to defeat and destroy the just objects of the state.

Suppose the citizen, under these circumstances, feels no gratitude, and is right in not feeling it, because nothing has been bestowed upon him to be thankful for !

No one now will be so hardy as to maintain that sub- jects must submit without resistance to a Heliogabalus. The allegiance of the French, who have sworn it within the last hundred years, has been to ever so many persons and governments. Nature binds us by a kind of instinct to the place where we received our first breath, but often some causes weaken or destroy this impression. The injustice or severity of the government may efface it. " The deep-rooted feeling of every true heart toward the nation to which we belong by blood would," writes Lieber, " have afforded a far better foundation for national alle- giance than a feeble one of gratitude : love to the country of our birth in many instances outlives our gratitude."

The meanest factory-boy in Manchester may still feel attached to England, but it would be very difficult to point out what reason he has for gratitude. Is he not quit with the state as to gratitude every evening after an unrequited day of overwhelming labor?

Who is bound to be grateful, the state, or the poor man who has always lived by his work, paid heavy taxes, and is finally pressed into sea service where he is crippled? All nations allow the state to force him to expose his life.

Colonization here presents itself for consideration. but before entering immediately upon it we desire to refer anew to obedience and the power of the state in its jural relation. We have seen that commanding and obeying are the two foundations of all human society; that society without laws would lose its moral character, and therefore man's destiny requires obedience to laws. To make, acknowledge, and obey laws is one of the high prerogatives as well as duties of man among all the animate beings of the visible creation.

"Stranger, tell the Lacedæmonians that we lie here in obedience to their laws." This was the simple inscription to commemorate the heroic and conscious devotion of the faithful band of Leonidas at Thermopylæ, and in which a nation of peculiar sagacity and promptitude of mind as well as ardor of soul for liberty, a nation with whom "freedom was what the sun is, the most brilliant and most useful object of creation, a passion, an instinct, thought to express the highest acknowledgment of a deed which every Greek remembered with national pride. It was the true expression of the public spirit. Of all that was noble and great in this patriotic act, the noblest and greatest seemed to them that the gallant citizens had been obedient to the laws and their country, even unto death."

The state must have power and authority for its government. Justice requires that every man shall have his due, and this cannot be accomplished without high authority and power to sustain the authority. The state through its government must protect every citizen against any violation of his rights by wrong-doers or enemies, must maintain its character as a society of right, and one of the main objects of the state is to obtain jointly that which is necessary for society, and cannot be obtained by individual exertion.

Public power is founded upon confidence reposed in him who has finally to carry out the law. However carefully limited and definite, the power granted may be abused. There exists likewise an intense desire to exercise, practice, and apply it. It is its very nature, and without it the world would be at a stand.

Our discourse will here proceed to the subject of colonization. A number of states or societies may associate or confederate together for their mutual security and advantage. In some respects such confederacies are to be considered as forming only one nation; in other respects they are to be considered as still retaining their separate political capacities, characters, rights, and powers. The word "colony," in Latin *colonia*, is derived from the verb *colo, colere*, to till or cultivate the ground.

The formation of colonies is among the oldest events in history. Maritime states, such as those of Phœnicia and of Greece, which possessed only a scanty territory, would have recourse to emigration as their population increased. Commercial enterprise seems to have led both to maritime discovery and to colonization.

All the different states of ancient Greece possessed, each of them, but a very small territory: and when the people in any one of them multiplied beyond what that territory could easily maintain, a part of them were sent in quest of a new habitation in some remote and distant part of the world, the warlike neighbors who surrounded them on all sides rendering it difficult for any of them to enlarge its territory at home. The mother city (state), though she considered the colony as a child, at all times entitled to great favor and assistance, and owing in return much gratitude and respect, yet considered it as an emancipated child, over whom she pretended to claim no direct authority or jurisdiction. The colony settled its own form of government, enacted its own laws, elected its own magistrates, and made peace or war with its neighbors as an independent state, which had no occasion to wait for the approbation or consent of the mother city.

Rome, like most of the ancient republics, was originally founded upon an agrarian law, which divided the public territory in a certain proportion among the different citizens who composed the state. The course of human affairs, by marriage, by succession, and by alienation, necessarily deranged this original division, and frequently threw the lands which had been allotted for the maintenance of many different families into the possession of a single person. To remedy this disorder, for such it was supposed to be, a law was made restricting the quantity of land which any citizen could possess to five hundred *jugera*, about three hundred and fifty acres. The law, however, though we read of its having been executed upon one or two occasions, was either neglected or evaded, and the inequality of fortunes went on continually increasing. The greater part of the citizens had no land; and, without it, the manners and customs of those times rendered it difficult for a freeman to maintain his independence. Among the ancient Romans, the lands of the rich were all cultivated by slaves, who wrought under an overseer, who was likewise a slave; so that a poor free-man had little chance of being employed either as a farmer or as a laborer. All trades and manufactures too, even the retail trade, were carried on by the slaves of the rich for the benefit of their masters, whose wealth, author-ity, and protection made it difficult for a poor freeman to maintain the competition against them. The citizens, therefore, who had no land had scarce any other means of subsistence but the bounties of the candidates at the annual elections. The tribunes, when they had a mind to animate the people against the rich and the great, put them in mind of the ancient division of land, and repre-sented that law which restricted this sort of private prop-erty as the fundamental law of the republic. The people became clamorous to get land, and the rich and the great were determined not to give them any part of theirs. To satisfy them in some measure, therefore, they frequently proposed to send out a new colony.

But Rome, Victrix Roma, in her career of conquest, was not, even upon such occasions, under a necessity of forcing out her citizens to seek their fortune through the wide world, without knowing where they were to settle. She assigned them lands, generally in the conquered lands of Italy, where, being within the dominion of the republic, they could never form an independent state, but were at best a sort of corporation, which, though it had the power of enacting by-laws for its government, was at all times subject to the correction, jurisdiction, and legislative au-thority of the mother city. The sending out a colony of this kind gave some satisfaction to the people, and often established a sort of garrison in a newly-conquered prov-ince, the obedience of which might otherwise have been doubtful.

A Roman colony, therefore, whether we consider the nature of the establishment itself or the motives for making it, was altogether different from a Greek one. Both institutions, however, derived their origin either from necessity or from clear and evident utility.

The establishment of the European colonies in America and the West Indies arose from no necessity: and its utility was not perhaps then well understood.

When Columbus returned from his first voyage of discovery, and was introduced, as we are told, with a sort of triumphal honor to the sovereigns of Castile and Aragon, St. Domingo was represented as a country abounding with gold, and an inexhaustible source of real wealth to the crown and kingdom of Spain. The council of Castile determined to take possession of countries of which the inhabitants were plainly incapable of defending themselves. The pious purpose of converting them to Christianity sanctified the injustice of the project. But the hope of finding treasure of gold there was the sole motive which prompted to undertake it; and to give the motive the greater weight, it was proposed that half of all the gold and silver that should be found there should be given to the Crown. This proposal was approved by the council. The other enterprises of the Spaniards in the New World, subsequent to those of Columbus, seem to have been prompted by the same motive.

It was the sacred thirst of gold, *auri sacra fames.* The same avidity, the same passion, which has suggested to so many people the absurd idea of the philosopher's stone, has suggested to others the equally absurd one of immense rich mines of gold and silver. The dream of Sir Walter Raleigh concerning the golden city and country of Eldorado may satisfy us that even wise men are not always exempt from such strange delusions. Every Spaniard who sailed to America expected to find an Eldorado. The first adventurers of all the other nations of Europe, who attempted to make settlements in America, were animated by the like chimerical views.

The colony of a civilized nation, which takes possession of a waste country, advances more rapidly to wealth and greatness than any other human society. It carries out with it a knowledge of agriculture and other useful arts, the habit of subordination, and some notion of government and the administration of justice and law in the mother country, and usually establishes something of the same kind in the new settlement.

The progress of many of the ancient Greek colonies seems to have been very rapid, but the progress of the Roman colonies seems never to have been very rapid. They were established in conquered provinces fully inhabited before, and allowed to manage their own affairs in the way that they judged most suitable to their own interest.

In the plenty of good land, the European colonies established in America and the West Indies resemble, and even greatly surpass, those of ancient Greece. In their dependency on the mother state they resemble those of ancient Rome. But their great distance from Europe alleviated more or less the effects of this dependency. Their situation placed them less in the view and less in the power of their mother country.[1]

These remarks on colonies, true in themselves, contain no reference to any special instance of colonial establishment, progress, and history.

In 1820 the Pilgrim Society of Massachusetts was formed, " to commemorate the landing and to honor the memory of the men who first set foot on Plymouth Rock," and Mr. Webster was invited to deliver a discourse on the " 22d of December, the close of the second century of the Fathers."

The discourse delivered by him in pursuance of the invitation stated the causes and the motives which in-

---

[1] Adam Smith, *Wealth of Nations.*

duced the first settlers of Plymouth to relinquish their
native country, and to seek an asylum in an unexplored
land, with a tribute to the memory of the Puritans, and a
touching picture of their sufferings on both sides of the
water; the progress of New England during the century
which had then elapsed, with some wise and profound
observations on the principles upon which society and
government are established in this country. It was an
eloquent and noble disquisition of the illustrious American.

Edward Everett declared, "The occasion of the address
attracted attention more immediately to the New England
colonies than to other English colonies then established."
True. But it filled the heart and mind of America, and
commanded the respect and admiration of every enlightened advocate of liberty; it embraced the whole body of
the republic, *totum corpus reipublicæ*, inculcated good
faith to all nations, obedience of men to the Creator and
Ruler of the Universe, leading us progressively from individual to social man, from society to colonies, from
colonies to independent states, thence to associated and
confederated states, and to states wisely and gloriously
united to form one country, one national constitution and
government, the imperial Republic of the United States
of America, — *E Pluribus Unum*, one formed from many,
to secure liberty and establish justice.

England had once acquired undisputed control over
the Indian tribes, still tenanting the forests unexplored
by the European man. She had established an uncontested monopoly of the commerce of all her colonies.
But forgetting all the warnings of preceding ages, forgetting the lessons written in the blood of her own
children through centuries of departed time, she undertook to tax the people of the colonies without their con-

sent, and had claimed the right to do so, and to bind them by her statutes in all cases.

Resistance, instantaneous, unconcerted, sympathetic resistance, like an electric shock, startled and roused the people of all the English colonies on this continent.

This was the signal, the first signal, of the North American Union. The struggle was for chartered rights, for liberties, English liberties, for the cause of Sidney and Hampden, for trial by jury, for the *habeas corpus* and Magna Charta. But the English lawyers had decided that Parliament was omnipotent, and Parliament in its omnipotence, instead of trial by jury and the *habeas corpus*, enacted admiralty courts in England to try Americans for offenses charged against them as committed in America: and, instead of the privileges of Magna Charta, nullified the charter of Massachusetts Bay, shut up the port of Boston, sent armies and navies to keep the peace and teach the colonies that Hampden was a rebel and Algernon Sidney a traitor.

English liberties had failed them. From the omnipotence of Parliament the colonists appealed to the rights of man and the omnipotence of the God of battles. " Union! Union!" was the instinctive and simultaneous cry throughout the land. Their Congress, assembled at Philadelphia, once, twice, had petitioned the king, had remonstrated to Parliament, had addressed the people of Britain for the rights of Englishmen in vain. Fleets and armies, the blood of Lexington, and the fires of Charlestown and Falmouth had been the answer to petition, remonstrance, and address.

Independence was declared. The colonies were transformed into states. Their inhabitants were proclaimed to be one people, renouncing all allegiance to the British Crown, all co-patriotism with the British nation, all claim to chartered rights as Englishmen. Thenceforth their

12

charter was the Declaration of Independence, their rights the rights of mankind, their government such as should be instituted by themselves under the mutual pledges of perpetual union, founded on the self-evident truths proclaimed in the Declaration.

The Declaration of Independence was issued in a civil war which raged with fury six years. It was a manifesto to the world of mankind to justify the one confederated people for the violent severance of the ties of their allegiance, for the renunciation of their country, and for assuming a station themselves among the potentates of the world, — a self-constituted sovereign, a self-constituted country.

The attempt of England to monopolize the trade of the colonies, and the continued effort on the part of the colonies to resist or evade that monopoly, demand further exposure. The English Act of Navigation was passed in 1660. Its first and grand object seems to have been to secure to England the whole trade with her plantations : none but English ships should transport American produce over the ocean, to be sold only in the markets of the mother country. It is unnecessary to detail other acts or laws, passed subsequently in a like spirit to make the interest of the whole people of the colonies subordinate to, and for the exclusive advantage of, another people.

The association of the American people into one body politic took place while they were colonies of the British Empire and owed allegiance to the British Crown. That the union of this country was essential to its safety, its prosperity, and its greatness had been generally known and frequently avowed long before the Revolution or the claims of the British Parliament. As early as 1643, a league, offensive and defensive, distinguished by the name of the United Colonies of New England, was entered into, and subsisted, with some alterations, for

upwards of forty years, and part of that time with the
countenance of the government in England. It was not
dissolved until 1686, when the charters of the New England colonies were in effect vacated by a commission
from King James II. The people of this country continued to afford other precedents of association for their
safety.

Passing at once to the interesting Congress held at Al-
bany, in the year 1754, of governors and commissioners from other colonies as well as from New England, to
consider the best means of defending America in case
of war with France, which was then impending, we find
that the object of the English administration in calling
this convention was in reference to friendly treaties with
the Indian tribes. But the colonies had more enlarged
views. One of the colonies, Massachusetts, expressly
instructed her delegates to enter into articles of union
and confederation with the other colonies, for their general security in peace as in war. The convention unanimously resolved " that a union of the colonies was absolutely necessary for their preservation." They rejected
all proposals for a division of the colonies into separate confederacies, and proposed " a plan of federal government." But this bold project of a continental union
had the singular fate of being rejected, not only on the
part of the Crown, but by every provincial Assembly.
We were destined to remain for some years longer separate, and in a considerable degree alien commonwealths,
emulous of each other in obedience to the parent state
and in devotion to her interests, but jealous of each
other's interest. So strong was this, and so exasperated
were the people of the colonies in their disputes with each
other concerning boundaries and charter claims, that
Franklin (one of the commissioners to the Congress that
formed the plan of union in 1754) observed, in the year

1760, "that a union of the colonies against the mother country was absolutely impossible, or at least without being forced by the most grievous tyranny and oppression."

The great value of a federal union of the colonies had, however, sunk deeply into the minds of men. The necessity of union had been felt, its advantages perceived, its principles explained, the way to it pointed out, and the people of this country were led, by the force of irresistible motives, to resort to union, the same means of defense and security, when they considered that their liberties were in danger, not from the harassing and irregular warfare of the Indian tribes, but from the formidable claims and still more formidable power of the parent state.

The assertion by the British Parliament of an unqualified right of binding the colonies in all cases whatsoever, and specifically of the right of taxing them without their consent, and the denial by the colonies of the right of taxation without representation, and the attempt of the king and Parliament to enforce it by the power of the sword, were the immediate causes of the American Revolution.

An extensive and general association of the colonies took place in September, 1774, and united to send delegates to Philadelphia, "with authority and direction to meet and consult together for the common welfare." In pursuance of their authority, this first Continental Congress took into consideration the afflicted state of their country: asserted by resolutions what they deemed the unalienable rights of English freemen: pointed out to their constituents the system of violence which was preparing against those rights; and urged them by the most sacred of all ties, the ties of honor and of their country, to renounce commerce with Great Britain, as being the most salutary way to defeat the one and to secure the other.

These resolutions received prompt and universal obedience, and "the union thus auspiciously formed was continued by a succession of delegates in Congress, and through every period of the war and through every revolution has been cherished as the solid foundation of national independence."

In May, 1775, a Congress again assembled at Philadelphia, and was clothed with ample discretionary powers. The delegates were chosen, as those of the preceding Congress had been, partly by the popular branch of the colonial legislatures when in session, but principally by conventions of the people in the several colonies. They were instructed to "concert, agree upon, direct, order, and prosecute" such measures as they should deem most fit and proper to obtain redress of American grievances; or, in more general terms, they were to take care of the liberties of the country. Soon after this meeting, Georgia acceded to and completed the confederacy of the thirteen colonies. Hostilities had already commenced in Massachusetts, and the claim of the British Parliament to an unconditional and unlimited sovereignty over the colonies was to be asserted by an appeal to arms. The Continental Congress, entrusted with the power and sustained by the zeal and confidence of their constituents, prepared for resistance. They proceeded immediately to levy and organize an army, prescribed rules for the government of their land and naval forces, contracted debts, emitted a paper currency upon the faith of the union, and gradually assuming all the powers of national sovereignty, at last, on the fourth day of July, 1776, took a separate and equal station among the nations of the earth, declaring the united colonies to be free and independent states.

It was thought expedient for security and duration to define with precision, and by a formal instrument, the nature of our compact, the powers of Congress, the residuary sovereignty of the states.

On the 11th of June, 1776, Congress undertook to digest and prepare Articles of Confederation, but it was not until the 15th of November, 1777, that Congress could so far unite the discordant interests and prejudices of thirteen distinct communities to agree to the Articles of Confederation, and the articles submitted were declared to be " the result of impending necessity and of a disposition for conciliation as the best system which could afford any tolerable prospect of general assent."

These Articles met great obstacles in their progress through the States. Most of the legislatures ratified them with a promptitude which showed their sense of the necessity of the confederacy and of the indulgence of a liberal spirit of accommodation. But Delaware did not accede to them until the year 1779, and Maryland at first rejected them, but assented to them on the 1st of March, 1781, upwards of three years from their first promulgation; and thus the Articles of Confederation received the unanimous approbation of the United States.

The government of the Union is considered to have been revolutionary in its nature from its first institution by the people of the colonies, in 1774, down to the final ratification of the Articles of Confederation, in 1781, and to have possessed powers adequate to every national emergency, and coextensive with the object to be attained. Kent says of the Articles of Confederation that they were in fact but a digest, and even limitation, of the sovereign powers, undefined, but delegated by the people of the colonies to Congress in 1775, and freely exercised and implicitly obeyed.

In the enthusiasm of their first union they had flattered themselves that no general government would be required. As separate states they were all agreed that they should constitute and govern themselves. The progress of the British arms excited apprehension for our safety. The

Revolution under which they were suffering and gasping, the war which was carrying desolation into their dwellings and mourning into every family, had been kindled by the abuse of power, the power of government. An invincible repugnance to the delegation of power had thus been generated by the very course of events which had rendered it necessary; and the more indispensable it became, the more awakened was the jealousy and the more intense was the distrust by which it was to be circumscribed.

Notwithstanding the undefined and discretionary sovereign powers which were delegated by the people of the colonies to Congress in 1775, and which had been freely exercised and implicitly obeyed, a remarkable instance of this original, dormant, vast discretion appears on the journals of Congress the latter end of the year 1776. The progress of the British arms had, at that period, excited the most alarming apprehension for our safety, and Congress transferred to the commander-in-chief for the term of six months complete dictatorial power over the liberty and property of the citizens of the United States. Such loose, undefined authority as the Union originally possessed was absolutely incompatible with any regular notions of liberty. Though it was exercised with the best intentions and under the impulse of an irresistible necessity, yet such an irregular sovereignty can never be durable. It will either dwindle into insignificance or degenerate into despotism. Disobedience to the laws of the Union must be submitted to by the government to its own disgrace, or those laws must be enforced by arms.

Story, in a brief history of the confederation, says: " One of the first objects beyond that of the immediate public safety which engaged the attention of the Continental Congress was to provide the means of a permanent union of all the colonies under a general government.

The deliberations on this subject led the Continental Congress, after various debates and discussions, to agree upon a frame of government in Articles of Confederation in November, 1777, which were sent to all the States for their adoption and ratification, but were not finally adopted until March, 1781, upwards of three years from their first promulgation, when they received the unanimous approbation of the United States."

The Articles of Confederation had scarcely been adopted before the defects of the plan as a frame of national government began to manifest themselves. It was remarked by an eminent statesman that they gave authority for the following purposes without being able to execute any one of them: "They may appoint ambassadors, but they cannot defray even the expenses of their tables. They may borrow money in their own name on the faith of the Union, but they cannot pay a dollar. They may coin money, but they cannot import an ounce of bullion. They may make war and determine what number of troops are necessary, but they cannot raise a single soldier. In short, they may declare everything, but they can do nothing."

The colonies relaxed their union into a league of friendship between sovereign and independent states. They constituted a Congress coextensive with the nation, but so hedged and hemmed in with restrictions that the limitation seemed to be the rule, and the grant the occasional exception. The Articles of Confederation, subjected to philosophical analysis, seem to be little more than an enumeration of the functions of a national government, which the Congress constituted by the instrument was not authorized to perform. There was no executive power.

The confederacy of sovereign states made itself known by its fruits. All agreed that something must be done to meet the exigencies of the occasion.

Story closes his remarks on the history of the confederation with declaring " that from the predominance of state jealousies, and the supposed incompatibility of state interests with each other, it became apparent that the confederation, being left without resources and without power, must expire of its own debility. It had lost all vigor, and even ceased to be respected, and the only question which remained was, whether the confederation should be left to a silent dissolution, or an attempt should be made to form a more efficient government."

Such was the condition of the founders of our independence when peace came, in 1783.

" Our fathers raised their flag against a power to which, for purposes of foreign conquest and subjugation, Rome, in the height of her glory, is not to be compared : a power which has dotted the surface of the whole globe with her possessions and military posts, whose morning drum-beat, following the sun in his course and keeping pace with the hours, circles the earth with one contiguous and unbroken strain of the martial airs of England." This description of English power by Mr. Webster points to the time when the fathers raised the national flag of the United States and proclaimed their independence to the world in 1776.

The Parliament of Great Britain asserted a right to tax the colonies in all cases whatsoever : and it was on this question our fathers made the Revolution turn. The amount of taxation was trifling, but the claim itself was inconsistent with liberty, and contained a seminal principle of mischief, the germ of unjust power. This, however plausibly disguised, did not elude the clear and steady eye of the colonists. They detected it, dragged it forth : did not wait till the government was overthrown, or liberty itself was put in extreme jeopardy. The claim, the assertion, threw the whole country into a flame. One mind animated the whole mass. They raised the flag against the British assertion, took up arms, declared war, and poured forth their treasures of blood and means in opposition to British assertion and power.

The government of the United States passed through three forms : (1) the revolutionary, (2) the confederate, (3) the constitutional. The first and the third proceeded equally from the people in their original capacity. The first was supported by Articles of Confederation. The Continental Congress conducted the national affairs until near the close of the Revolution, and extended only to the maintenance of the public liberties of all the States during the contest with Great Britain, and it would naturally terminate with the return of peace and the accomplishment of the ends of the revolutionary contest.

How great, then, would be the danger of the separation of the confederated states into independent communities, acknowledging no common head and acting upon no common system, presented to the consideration of Congress !

The Articles of Confederation constituted a system elaborated with great, persevering, and anxious deliberation, animated with the most ardent patriotism, put together with eminent ability and untiring industry, but vitiated by the difficulty of combining in one general system the various sentiments and interests of a great extent of country divided into so many sovereign and independent communities. It is an error, a popular error, to suppose that the Articles of Confederation carried the country through the war. Those Articles were not finally adopted till the spring of 1781, a few months before the war was virtually brought to a close by the surrender at Yorktown.

Peace came. The United States of America were recognized as free and independent, and, as one people, took their station among the powers of the earth. When the perils of war ceased, and the formal treaty of peace was signed with Great Britain, the confederacy, the Articles of Confederation, proved as incompetent to guard our fathers, conduct and govern them in peace, as it had been to conduct them in war.

COMMERCE.

[Delivered as an introductory lecture to the law students of the University of Louisiana, before treating in detail the various branches of commercial law.]

THE commercial intercourse of nations and that of individuals establish relations, impose duties and obligations, and give birth to contracts often of a peculiar nature. These contracts may be governed by the law of nature and of nations, or by the civil and municipal law, or by the special agreement and stipulations of the parties to them. A just idea of commerce and its operations is necessary to understand its jurisprudence.

I commence, therefore, with an essay on its origin, progress, true character, and nature, and will next consider the history of the law that governs it, the general rules of nature and justice recognized by custom as part of that law, and the special rules of civil or municipal authority applicable to and affecting it.

I propose, then, to treat more in detail of commercial law, in the following order, adopted as the simplest and most comprehensive: (1.) Of mercantile persons, or those by whose intervention trade is carried on. (2.) Of mercantile property, or that which they seek to acquire. (3.) Of mercantile contracts, or the arrangements they may adopt to effect this acquisition. (4.) Of mercantile remedies, or the mode in which these arrangements and their proper execution may be enforced.

The origin of commerce is lost in the mists of antiquity. It is coeval with the first dawn of civilization. It is the first offspring of the right of property.

The buffalo hide, the deerskin, the jerked meat, the gathered corn of an Indian, the cabin itself, with all the accumulated fruits of the earth and the products of the chase in it, are the property of the owner, being the result of his own labor and savings. Having more than his own immediate necessities require, he may labor for what is merely convenient. He may make bows and arrows, or he may trap bears and otters for their skins, and he may exchange these for other articles. Hence the origin of barter, or the exchange of commodities for commodities ; in a word, commerce, *commutatio mercium.* The moment that individuals ceased to supply themselves directly with the various articles and commodities they made use of, that moment must a commercial intercourse have begun to grow up among them.

If the exchange of different products were carried on by the producers themselves, they would necessarily lose a great deal of time and experience much inconvenience, while the work of production itself would meet with perpetual interruption. To obviate this inconvenience, a distinct class of persons — merchants — sprang up, whose business it was to collect the surplus products of men's labor and to exchange these with individuals, who might offer in barter other articles made by themselves. To supersede the necessity of bartering, or exchanging, the innumerable variety of commodities, some measure of value, some common standard of exchange, was requisite, in reference to which every article might be valued : and in most civilized countries the precious metals, gold and silver, as having an intrinsic value which fluctuates very little, were adopted for the purpose.

In some parts of Africa the money consisted of the shells called cowries, in other parts of bars of iron. In Virginia, for a long time, tobacco was the common standard of reference, the money of the country. Sir James

Stuart distinguished it in his political economy as " money of account." in contradistinction from money coin.

Homer, whose writings abound with descriptions of ancient manners and customs, draws a striking picture of barter as it was carried on some three thousand years ago. At the close of the seventh book of the Iliad he describes the arrival of a fleet of merchant vessels from Lemnos freighted with wine, and the Greeks hastening to exchange for it brass, gleaming iron, hides, cattle, and slaves : —

> " Of wine they purchased at their proper cost ;
> And well the plenteous freight supplied the host.
> Each, in exchange, proportioned treasure gave :
> Some, brass or iron ; some, an ox or slave.
> All night they feast, — the Greek and Trojan powers :
> Those in the fields, and these within their towers."
>
> POPE, *Iliad*, Book vii.

But we have an instance of the use of money, and of the custom of merchants at an earlier date, recorded in holy writ, where Abraham is described as weighing to Ephron " four hundred shekels of silver, current money with the merchant." (Gen. xxiii. 16.)

Merchants are generally divided into two classes, the wholesale dealers and the retail dealers. The wholesale dealers purchase various products in the places where they are produced, or are least valuable, and carry them where they are more valuable or more in demand. The retail dealers, having purchased the commodities of the wholesale dealers or the producers, collect them in shops, and sell them in such quantities as may best suit the public demand. Each dealer confines himself to one business, and the necessary business of retail is best conducted by a distinct class of dealers.

The great commerce of every nation is its internal commerce or home trade, — that which is carried on at home, within a nation, and more especially that which is carried on between the inhabitants of the town and those of the country. It consists in the exchange of rude, raw materials for manufactured produce. This exchange is sometimes made immediately, but it is generally effected by the intervention of money, or of some paper that represents money. The country supplies the town with the means of subsistence and the materials of manufacture. The town repays this supply by sending back a part of the manufactured supply to the country. This is mutually beneficial. The country purchases from the town more manufactured goods with the produce of its own labor than it must have employed in preparing them itself. The town affords a market for the surplus produce of the country. The greater the number and revenue of the inhabitants of the town, the more extensive and advantageous is the market. Adam Smith says: " Among all the absurd speculations that have been propagated concerning the balance of trade, it has never been pretended that the country loses by its commerce with the town, or the town by that with the country, which sustains it."

When there is a surplus of rude and manufactured articles for which there is no demand at home, they must be sent abroad, in order to be exchanged for something for which there is a demand at home. As men improved in arts and refinements, their relations gradually became more extended. They learned to trust their lives and property in vessels, to cross rivers, to traverse seas, and to exchange the products of different countries and different climes.

It follows, then, that as subsistence is prior to convenience and luxury, and as the industry which procures the former must be prior to that which ministers to the latter, the cultivation and improvement of the country must have been prior to the establishment of any considerable towns, and some sort of manufactures must have been carried on in those towns before the inhabitants could well think of employing themselves in foreign commerce. And this order of things, we are informed, has always been in some degree observed in every society that possessed any territory.

In illustration of this it may not be useless or uninteresting to trace the rise and progress of civilization and of government in the western part of Europe, from the ruin and degradation which followed the fall of the Roman Empire. Nowhere has this been done better than by Adam Smith in "The Wealth of Nations."

When the German and Scythian hordes overran the western provinces of the Roman Empire, the confusion which followed so great a revolution lasted for several centuries. The rapine and violence exercised against the ancient inhabitants interrupted the commerce between towns and the country. The towns were deserted, the country was left uncultivated, and the western provinces of Europe sank into the lowest state of poverty and barbarism.

The chiefs and principal leaders of those nations acquired to themselves the greater portion of the lands of the provinces. Land was considered the means of power and protection. Every great landlord was a sort of petty prince: his tenants were his subjects. In peace, he was their legislator and judge: in war, their leader. He made war, too, at his discretion, against his neighbor or his sovereign.

The security of a landed estate, and the protection which the owner could give to those who dwelt on it, depended on its greatness. To divide it was to ruin it and expose it to the incursions of its neighbors. Hence, the law of primogeniture was, in process of time, applied to the succession of landed estate; and although, says the author of "The Wealth of Nations," the proprietor of a single acre of land, in any state of Europe, is at present as secure of his possession as the owner of a hundred thousand acres, still the law of primogeniture prevails. The law of entails was a natural consequence of the law of primogeniture, and aided in keeping in the hands of a few individuals immense quantities of land. Large tracts of land were thus engrossed and kept together in particular families.

In the disorderly times which gave rise to those institutions, the great proprietor seldom thought of improving his land. He found sufficient employment in defending his own territories and extending his jurisdiction over those of his neighbors. He had neither leisure nor inclination to attend to the cultivation or improvement of his land.

Those who occupied the land under him were mere tenants at will. They were almost all slaves. They were supposed to belong more directly to the land than to their master. They could be sold with it, but not separately. They could marry, provided it was with their master's consent; and he could not afterwards sell the man and wife to different persons. If he maimed or murdered one of them, he was liable to some small pecuniary penalty. But they were not capable of acquiring property. All that they acquired, they acquired for their master; he could take it from them at pleasure. If little improvement, then, was to be expected from the great proprietors, still less was to be looked for from the degraded tenants.

Such was the condition of the inhabitants of the country after the fall of the Roman Empire. The condition of the inhabitants of the towns and cities was not much better.

13

The great proprietors of land generally lived in forti-fied castles on their own estates, in the midst of their own tenants and dependents. The towns were chiefly inhabited by tradesmen and mechanics, who seem to have been, in those days, of servile or nearly servile condition. The privileges granted to the inhabitants of some of the prin-cipal towns in Europe by ancient charters show what they were before these grants. It was granted as a privilege that they might give away their own daughters in marriage without the consent of their lord; that, upon their death, their own children, and not their lord, should succeed to their goods; and that they might dispose of their own ef-fects by will. They seem to have been a very poor, mean set of people, who used to travel about with their goods from place to place, and from fair to fair, like the hawk-ers and peddlers of the present day. Taxes were levied upon their persons and goods when they passed through manors, when they went over certain bridges, when they carried their goods from place to place in a fair, when they erected a booth or stall therein. These taxes were called in England passage, pontage, lastage, and stallage.

But how servile soever may have been originally the condition of the inhabitants of the towns, they arrived at liberty and independence much earlier than the occupiers of land in the country. Sometimes the king, sometimes a great lord, would grant to particular traders a general exemption from their taxes. Such traders were, upon this account, called free traders. They, in return, usu-ally paid to their protector a sort of annual poll-tax. These taxes and these exemptions were, at first, altogether personal, and affected only particular individuals. The part of the king's revenue arising from poll-taxes in any particular town gradually increased, and it became usual to farm it out for a certain rent, — sometimes to the sheriff of the county, sometimes to other persons. The burghers themselves frequently got credit enough to be allowed to farm the revenues of this sort, arising out of their own town, for a term of years. In process of time, however, it became usual to farm the revenues to them by way of a grant in fee : that is, forever reserving a certain rent, never afterwards to be augmented. The payments having thus become perpetual, the exemptions also became perpetual, and ceased to be personal. They were no longer considered as belonging to individuals as individuals, but as burghers of a particular burgh, which, for this reason, was called " a freeburgh." Along with this grant, the privileges already mentioned were generally bestowed on the burghers of the town, who thus lost the attributes of slavery and villanage, and really became free. They were also generally, at the same time, erected into a corporation, with the privilege of having magistrates and a town council of their own, of making by-laws for their own government, of building walls for their own defense, and of keeping watch and ward. Corporations of this kind were a sort of independent republics erected in the midst of despotism.

In this manner, order and good government were established in towns at a time when the occupiers of land in the country were exposed to every kind of violence.

The inhabitants of towns, by the gradual improvement of their own manufactures, and by importing from abroad the improved manufactures and expensive luxuries of richer countries, furnished the great proprietors of land with something for which they could exchange their surplus produce. By affording a large and ready market for the rude produce of the country, they encouraged its cultivation and further improvement. The wealth acquired by them was, not unfrequently, employed in purchasing land, of which a great part was uncultivated, and they became the best of all improvers, carrying into their

new business their characteristic boldness, energy, and
spirit, with habits of order, economy, and attention.
Thus the manufactures and commerce of the towns contributed to the improvement of the country, and gradually introduced among its inhabitants the like order and
good government which had been previously established
in the cities.

Paley says: " In the neighborhood of trading towns,
and in those districts which carry on a communication
with the markets of 'trading towns,' the husbandmen
are busy and skillful, the peasantry laborious; the land is
managed to the best advantage, and double the quantity
of corn or herbage (articles which are ultimately converted into human provision) raised from it of what the
same soil yields in remoter and more neglected parts of
the country. Wherever a thriving manufactory finds
means to establish itself a new vegetation springs up
around it. Agriculture never arrives at any considerable
degree of perfection when it is not connected with trade :
that is, when the demand for the produce is not increased
by the consumption of trading cities."

This is undoubtedly true. Agriculture never ap-
proaches to perfection in a merely agricultural country.
Knowledge and exertion are stagnant in such a country,
because the stimulants to labor and the means of enjoying
life to the utmost are wanting.

An able and thoroughly informed writer on political
economy remarked some sixty years ago: If we turn our
eyes to Poland, devoid of manufactures and commerce, we
shall behold a picture not unlike this : a few overgrown
landholders living in gross and barbarous magnificence :
the land cultivated by an ignorant peasantry, in a condition that may well be called slavish, where the produce
often rots on the soil, when there are no means of
exporting it and not mouths enough to consume it ! The

agriculture of such a country must be destitute of all spirited improvement, and exertion be paralyzed in both master and slave.

It is obvious that the more sources of wealth there are in a country, the more means of enjoyment, the more and greater incentives to exertion and accumulation, and the more varied and desirable the produce, the greater will be the industry and wealth of the country. A great stimulus to scientific attainments has been the result of manufactures. The great sources of improvement in the comforts and enjoyments of life have been manufactures and commerce.

The inhabitants of the richest and most extensive country, provided it were divided into smaller portions, without any intercourse with each other or with foreigners, could not be otherwise than poor and miserable. Without such intercourse, without commerce or the exchange of commodities, every man would be obliged to subsist exclusively upon the products of his labor. No one could devote his time to any particular pursuit. The necessity which would compel him to turn from one employment to another would prevent him from excelling in any species of work, and diminish the products of his labor. There would be no distinction of employments and professions resulting from a division of labor, no arts or sciences of any sort.

By means of commerce every individual is enabled to avail himself to the utmost of the peculiar advantages of his place, to work on the special materials with which nature has furnished him, to humor his genius or disposition, to betake himself to the task in which he is peculiarly qualified to succeed. The inhabitant of the mountain may betake himself to the culture of his woods and the manufacture of his timber, the owner of the clay pit to the manufacture of his pottery, the owner of

pasture lands to the care of his herds, and the husband-
man to the culture of his fields or the rearing of his
cattle. Any one commodity, it is true, would form but a
small part in the accommodations of human life, but it
may, under the facilities of commerce, be exchanged for
what will procure any or every other part. Thus genius
is stimulated, industry and the mechanic arts flourish, and
the liberal arts themselves are refined.

Man was created not only to inhabit the earth as the
beasts inhabit it, but to subdue it, and to exercise through
natural laws vast power over all the elements when the
energies of his will are directed by wisdom, and when
his choice of methods is founded upon knowledge.

There be three things, says wise Bacon, which make a
nation great and prosperous, — a fertile soil, busy workshops, and easy conveyance of men and things from one
place to another. Where there are no facilities of transport the people are in a state of barbarism. As they
emerge from this condition, their commerce is at first carried on in the rudest manner. Then the peddler and the
pack-horse are seen treading the pathways along the beds
of streams, avoiding the steep hills and rugged mountains which a direct course would require more labor to
cross.

The work of improvement slowly progresses. Commerce, whose increasing benefits are felt in every part
and territorial division of the state, calls for further
means and facilities of transporting and distributing its
various, numerous, and important materials. To enable
the inhabitants of large towns to supply themselves with
the bulky products of the soil, new roads and canals are
necessary and must be established, intersecting the country, and opening an easy access to its remotest extremi-
ties.

Roads, good roads, canals, and rivers have been

denominated national veins and arteries. They are essential to the healthy existence and strength of the state. They diminish the expense and increase the speed of carriage and conveyance of products from place to place, and so enable them to be sooner applied to the purposes for which they are intended. The inhabitants of the town are in this way supplied with the bulky products of the country almost as cheaply as if they lived in country villages; securing them the advantages of concentration, perfecting the division of labor, and supplying the country with proportionally cheap manufactured goods, conveyed at an extremely small expense to its remotest parts. The direct advantages of good roads and canals to agriculture are equally important in the carriage of supplies of manure and other heavy articles, to enrich the luxuriance of fertile soils, and to render those that are poor productive.

Nothing in a state enjoying great facilities of communication is separate and unconnected. All is mutual, reciprocal, and dependent. At length the civil engineer appears and applies his art, and the modern road is constructed. Forests are felled, hills leveled, valleys filled up, mountains excavated, marshes drained, chasms and rivers bestridden with bridges. Through the solid rock beneath the surface of the earth, under the beds of great rivers on whose bosoms navies ride, the road is carried on. The triumph of science is complete. The products of labor are conveyed from place to place by the railway with a swiftness outstripping the speed of the wind. Knowledge, intelligence, the product of thought, are instantaneously transmitted across the ocean, around the world, by the electric telegraph, which literally annihilates both space and time.

The application of steam to the transportation of persons and goods on the land and on the water, to the navi-

gation of rivers, internal lakes, and the ocean, and to
railroad purposes, created a new era in commerce, and
has given new vigor to the march of civilization.

At the opening of the Northern Railroad to Grafton,
N. H., in 1847, Mr. Webster happened to be present, and
was unexpectedly and in the most enthusiastic manner
called upon to address a large number of persons who
were there to witness the ceremonies of the occasion.
He readily complied with the summons. Among other
things, he said: " Fellow-citizens, this railroad may be
said to bring the sea to your doors. You cannot, indeed,
snuff its salt water, but you will taste its best products
as fresh as those who live on its shores. I cannot conceive of any policy more useful to the great mass of the
community than the policy which established these public
improvements. Let me say that in the history of human
inventions there is hardly one so well calculated as that
of railroads to equalize the condition of men. The richest must travel in the cars, for they travel fastest; the
poorest can travel in the cars, while they could not travel
otherwise, because this mode of conveyance costs but
little time and money. Probably there are in the multitude before me those who have friends at such distances
that they could hardly have visited them had not railroads
come to their assistance to save them time and to save
them expense. Men are thus brought together as neighbors and acquaintances who live two hundred miles apart."

The easy intercourse of men, so simply and plainly
stated, their various pursuits and occupations, and the
pleasures which are the fruit of their labor, their education, practical skill, and experience, especially when
enriched with science, advancing industry, and refinement
in the mechanical arts, and commonly producing some
refinements in the liberal, all join in rendering the intercourse of persons more frequent, easy, familiar, and

sociable. They love to talk over their several pursuits, skill, and improvements, to receive and communicate knowledge. So that, as Mr. Hume concludes, besides the improvements which they receive from knowledge and the arts, it is impossible but they must feel an increase of humanity, from the very habit of conversing together and contributing to each other's pleasure and entertainment. Thus, industry, knowledge, and humanity are linked together by an indissoluble chain. Profound ignorance is totally banished, and men enjoy the privilege of rational creatures to think as well as to act, to cultivate the pleasures of the mind as well as those of the body. The same age which produces great philosophers and politicians, renowned generals and poets, usually abounds with skillful weavers and ship-carpenters.

If we turn to foreign trade, and consider commerce as the interchange of the products of industry between different countries and different people, we behold on an extended survey the benefits which are conferred by a division of labor on all the countries of the world.

Providence has disseminated its blessings among the different regions of the world. Each country produces some peculiar fruits which cannot be profitably procured elsewhere. *Non omnis fert omnia tellus.* We cannot acclimate beneath a Southern sky the productions of the North, nor under a Northern sky the productions of the South.

> " This ground with Bacchus, that with Ceres suits ;
> That other loads the trees with happy fruits ;
> A fourth, with grass, unbidden, decks the ground."

No nation is abundantly supplied with any considerable variety of articles of domestic growth, or is content to live upon the productions of its own labor and its own soil. Nature has implanted in every people desires for the productions of other soils and other climates. At the same time their own products are infinitely more in quantity than they themselves need. By means of mutual intercourse and traffic, nations are thus enabled mutually to supply one another's wants, and multiply and cheapen the conveniences and enjoyments of life. They are made in some sort dependent upon one another, and are united together by their common interest.

Observe for a moment how many of our comforts and even necessaries are derived from commerce and intercourse with strangers. The ships at our levee are laden with the harvest of every clime; our stores are furnished with the choicest manufactures of foreign artisans, — silks, cottons, hardware, porcelain, jewelry, laces from Brussels, Lyons, Paris, Geneva, Sheffield, Manchester, Liverpool, London; our tables are supplied with spices, oils, wines; China furnishes us with tea, and the remotest corners of the earth contribute to our pleasures or wants. Addison's pleasing description of a lady's dress more than a century and a half ago continues to describe the dress of the present day: "The single dress of a woman of quality is often the product of an hundred climes. The muff and the fan come together from the different ends of the earth. The scarf is sent from the torrid zone, and the tippet from beneath the pole: the brocade petticoat rises out of the mines of Peru, and the diamond necklace out of the bowels of Indostan." Mr. McCulloch states that the people of Great Britain owe more than half of all they enjoy to their intercourse with others. It is to the products and the arts derived from others, and to the emulation inspired by their competition and example, that we are mainly indebted for the progress we have made, as well as for that we are yet destined to make.

It is certain that in most nations foreign commerce has preceded any refinements in home manufactures or such as were fit for distant sale. It supplies men with new commodities, and awakens new desires and new tastes. The temptation is stronger to make use of foreign commodities, which are entirely new to us and ready for use, than to make improvements on any domestic commodities, which always advance by slow degrees, and never affect us by their novelty.

The profit in exporting what is superfluous at home to nations abroad, and importing foreign commodities, useful, pleasant, novel, improved, refined, is great. The trade stimulates domestic industry, improves every branch of commerce, of agriculture, and of manufactures, and stirs up a spirit of enterprise, of invention and competition in making us acquainted with foreign arts. Imitation soon diffuses all those arts, while domestic manufacturers emulate the foreign in their improvements, and work up every home commodity to the utmost perfection of which it is susceptible.

But foreign commerce imparts not merely the commodities, but with them the knowledge, experience, and useful practices of other nations. It diffuses knowledge, and conveys its pleasures and the blessings of civilization to the remotest regions. It distributes the gifts of science and art, and gives to each particular country the means of profiting by the inventions and discoveries of others. The inventions and discoveries of Fulton and Whitney, of Arkwright the cotton spinner, of Watt and Bolton the engineers, of Wedgwood and Bentley the potters, and the labors and speculations of Galileo, Kepler, Lavoisier, Laplace, Newton, Black, and others, have benefited all nations.

Everything in the world is to be acquired by labor, and labor is to be performed by natural law directed and applied by reason and wisdom. It is by compelling nature to work for us that the great improvements of

modern times in manufactures and in commerce have
been made. This it is that raises us so much above the
savage state of society; that makes us equal to the most
gigantic efforts, and endows us with almost superhuman
power. We have put in requisition the powers of wind
and water, of heat and cold, of magnetism and electricity.
We have made the planetary system subservient to our
hourly enjoyments, and we are proceeding daily in the
glorious career of overcoming the obstacles which nature
has placed in the path of our wishes, and of subjecting
all her elements to our control. This has been done
by mathematicians, natural philosophers, chemists, and
mechanics, rich, beneficent, ennobling, and enduring gifts
of science.

From the character and nature of commerce, its connection with and influence upon good order, faith, and
just government, and its diffusion of knowledge, various
materials, comforts, pleasures, and ornaments of life, it
must ever flourish in a wise and free government. The
spirit of commerce is congenial with liberty. And if we
trace her, in her progress through Tyre, Athens, Syra-
cuse, Carthage, Venice, Florence, Genoa, Antwerp, Hol-
land, England, the United States, we shall always find
her to have fixed her seat in free governments.

Milton, great poet and great man, speaks of "the
mountain nymph, sweet Liberty." From her lofty seat
she looks down upon and visits the valleys, the plains,
and seashores, imparting knowledge, truth, courage, enterprise, wisdom, love of law, and protection of equal human
rights. A distinguished American historian says: "The
seaboard would seem to be the natural seat of liberty.
There is something in the very presence, in the atmosphere of the ocean, which invigorates not only the physical, but the moral energies of man. The adventurous
life of the mariner familiarizes with dangers, and early

accustoms him to independence. Intercourse with various climes opens new and more copious sources of knowledge; and increased wealth brings with it an augmentation of power and consequence. It was in the maritime cities scattered along the Mediterranean that the seeds of liberty, both in ancient and modern times, were implanted and brought to maturity."

Foreign trade is to all the countries of the world what home trade is to the different portions and provinces of the same country. It is an extension of the benefits conferred upon man by a division of labor. As individuals are benefited in trade and riches, and the several States of our Union are rendered happier and wiser, more opulent, refined, and powerful, by the division of labor and free commerce and unrestricted intercourse one with another, so our imperial republic, controlling our foreign relations and trade under its national, democratic, federal government, — *E Pluribus Unum*, — increases in power, wealth, and happiness, in proportion to our extensive commerce and varied labor in manufactures and agriculture, inseparable from it. The same train of consequences is observable in the world at large.

The Creator gave man dominion over the earth, and over the sea, and over the air : to master them, to make them minister to our highest power. The application of science to the arts imparts skill and strength, intellectual and moral energy. Mind conquers and controls matter. Every natural agent, wind, water, gravity, is made to work. Machinery performs what formerly was the task of human hands.

The application of steam to commercial purposes, and the transportation of goods and persons, on the land and on the water, has been already noticed. The newspaper press informs us that a calculation has been made by some foreign arithmeticians of the potent agency of steam

in the world. The calculation states the horse power of
England per annum, of the United States, of Germany,
of France, of Austria, exclusive of locomotive power;
then states the horse power of the locomotives in France,
of fixed engines, of steamers, etc., and concludes: "The
total horse power of all the machines and engines worked
by steam in the world is estimated at 80,000,000. Now
each horse is equal to ten men, so that the whole steam
power of the globe represents a daily working power of
800,000,000 men. Two German savants reckoned the
population of the globe at 1,455,923,000, and the number
of males between sixteen and sixty-five at about one third
of the population, making the total of men of working age
500,000,000. As steam does the work of about 800,000,000
men, it follows that the power of laborers and resources
of industry have nearly trebled in fifty years, since the
steam engine spread its beneficent influence over all civilized countries."

It may not be superfluous to state how, under the power
of mind, steam, one of the most powerful forces of nature,
has been reduced to obedience — governed, controlled,
and made subservient to the human family — by subjecting its invariable energies to the variable conditions of
adjustment: blending mental and material laws, and intimately connected with commerce, home and foreign. Mr.
Webster described its potent agency in a lecture before
the Mechanics' Institution, in 1828: —

"Everywhere practicable, everywhere efficient, it has
an arm a thousand times stronger than that of Hercules,
and to which human ingenuity is capable of fitting a
thousand times as many as Briareus. Steam is found in
triumphant operation on the seas, — we may now add the
oceans, — and, under the influence of its strong propulsion,
the gallant ship

'Against the wind, against the tide,
  Still steadies, with an upright keel.'

It is on the rivers, it is on highways and along the courses of land conveyance, it is at the bottom of mines a thousand feet below the earth's surface, it is in the mill and in the workshops of the trades. It rows, it pumps, it excavates, it carries, it draws, it lifts, it hammers, it spins, it weaves, it prints. It seems to say to men, 'Leave off your manual labor, give over your bodily toil; bestow but your skill and reason to the directing of my power, and I will bear the toil, with no muscle to grow weary, no nerve to relax, no breast to feel faintness.' "

It is impossible to conjecture to what further uses and improvements in mechanical arts and operations this tremendous force may be applied, or to ascribe any limit to its progress.

The greatness of a state and the happiness of its people are inseparable in regard to commerce. It augments the power of the state by increasing its stock of labor, as well as the riches and happiness of individuals by increasing employment, the multitude of mechanic arts and their products, and the persons who are employed in producing them and who share in their product. It stimulates industry : it imparts and diffuses knowledge and skill ; it supplies new objects of desire and materials for labor ; it leads to imitation, skill, rivalry, improvement, social intercourse, refinement, and humanity : it gives a lively spirit, healthy activity, strength, and energy to the mind.

Mr. Everett truly states that merchants have ever been friends of learning and liberty, and enemies of tyranny and despotism. It was certainly so with American merchants during our revolutionary struggle.

In the dawn of civilization alphabetical writing was used among the Phoenician merchants. One thousand years after, these merchants were the champions of liberty.

When Alexander carried on his crusade against Asia, the merchants of Tyre detained him by arms longer than Darius could with all the armies of the East.

When, in succeeding centuries, the Romans were marching to universal empire, the commercial city, Carthage, checked their progress.

The emancipation of Europe from the iron despotism of the barons, under the feudal system, began with the privileges granted to the cities.

The colonization of our country sprang mainly from religion and commercial adventure.

The British navigation act was the foundation of colonial grievances. The colonists complained and struggled against the monopoly of the mother country. They saw no barriers on the sea, and could not patiently submit to artificial restraints. But when these restraints were removed, commerce went forth, like an uncaged eagle, who rushes out at length to his native element, and exults as he bathes his undazzled eyes in the midday sunbeam or pillows his breast upon the storm. Not content with the broad circuit taken by the trading nations of Europe, the commerce of America penetrated not only the remotest haunts of European trade, — the Mediterranean, the Baltic, and the White seas, — but engaged in the trade with Hindostan and China, explored new markets on islands and coasts, before unapproached by modern commerce, and opened the way for traffic with Japan.

A word or two more in regard to American commerce.

During the revolutionary war our commerce was nearly annihilated by the superior naval power of our enemy, and the return of peace enabled foreign nations, and especially Great Britain, to monopolize our home trade. The Articles of Confederation conferred no power on the confederacy to regulate commerce, but left it to the control of each State for itself. It was found impossible to excite or foster enterprise in trade under the influence of jarring state regulations. Thirteen States, each with power to regulate commerce, and each looking only to its own interest! A navigation act passed by one State was defeated by the legislation of another. Duties were levied in one State, while free trade was adopted in another. We were thus the victims of our own imbecility, and reduced to a subjection to the commercial regulations of other nations, notwithstanding our boasted freedom. The country was losing all the advantages of its position. American navigation could not compete with foreign. Foreign ships had free admission into our ports, while American ships were loaded with heavy exactions or prohibitions abroad. Foreign supplies flooded the country. The national industry was paralyzed, and the Revolution itself was beginning to be regarded as a doubtful blessing. Every attempt to bring the state legislatures into any harmony of action or any pursuit of a common object had failed, when, in 1786, Virginia proposed a general convention of delegates from all the States, " to consider how far a uniform system of commercial regulations may be necessary to their common interest and permanent harmony." This was the first step in the train of measures that led to the adoption of the Constitution of the United States.

Other objects and other considerations, besides pressing commercial necessity, influenced the fathers of our country in framing that Constitution. The confederacy had made itself known by its bitter fruits; it was a failure, — in the words of Mr. Adams, "a wretched and ignominious failure." The Articles of Confederation enumerated the functions of a national government, which the Congress instituted by the instrument was not authorized to perform. The jealousy of delegated power pervaded

14

every part. There was no executive power. Congress
was authorized to make war and conclude peace, to contract debts and bind the nation by treaties of commerce,
yet the Articles of Confederation had withheld from Congress the power of regulating the commerce of the Union
and levying money by taxation upon the people: they
could contract, but could not perform.

The revolutionary debt remained unpaid, the national
treasury was bankrupt, the country was destitute of
credit, and, to defray its necessary expenses and charges,
the only power of Congress was to issue its requisitions
to the States, which they neglected. The whole government, therefore, was little more than a name, incapable
of securing and protecting the interests of the country,
and made subservient to the policy of foreign nations.

Such was the painful, feeble, disgraceful condition of
the country, when, after a mature, patriotic deliberation,
the people of every State came to the conclusion that,
for the rescue of their character, their interest, liberty,
power, and dignity, a national government ought to be
established. Prudently and wisely this task was performed.

The framers of the Constitution of the United States
were wise, patriotic, and experienced. They were great
reformers, and, when they assembled in federal convention, deemed it a solemn duty to frame an efficient plan
of government for the United States, to be submitted to
the people of the States for their mature consideration and
judgment, and adoption or rejection.

And the people of the several States calmly and deliberately set aside and abolished the imbecile, impotent government of the confederation, and adopted the Constitution of the United States. The Constitution was then
promulgated to all the nations of the earth with this preamble or proclamation : " We, the people of the United

States, in order to form a more perfect union, establish justice, insure domestic tranquillity, provide for the common defense, promote the general welfare, and secure the blessings of liberty to ourselves and our posterity, do ordain and establish this Constitution for the United States of America."

The organization of the government conformably to the Constitution and to give it practical operation was effected in 1789, under the administration of Washington. Life, vigor, power, and new character were at once imparted to it. Congress proceeded to exercise the powers conferred upon it. A comprehensive system of revenue was adopted; taxes, imposts, and duties were laid and collected by the government without any requisition on the States; provision was made to pay the public debt and provide for the general welfare; the foreign commerce was wisely regulated, the interests of the country were duly protected, and its other foreign relations were considered and treated with ability, with dignity, with a becoming spirit, — the spirit of nationality, the nationality of America. The laws of the United States were executed and carried into effect in every part of the Union.

In regard to commerce, the main subject of this disquisition, the Constitution ordains : " The Congress shall have power to regulate commerce with foreign nations and among the several States, and with the Indian tribes." The grant is plenary and exclusive; it embraces the whole and each and every part of the country, and the whole and each and every subject of commerce. The power is vital to the Union. It put an end to the serious dissension among the States themselves, and to the irritation and jealousy caused by the difference of their regulations. It established a uniform system, and harmony, and coöperation for the general welfare; one rule, one commercial law and regulation among the States that stand upon the territory of this grand republic, annihilating the causes of domestic feuds and rivalries, compelling every State to regard the interest of each as the interest of all, and diffusing over all the benefits and blessings of a free and rapid exchange of commodities upon the footing of perfect equality.

In nothing has the Constitution displayed more profound wisdom than in the grant of this power. It served to consolidate the Union and render it more perfect. It gave to our commerce in every foreign market an American national name and influence. As we were one people in making war and one people in making peace, so were we one in regulating commerce. It enabled the government to place the United States upon a just and rightful equality with foreign nations, to compel them to abandon their unjust and selfish policy, and to protect our commercial interests against their injurious competitions.

It seems to be agreed among all enlightened men that the effects produced by commerce are national wealth, circulation of capital, augmentation of the public revenues, of the general ease, comfort, and prosperity of the people, and of the power of the state.

England furnishes an illustrious example of this, and our national progress confirms it. Statisticians, statesmen, historians, orators, philosophers, have contrasted the feeble and disheartening condition of our forefathers under the government of the confederacy, with its ill-regulated and defective system, which withheld from Congress the power to regulate commerce, and our present condition under the government as it has been formed and modified by the Constitution of the United States.

They observe the vast extent to which our country has extended herself, stretching from the British possessions, the waters of the St. Lawrence, and the great lakes of the continent to Mexico and the waters of the Rio Grande, and from the Atlantic Ocean to the Pacific Ocean, — the thirty-eight sovereign States, the Territories, and the public land. They observe her rapid and steady progress in all the arts, mechanic, useful, refined; in science, and its agency and application to the wants, the comforts, the pleasures, the refinements, and pure enjoyments of human life. They point out her highways, roads, canals; the network of railroads and telegraphic lines by which the country is reticulated, developing her resources, and uniting emphatically, in metallic bands, all parts of the Union; her seacoast towns; her harbors and ports and lighthouses; the paths of her commerce, wide as the world, on the great seas, and her navy, which takes no law from superior force: the glory and the name of the great republic, the great example of popular government, of freedom and industry, of justice and equality, — stimulating and quickening the spirit and energy of its active, enterprising, adventurous, and well-informed citizens to emulate the virtues and actions of their ancestors, who established public liberty in America, to the safety, honor, and welfare of the country.

ADDRESS TO LAW STUDENTS.

[Delivered in 1877 to the graduating class of law students by Mr. Hunt as president of the University of Louisiana.]

GENTLEMEN, — In pursuance of the duty assigned me as President of the University of Louisiana, under the Constitution and laws of the State, I do now publicly confer upon each of you here presented by the Dean and Faculty of the law department, with the approval of the administrators of the University, therefore, the degree of Bachelor of Laws, with all the rights, honors, dignities, and privileges appertaining to that degree.

Diplomas, written evidence of the degree conferred, are in the hands of the Dean, and will be delivered to those entitled to them.

Circumstances unhappily preventing the learned Dean of the Faculty from delivering, according to appointment, the usual appropriate address on the graduation of the class, at his desire and on your request I have undertaken to perform the duty on this occasion, and must ask your indulgence, your kind consideration and judgment, for the plain discourse you are about to hear.

Gentlemen graduates, you have completed the course of your collegiate studies, and are about to enter upon the active business of life, to exert your powers and virtues, and to convert to private and public use the learning and ability which you have acquired in the law school of the University. You are just going forth to attempt the practice of law, to do its hard work, to kindle with its excitations, to be agitated by its responsibilities, to sound its depths and shoals of honor. Some of you may be exposed to difficulties. Determine to surmount them with courage, or to bear them with resignation. Be prudent, industrious, and ever instant in the pursuit of knowledge.

In discharging the official duty of addressing you, I am moved by a solicitude for your personal welfare, and a regard for the profession and divine nature of law.

Whatever progress you have made in jurisprudence, you must be sensible that if, relying on your present attainments, you abandon study, you can never become distinguished. If you aspire to respectability and to eminence, you must labor long and hard, cheerfully and heartily. Labor is the condition of success and greatness. It is a fine remark of Chancellor Kent that "it appears to be the general order of Providence manifested in the constitution of our nature that everything valuable in human acquisition should be the result of toil and labor."

Nor should this truth discourage you. *Labor vincit omnia.* And labor is in itself agreeable to the well-organized mind, anxious for improvement and rejoicing in its progress. At this day, no mere force of genius however extraordinary, no combination of natural faculties however rare and exquisite, no general information however vast and extensive, unaccompanied with a profound knowledge of jurisprudence and of the peculiar system of laws in a commonwealth, can constitute an efficient practical lawyer. The progress you have already made in the law must convince you of this, while that very progress gives assurance of success to the persevering student.

But you should by no means neglect the general culture of letters and of the arts and sciences, merely because your labors are to be chiefly devoted to the law. The different branches of learning bear an intimate relation to one another. Consider for a moment what a lawyer must know and what he has to do if he be in good practice.

He must be more or less acquainted with the mechanical arts and sciences, with modern inventions and discoveries, with the details of trade, commerce, and manufactures. He must put himself in the way of all the liberal opinions which modern investigation has brought into view. He must trace the laws from the first rough sketches to the more perfect draughts, from the causes that produced them through all the effects, good and bad, that they produced.

The perfect lawyer should be familiar with every study. He must pry into the secret recesses of the human heart, and explore to their sources the passions and appetites and feelings of mankind. He should watch the motions of the dark and malignant passions as they silently approach the chambers of the soul in its first slumbers. He should catch the first warm rays of sympathy and benevolence as they play around the character. He should unlock the treasures of history for instruction and admonition. He must drink in the lessons and the spirit of philosophy, which is conversant with men's business and interests : which dwells, says Story, not in vain imaginations and platonic dreams, but which stoops to life, and enlarges the boundaries of human happiness, sits by us in the closet, cheers us by the fireside, walks with us in the fields and highways, kneels with us at the altar, and lights up the enduring flame of patriotism.

The morals of the law are pure and just. No men are so constantly called upon in their practice to exemplify the duties of good faith, strict integrity, and chivalric honor as lawyers. To them is often entrusted the protection of the peace and comfort as well as the property of whole families, of personal rights and personal character, of domestic harmony and parental authority, or it may be the vindication of innocence against private injustice. Rank and wealth and patronage may be on one side, and poverty and distress on the other. The oppressor may belong to the very circle of society in which they love to move, and where many seductive influences may be employed to win their silence. Some crafty pretext, some captivating delusion, may mask the real design of the oppressor. The press may be employed to poison public opinion, and to intimidate the sufferer who resorts to a court, the citadel of public justice, the true guardian in all governments, and, especially in free governments, of the whole community. He calls upon his advocate, the lawyer, to maintain the supremacy of the law against power and wealth, to vindicate his rights, to require damages, as the case may be, from the violator of his domestic peace, or to expose to scorn the subtle contrivances of fraud. In such cases, the attempt to unravel the fraud and expose the injury may be full of delicacy, and may incur severe displeasure among friends. But it is on such occasions the advocate rises to the dignity and the great moral obligations of his profession. It may be that his profession calls him to different duties. He may be required to defend against the arm of the government a party standing charged with some odious crime, real or imaginary. He is not at liberty to desert even the guilty wretch in his lowest estate, but he is to take care that even here the law shall not be broken or bent to bring him to punishment. He will at such times, from a sense of professional duty as well as from compassion, freely give his talents to the cause, and never surrender the victim until the judgment of his peers has convicted him upon legal evidence.

Bear this in mind: when once you undertake the cause of a client, you make it your own, and it becomes entitled to the same attention and earnest interest which you give to your own affairs. Nay, you are bound to protect that client at all hazards and costs even to yourselves. I will not say that you are to have no scruples about any act whatever that may benefit your client, for such a rule would overturn all morals. Nor will I say that you should separate the duties of a patriot from those of an advocate. The administration of justice is the great end of human society, and justice the great end of law, sovereign law, which,

> "O'er thrones and globes elate,
> Sets empress, crowning good, repressing ill."

I repeat, the law is the only recognized sovereign of freemen. Upon her supreme and steady rule depends the secure enjoyment of life, of liberty and property. It is the remark of a wise, learned, and philosophic jurist and statesman that in all the elaborate policy by which free states have sought to preserve themselves, there is none so sure, so indispensable, as justice, justice to all: justice to foreign nations of whatever class of greatness or weakness, to public creditors, alien or native; justice to every individual citizen, down to the feeblest and the least beloved; justice in the assignment of political and civil rights; justice between man and man, every man and every other. To observe and to administer this virtue steadily, uniformly, and at whatever cost, this, the best policy and the final course of all governments, is preëminently the policy of free governments. It is the true interest, the best, the only policy, and the highest glory of a country.

Mr. Choate, an eminent lawyer of Massachusetts, declared: "In all political systems and in all times, the profession has seemed to possess a twofold nature, to be tired by the spirit of liberty, and yet to hold fast the sentiments of order and reverence, and the duty of subordination. It has recognized and vindicated the rights of man, and yet has reckoned it always among the most precious of those rights to be shielded and led by the divine nature and the immortal reason of law."

The love of liberty and the love of law characterized the wise and illustrious fathers of our country; and liberty and law, intimately united, were made the basis of justice and American government. The profession of law, useful, honorable, and distinguished, is, undoubtedly, the great ornament and one of the defenses and securities of free institutions, indispensable to and conservative of public liberty. Without liberty, law loses its nature and its name, and becomes oppression. Without law, liberty also loses its nature, and becomes licentiousness. Locke says, " Where there is no law, there is no freedom." And Lord Chatham, after his fashion, declared, "This I know : where law ends, tyranny begins."

The rightful end of all civil government is to secure freedom. Its highest office is to watch over the liberties of each and all. Its very chains and prisons have the general freedom for their aim ; they are just only when used to curb oppression and wrong, to disarm him who wars against others' rights, who, by invading property or life, would substitute force for the reign of equal laws. Checks on licentiousness that would trespass on right, wholesome restraints on others to keep off from us, the checks and restraints on legislative, executive, and judicial powers in our American system of government, are safeguards of individual rights, a bulwark, fortress, security of public liberty.

In all the past period of our history, the lawyers of the country have been conspicuous for an ardent spirit of liberty. inflexible adherence to principle, intrepidity, and knowledge of their rights. Many of those who stirred up and made the people ready for revolution were lawyers. They argued, they refined, distinguished, explained about their rights, and were prepared to maintain them with unflinching courage. They were foremost in vindicating the true interpretation of the charters of the colonies, and

in exposing the infringements which led to the Stamp Act
and tea tax, and to the Revolution and our national independence. "A love of freedom," said Mr. Burke in
1775, " is the predominating feature in the character of
the Americans. And this is to be attributed, in no mean
degree, to their education. In no country, perhaps, in the
world is the law so general a study . . . *abeunt studia
in mores*. . . . In other countries, the people, more simple
and of a less mercurial cast, judge of an ill principle in
government only by an actual grievance ; here they anti-
cipate the evil and judge of the grievance by the badness
of the principle. They augur misgovernment at a distance, and snuff the approach of tyranny in every tainted
breeze."

So it was ; and it has been claimed, truly and justly
claimed, that in the following time the American bar, —
springing into existence by revolution, and justifying that
revolution only on a principle of natural law, — by its
professional appreciation of order, obedience, restraint,
its free and lofty spirit, its profound and wide intimacy
with all liberty, and, above all, English liberty, displayed
the wisdom of statesmen in framing a constitution for
the United States, and completing the revolution with an
original system of government, free republican government, and a grand written code of public laws, approved,
ordained, and established by the free people of the several
States.

I do but repeat what has been often and commonly
remarked, and is undoubtedly true, when I say our system of government is peculiar and complicated. It is
original in its character, truly and emphatically our own,
American, without example or parallel. We have state
sovereignties, each exercising legislative, executive, and
judicial powers, and all standing on an equal footing,
and we have a general government, under which all these

States are united: and it is the very beauty of our system that the federal and the state governments are thus kept distinct. The people of each State formed the Constitution of the State. The people of the United States ordained and established the Constitution of the United States. Mr. Webster said he defied the wit of man to devise anything preferable, and anything more suitable on the whole for the great interests of a great people spread over a large portion of the globe, than the provision of local legislation for local and municipal purposes, with a general government for general purposes. The States are united,

> "Not chaos like, together crushed and bruised,
> But, like the world, harmoniously confused :
> Where order in variety we see,
> And where, though all things differ, all agree."

In constructing the American Constitution, with the reconciliation of universal liberty with the philosophy of government, the distribution of its powers into separate departments, the checks and balances necessary to make it a government of laws, and not of men : in recognizing the right of the people to make all the laws and to make the Constitution, and the wisdom of the people in restraining themselves from the disorderly exercise of power by the supremacy of the Constitution while it exists, and by the establishment of a fundamental organic rule to test the legislation of the day by the standard of truth and time, the lawyers and other wise, experienced, and patriotic men united and coöperated to secure the blessings of liberty and establish justice.

The Articles of Confederation, a mere compact of state governments, had proved a miserable failure. The federal Constitution was framed and a united government was established, with power to act on the individual citizen, by the concurrent vote of Congress, the States, and the people. The separate state governments remained unimpaired for all the purposes of purely local administration, the people of the several States forming the people of the Union; and the Constitution of the United States, and the laws made in pursuance thereof, are declared to be the supreme law of the land, anything in the Constitution or laws of any State notwithstanding.

It is this system of government and these political principles, reconciling the strength of a great with the freedom of a small State, that form what has been called "a decentralized republican empire." The working of the system appears from the changes that have been wrought in the condition and prospects of the American people. On the 30th of April, 1789, the chancellor of the State of New York, from the balcony of the City Hall, administered to George Washington the solemn oath, "faithfully to execute the office of President of the United States, and, to the best of his ability, to preserve, protect, and defend the Constitution of the United States."

His administration fixed the character of the Constitution as a practical system of government, and settled upon firm foundations the execution of the Constitution and laws. He laid the corner-stone of the original Capitol on the 18th day of September, 1793. He was then at the head of the government, which at that time was weak in resources, burdened with debt, just struggling into political existence and respectability, and agitated by the heaving waves which were overturning European thrones. On the 4th of July, 1851, Millard Fillmore, President of the United States, laid the corner-stone of the addition to the Capitol, and Daniel Webster, Secretary of State of the United States, at his request, delivered an address to the people assembled to witness the ceremony, — wise and patriotic, describing a degree of national progress with which the world can furnish no parallel.

It is impossible to review the course of that progress to the year 1876 without wonder and amazement at every step. See the vast area of territory to which our country has expanded herself; her advance in science, and its application to the useful arts, in commerce, manufactures, and development of resources; in justly acquiring the name of the great republic, demanding nothing wrong and submitting to nothing wrong in her intercourse with foreign nations, and dispensing justice according to the Constitution and laws of the land at home.

Gentlemen, it is the duty of the present American bar to aid in the interpretation of these Constitutions, state and federal; to ascertain their true construction, the powers vested in the state governments by their respective state Constitutions, or remaining in their people, and to administer and maintain them : to interpret, administer, and maintain the Constitution of the United States in the plenary grant of its specific powers, given expressly or by necessary implication to the government of the United States, which the people have made the supreme law of the land. In the performance of these duties the profession is raised to a function by which the republic may be saved.

I desire to impress upon you the value of storing your minds with the learning of former ages. Some knowledge of the ancient languages is essential to the civil lawyer. A great English jurist remarks : " You can scarce find an eminent man in modern times who has not formed his genius and improved his taste and talents for executing works of immortal renown by a thorough study of the Greek and Roman classics." Not that their ideas are more just or that their learning is more profound than those of many moderns, but because from their writings you will imbibe the spirit of true genius and liberty. and habituate yourselves to their copiousness and elegance. The speeches of Demosthenes are models of eloquence, and kindle within us the fire of ancient times and of liberty. I need not urge you to cultivate this noble art of persuasion. The just estimation of eloquence depends upon the virtuous and rational use made of it. " In peaceful times," said the Roman orator, " she flourishes, protectress of liberty, patroness of improvement, guardian of all the blessings that can be showered upon the mass of humankind. Nor is her form ever seen but on grounds consecrated to free institutions." But no splendor of talents, no perfection in art, can compensate for the want of moral principle. Personal virtue is the foundation of all real worth, of true dignity of character, of genuine piety, and of the most extensive usefulness. No man wholly destitute of moral principle can ever be a great lawyer. It is almost impossible to separate the impression made by the character of a speaker from the things he says. An opinion of honor and probity in the person who undertakes to persuade adds to the influence of his speech : a contrary opinion detracts from its authority.

In the practice of your profession, gentlemen, you should eschew and discountenance all chicanery, all petty and vexatious quibbles and artifices. Such things are a reproach to public justice, and never fail to bring those who resort to them into contempt and odium.

Be frank and honorable, the avowed advocates of truth and justice. Never violate them yourselves, and never advise others to violate them. In your intercourse with your brethren of the bar, you should be obliging, kind, and courteous. Never treat with arrogance or contempt those who possess talents inferior to your own. God has seen fit to bestow on different individuals different kinds and degrees of mental and corporeal endowments. You should be especially careful, if you possess extraordinary powers of wit and sarcasm, not to exercise those powers unjustly and unkindly, nor to indulge in ridicule and personalities unprovoked and uncalled for.

Gentlemen, graduates, lawyers, in the discharge of your professional duties you should always be faithful, undaunted advocates of civil and religious liberty, of justice and the rights of individuals. The true American lawyer, informed, prompt, bold, will be foremost in upholding and protecting the rights of the people, in inculcating a proper regard for law, and in enforcing a steady devotion to constitutional government. Kind-hearted and generous, his ear will ever be open to cries of injured innocence, and his heart will beat in sympathy with the distresses of wronged and suffering humanity. He will never aid the unjust man by wresting the law to his purposes, to despoil another of his property, or to obstruct him in obtaining possession of it. To the poor and just man. overwhelmed by inevitable misfortunes, and involved in difficulties by the suspicions and persecutions of disappointed gain or malignant avarice, he will prove a stay and support, a friend and champion, a guardian angel to guide him through the mazes of a legal labyrinth to security and peace.

I feel that I need not impress upon you the duty of cherishing a love for your Alma Mater, and of advancing, for the honor of Louisiana, her fame and usefulness. The principles and the learning which you carry home with you are the best evidence of her charter. She now sends you forth into the field of competition and labor. The affection, the good wishes, the confidence of all her professors attend you.

15

REPORT UPON THE LAW OF EVIDENCE.

[In 1861 the Senate of the State of Louisiana, having had
under consideration a proposed amendment to the law of evidence of the State, listened to the following report of Mr. Hunt
in behalf of the Judiciary Committee.]

AT the last annual session of the legislature a bill was
introduced similar to that now before the Senate, for the
amendment of the law of evidence in this State. It was
referred to the Committee on the Judiciary, who reported
it back favorably to the Senate, but no further action was
had upon it. They did not press the immediate consideration of the bill, because the change which it proposed
to make in the law of evidence is radical, and overturns
rules long established, and which, until a comparatively
recent date, received the commendation of the ablest
jurists of Europe and America. It is true, the principles
embodied in the bill had been thoroughly discussed by
Jeremy Bentham and his followers, and had, under the
lead of Lords Denman, Campbell, Brougham, and others,
been successively adopted by the British Parliament and
made part of the English law. They had been advocated
with masterly ability by Edward Livingston in the introductory report to the Code of Evidence, prepared under
the authority of a law of the State passed in 1822.
They had been adopted, too, by States of our late Union,
eminent for their polity and the wise administration of
justice. But the attention of the legislators and jurists
of Louisiana did not appear to have been turned to the
subject; and it was deemed prudent to defer final action
upon the matter until the present time.

The object of the bill is to render large classes of persons competent to testify, whose testimony is excluded by the existing law.

The law excludes the testimony of persons in a case who are interested in its result.

It excludes the testimony of parties in their own favor.

It excludes the testimony of husband and wife for or against one another.

It excludes the testimony of ascendants and descendants in civil cases.

It excludes the testimony of persons who are deficient in religious belief.

It excludes the testimony of persons who have been convicted of an infamous offense.

The bill proposes to alter the law in these particulars, and to receive the testimony of the persons now repudiated as witnesses, leaving its value to be estimated by the judging power.

Before entering upon the examination of the several provisions of the bill, the committee desire to advert to some general principles connected with them all.

Every person who institutes a suit is bound to state such facts as will show his claim to be founded in law. The facts may be either admitted or denied. If admitted, it becomes the duty of the court to determine what the law is upon the facts; if denied, they must be proved, and this proof must be made by evidence. The duty of judicial tribunals embraces the investigation of facts, as well as the application of the principles of law to such as are ascertained. Law, indeed, can be administered only on the assumption of the truth of the facts to which it is applied.

The object of evidence is the establishment of truth. Courts of justice employ the same means of investigating and determining disputed facts as mankind in general make use of, except so far as positive laws interfere. It has been truly said that the organization of courts, the enumeration of rights, the means of asserting them, the denunciation of penalties for infringing them, and the rules of procedure are only preparatory steps to the trial, which in itself is but the examination of evidence. So that ultimately the whole machinery of jurisprudence in all its branches is contrived for the purpose of enabling the judging power or tribunal to determine on the truth or falsehood of every litigated statement. This can only be done by hearing and examining everything that will contribute to bring the mind to the determination. If we refuse to hear anything that will produce the effect, we determine on imperfect evidence, and of course are subjected to the chance of making an erroneous decision. All exclusions of evidence are, therefore, injurious to the object of all investigation, — the discovery of truth. In the ordinary affairs of life, in the investigation of truth, no evidence is rejected. Suppose you wish to inquire concerning some delinquence that has occurred in your house, and that you have an inmate who saw what occurred: would you refuse to ask him any questions, or to hear him, because you know he has been heretofore guilty of lying? No, you would hear his statement, and, allowing for his propensity, judge whether it affected him in the case before you. In all other matters of inquiry and investigation, everything is examined, every one is heard, and he who is to judge relies upon his own power to discriminate. In law alone he is taught to distrust that power, and to reject all evidence that may possibly lead him astray. Is this reasonable?

To this question the common and the civil lawyers answer "Yes," and extol the wisdom of the rules which exclude the testimony of certain classes of persons. In this respect they argue: "The law follows the common experience of mankind. The purposes of justice require that such evidence as is more likely than otherwise to mislead should be excluded. If this were not the case, a witness unworthy of credit might often receive as much consideration as one worthy of the fullest confidence. We must, therefore, guard against incorrect decisions by the absolute rejection of persons whose testimony, either from interest in the matter in dispute or any other visible cause, seems likely to prove untrustworthy."

On the other hand, it is contended that no kind of evidence whatever, capable of throwing light on the question agitated, ought to be rejected, unless its exclusion can be justified by the inconvenience and expense of obtaining it, or by the vexation and delay that would attend it. In illustration of the latter part of this proposition, the following case has been put: "By laying a barrowful of rubbish on a spot on which it ought not to have been laid (the side of a turnpike road) Titius has incurred a penalty of five shillings. No man was witness to the transaction but Sempronius; and in the station of writer Sempronius is gone to make his fortune in the East Indies. Should Sempronius be forced, if he could be forced, to come back from the East Indies for the chance of subjecting Titius to this penalty? Who would think of subjecting Titius to this vexation? Who would think of subjecting Sempronius or anybody else to this expense?" It is obvious that the vexation, expense, and delay in obtaining the testimony would amount to a preponderant evil, and justify its exclusion. But it is insisted that where this is not the case, all objections to the admissibility of a witness should be at once annihilated and classed under objections to his credibility, varying according to circumstances; that in many cases the excluding of a casual witness to a fact would be to exclude all attainable evidence on the question in dispute, and offer by

impunity a premium to dishonesty, fraud, and crime.   If
it be said that, owing to unsoundness of mind, deficiency
of religion, antecedent misconduct, or personal interest,
the evidence is likely to prove unsafe, the answer is, that
any line drawn on the subject must be in the highest
degree arbitrary.   It is impossible to enumerate *a priori*
the causes which may distort or bias the minds of men
to pervert or misstate the truth, far more to estimate their
weight in each individual case or with each individual
person.   This is the settled opinion of the ablest English
writers and jurists, after a careful examination of the
arguments concerning the incompetency of witnesses and
a practical experience of years ; and the opinion is well
founded.

Let us consider the matter.   For what purpose does
the court sit?   To decide correctly the cause before it.
What then is the evil to be guarded against?   Erroneous
decision, or " misdecision," as Bentham calls it, produced
by false testimony.   Now, the testimony offered and rejected was either necessary to the cause of the party producing it, or it was not absolutely necessary.

First, suppose it necessary, the party offering it
having no other testimony to establish his right.   It is
plain, in that case, that by excluding it you certainly
produce an erroneous decision, for fear of a *possible*
erroneous decision from false testimony, " as a panic-
struck bird is said to fly into the serpent's mouth, or as a
man jumps overboard for fear of being drowned."   If the
testimony be admitted, you may be on your guard and
correct the evil.   If it be rejected, there is no alternative.
Misdecision is inevitable if testimony, without which a
just decision cannot be had, be rejected.   You owed a
thousand dollars : you paid it in the presence of Primus :
Primus is convicted of an offense destroying his compe-
tence to testify : his testimony is rejected : you lose your

cause. Could more injustice be done if he were admitted?
False testimony is given every day in some cause or
other; cross-examination or counter-testimony almost invariably corrects it. The opposite party, the counsel, the
judge, the jury, are all on their guard, and it is nearly
impossible for perjury, suspected beforehand, to succeed.

Suppose, next, the evidence excluded to be not absolutely necessary, because the party offering it has other
testimony. If the decision be given on that other testimony, the exclusion can produce no beneficial influence on the decision of the cause; it only puts the party
to expense to procure different evidence. A witness
knowing the suspicions concerning him, and how much
every one is on the alert to convict him of falsehood,
would not commit perjury gratuitously. If he have any
special motive to bear false testimony, this motive is
extraneous to the legal motive for rejecting him. Even
from a witness desirous of deceiving, examination and
cross-examination will generally elicit useful truths. Mr.
Best says: " We have read somewhere of a whole nation
who purposely gave false answers to all questions respecting the topography of their country. Still, a traveler was
enabled to ascertain it by questioning upon incidental
facts, when the truth naturally oozing out supplied him
with materials for arriving at the knowledge sought."

The rules of evidence by which our courts are governed have been borrowed in a great part from the
English law. In revising the Civil Code in 1825, it was
intended to prepare a separate code of evidence. But
this has not been done, and our Civil Code contains only
some general leading principles of evidence in civil cases.
On the subject of exclusion, which is now under consideration, the systems materially differ, and are more or
less uncertain in their provisions.

Various classes of persons were rejected by the civilians

of mediæval Europe and by the old English lawyers upon the ground that giving evidence in a court of justice is a right rather than a duty, and consequently that incompetency to testify is a fitting punishment for matters to which the law is desirous of attaching the stigma of disgrace.

The ancient practice in England affixed the brand of incompetency to holding obnoxious opinions; thus not only punishing the delinquent, but inflicting ruin on a party to a suit whose life, property, or honor might be saved by the evidence of the rejected witness.

There can be no doubt that this principle was borrowed from the civil law of the Middle Ages.

In that law, the list of persons liable to be rejected as incompetent to bear testimony was exceedingly large. In some instances entire classes were rejected. The celebrated Constitution of the Greek Emperor Anastasius declared that Pagans, Manichæans, and members of some other sects were disqualified from giving evidence under any circumstances; while heretics and Jews were allowed to do so only in causes in which they were parties, and, except in peculiar cases, could not bear testimony against orthodox Christians. Similar principles prevailed in the canon law.

The law of ancient Rome refused the testimony of women in certain cases, and the civil and canon laws in the Middle Ages carried the exclusion further. In Scotland, until the beginning of the eighteenth century, sex was a cause of exclusion in the great majority of cases. Even the old English lawyers occasionally rejected the evidence of women, on the ground "they are *frail.*" The reason is not unlike that of the civil law, which is said to be "because women are usually *fraudulentæ, fallaces, et dolosæ,*" or the reason assigned by the doctors of the canon law, who declared, in the language of Virgil,

" *varium et mutabile, semper femina.*"   Undoubtedly
there were many exceptions to these rules.   But even
after women had been admitted to bear testimony in
France, their evidence was not considered equivalent to
that of a man ; and it seems to have been a principle that
a virgin was entitled to greater credit than a widow, —
" *magis creditur virgini quam viduæ.*"

Under the civil law system, all questions of law and
fact were decided by a single judge.   The examination of
witnesses was secret, and was made by judges unacquainted
with the circumstances of the case, without confrontation,
personal cross-examination, or publicity ; the parties themselves were not allowed to be present.   Under such a
system, the difficulty of detecting falsehood afforded a
plausible pretext for an extended prohibition of suspected
witnesses, though nothing can give a colorable excuse for
the enormous extent to which it was carried.

How different is the common law system and our own !
Under these, the evidence of witnesses is given *viva voce*,
in presence of the party against whom they are produced,
and he is allowed to cross-examine them.   The great tests
of the truth of a narrative are the consistency of its several parts and the probability of the matters narrated.
Stories entirely false are comparatively rare : it is by misrepresentation, suppression of some things and addition
of others, that a false coloring is given to the acts of
men ; and it is only by a searching inquiry into the surrounding circumstances that the whole truth can be
brought to light.   The party against whom false testimony
is directed is interested in exposing it, and is the person
best acquainted with the facts as they really have occurred,
and is, therefore, most able to furnish means for the detection of the falseness of the testimony.   Besides, it is
very difficult for a witness to come prepared with his story
to meet every question which may be put to him suddenly

on a cross-examination. And further, what is perhaps of still greater importance, courts of justice are, by the common law and by the law of Louisiana, open to all. The publicity of the examination of the witness operates as a check upon mendacity and incorrectness. Environed, as he sees himself, by a thousand eyes, contradiction, should he hazard a false tale, will seem ready to rise up in opposition to him from a thousand tongues. Many a known face, and many an unknown one, presents to him a possible source of detection, from whence the truth he is struggling to suppress may, through some unsuspected channel, burst forth to his confusion.

Under such a system, the principle of exclusion is wholly misplaced. Accordingly, the inclination of modern judges and law-givers in England and the North American States is in favor of receiving the testimony of witnesses, leaving its value to be properly estimated.

The committee might rest content with this general statement of the argument in favor of the bill: but they will proceed to examine more particularly the grounds on which the several clauses of the bill are based. And first, the law excludes the testimony of persons who are interested in the result of the suit. The rule, it is said, is founded on the known infirmities of human nature, which the law deems too weak to be generally restrained by religious or moral obligations, when tempted and solicited in a contrary direction by temporal interests. Its object is to guard against the danger of perjury, and to shut out testimony unworthy of credit in judicial investigations. "There is," said Lord Chief Baron Gilbert, "from the nature of human passions and actions, more reason to distrust such biased testimony than to believe it."

The principle upon which the rule rests is altogether unfounded. It assumes that, in the great majority of instances, men are so corrupt that, from a mere regard to their interest, however small that interest may be, they will violate the duties of morality and religion, and run the risk of incurring the penalties of the law by committing perjury, for the chance of imposing upon the judge and jury, after counter-testimony and strict cross-examination, before the public, in open court, where every one who hears them testify is aware of their bias and on his guard against deception by false testimony. For although other strong motives to produce mendacity may be secret, yet interest, pecuniary motive, before it can render a witness incompetent, must be proved and known to the court and jury. The assumption is contrary to all experience. In general, witnesses are honest, however much interested; and in most cases of dishonesty the falseness of the testimony is detected, and misleads none.

Let it be remembered that the great object to which all the rules of evidence should be directed is the discovery of truth; and that the only question is, Will the object be better effected by the admission or by the exclusion of the witness? No one who has an enlarged knowledge of human nature, or any respect for the society in which he lives, would hesitate to admit the witness.

Undoubtedly, interest may be a motive with some persons for mendacity and perjury, but its influence varies upon different persons. The amount of the interest, the condition of the witness, his standing in society, his fortune, education, sensibility, and other circumstances may affect and control the influence. Who can believe that the loss or gain of five dollars would have affected the testimony of George Washington or of John Marshall? On the other hand, suppose, with Mr. Bentham, an ill-educated laborer, with a wife and children on the point of starving: is there any analogy between the cases?

Now, the truth is secured among men in their mutual intercourse by powerful sanctions or guarantees: (1.) By the natural sanction, which is a sort of instinct that impels man to speak the truth, and makes him do violence to himself whenever he betrays it and injures another. (2.) By the moral or popular sanction, which punishes, with disgrace, the liar. (3.) By the religious sanction, which is founded on the dread of future punishment. (4.) By the legal sanction, which punishes false testimony in a judicial proceeding, and renders it difficult to devise a falsehood that will pass examination in a court of justice. All these sanctions are in continual operation to secure the truth of testimony before the courts. If it be admitted that men may occasionally be found in whom motives of interest preponderate over the powerful restraining motives just enumerated, it cannot be denied that they constitute a very small number in comparison with those to whom the interest is too trifling to be an object compared to their fortune and situation in life; those who, under the influence of a strong interest, would be restrained by the stronger motives of religion or morality; those who would be deterred by the fear of shame or of punishment; and those who, without these restraints, find their hearts to fail them from the difficulty of framing false testimony so as to give it the semblance of truth.

Ought we then to exclude the numerous interested witnesses who would tell the truth, because a few interested would commit perjury at the risk of detection and punishment?

Remember the law has drawn no line of pecuniary interest; it makes no distinction between interests of different amounts, or between interested witnesses of different characters; it quite overlooks the ratio between the sum in question and the pecuniary circumstances of the witness. No matter what the amount of interest is, one cent, one dollar, one hundred, one thousand, one million, the effect is the same, the witness is excluded. It is true, the interest appears, and if the law would permit the witness to be heard his testimony might be weighed and his motives judged. But no : by the law of exclusion for pecuniary interest, a cent may render a man venerated for his holy life, of the highest sense of honor, and worth a million of dollars, a witness too suspicious to be credited on his oath. And this is law : "founded," says Lord Erskine, "in the charities of religion, in the philosophy of nature, in the truths of history, and in the experience of common life."

Who is the person suffering? The innocent suitor. Suppose the excluded testimony is necessary to save the character or life of the party offering it. One man is presumed to be a perjurer, and therefore another man is disgraced for life or punished with death.

Our law excludes, in civil cases, all persons from testifying who are interested, directly or indirectly, in the result of the suit. This is imperatively expressed in Article 2260 of the Civil Code. But our courts have, by a long series of decisions, adopted the English rule, and excluded only those who are directly interested ; they have admitted all the exceptions contained in the English law. Now, the interest which excluded at common law was a legal interest ; that is, a direct certain interest in the event of the case, or an interest in the record for the purposes of evidence, however minute that interest may have been. This rule, so wide and extensive in its terms, gave rise to constant questions and doubts, and the courts gradually relaxed it by making numerous and important exceptions to it, irreconcilable with the principle of the rule itself. Thus, a certain legal interest, to the amount of a dollar, excludes ; a contingent interest, to the amount of a million, is unnoticed. The consequence is that parties are often competent to give evidence who are swayed by the strongest moral interest to pervert the truth. Again, a factor, or any other agent, who is to receive a commission on the amount of a contract or sale, is declared a competent witness to prove the sale or contract for his principal. A servant employed to deliver goods to a purchaser, or a clerk employed to pay money to a creditor, is a good witness to prove the delivery or the payment, as the case may be. But if the cause depend on the question whether the agent or servant has been guilty of neglect or misconduct, he is not a competent witness for his principal without a release, because he is liable over. Cases without number, of a similar character, might be cited, wherein the disqualification from interest was found so inconsistent with public policy as to cause constant inroads to be made upon the principle of exclusion. These cases are frequently entirely contradictory to each other, or supported by decisions abounding in flimsy and subtle distinctions, and occasionally, by their contrariety, creating much legal doubt. In order to meet the difficulty, various expedients, by means of release, etc., were resorted to, for the purpose of restoring the competency of interested witnesses. Speaking of release, Lord Brougham, then Mr. Brougham, in his celebrated speech on law reform, in the House of Commons, in 1828, said: "Evidence is thus often cooked up for the court, nay, in the court, while the witness is in the box, which, according to the existing rules, is not admissible without this process of release. Now, what is the real effect of the release on the mind of the witness? Just nothing; for if he be an honorable man, he gives it up the moment he leaves the box, and while swearing he knows that he is to do so."

The courts in England still further relaxed the rule of exclusion in the case of Bent *v.* Baker, in which it was decided that, in an action, one underwriter of a policy was a competent witness for another underwriter of the same, even though his evidence substantially settled the case as to both. Without dwelling further upon the decisions of the courts, it will suffice to observe that the practical inconvenience of so extensive an exclusion of witnesses as that on the ground of interest being found intolerable, Parliament at length interfered, and in 1834, by the Statute 3d and 4th William IV., rendered competent the whole class of witnesses excluded by an interest in the record as an instrument of evidence; but provided that the record should not be admissible in evidence in another cause, for or against such witnesses. It would seem that this statute introduced no new principle, but merely removed the interest which would otherwise have disqualified the witnesses, like the notable expedient of a release described by Brougham.

But this was superseded in 1843 by the Statute 6th and 7th Victoria, 85, commonly known by the name of Lord Denman's Act. After reciting that " the inquiry after truth in courts of justice was often obstructed by incapacities created by the present law, and it was desirable that full information as to facts in issue, both in criminal and civil cases, should be laid before the persons appointed to decide upon them, and that such persons should exercise their judgment on the credit of the witnesses adduced and on the truth of their testimony, it enacted that no person offered as a witness shall be excluded, by reason of incapacity from interest, from giving evidence in any cause, except in certain cases therein afterwards specified." At length came Lord Campbell's Act, 14th and 15th Victoria, c. 99, August, 1851, to amend the law of evidence, which has effectually expunged from English jurisprudence the title of " incompetency of witnesses from interest."

The example of England has been followed in the

States of America very generally, — in Connecticut, New York, Ohio, Massachusetts, Mississippi, and other States.

The committee conclude their report on this portion of the bill by citing the uniform testimony of the English lawyers upon the subject, who declare that "of all the acts in their statute book, these which render interested witnesses competent contain in the smallest compass the greatest amount of good. They settle the law upon an intelligible, reasonable, and satisfactory basis, put an end to some of the most intricate perplexities of the law, and reject a principle which was unsound in theory, and in practice often led to results most unfavorable to the due administration of justice."

The time has come when Louisiana should act upon this matter, and, gaining wisdom from the experience of others, admit the evidence of interested witnesses without exception, leaving the weight of the evidence to be determined by the judging power.

The committee will next proceed to the consideration of the provision in the bill for the repeal of the rule which excludes the testimony of the parties in a civil suit. This exclusion is substantially embraced in that which has just been considered. It rests upon the ground that it removes the temptation to perjury, and secures judicial tribunals from being deceived by false testimony and led into erroneous decisions.

To a certain extent our present law has repudiated this argument. It allows one party to the suit to examine the adverse party. A plaintiff may interrogate the defendant, and the defendant the plaintiff. The bias of a party in his own favor is known, and every corrective is ready to be used against him: cross-examination, counter-evidence, publicity, experienced counsel, judge, and jury. Surely there can be no great danger of being misled by false testimony under such circumstances.

There are two defects in our present law upon the subject. The first consists in the mode of examining, and in the effect given to the evidence; the second, in not allowing a party to be examined whenever he himself chooses. The parties are generally those best acquainted with the facts of the case, and best able to state them. If it be desirable to hear them, there can be no reasonable objection to extract from them the whole truth by a public examination in the same way as we extract truth from other witnesses. The testimony of every witness should be left to have that weight which his character or other circumstances justly entitle it to. The declaration of a party may not be believed by the judge and jury. He is certainly a suspicious witness, and yet the law declares that his oath shall be *conclusive*, unless contradicted by two witnesses, or one witness corroborated by circumstances or written proof. The true rule is to put his testimony on a footing with that of any other witness.

The exclusion of a party's testimony in his own favor strikes at the great principle of legal evidence, that the best evidence should be adduced. It renders inferior evidence necessary, at the hazard of delay, vexation, and expense, parties generally knowing most about the matter in dispute.

Why should a party be deprived of the right of being heard, of clearing up doubts, and rectifying errors which may have been produced by the inattention or design of witnesses, or the ambiguity of other evidence? Why exclude that which is calculated to throw most light upon the subject?

The rule of exclusion is broken in upon in all motions upon affidavit, — an affidavit drawn by his lawyer, and heard without cross-examination: in the affidavit to hold to bail; in the affidavit to attach, and in the affidavit to sequester property; in the affidavit for an injunction,

16

and in the various affidavits used in the progress of a
cause.   It is broken in upon in the oath *in litem:* first,
in cases where the party against whom it is offered has
fraudulently or unwarrantably intermeddled with the
plaintiff's goods, and no other evidence can be had of the
amount of the damages; and second, when on grounds of
public policy it is deemed essential to the purposes of
public justice.   In a word, the exceptions are so numerous
that the rule itself serves only the purposes of deception;
it no longer prevails in England.

Shortly after the passing of Lord Denman's Act, the
statute for the establishment of county courts, which
superseded a large number of minor tribunals in England,
was promulgated.   It provided that parties in those new
courts should be witnesses on either side.   This was not
an innovation, for the old Court of Conscience and Court
of Requests contained similar provisions.   By the old
bankruptcy acts, passed under James I., every bankrupt
was made a competent witness in relation to the bankruptcy, and this principle is incorporated into the present
bankrupt law of England.

By far the greater portion of the numerous demands
recoverable in the county courts were recoverable in the
superior courts.   In the former, the evidence of the party
weighed: in the latter, it was deemed wholly unworthy of
trust.   It thus appeared as if the superior courts had less
efficacious means of testing the truth of evidence and detecting falsehood than the inferior tribunals.   The plaintiff (who had his option as to where he would sue), if his
own testimony would be adverse, or he knew the evidence
of the defendant would establish the defense, sued in the
superior court, and excluded the evidence.   The jurisdiction of county courts having been considerably enlarged,
and the evidence of parties having proved beneficial to
the administration of justice, it was deemed unreasonable

to preserve a distinction between the rules of evidence in the tribunals. By the act to amend the law of evidence, passed 7th August, 1851, 14th and 15th Victoria, c. 99, all the parties to a suit, and those in whose behalf a suit is brought, are admissible witnesses, on behalf of either or any of the parties to the suit.

The committee have felt and still feel much doubt whether this principle should be extended to criminal cases. They are inclined to think the provision in Lord Brougham's Act, which declares that no person shall be compelled to criminate himself, or to give evidence against himself upon any charge brought against him for a criminal offense, is founded in philosophy as it is undoubtedly in clemency. They have, therefore, retained the provision in the bill before the Senate.

By our code, as well as under the common law, the rule by which parties are excluded from being witnesses for themselves applies to the case of husband and wife; neither of them being admissible as a witness in a cause, civil or criminal, in which the other is a party or has interests involved. The exclusion is founded partly on their legal identity, and partly on public policy, which requires that the confidence between husband and wife should be sacredly protected and cherished as the best solace of human existence.

The committee have stated this exclusionary rule and the reasons assigned for it in the language of Mr. Greenleaf. If the rule were limited to the protecting from disclosure matters communicated in nuptial confidence, or facts the knowledge of which has been acquired in consequence of the relation of husband and wife, the committee would not recommend its repeal, but it is an absolute prohibition of the testimony of the witness to any facts affecting the husband or wife, as the case may be, however the knowledge of these facts may have been acquired. The rule only applies where the husband or wife is party to the suit, and does not extend to a collateral suit between third parties. And the declarations of a wife, acting as the agent of her husband, are evidence against him, like the declarations of any other agent.

The exceptions to the rule are important. In cases where a personal injury is threatened or inflicted by one on the other, the law does not allow the legal identity of husband and wife to supersede the great principle that the state is bound to protect the life and limbs of its citizens ; and it generally happens that offenses of this kind cannot be proved without the evidence of the injured party. In such cases, therefore, the injured husband or wife may testify against the other. And yet, with what has been called "a cruel absurdity," in a case of bigamy, the first wife is not a competent witness against the accused, she is prohibited from proving the fact of her marriage, her mouth is stopped against him, while, with strange inconsistency, she is allowed to prove the fact in a collateral suit between third persons !

As early as 21 Jac. 1, c. 19, commissioners in bankruptcy were authorized to examine the bankrupt's wife to discover any property concealed by him ; and the provision was reënacted under George IV. The examination of the bankrupt and wife in a modified form was retained under the present Queen of England. The county courts, Acts 9 and 10 Victoria, which rendered parties to suits competent witnesses in those courts, extended "to their wives and all other persons." And finally, the statute of 1853, 16 and 17 Victoria, c. 99 (Lord Brougham's Act), not overlooking the temptation, naturally arising out of the marriage connection, to induce husband and wife to favor each other, but considering it, like any other known bias, to be guarded against and allowed for, enacted that husband and wife should be competent witnesses for

and against each other in all civil cases, except in proceedings in consequence of adultery; but they were not
competent in any criminal proceedings against each other,
nor compellable to disclose any communication made by
one to the other during the marriage. This statute has
been substantially copied and adopted by the leading
States of the late Union, and its provisions are embodied
in the bill referred to the committee. They are recommended to the adoption of the Senate, as founded in
principle and sanctioned by experience.

If the reasoning in this report is correct, it necessarily
follows that the rule of our Civil Code which excludes the
testimony of ascendants and descendants for or against
each other should be repealed. The rule does not prevail in criminal cases. Pride, passion, affection, friendship, blood relationship. the love of parents and of children, are no disqualification of a witness in a criminal
prosecution affecting the life, liberty, property, or honor
of the accused. But let the case be a civil one involving
a claim of twenty dollars, and our law will not permit
an ascendant or descendant to testify for or against each
other when a party to the suit. Are there not the same
means of ascertaining whether the father or son tells
the truth in a civil suit as in a criminal suit? If admitted as a witness in the latter, ought he not also to be
admitted in the former case? Cannot the weight of his
evidence be equally considered in each case? The committee are of opinion that the proposed alteration, which
will admit the evidence of ascendants and descendants in
civil as well as in criminal cases, should be made.

It remains for the committee to examine the rules
which exclude the testimony of witnesses who do not believe in the existence of a God and a future state of rewards and punishments, and of witnesses who have been
convicted of any infamous offense.

The sanctions by which mendacity is restrained and truth is secured — natural, moral, religious, and political — have been pointed out already; the difficulty of devising a falsehood that will pass examination in a court, the fear of legal punishment, the fear of disgrace and loss of character, the pain of falsehood and injustice, the dread of future punishment. Of these sanctions, one only, the religious sanction, has no influence on the mind of the atheist. The other sanctions operate with full force upon him. "Atheism," says Lord Bacon, "leaves a man to sense, to philosophy, to natural piety, to laws, to reputation: all which may be guides to an outward moral virtue, though religion were not."

Ought atheism, then, and other forms of infidelity which deny all exercise of divine power in punishing falsehood, to be recognized as a sufficient ground to render a person incompetent to testify? The committee think they ought not.

The law presumes that every man brought up in a Christian land, where God is generally acknowledged, does believe in Him and fear Him. The witness himself cannot be questioned as to his religious belief, because this would be a personal scrutiny into the state of his faith and conscience foreign to the spirit of our institutions. No man is bound to avow his belief: but if he does avow it, the avowal may be proved, like any other fact, by third persons.

Now, it is argued by Mr. Bentham, and those who have succeeded him, that he who runs counter to the religious persuasions of the community is sure to meet with much obloquy and great personal inconvenience. Suppose such a man produced as a witness. In a conversation with several persons he had avowed himself to be an atheist, and had, by so doing, marred the prospects of success that he entertained for himself and his family. Nothing prevented him from affirming the contrary, or concealing his opinion and escaping the injury and the stigma which his avowal fastened on him, but a regard for truth and a respect for his own character in society and in his own family. This is deemed a sufficient ground to disbelieve him, and he is rejected as incompetent to testify. His declaration of atheism renders him utterly incompetent.

We read of conspirators in crime who, in order to secure impunity, bind each other by solemn oaths never to reveal the part taken by any of them in the perpetration of the crime. How much more efficacious is the mode furnished by this rule of evidence! Let a man who proposes to join in committing a crime make his associates avow themselves to be atheists, and he will be perfectly secure as against them. In this way, any knot of criminals may combine and secure impunity, and any man whatever may get rid of the inconvenience of giving testimony. A man is indicted for a crime. Paul was present at the time of its commission, and knows all the circumstances. He is summoned to testify. He wishes to screen the culprit. He declares to the friends of the prisoner, or to other persons, that he is an atheist, and suggests to the counsel of the accused, " Ask Primus, Secundus, Tertius, if I did not avow myself to be an atheist." The objection is taken, the witness is dismissed, the culprit is set free.

Is it wise to leave it in the power of any man whose breast is the repository, perhaps the sole repository, of evidence affecting the lives and fortunes of others, to stifle that evidence by pretending to hold erroneous views on the subject of religion ? But even if we suppose the want of religious faith to be genuine, is it not more properly an objection to the credit than to the competency of the witness ?

In England, the Statute 6 and 7 Victoria, c. 22, allowed

the unsworn testimony to be received of the members of certain barbarous races in the British colonies, who are described in that statute " as destitute of the knowledge of God and of any religious belief," and left but a little more to be done in order to destroy the mischievous principle of the old law, which punished the holder of obnoxious opinions by rendering him incompetent to give evidence.

Under the rule which rejects the testimony of persons insensible to the obligations of an oath, the law excludes infamous persons ; that is, persons who have been guilty of those heinous crimes which men generally are not found to commit, unless when so depraved as to be unworthy of credit for truth. It is unnecessary, and it would be somewhat difficult, to enumerate with nicety the offenses deemed infamous by law. In order to test the propriety of this exclusion, the case of perjury may be selected.

Does it follow that a man, because he has been once convicted of perjury and suffered the penalty of the law therefor, will, whenever he may be called on to testify, commit another perjury, and render himself liable to renewed punishment? And that, too, in cases where no motive could exist or be surmised for his perjury? Suppose the offense to have been committed in the folly tide of youth, under motives of kindness intermingled with temptations, and to have been repented of for fifty years. Ought this to be imputed to him after living half a century of virtue and truth? And must an innocent man, who has no other witness to prove the groundlessness of a charge against him, be unjustly condemned because the witness was guilty of a delinquency so many years before? All exclusions operate as a punishment on the parties who need the testimony excluded. A perjured person cannot be a witness on behalf of another person, but may in behalf of himself. In his own cause he may make any affidavit necessary to his exculpation, or defense, or personal protection, or for relief against an irregular judgment, or the like. And in the very teeth of the rule which excludes persons infamous, " *repellitur a sacramento infamis*," a man may, in legal strictness, be convicted even of a capital offense, on the unsupported evidence of a person avowing himself an accomplice in his crime, who is taken out of jail to bear testimony against his companion, and gives his testimony *in vinculis*, in custody with a rope round his neck, being liable on his own confession to execution if the government be dissatisfied with his conduct in this respect.

A witness of depraved and abandoned character, Mr. Starkie says, may not be unworthy of credit where there is no motive for misrepresentation; for there is a constant tendency to declare the truth which is never wholly eradicated even from the most vicious minds, and the danger of detection and the risk of temporal punishment may operate as restraints upon the most unprincipled, even when motives of veracity of a higher nature are wanting.

In England, all objections to the competency of witnesses on the ground of infamy have been removed by the act on evidence, 6 and 7 Victoria, c. 85, Lord Denman's Act, which declares, " No person offered as a witness shall hereafter be excluded by reason of incapacity from crime from giving evidence in any court, but every person so offered shall be admitted to give evidence, notwithstanding he may have been previously convicted of any crime."

The committee have now laid before the Senate the theory of human nature on which the exclusionary rules of evidence that the bill proposes to abolish are based, and have shown that the theory is false and degrading to the society in which we live, while the rules themselves

have been in so many particulars impaired and overthrown by admitted exceptions conflicting with them as
to involve the law upon the subject in obscurity, doubt,
and difficulty, to obstruct the inquiry after truth in
courts of justice, to deny to innocence the proper and
natural means of protection, and in many instances to
secure impunity to fraud and crime. They have shown
that the theory and the rules have been repudiated and
repealed in England and in most of the late United States
of America, and that the true principle of evidence is
that now adopted in the courts of those countries : put
everybody on the stand who knows anything about the
case, and let the persons appointed to decide upon the
facts in issue, both in civil and criminal cases, exercise
their judgment on the credit of the witnesses adduced
and on the truth of their testimony.

In stating the arguments for and against the rules now
existing, the committee have freely used the language
employed by the courts, and by the common lawyers, and
by the most distinguished advocates of reform.

It is time to throw off the trammels and prejudices
generated by the long habit of thinking and acting in a
legal routine, and to legislate upon correct principles.

It certainly would be desirable, if practicable, to have
perfect witnesses in every case. " But perfect men do
not exist : and if the earth were covered with them,
delinquents would not send for them to be witnesses of
their delinquency. The legislator, then, has this option,
and no other : to open the door to witnesses, or to give
license to crimes. For all purposes he must take men as
he finds them : and for the purposes of testimony he must
take such men as happen to see and know what, had it
depended on the actors, would not have been seen and
known by anybody."

The amendments proposed were as follows : —

AN ACT RELATIVE TO THE LAW OF EVIDENCE.

Whereas the inquiry after truth in courts of justice is often obstructed by incapacities created by the present law of evidence ; and whereas it is desirable that full information as to the facts in issue, both in criminal and in civil cases, should be laid before the persons appointed to decide upon them, and that such persons should exercise their judgment on the credit of the witnesses adduced and on the truth of their testimony :

SECTION 1. *Be it enacted by the Senate and House of Representatives of the State of Louisiana, in General Assembly convened,* No person shall be incompetent as a witness because of his or her conviction of crime, or his or her interest in any issue or question before any court or officer authorized to administer oaths.

SEC. 2. *Be it further enacted, etc.,* Nothing herein shall render any person who in any criminal proceeding is charged with the commission of any offense against law competent or compellable to give evidence for or against himself or herself, or shall render any person compellable to answer any question tending to criminate himself or herself.

SEC. 3. *Be it further enacted, etc.,* Parties shall be competent and compellable to testify on behalf of themselves or of others, in any suit or other proceeding pending in a court, or before any person authorized to administer oaths. And the husbands and wives of the parties shall, except as hereinafter excepted. be competent and compellable to testify on behalf of any party to the suit or other proceedings.

SEC. 4. *Be it further enacted, etc.,* Nothing herein shall render any husband compellable to give evidence for or against his wife, or any wife competent or compellable to give evidence for or against her husband, in any criminal proceeding, or in any proceeding instituted in consequence of adultery.

SEC. 5. *Be it further enacted, etc.,* No husband shall be competent or compellable to disclose any communication made to him by his wife during the marriage, and no wife shall be competent or compellable to disclose any communication made to her by her husband during the marriage.

Sec. 6. *Be it further enacted, etc.*, Ascendants and descendants shall be severally competent witnesses for or against each other in all suits or proceedings, civil or criminal.

THE RIGHTS OF THE STATES.

[The following extracts must have been written about the conclusion of the civil war. They serve to show the views of Mr. Hunt upon the policy to be pursued by the general government towards the States, which had joined the Secession movement.]

To exclude the citizens of the Southern States from all share in the government of our common country; to deny them all voice in it; and, not content with having forced them to change their domestic institutions, to hold them in absolute subjection under a military rule more despotic than that of a Roman proconsul or propraetor!

The people of Louisiana are loyal. There are doubtless a few individuals to be found scattered here and there in the State who are unwilling to submit to the national government and are not to be trusted. But the determination to support and obey the Constitution and the laws of the United States is almost universal. I know no man of character and talent who has taken the oath of allegiance to the government who is disloyal. I know no such man who can take the "test oath," according to my interpretation of it. Mr. Clingman, in a letter to the "New York Times" (December 8, 1865), expressed his belief that no man in North Carolina can take it without perjury. If the oath be insisted on, the South cannot have real representatives in Congress, although they may have nominal or counterfeit representatives, which would be worse than to have no representatives at all. Is it not then the dictate of true wisdom and policy to allow men of talent and consideration, loyal and true to the Constitution, to represent the States, and thus to secure to the national government and administration the entire political and moral support of the South? The government of the United States can have the entire people of the South true to it by accepting them as such. The Southern States acknowledge their errors, have complied with all the requisitions of the President, are anxious to be restored to the Union as its friends and supporters. The United States can at once and forever secure this friendship and support by allowing them to exercise the privileges that belong, according to the Constitution, to all the States of the Union. But if, without any necessity or reason, they be kept under military rule, disaffection may be produced and the expenses of the government increased, to the injury of the government as well as of the South. Some designing politicians and placemen, and some persons still inflamed with a desire for vengeance, will persist in still regarding the South as an enemy to be punished. But good and reflecting men cannot fail to remember that the Southern States have suffered more severely than any community in modern times. Two thirds of their property is gone: four millions of slaves emancipated; their land and personal property depreciated: the entire country desolated and laid waste: many — alas, how many! — of their best men and noblest youths wounded and killed: universal grief pervading the land: women, children, and aged men at the point of starvation! Overwhelmed by numbers, and unable longer to resist, the South have abandoned their contest against the power of the North. In attempting to secede from the Federal Union they acted under a mistaken but earnest and honest conviction that they had the constitutional right to secede, and that their interest and the security of their slave property required them to resort to the exercise of that right. Nor were they alone in that opinion. The extreme doctrines of state rights, as taught by Mr. Calhoun and his followers in the South, were the avowed doctrines of a large portion of the leading Democrats of the North. These doctrines necessarily led to the conclusion that the several States possessed the right of seceding. It is true that President Buchanan, the last Democratic President of the United States, after South Carolina had by a convention declared that she was no longer a member of the Union, did, in a message to Congress, enter upon an argument to prove that no State had a right to secede. But it will be remembered that he at the same time declared that the national government had no power to coerce the State. This extraordinary position of the President of the United States gave heart to the advocates of secession and paralyzed the advocates of the Union in the South, until at length, when Mr. Lincoln succeeded to the presidency, the South presented an unbroken hostile front to the government of the United States. Every department of that government — executive, legislative, judicial — then denied the right that the South had asserted, and war, bloody, desolating war, ensued. All candid persons admit that slavery was the true cause that led to it. The issue of the war has decided against the doctrine of secession as taught in the state-rights school of politics. The desperate, sanguinary, and desolating struggle between the two sections of the Union has settled forever this question. No wise or patriotic man will ever again endeavor to persuade the people that secession is a peaceful remedy, or urge them to a new trial of the fearful issue. The war has also settled that slavery is and shall forever be absolutely exterminated in all the States of the Union. The people of the South, with manly fortitude and frankness, acknowledge these facts and acquiesce in the result with extraordinary unanimity. President Johnson, himself a Southerner and thoroughly acquainted with the people of the South, has, with enlightened humanity and a wise policy, encouraged the people in their desire to return to their loyalty and to reconstruct the Union and the government at once.

Of course the Constitution of the United States recognizes the existence of States. One branch of the legislature of the United States is composed of senators appointed by the States in their state capacities. The Constitution of the United States says that " the United States shall guarantee to each State a republican form of government, and shall protect the several States against invasion." According to our system, it devolves upon the President to determine in the first instance what are and what are not governments. He recognizes governments, foreign governments, as they appear from time to time in the changes of the world. The provision of the Constitution that guarantees to every State in this Union a republican form of government, protection against invasion, and under certain circumstances against domestic violence, and the law of Congress making provision for carrying this constitutional duty into effect in proper cases, make it the duty of the President to decide what is the rightful government of the State in cases of commotion. He cannot avoid the decision.

We know that the executive in the first instance treated, and in his proclamations expressly designated, the rebellion of the States as " an insurrection," and we know, too, that Congress subsequently joined him in so treating and designating it. The executive has now recognized the existence of the several States of the South and their respective governments. He has aided in reorganizing them. He has counseled them in regard to changes in their fundamental laws. He has submitted to them for ratification proposed amendments to the Constitution of the United States under the provision of the Constitution which declares that amendments proposed by two thirds of both houses shall be valid when ratified by three fourths of the legislatures of the several States. He has, through the Secretary of State of the United States, solemnly proclaimed that those amendments have been adopted by the concurrent votes of some of the States of the South. He is daily proceeding in the glorious work of reconstructing the Union through the agency of the people and the governments of the States of the South. He has extended to them the hand of friendship and confidence, and recognized them in every way within his power as members of the Union.

From his provisional governors and special agents deputed to gain information, the President has had the best opportunity of learning the true condition of the South and the present sentiments of the people ; and whether, in seeking again the constitutional right of representation, they are prepared to comply with all their constitutional obligations, and whether their elections were made in a proper way.

True policy requires Congress to expedite rather than delay the recognition and readmission of the Southern senators and representatives. In the present condition of things, the functions of these States are suspended. They are excluded from all representation in the national legislature. They have not even a territorial voice, but are as speechless as if they were dead. It is not right, it is not consistent with the principles of the Constitution of the United States, nor with the public safety, for any part of the country to legislate for any other part of the country without giving it a voice in that legislation. Representation is the vital principle of American republican institutions. Its denial to any extent mars and destroys

17

the regular operation of the government, and gives rise
to every kind of abuse.   If the South is to be deprived of
all representation and made subject to laws in framing
which it has had no part, it will be impossible to avoid
the spirit of sectionalism and discrimination against it.
The natural effect of this must be to beget a sense of
grievous oppression and wrong, which must inevitably lead
to an intense hatred on the part of the Southern people
of their oppressors.   Observe the present condition of the
South.   They have submitted.   They have complied with
all the requisitions of the North.   They are anxiously waiting to see how their submission and compliance will be
received and treated ; whether the Northern people desire
again to fraternize with them, or mean only to be their
masters.   A generous and magnanimous policy by Congress in admitting their representatives and burying the
past would completely extinguish every lingering and
smouldering feeling of resentment, and remove the
last sense of humiliation that cannot exist without
some bitterness.   A harsh and jealous treatment would,
on the other hand, not only repress the better impulses of
the Southern heart, but fill it with a determination to
oppose the government, and would perpetuate that spirit
of sectionalism of which the North so loudly complains,
and would give to it intensity in the worst form.   It is
impossible to shut out all Southern representation without producing the impression that the North means to
domineer and degrade.   If it be said that the new loyalty
of the South is defective and immature, I answer that the
assertion is not correct.   I know the people of Louisiana.
I know that there are among them not a few who are discontented and sullen, but the vast majority of them accept
their situation with manly frankness, and admit their errors : they have not only adopted and approved the amendments to the Constitution of the United States, but have

returned to their allegiance with a firm resolve to be true to it. Nothing could have a more powerful and a more blessed influence upon the discontented than that the Northern heart is ready for a complete reconciliation. What better means can be imagined, what more thorough, prompt, and convincing, than to admit the Southern representation in the halls of Congress? Suppose the worst, — suppose that a portion of the South should continue factious and discontented. What could they do, what possible harm? Why, even if the entire South were disaffected and of doubtful loyalty, they would still form but a wretched minority in the house. Nay, let me go a step further. I appeal to the great Union sentiment which pervades this Congress, to the overwhelming strength which it possesses, and which no possible elements of opposition, however combined, can prevent from working its will. Let Congress trust to that strength, and act with generous fearlessness. Uninfluenced by any feelings of bitterness and resentment or theoretical dogmas, let them admit into their bosom the truly accredited representatives of the South, so that they may have full knowledge of the condition of every part of our land, and act justly for all. The spirit of liberty and of national concord and of the Union demands this at their hands.

How can Northern statesmen, who so often and so eloquently express their sympathy for oppressed Ireland, simply because its people have been deprived of an equal right and equal voice in the government of Great Britain, reconcile these enlarged and liberal views with that policy which would deprive the people of the South of any voice whatsoever in making laws by which they are to be governed, or in the administration of the national affairs of our common country?

There is no reason to doubt that the persons who have been pardoned by the President have taken the oath of allegiance in good faith. They may be as securely relied on as any class of people in the South. They have no motive to break the oath. If the test oath was intended simply to be protective, it is plain that it is no longer necessary for that purpose, because there is no longer treason, actual or potential. Nobody believes a renewal of the rebellion possible. The test oath never was intended as punitory. It is not fit that representatives and senators elect should be excluded from Congress merely as a punishment. If it is best to punish them, it should be done in the usual way, with the regular pains and penalties of the law visited upon persons and property. There is no such independent punishment known to our statute as exclusion from places of public trust; that exclusion is only incidental to some high penal conviction.

If it be said that men so lately covered with treason ought not to be admitted to the national Congress, I ask, in reply, " Is such a feeling as this to be indulged, at the expense of the best interests of the country, which imperiously call for an early reconstruction? Is there anything in it to justify the continuance of the suspension of the representative principle, which is the very vital essence of the American system of government?" The President's magnanimous policy upon this subject has been attended with the happiest results. Let the action of Congress harmonize with his, and the republic will at once be restored to all its constitutional and glorious working.

Extraordinary as has been the history of our country for the last four years, — the war, its commencement, its progress, its close, the immense amount of treasure expended, the number of lives lost, the armies raised, the wealth, power, and resources of the country, — nothing is more surprising than the fact that the Southern people, so soon after they had been defeated, resumed the pursuits of agriculture, commerce, and the general business of life with a cheerful and proper spirit; they have exhibited no inactivity or indolence, no indifference to the ordinary ambitions of men. During the last nine months their progress in material activity and development has been great and steady. The cash received for the large amount of cotton which it turned out that the South had preserved, — upwards of eleven hundred thousand bales, — amounting to four hundred millions of dollars, and the large amount of Northern capital invested there, together with the tide of immigration turning towards the South, give hopes for its attainment of a condition of national prosperity unequaled in the past, and for a return of amity between all parts of the Union, if the South be promptly admitted to the enjoyment of its right of representation in the councils of the nation, and of local self-government, according to the Constitution of the United States.

Nothing, in my opinion, illustrates more clearly the sterling worth of character of the Southern people than the manner in which the officers and soldiers of the late Confederate armies have deported themselves since the failure of that cause to which they had devoted their most earnest work and hearts. Generals and privates, all have met their fate like men, and addressed themselves to the task of building up their ruined fortunes. They are to be seen in every position, — in the universities and colleges of learning, in the temples and houses of religious worship, in the halls of medical science and of jurisprudence, in the counting-house and in the workshop, in the field, and on the rivers and lakes and oceans, — in every honorable and honest pursuit; laboring, toiling, intent upon obtaining an honest livelihood, and, as I have already said, returning to their common country, repentant and loyal, like the prodigal son to the home of his father. Will that parent receive them with kindly heart, or with cruel reproaches and suspicion? Rest as-

sured that persons of such character, though in returning
to their old places they may find strangers occupying for
a time stations of high authority, will certainly be called
again to guide and direct the interests of their own land.

With regard to Louisiana, the President of the United
States has recognized the state authorities, maintained
them in their functions, and refused to appoint a provisional governor and other state officers. In a word, he
has recognized the state organization and state government, and left it uncontrolled, save by that martial law
which, wherever it prevails, overrides all other laws and
constitutions.

Nor has the popular branch of the national government
failed to recognize the constitutional existence of the State
of Louisiana. While the war was yet raging, Flanders
and Hahn were elected members of the House of Representatives in the Congress of the United States, went to
Washington, were admitted to the seats they claimed,
and participated in the debates and legislation of our
common country.

It is true that the Senate of the United States did not
permit Mr. Smith and Mr. Cutler, who were elected to be
members of that body by the legislature of Louisiana, to
take their seats. But this was not upon the ground that
Louisiana was not a State of the Union, but because the
legislature, so called, that elected them represented only
an insignificant portion of the territory and of the population of the State. Now the legislature of Louisiana
represents the entire people and the entire territory of
the State, and that legislature has elected two citizens
of the United States to fill the places which Smith and
Cutler had been improperly chosen to fill. Observe how
Senator Howard, of Michigan, spoke: "The measure
before you proposes to acknowledge eight thousand citizens of Louisiana as the State, and to give them the

rights and privileges belonging to more than fifty thousand." Hear Mr. Wade, of Ohio: "Is it not exceedingly important that we shall have here for four or five days, side by side with us in the senate chamber, two men from Louisiana, representing nobody and nothing except the will of the commander-in-chief of the army of the United States?" Senator Sprague, of Rhode Island, declared his ability to prove that thirty of the state legislature that elected Mr. Smith and Mr. Cutler were officers of the general government from the Northern States; and Mr. Grimes, of Iowa, said he "was prepared to prove that the voters whose votes were polled in the outlying parishes were carried in army transports to the places where they voted, — being discharged soldiers and persons belonging in New Orleans, — and were brought back again to New Orleans that night" (7th February, 1864).

On the 3d of December, 1865, the President, by Mr. Seward, congratulated Alabama as being the State, the twenty-seventh, which completed the adoption of the amendment of the Constitution of the United States and altered the organization of the whole Union. The Constitution of the United States declares that amendments to the Constitution proposed by Congress shall be valid when ratified by the legislatures of three fourths of the several States, or by conventions in three fourths thereof, as the one or the other mode of ratification may be proposed by Congress. In the amendment just made Congress decided that the legislatures of the States should act. It was accordingly submitted to the legislatures of Louisiana, Arkansas, Virginia, North Carolina, South Carolina, Georgia, Tennessee, and Alabama. The action of all these legislatures was considered by the President the action of state legislatures. It is only in this point of view that the ratification by the State of

Alabama can be considered, as the twenty-seventh State which was necessary to form the complement of votes required to make the three fourths of the state legislatures required by the Constitution. If the Congress of the United States, directly or indirectly in its legislation, accept the ratification by these States, the Southern States will be thereby accepted as within the Union; for the highest act a State can exercise is to alter the Constitution, the fundamental law of the country. It is true that Mr. Sumner has introduced a resolution into the Senate declaring the amendment to be adopted by three fourths of the States represented in Congress. By this resolution only twenty-five States are considered to be in the Union, while eleven provinces, or dependencies, — for such he considers the rebellious States, — must be legislated for as void of all right of local self-government, and subject now to military rule, and hereafter to such form of government as Congress may substitute therefor. A doctrine so monstrous is not to be discussed!

I have stated the extraordinary doctrine of President Buchanan. A State has no right to secede, but the United States has no right to prevent a State from seceding. The laws of the United States are supreme, but a State cannot be compelled to obey them. The violation of those laws may be a crime, but no person violating them under state authority can be punished. I do not desire to dwell upon the abstract theories and antagonisms, section jealousies and disputes, enlisting the evil passions of humanity, kindling the fires of discord and hatred until they burn fiercer and fiercer for a series of years, and at length the American people, abandoning reason, forgetting their memories of common sufferings and common triumphs, regardless of the glory that awaited them as a united people, looking upon each other with mutual aversion and deadly hatred, drew the sword, and each section of the country, in a desire for triumph, assuming the specious garb of patriotism, relied for the arbitrament of their differences upon the wager of battle. For four long years the contest has been waged; the award is against the South as a party to the issue, and the whole people have accepted that award as by the will of one man, and have wisely renounced that which they could not by valor achieve. They have solemnly, in remodeling their Constitutions, declared the supremacy of the Constitution and laws of the United States, meaning thereby to pledge their fidelity to the whole country, to recognize their duty to and interest in the whole country, and look with confidence to the discharge of their reciprocal obligation by the people of the entire country. They have not been discouraged by the suspicion and distrust openly expressed towards them by the more violent politicians of the North. Determined faithfully to observe and obey the behests of the federal Constitution, repressing all improper and narrow promptings of mere sectional feelings and interests, sustained by conscious rectitude, they will maintain with calm dignity and unshaken resolution the position they have assumed. A storm of dreadful violence and fury has swept over them. As the billows of the mighty deep continue to roll mountains high, even after the tempest has subsided and the winds have lulled, so the fierce and angry passions roused by the terrible war which raged for four long years were not at once calmed, but continued to swell and toss the public mind after peace was restored. But they are fast subsiding, and the atmosphere, although somewhat troublous, is rapidly clearing. The clouds are vanishing, prejudices disappearing, and reason is rapidly resuming its sway. The North cannot fail to perceive that the South, however wrong in principle, acted without any taint of duplicity in endeavoring to separate herself from the United States. However unwise and erroneous her conduct, it was open, marked with courage and with truth, the inseparable companions of magnanimity. The Southern people now, in returning to their allegiance, do so with sincerity, and those who distrust them or regard them with suspicion will in due time learn to respect their character, and marvel less at their approved fealty than at their own ungenerous tardiness in discovering it.

There is evidently a class of politicians, represented by a number of members of Congress, whose counsels and actions indicate a settled purpose of opposing the reconstruction of the Southern States. The numerous and extraordinary requirements and conditions they seek to impose, the captious, exacting, implacable spirit of sectional hatred and strife that actuates them, leave no room to doubt their object, — an object dangerous to the financial prosperity of the country and disgraceful to the republican name. Who can doubt that the Southern people are sincerely desirous of a genuine reconciliation? They have almost with one voice acknowledged themselves overcome ; they unhesitatingly and without reserve accepted the amnesty oath of President Johnson ; they accepted the provisional governors that he appointed, and treated them with respect and confidence, though many of them were persons never really of their choice. They elected conventions of men in full sympathy with the government, and remodeled their state Constitutions in accordance with the suggestions of the President. They elected legislatures anxious to satisfy the government at Washington, and adopted every measure calculated to facilitate the work of reconstruction. They have returned to the pursuits of industry, and in no part of their wide territory is there any attempt or desire to oppose the government of the United States. They are churlish, thwarting, mutinous, but submit with a good grace, such as nobody could have ventured to predict one year ago.

Does the interest of the nation, does an enlightened policy, justify Congress in meeting this display of good sense and good feeling in the Southern people with distrust and aversion or with friendly encouragement? If we consider the North as victors in the war, are they not bound by a generous manly policy to a speedy reconciliation? If we consider them as Union men, are they not morally bound, in a devotion consistent with that cause in the name of which this terrible war was carried on, to do their utmost to have the Union restored as soon as it can be done with safety and without violation of principle? Should a mere feeling of animosity and resentment prevent the discharge of this high and important duty?

The Southern people are a suffering people; the war has left them desolate from the Atlantic to the Rio Grande. No change is possible until their constitutional rights are restored. Without that restoration they cannot be relieved from uncertainty. Their political and social system requires that stimulus which can come only from a participation in all those rights. This is as necessary for the nation at large as for the South. All reflecting men must admit that the national finances, resting on a foundation of irredeemable paper, are in a dangerous if not alarming condition. To support the national credit and restore soundness to all 'the business operations of the country, the old conditions of trade between the United States and foreign lands must be reëstablished; and for this purpose it is essential that the great Southern staples shall be reproduced and supplied for exports, which can never be hoped for unless the reconstruction of the Union is complete. Keep the South under a despotic military rule, and she will be without energy. Treat her with harshness, and she will become discouraged, or, still worse, rancorous and vindictive. He who favors such a policy would perpetuate bitterness, and ought to be accounted a public enemy.

It is scarcely twelve months since the South was engaged in the most desperate war of modern times, with every circumstance of passion and fury. To expect that the people should look with positive affection on their conquerors, condemn their most eminent countrymen as traitors, and repudiate as abominable the principle for which they sacrificed their fortunes and staked their lives is beyond all reason. It is enough if they know themselves beaten, accept the results without reserve, cherish no idea of deferred rebellion, and are prepared to return to their former position with a resolution to perform all their duties as citizens, and a resolution to receive the warmest impressions that time and intercourse may bring. More cannot be expected; but if more is desired, it can be secured only by the policy that the radicals so fanatically denounce. If the citizen of the South is to be made to look on the Union as he did ten years ago, it can only be accomplished by liberal and conciliatory conduct on the part of the government, passive acquiescence in a cordial sympathy, — by kind and generous treatment. Radical policy is stultified by its own professions. Radicals pretend to desire a more sympathizing South than they have, and then, to improve Southern feeling, they propose to inflict political disgrace and humiliation on the Southern people. They pronounce them to be still disaffected and not sufficiently well affected, and by way of conciliating them would condemn them to alienation and outlawry. No reasonable person can expect a Southerner to look upon the United States government exactly like a New Englander. Enough for purpose of prudent reconstruction if the States lately in secession have abandoned all idea of independence, and are prepared to make the best of their position as members of the Union once more. The rest must be a work of time, and will be accomplished most speedily and surely by the President's policy. He does not claim to swamp the South with black voters, or place the negro in perilous antagonism to the white. He asks only profession of political honesty, — that the South shall forego their views of secession, acknowledge and confirm the abolition of slavery now and forever, deal fairly with the enfranchised slave, and repudiate the debt contracted for the purpose of rebellion ; and then open the doors of Congress and restore the Union. The radicals desire impossibilities, require the South humbly and thankfully to kiss the rod after the fashion they prescribe. The first is a policy of moderation and promise, and will bring back the South to those sentiments of perfect concord that the radicals pretend to demand. The second is a policy of provocation and oppression continued after victory, and must intensify and perpetuate the very hostility which it is intended to expurgate.

THE LOUISIANA STATE LOTTERY.

[Mr. Hunt was anxious that the State of Louisiana should refuse all legislative aid to the Louisiana State Lottery. But a few years before his death he wrote a number of articles denouncing the business of lotteries generally, and particularly the existence of the Louisiana State Lottery. His views are expressed in the following paper.]

LOTTERIES fall within the class of hazardous contracts. A contract is hazardous when the performance of that which is one of its objects depends upon an uncertainty. The word "hazard" means chance, risk. In a state of nature every individual is obliged to bear the entire burden of his own destiny; in a state of society he is able, at least partially, to relieve himself of the burden by dividing it with or shifting it upon others. This is the principal object of contracts of hazard. They spring from our hopes and from our fears. Some persons desire to tempt Fortune; others, to secure themselves against her caprices. Accordingly, we find that in every age there has existed a traffic or dealing in regard to things uncertain and eventual. The most ancient laws known to us prove that men have constantly sought to grasp and include within their compacts and agreements things which they can scarcely attain by their own weak prescience. They have undertaken to subject to calculations and speculations that which does not belong to us, and is beyond human control, hazard itself, mere chance to weigh destiny and calculate the future. The effect or result of these agreements is obvious, and witnessed every

day. We increase and multiply our possessions and
wealth by assigning an actual value to probabilities more
or less remote ; mere expectations become real riches ;
evils that otherwise may perchance, some day, be too real
and afflicting are averted or alleviated in advance by the
wisdom of our arrangements and combinations. We
render innocuous the blows of fate against individuals by
associating to divide their force, and sharing it when
divided and distributed.

The statement of the principle of contracts of hazard is
a sufficient justification of them. What can be more in
accordance with an enlarged and enlightened social justice,
what more legitimate, than to make, as it were, a common
stock of our fears, our hopes, and all our affections, so as
not to leave entirely to chance that which may be regulated by prudence and consultation, but to aid one another
by salutary and beneficial compacts in dividing and running with less danger the risks of life?

But this reasoning is not applicable to every species of
hazardous and aleatory contracts. There is a great difference between a contract that depends upon an uncertain
event and a contract that has no other cause or consideration whatever than the uncertainty of an event. The first
may be supported and favored on considerations of private
individual and public good. The latter is without any
useful rational motive.

There can be no valid contract without a cause or consideration. And the law requires something more solid
and real than an extravagant and wild desire of trusting
to the caprices of fortune to serve as a lawful foundation
or just cause of obligations among men. By way of
examples, a gambling contract is first examined, and then
a contract of insurance.

What is the cause or consideration upon which the
gambling contract rests? Nothing but the uncertainty

of gain or loss. It is impossible to assign another cause. Two gamesters enter into an agreement as to a stipulated sum. Each, relying on his own good fortune and confident that he will gain it, leaves the disposal of it to the blind arbitrament of chance. The desire and the hope of gain are the only motives that induce the parties to enter into the contract. This desire and this hope depend upon no action and look to no reciprocity of services. Each gamester hopes only in his own good fortune, and can gratify his desire only by the misfortune of the other. He can be happy only at the expense of others, and in their misery. He is reduced to envy and curse the good that comes to them at his expense, and to rejoice over their ruin. In contrast to ordinary contracts which give employment to labor and bring men together in social friendship, these gaming contracts isolate and keep them apart, encourage idleness by separating the idea of gain from that of labor, and stifle all kindly sentiment. Where the object is an ill-regulated desire of gain, of enriching one's self at the expense of another without doing him or the community any service, the contract is contrary to good morals and the fundamental principles of society.

On the other hand, when contracts of insurance are carefully examined and considered, it will be at once perceived that, although they are based upon the uncertainty of an event, they are founded upon considerations of individual and general public good that entitle them to the favor of the law.

Property, in spite of all that may be done by government and the vigilance of individuals, must still be exposed to casualties by fire, shipwreck, and other unforeseen disasters. Hence it is important to inquire, when they do occur, how such unavoidable losses may be rendered less injurious. The conflagration of a sugarmill or cotton-mill, or the loss of a ship at sea, would press heavily on the richest individual. But were the loss distributed among several individuals, each would feel it proportionally less ; and provided the number of those among whom it was distributed were very considerable, it would hardly occasion any sensible inconvenience to any one in particular. Hence the advantage of individuals combining to lessen the injury arising from the accidental destruction of property. It is this diffusion of loss over a wide surface and the valuation of the risk that form the employment of those engaged in insurance. The contract of insurance is a contract of indemnity. Its very essence, its sole object, is indemnity, to prevent the assured from suffering loss by means of any of the perils insured against. Its whole spirit would be violated if the assured could make the occurrence of any such casualties a means of gain, for this would be to give him an interest in procuring losses, which would be contrary to every principle of public policy.

From these remarks we turn to a more special notice and consideration of lotteries, their nature and their effects upon society for good or evil.

Webster, in his dictionary, has given us a correct definition of the term " lottery," and has accompanied it with a wise and practical remark as to the effects of lotteries in general, namely: " Lottery, a scheme for the distribution of prizes by chance, or the distribution itself. Lotteries are often authorized by law, but many good men believe them immoral in principle, and almost all men concur in the opinion that their effects are pernicious."

All philosophers, moralists, and writers of eminence of the present day unite in condemning lotteries. All encyclopædias, dictionaries of the sciences and arts, storehouses not only of literature, but also of history, the

18

principal facts, principles, laws, and practices of different countries and peoples, digested under proper titles, contain conclusive proof of their impolicy and mischievous effects.

The term "lottery" may be applied to any process of determining prizes by lot, whether the object be amusement, or gambling, or public profit. The overweening conceit which the greater part of men have of their own abilities is an ancient evil, remarked by the philosophers and moralists of all ages. Their absurd presumption in their own good fortune has been less taken notice of. It is, however, if possible, still more universal. There is no man living who, when in tolerable health and spirits, has not some of it. The chance of gain is by every man more or less overvalued, and the chance of loss is by most men undervalued.

That the chance of gain is naturally overvalued we may learn from the universal success of lotteries. The world never saw, nor will it ever see, a perfectly fair lottery, or one in which the whole gain compensated the whole loss — because the undertaker would make nothing by it.

In the state lotteries, the tickets are really not worth the price which is paid by the original subscribers, and yet commonly sell in the market for twenty, thirty, and sometimes forty per cent advance. The vain hope of gaining some of the great prizes is the sole cause of this demand. The soberest people scarce look upon it as a folly to pay a small sum for the chance of gaining ten or twenty thousand dollars, though they know that even that sum is perhaps twenty or thirty per cent more than the chance is worth.

In a lottery in which no prize exceeded one hundred and fifty dollars, though in other respects it approached much nearer to a perfectly fair one than the common state lotteries, there would not be the same demand for tickets. In order to have a better chance for some of the great prizes, some people purchase several tickets, and others small shares in a much greater number. There is not, however, a more certain proposition in mathematics than that the more tickets you adventure upon, the more likely you are to be a loser. Adventure upon all the tickets in the lottery, and you lose for certain; and the greater the number of your tickets, the nearer you approach to this certainty.[1]

The "American Cyclopædia" says : "Lottery is a sort of gaming contract, by which, for a valuable consideration, one may, by favor of lot, obtain a prize of value superior to the amount or value of that which he risks." The word is derived from "lotto," a lot which decides. Almost all modern states have, at some periods of their history, employed lotteries as a means of revenue, but they have always been found to exert a mischievous influence upon the people. The poor are invited by them rather than the rich. They are diverted from persistent labor and patient thrift by the hope of sudden and splendid gains; and as a large part of their receipts is withheld, a necessary loss falls upon a class which, of all in the community, can least afford to bear it. Between 1816 and 1828, the French government derived an annual income of 14,000,000 francs from lotteries. In 1829, a law for the extinction and suppression of the royal lottery abolished and closed its offices in 28 departments. — *supprimant d'abord les bureaux de 28 départements.* In January of the next year, 525,000 francs more were found to be in the savings-banks in Paris alone than in the same month of the preceding year.

We repeat that lotteries have been established and en-

[1] Adam Smith, *Wealth of Nations.*

couraged by some states for the purpose of raising a revenue.

In the Italian republics of the sixteenth century, the lottery principle was applied to encourage the sale of merchandise. The lotto of Florence and the semiharis of Genoa are well known; and Venice established a monopoly, and drew a considerable revenue for the state.[1]

In France, the system of state lotteries for revenue was very long carried on by the government, and had a pernicious and demoralizing effect on French society, — a demoralization greater even than that produced in England by a like cause. The eloquent Bishop of Autun denounced lotteries as no better than the lowest, vile street games of the worst description; and the wise and illustrious Turgot condemned state lotteries as an immoral, unequal, unjust source of public revenue. State lotteries have been abolished in France, as already mentioned.

In England, the earliest lottery of which there is any record was in 1569, when 40,000 chances were sold at ten shillings each. The prizes consisted of articles of plate, and the profit was employed for the repair of certain harbors. The spirit of gambling in this direction appears to have materially increased in the course of the following century, for private lotteries were, early in the reign of Queen Anne, suppressed as "public nuisances."

The financial condition of France, *la pénurie des finances*, caused her to create in 1700 a public lottery of ten millions, which was soon followed by the establishment of other lotteries in the provinces; and in 1777 a special administration of them was organized. A decree of the convention (*du 28 Vend. an 12*) continued the lottery of France, and suppressed all other lotteries of every kind. But one month later a decree abolished lotteries

[1] *Encyclopædia Britannica.*

entirely. *Fléau inventé*, said the deputy who moved for the abolition, *par le despotisme, pour faire taire le peuple en sa misère, en le leurrant d'une espérance qui aggravait sa calamité.* Reëstablished by the Directory, the national lottery continued to subsist during the Consulate, the Empire, and the Restoration ; and lotteries of every kind were again prohibited by the law of May, 1836.

The evils attendant on lottery speculations attracted in 1819 the attention of the English people, and were thoroughly discussed in Parliament. In 1823 public sentiment had become so far adverse to the further approval of them that a lottery was tolerated in that year only because it was to be the last ; and the act was accompanied by provisions for the future suppression, entire suppression, of lotteries, which had long before been denounced by Parliament as " common nuisances, by which children, servants, and other unwary persons had been ruined." The " Cyclopædia of Universal Knowledge," London, states correctly that lotteries have been very common in the United States, and have been sanctioned by the several States, not so much as a means of raising money for state purposes as with the view of encouraging, as they supposed, many useful objects, such as canals, schools, etc. It adds : " The numerous frauds practiced in lottery schemes in the United States have perhaps done more to open the eyes of the people to the mischief resulting from them than any investigation into the true principles of lotteries." Perhaps so. But the sight of the mischief and the knowledge of its cause have led wise and reflecting men carefully to examine the nature and character of lotteries, the object which the proprietors and undertakers have in view, the scheme and manner of conducting them, the temptation held out to purchasers of tickets, the practical effect on the poor

and deluded class of the people, the certain success of
the undertakers and proprietors of the lotteries; and,
after careful examination and consideration, to pronounce
them unworthy of the favor and support of a good government.

The impolicy and ill effects of a state's resort to a
lottery, instead of to more honest direct taxation, to increase its revenue, require no further exposure. A philosophic, learned, and vigorous writer on political economy,
in 1826, sternly remarked: "Taxes by way of lottery
have received the decided reprobation of every good
writer in Europe. What right has a government to use
a gallows that encourages lotteries? It is really deplorable that at this day writers on political economy have
to preach against a system of gambling, the parent of
improvident adventure, of fraud, of theft, of disappointment, of despair, — a system encouraged by law, encouraged by the clergy!" (See Gaesit sur les revenues pub-
liques.) Elsewhere, in a note to the rule "that no law
should restrain or control the acquisition or disposal of
property but what the good of society calls for," he adds:
"Perhaps what the manifest principles of morality require. Can a tax upon gambling-houses be defended?
Can lotteries be defended? Especially in this country,
where our financiers are not driven to their wits' end to
find out ways and means, etc. Even the clergy . . . seem
not averse to build churches by lotteries. This is calling
in the good offices of the devil to aid in building the
house of God!"

Mr. Jefferson, on his retirement from the presidency of
the United States to the station and pursuits of a private
patriot citizen, applied to the Virginia legislature for
permission to sell his own property freely to pay his own
debts: to sell it, — not to sacrifice it, not to have it
gobbled up by speculators to make fortunes for them-

selves, leaving unpaid those who had trusted to his good faith, and himself without resource in the last and most helpless stage of life. This induced him to prepare an essay entitled "Thoughts on Lotteries," February, 1826.[1]

It was an adroit and successful address to the legislature to allow him to dispose of his large landed estate, to repair his fortune broken by unavoidable neglect in a long course of important public services at home and abroad, — an ingenious, elaborate, eloquent, but sophistical petition, skillfully flattering the pride and lauding the past action of the legislature. It makes a grand display of good works effected by the granting of lotteries for useful purposes, namely: for public revenues of the State of Virginia, for schools and colleges, for public roads and canals, for religious societies, for private societies, for the benefit of private individuals.

But, properly weighed, it shows a mistake, a grave error, in the policy of legislation then prevalent in the Old Dominion, — the use of a bad passion in man, of the love of gain without labor, of the hazard of the small means of the poor, insufficient often for the comfort and support of their families or of themselves individually, to obtain large sums on remote possibilities.

Doubtless some good has resulted occasionally from lotteries as described; but the means of obtaining such good are not to be lost sight of, and not to be employed if they are pernicious to public morals, if they excite the lust of the greater number, and especially of the poor, to jeopard their hard earnings and small means on false and delusive schemes of profit without labor.

Mr. Jefferson, not wisely and truly, would artfully and for his purpose resolve all the pursuits of human industry into games of chance. He says: "In all these pursuits

---

[1] *Jefferson's Works*, vol. ix. p. 500.

you stake some one thing against another which you hope
to win. But the greatest of all gamblers is the farmer.
He risks the seed he puts into the ground, the rent he
pays for the ground itself, the year's labor on it, and the
wear and tear of his cattle and gear, to win a crop which
the chances of too much or too little rain and general
uncertainty of weather, insects, wastes, etc., often make
a total or partial loss."

This is certainly an abuse of terms and of right reason.
God gives man reason and the means of providing for
himself. The use of that reason and of those means in
the practical labor of production cannot be justly and
fairly assimilated to the remote chance or probability of
gain in a lottery. The ways of Providence are not
always known to us. We cannot foresee storms and
tempests, earthquakes and inundations. But we have
good ground to rely upon our labor for protection and
support in the justice, mercy, and loving-kindness of the
Creator who has fitted us for our state, and not made us
for suffering and want.

Mr. Jefferson himself is obliged to qualify his system
of chance in all the pursuits of life. There are some pursuits, he admits, entirely unproductive, doing good to
none, injury to many, so tempting and seducing that it
is the duty of society to suppress them entirely; but lotteries which had been found useful by the legislature of
Virginia to the whole State, to public revenues, to private
societies, and to individuals, under circumstances which
claimed favor or indulgence, are placed under the discretion of the legislature, to which he submits whether the
devotion of threescore years and one of his life, devoted
uninterruptedly to the service of his country, to good
government, to liberty, to a share in the merits of the
great work of American independence and in the benefits
of the Constitution of the United States wisely adminis-

tered, — whether he or his situation would justify the legislature in permitting him to avail himself of the mode of selling by lottery for the purpose of paying his debts.

The raising of money by lotteries for public purposes in Virginia had its origin in times of public disturbance and general poverty. It was a sort of legislative ruse to draw money from individuals in small sums by operating on the chance prospect of gain, when laying of a tax upon property avowedly for the same purpose would have excited general complaint and opposition. The system was popular and of long continuance. It was under the prevalence of that system that Mr. Jefferson sought relief from poverty in his old age by a petition for leave to dispose of his large but unprofitable landed estate by a lottery. Virginia granted the prayer, but it would have been better for her fame to have relieved her noble son, the author of the Declaration of American Independence, by a special appropriation or tax for the purpose.

More than half a century has since elapsed. At the present day the moral and enlightened patriot, no longer deceived and misled by the false and delusive expectation of immoral gain, condemns the system of lotteries as inconsistent with and prejudicial to good morals, and injurious to the pursuits of useful industry by which man can alone provide properly for his wants, and secure the peace, prosperity, and good order of civilized life.

Edward Livingston, one of the wisest, most philosophic and eminent statesmen of our country, in a report to the legislature of Louisiana on a criminal code prepared by him under the appointment of the General Assembly of the State, thus stated " a common fault in the legislation of our country. We shape our laws to fit the principal end which is proposed without sufficiently examining whether the same object could be obtained by other means. . . . that avoid dangers which, in our eagerness to obtain some doubtful good by a straightforward off-hand legislation, have totally escaped our attention. Thus, to raise a revenue for some useful purpose, we license gambling-houses; to promote education and to provide for the building of churches, we establish lotteries. . . . We do this without sufficiently inquiring whether the requisite revenue might not be obtained by some other and better means than giving the sanction of law to the worst of vices: whether a purer source could not be found from which to draw the means of supporting religious and scientific education than one that corrupts morals, encourages idleness, and leads the poorer classes to poverty and vice."

This view of the impolicy and immoral tendency of lotteries would lead a member of Congress, duly regardful of the general good and dignity of the nation, to oppose any legislation in support of a lottery, however specious in the purposes it proposed, and any offer of employment to favor and procure such legislation. The legal rights of the lottery company, whatever they may be, can be properly settled in a due course of law without any undertaking on his part, and non-intervention in a matter coming before Congress touching the lottery would leave him free from all embarrassment to act according to his views of justice, public policy, and constitutional duty.

The special instance of the Louisiana State Lottery Company will now be examined.

Louisiana, in 1845, ordained as follows in the Constitution of the State: " No lottery shall be authorized by this State, and the buying and selling of lottery tickets within the State is prohibited." This Constitution was revised and amended in 1852: many articles were added to it, many altered or modified, but the Constitution of 1852 retained the fundamental law of 1845 in regard to lot-

teries and repeated in its very words, *ipsissimis verbis:*
"No lottery shall be authorized by this State, and the
buying and selling of lottery tickets within the State is
prohibited."

In the "compilation of the state Constitutions and the
Constitution of the United States," printed by order of
Congress, we find, in a note to the publication of "the
Constitution of Louisiana, 1864," p. 711, that "the Constitution was formed by a convention which met at New
Orleans under the auspices of General Banks, then commanding the military department of the Gulf, April, 1864,
was submitted to the people in September, and was proclaimed ratified by a vote of 6,836 against 1,566 ; but the
state government organized under it was not recognized
by Congress."

The small vote taken on the so-called Constitution of
1864 shows that it had no real popular character, consideration, and authorization, and was not an expression of the
opinion of the people of Louisiana. It was not in any
just and honest sense a ratification of the Constitution
submitted to them. The truth of this conclusion is confirmed by the fact that a new Constitution, superseding
that of 1864, was formed by a convention called under the
reconstruction acts of Congress, which met in December,
1867, and completed its work in 1868. The new Constitution was submitted to the people of Louisiana in 1868,
and was ratified by a vote of 66,152 against 48,759.

The Constitution of 1864 contained the following article,
to wit : " Constitution of Louisiana, 1864. Article 116. The
legislature shall have the power to license the selling of
lottery tickets and the keeping of gambling-houses. Said
houses in all cases shall be on the first floor, and kept
with open doors, but in all cases not less than $10,000
per annum shall be levied as a license or tax on each
vender of lottery tickets and on each gambling-house,

and $500 on each tombola." The Constitution of 1868 contained no provision for the granting or the prohibiting of lotteries, or the licensing of gambling-houses.

It thus appears that Louisiana, by her state Constitutions from 1845 to the civil war of secession, under the dominion of peace and American moral influences, ordained that no lotteries should be authorized by the State, and that the buying and selling of lottery tickets was prohibited. And it further appears that a power conferred upon the legislature to license the selling of lottery tickets and the keeping of gambling-houses was the offspring of abused military authority and influence for licentious and tyrannical gain by an anti-American, immoral, and pretended exercise of constitutional power.

The charter of the Louisiana State Lottery Company will now be considered. The company was incorporated by the state legislature in 1868. See Acts of Louisiana, 1868, No. 25, p. 24.

The first section enacts that, whereas many millions of dollars have been withdrawn from and lost to this State by the sale of Havana and other lottery tickets, etc., and fractional parts thereof, it shall hereafter be unlawful to sell, offer, or expose for sale any of them or any other lottery, except in such manner and by such persons as shall be hereinafter authorized.

By a provision in a subsequent part of the act, any person or persons violating the above enactment, or the rights and privileges herein granted to this corporation, shall be liable to said corporation in damages in a sum not exceeding $5,000 nor less than $1,000 for each offense; and in a section immediately following the term of duration of the corporation is fixed, to be and continue during twenty-five years from the first day of January, 1869, for which time it shall have the sole and exclusive privilege of establishing and authorizing a lottery or a series of lotteries, and selling and disposing of lottery tickets, etc., and fractional parts thereof.

It was further enacted that the corporation shall have the sole right and privilege, during the whole term of its existence, to dispose of by lottery or series of lotteries any land it may become possessed of by purchase or otherwise.

The fifth article of incorporation, in its first section, provides : " The corporation shall pay to the State of Louisiana the sum of $40,000 per annum, payable quarterly in advance to the state auditor, who shall deposit it in the treasury of the State, to be credited to the educational fund. And said corporation shall be exempt from all other taxes and licenses of any kind whatever, whether from state, parish, or municipal authorities."

The charter of the company should be further examined and scrutinized. The act creating the corporation is entitled " An act to increase the revenues of the State. and to authorize the incorporation and establishment of the Louisiana State Lottery Company, and to repeal certain acts now in force."

The company is then constituted and declared a corporation, with the powers and privileges set forth in the act, and for the purposes and objects specified in articles of incorporation.

" Article 1. The name and title of this corporation shall be the Louisiana State Lottery Company, and its domicile shall be in the city of New Orleans, State of Louisiana.

" Article 2. The objects and purposes of this corporation are, first, the protection of the State against the great losses heretofore incurred by sending large amounts of money to other States and foreign countries for the purchase of lottery tickets and devices, thereby impoverishing our own people ; second, to establish a solvent and reliable home institution for the sale of lottery, policy, and combination tickets, etc., and fractional parts thereof, . . . to insure perfect fairness in the distribution of prizes; third, to provide means to raise a fund for educational and charitable purposes for the citizens of Louisiana." All to be accomplished through the instrumentality of the Louisiana State Lottery!

The title of the act, the name of the corporation, the statement of the objects and purposes of the company, are alike deceptive and fraudulent.

The immoral character of lotteries has been sufficiently shown by their pernicious effects upon society, and the pretended object of the act, "to increase the revenues of the State," is glaringly false, and too ridiculous and contemptible for serious notice.

The grant sought and obtained was to enable the corporators, a number of avaricious speculators, to enrich themselves by a lottery or delusive scheme, at the expense of the people at large, but chiefly of persons of small means and in narrow circumstances, whose wants and greedy hopes of gain would induce them to part with their small sums, for the chance, the very remote and improbable chance, of rich prizes.

The grave and solemn declaration that the objects and purposes of the corporation are, first, to protect the State from great losses and the people of the State from impoverishment by sending money abroad to purchase foreign lottery tickets, and second, for the accomplishment of this great object, to establish a home institution for the sale of lottery tickets and fractional parts thereof, is an audacious and deceptive statement, a false pretense, to obtain and secure to itself, the corporation, the custom and support of purchasers of lottery tickets.

This is apparent on the face of the act, which enacts that the corporation shall continue twenty-five years, and shall have the sole and exclusive privilege of establishing a lottery or series of lotteries, and selling or disposing of lottery tickets and fractional parts thereof; and subjects any person selling or exposing for sale any lottery ticket or fractional part, in violation of the privileges granted to the corporation, to the heavy penalties stated already.

In 1778 an English lottery act was passed. It limited the subdivision of chances or fractional parts of the lottery tickets to a certain portion or minimum. This was intended to prevent the laboring population from risking their earnings; but we are told the limitation was extensively evaded by means which aggravated the evil; and a growing repugnance was, in consequence, manifested in Parliament to this method.[1] No minimum fractional part of a ticket limits the Louisiana Company. It is free to subdivide its tickets, according to its own interest and policy and greed of gain.

The charter provides that, for the sole and exclusive rights and privileges granted to the company for twenty-five years, — guaranteed and fortified by severe penalty against violation, — this odious monopoly of a pernicious institution, "the corporation shall pay to the State of Louisiana the sum of $40,000 per annum, . . . which sum shall be credited to the educational fund; and the said corporation shall be exempt from all other taxes and licenses of any kind whatever, whether from state, parish, or municipal authorities."[2]

On the first day of August, 1883, Mr. M. A. Dauphin published an address to the public, in the "New Orleans Picayune," in regard to the Louisiana State Lottery Company, of which he is the president. He states that the company was incorporated for twenty-five years by the legislature for educational and charitable purposes, with a

[1] *Encyclopædia Britannica.*
[2] Acts of the State of Louisiana, 1868.

capital of $1,000,000, to which a reserve fund of over
$550,000 has since been added, making together $1,550,-
000; its stock has been sold at the board of Louisiana
brokers; its standing is conceded by all who investigate.
Many of our citizens own stock in the company. It has
"semi-annual drawings;" its "grand single number
drawings" take place "monthly;" and Mr. Dauphin
might have added, its "combination numbers drawings"
with one dollar tickets, and with their fractional minimum parts of twenty-five cents, are made every day. The
prizes drawn in the lottery have been promptly paid, the
semi-annual and monthly drawings have been under the
supervision and management of two popular citizens, and
the whole business of the company has been so cunningly
and successfully conducted as not only to add to its capital of $1,000,000 a reserve fund of over $550,000, and so
to the enhancement of its stock, but also to enrich the
individual members of the corporation by dividends of
profits, calculated by them to be realized from their
scheme, of not less than hundreds of thousands of dollars
per annum.

The declaration that the "third object of the corporation was to provide means to raise a fund for educational
and charitable purposes" is sheer hypocrisy.

The moralist will judge for himself of this lottery
mode of increasing the revenues of the State, and raising
a fund for education and charity for the citizens of
Louisiana, by paying $40,000 per annum for a license to
plunder the public and establish an odious and pernicious
monopoly.

It is to be observed that Dauphin's address regards
only the prizes in the lottery between January, 1879, and
the first of August, 1883, a period of three years and
seven months; and that the payment by the company of
$40,000 per annum was to be made on the express condi-

tion that the corporation shall be exempt from all other taxes and licenses of any kind whatever, whether state, parish, or municipal; and that, according to the rule of uniform and equal taxation prescribed in the Constitution of Louisiana, the taxes of the company would far exceed the price paid for the exemption. The true aim of legislation should be the good and expediency of the entire community. The intention of the legislator is to guard and secure the equal rights of every citizen; not to grant and lavish upon a favorite extraordinary privileges and exemptions, in disregard of justice, the well-being and morality of the community.

In 1879, a Constitution superseding the state Constitution of 1868 was adopted, as it has been heretofore stated, by the people of Louisiana. It contains two articles which will now be noticed (167 and 172):—

" Article 167. The General Assembly shall have authority to grant lottery charters or privileges, provided each charter or privilege shall pay not less than $40,000 per annum into the treasury of the State; and provided, further, that all charters shall cease and expire on the first of January, 1895, from which time all lotteries are prohibited in the State."

The charter of the so-named Louisiana State Lottery Company was for twenty-five years from January 1, 1869, and the Constitution of 1879 ordained that all charters granted under the grant of power in Article 167 should expire in the same year, and all companies should pay into the state treasury $40.000 per annum for each charter; thus seeming to place new lottery charters on an equal legal footing with that already in existence. But it omitted to grant any new lottery an exemption from taxes of any and every kind, in consideration of the $40,000 per annum to be paid the State, thus destroying the equality of privileges.

19

The same article declares that the charter of the Louisiana State Lottery Company, granted in 1868, is recognized as a contract binding on the State (a matter previously doubted by many), except its monopoly clause, which is " hereby abrogated, etc., . . . provided said company shall file a written renunciation of all its monopoly features, in the office of the Secretary of State, within sixty days after the ratification of this Constitution." Of the additional sums raised by licenses on lotteries, — $40,000 per annum on each lottery, — the hospital at Shreveport shall receive $10,000 annually, and the remaining sum shall be divided each year among the several parishes in the State for the benefit of their schools.

The address of President Dauphin on the character and business operations of his company, its capital and additional reserve fund from January, 1879, to August, 1883, etc., with the notice thereof and comments thereon, may render superfluous any further review of this article. Time has shown the folly of anticipating and the futility of suggesting an increase in the revenue of the State from the sums to be paid for future grants of lottery charters or privileges by the General Assembly, — sums to be sufficient to furnish the Shreveport hospital yearly $10,000, and to leave a remainder to be divided each year among the several parishes of the State, fifty-eight in number, for the benefit of their schools! In the time that has elapsed, now over three years, since the adoption of the Constitution of 1879, no lottery charter has been granted by the State; none has been sought, — no, not one. The Louisiana State Lottery Company stands alone in its bad eminence of lottery gamblers. Its sordid, covetous, and avaricious desire of gain, not content with what has been acquired, urges the corporation to pursue its object with unremitting greed. True, it has renounced its monopoly charter clause and paid the amount of its license. But the monopoly clause had ceased to be useful to the company, and the word " monopoly " was unpopular. Other clauses of the charter : the rights and privileges granted, secured, and enforced by penalties against any violation of them ; the exemption from all other licenses and taxes of any kind whatever, — state, parish, or municipal, — and the large amount of money and other property thus already acquired and held free from all taxation ; the manner in which its business was conducted, its constant and persevering temptation held out to all, and especially to the poorer and laboring classes of society, — all these combined have continued to secure the sole and exclusive use of lotteries in this Commonwealth in the hands of this corporation.

Enough has been said to show the immoral character of lotteries by their pernicious effects upon society, and to expose the real objects of what is called the Louisiana State Lottery Company. It is a monument of legislative folly and popular deception, and of successful individual cupidity.

The " American Cyclopædia," in its last edition, 1875, informs us that the action in most of the States in prohibiting the further establishment of lotteries should be mainly attributed to the efforts of a Pennsylvania society. In no fewer than twenty-six of the States the Constitution expressly forbids the legislature to authorize them, and in nearly all the States parties concerned are subjected to heavy penalties : but lotteries are still permitted in Kentucky, and in Louisiana a general law prohibiting lottery companies was suspended in 1868, by an act chartering a company, and giving it an exclusive privilege of selling lottery tickets for twenty-five years.[1]

It is to be observed that the state Constitution of 1879, which gave the General Assembly power to grant char-

---

[1] *American Cyclopædia*, vol. x., " Lottery."

ters to lotteries up to 1895, itself conveys a condemnation of the policy of such a grant by providing that "from that time all lotteries are prohibited in this State:" and this condemnation is conveyed anew in Article 172, to wit: "Gambling is declared to be a vice, and the General Assembly shall enact laws for its suppression." Wise for the future, provident for the protection of posterity against the immoral, mischievous, and baleful influence of a lottery system, but too weak to resist the pernicious influence of those interested in the system, the members of the convention, heedless of the present, passed by without notice the great injury to society, to the individual daily comfort and necessities of its members, to the fame of Louisiana, and yielded the constitutional sanction of the State to the charter of the Louisiana State Lottery Company.

It is a shame to us that such things can be reported, and that they cannot be refuted!

Passing by an easy transition from the mistaken policy and law of Louisiana on the subject of lotteries, and from the general prohibition of lotteries by the several other States of the Union, attention will now be turned to the laws of our general government, and to the rights asserted and claimed by the Louisiana Lottery Company under the Constitution of the United States.

The company has published an address, headed New Orleans, August 1, 1883. "To the public! Investigate for yourselves."

The address contains a statement "in regard to the standing of the company, the reputation and value of its stock, which is sold at the board of brokers and owned by many citizens, the fairness of its conduct, and the payment of prizes to the amount of $4,881,060, from January 1, 1879, to August 1, 1883, made up of $887,350 paid to nine banks in New Orleans, specially named; of $1,366,300 to express company, T. M. Wescoat, manager; and of $2,627,410 paid in sums of under $1,000 at the various offices of the company throughout the United States."

To this is appended in a footnote " that to the capital of the company of $1,000,000 a reserve sum of $550,000 has since been added;" and, in a further note, "agents and purchasers and holders of lottery tickets or funds are instructed, ' Address registered letters and make money orders payable to New Orleans National Bank, New Orleans, Louisiana. Remit by postal note, American express order, New York Exchange, or draft on New Orleans. Express charges on all sums of five dollars or upwards we pay.' "

The address states nothing of the receipts, the profits, the gain of the company, on what is termed " its grand single number drawings monthly," or on " its semi annual drawings," with their flaming, tempting advertisement, namely, " A splendid opportunity to win a fortune," or on its daily " combination numbers drawings," — nothing of the dividends paid to its individual members; but leaves the whole matter of the lottery success and benefit of the company for the " investigation of the public," upon its statement and alleged payment of prizes.

This address is evidence, not merely persuasive, but conclusive evidence, that the Louisiana Lottery Company has used, and now continues openly and avowedly to use, the United States mail to transport corrupting publications and articles injurious to the public morals from the State of Louisiana to other States of the Union, which have prohibited the establishment of lotteries, and the sale of lottery tickets, devices, or certificates, etc., of any kind whatever: and that the company has, for the sole purpose of lucre, without any other reasonable and assignable motive, extended its grasping hand beyond Louisiana, and carried and plied its pernicious business, with artful temptation and seductive success, by agents and employees at the various offices of the company throughout the United States, so as to delude their citizens, and induce them, in violation of their several state laws and state policy, to enter in considerable numbers into forbidden contracts, in buying and dealing in the lottery tickets of the Lottery Company, — a hazardous and unfair species of gambling, perhaps the most certainly unfair, demoralizing, and hurtful!

Assuming for the sake of argument that the charter of the Lottery Company is a valid grant by the State of Louisiana, the right of the company to use the mail, the post-offices, and the post-roads of the United States, in the manner and for the purposes claimed, will be considered.

The Constitution of the United States provides Congress shall have power to establish post-offices and post-roads.

Story says the nature and extent of this power, both theoretically and practically, are of great importance. "Nothing," observed "The Federalist," "which tends to facilitate the intercourse between the States can be deemed unworthy of public care." It is universally agreed that the post-office establishment is one of the most beneficent and useful establishments under the national government. It circulates intelligence of a commercial, political, intellectual, and private nature, administers to the comfort, interests, and necessities of individuals, cheers millions of hearts, imparts new influence and impetus to private intercourse, and, by a wider diffusion of knowledge, enables political rights and duties to be performed with more uniformity and sound judgment. It is effective as an instrument of the government in its own operations, in peace and in war, enabling it to send its orders, direct its measures for the public good, transfer its funds, and apply its powers with greater facility and promptitude. The establishment in the hands of the States would have been wholly inadequate to these objects; it requires a power which pervades the Union, and which the national government alone can safely or effectually execute.

The power of Congress over the post-office and the mail is an exclusive one. The States have no post-office department. The power to establish that department is delegated entirely to the general government.

" The power possessed by Congress embraces the regulation of the entire postal system of the country. The right to designate what shall be carried necessarily involves the right to determine what shall be excluded."

" The validity of legislation, prescribing what should be carried, and its weight and form, and the charges to which it should be subjected, has never been questioned. What should be mailable has varied at different times, changing with the facility of transportation over the post-roads. At one time, only letters, newspapers, magazines, pamphlets, and other printed matter not exceeding eight ounces in weight were carried. Afterwards books were added to the list, and now small matters of merchandise not exceeding a prescribed weight, as well as books and printed matter of all kinds, are transported in the mail.

" The difficulty attending the subject arises, not from the want of power in Congress to prescribe regulations as to what shall constitute mail matter, but from the necessity of enforcing them consistently with rights reserved to the people, of far greater importance than the transportation of the mail. In their enforcement, a distinction is to be made between different kinds of mail matter, — between what is intended to be kept free from inspection, such as letters and sealed packages subject to postage, and what is open to inspection, such as newspapers, magazines, pamphlets, and other printed matter purposely left in a condition to be examined. Letters and sealed packages of this kind in the mail are as fully guarded from examination and inspection, except as to their outward form and weight, as if they were retained by the parties forwarding them in their own domiciles. The constitutional guaranty of the right of the people to be secure in their papers against unreasonable searches and seizures extends to their papers thus closed against inspection, wherever they may be. Whilst in the mail they can only be opened and examined under like warrant, issued upon similar oath or affirmation, particularly describing the thing to be seized, as is required when papers are subjected to search in one's own household. No law of Congress can place in the hands of officials connected with the postal service any authority to invade the secrecy of letters and such sealed packages in the mail; and all regulations adopted as to mail matter of this kind must be in subordination to the great principle embodied in fourth amendment of the Constitution.

"Nor can any regulations be enforced against the transportation of printed matter in the mail which is open to examination, so as to interfere in any manner with the freedom of the press. Liberty of circulating is as essential to that freedom as liberty of publishing; indeed, without the circulation the publication would be of little value. If, therefore, printed matter be excluded from the mails, its transportation in any other way cannot be forbidden by Congress." [1]

The court proceeded to state that in 1836 the power of Congress to exclude publications from the mail was discussed in the Senate. President Jackson had, in a previous message, suggested to Congress the propriety of

[1] S. C. U. S. *Ex parte* Jackson, 6 Otto, 733.

passing a law prohibiting the circulation of incendiary publications to stimulate the slaves in the Southern States to insurrection, and preventing the post-office department, which was designed to foster an amicable intercourse and correspondence between all the members of the Confederacy, from being used as an instrument of an opposite character. That part of the message was referred, on motion of Mr. Calhoun, to a select committee of which he was made chairman, and he made an elaborate report on the subject, with an accompanying bill condemning in the strongest terms the circulation of the publications. He insisted that Congress had not the power to prohibit their transmission through the mail, on the ground that it would abridge the liberty of the press. At the same time he insisted that when a State had pronounced their circulation to be dangerous, and had prohibited it, it was the duty of Congress to respect its laws and coöperate in their enforcement, and to prevent delivery by the postmasters in the States where the circulation was forbidden.

"These views," said the court, "were founded on the assumption that it was competent for Congress to prohibit the transportation of newspapers and pamphlets over postal routes in any other way than by mail; and of course it would follow that if, with such a prohibition, the transportation in the mail could also be forbidden, the circulation of the documents would be destroyed, and a fatal blow given to the freedom of the press. But we do not think that Congress possesses the power to prevent the transportation in other ways, as merchandise, of matter which it excludes from the mails. To give efficiency to its regulations and prevent rival postal systems, it may, perhaps, prohibit the carriage by others for hire over postal routes of articles which legitimately constitute mail matter in the sense in which that term was used when the Constitution was adopted, consisting of letters, and of newspapers and pamphlets, when not sent as merchandise; but further than this its power of prohibition cannot extend.

"Whilst regulations excluding matter from the mail cannot be enforced in a way which would require or permit an examination into letters or sealed packages subject to letter postage without warrant issued upon oath or affirmation in the search for prohibited matter, they may be enforced upon competent evidence of their violation obtained in other ways, as from parties receiving the letters or packages, or from agents depositing them in the post-office, or others cognizant of the facts. And as to objectionable printed matter which is open to examination, the regulations may be enforced in a similar way by the imposition of penalties for their violation, through the courts, and in some cases by the direct action of the officers of the postal service. In many instances these officers can act upon their own inspection, and from the nature of the case must act without other proof, as when the postage is not prepaid, or where there is an excess of weight over the amount prescribed, or where the object is exposed and shows unmistakably that it is prohibited, as in the case of an obscene picture or print. In such cases no difficulty arises and no principle is violated in excluding the prohibited articles or refusing to forward them. The evidence respecting them is seen by every one, and is in its nature conclusive.

"In excluding various articles from the mail, the object of Congress has not been to interfere with the freedom of the press, or with any other rights of the people, but to refuse its facilities for the distribution of matter deemed injurious to the public morals. Thus, by act of March 3, 1873, Congress declared 'that no obscene, lewd, or lascivious book, pamphlet, picture, paper, print, or other

publication of an indecent character, nor any article or
thing designed or intended for the prevention of conception or procuring of abortion, nor any article or thing
intended or adapted for any indecent or immoral use
or nature, nor any written or printed card, circular,
book, pamphlet, advertisement, or notice of any kind,
giving information, directly or indirectly, where, or how,
or of whom, or by what means either of the things before
mentioned may be obtained or made, nor any letter upon
the envelope of which, or postal-card upon which, indecent or scurrilous epithets may be written or printed,
shall be carried in the mail; and any person who shall
knowingly deposit or cause to be deposited for mailing or
delivery any of the hereinbefore mentioned articles or
things . . . shall be deemed guilty of a misdemeanor, and
on conviction thereof shall for every offense be fined not
less than $100 nor more than $5,000, or imprisonment
at hard labor not less than one year nor more than ten
years, or both, at the discretion of the judge.'

"All that Congress meant by this act was that the
mail should not be used to transport such corrupting publications and articles, and that any one who attempted to
use it for that purpose should be punished. The same
inhibition has been extended to circulars concerning lotteries, institutions which are supposed to have a demoralizing influence upon the people. . . . The only question
for our determination relates to the constitutionality of
the act, and of that we have no doubt."

"The commitment of the prisoner to the county jail,
until his fine was paid, was, within the discretion of the
court, under the statute."

The statement of the case thus decided shows that
"Section 3894 of the Revised Statutes U. S. provides:
No letter or circular concerning 'illegal' lotteries . . .
shall be carried in the mail. Any person who shall know-

ingly deposit or send anything to be conveyed by mail in violation of this section shall be punishable by a fine of not more than $500 nor less than $100, with costs of prosecution." By an act of July, 1876, the word "illegal" was stricken out of the section. Under the law as thus amended, Jackson was indicted in the Circuit Court U. S., southern district of New York, for knowingly and unlawfully depositing, on the 23d February, 1877, in that district, in the mail of the United States, to be conveyed in it, a circular concerning a lottery offering prizes inclosed in an envelope to one I. Ketchum at Gloversville, New York. He was tried, convicted, sentenced to pay a fine of $100 with costs, and committed to the county jail until the fine and costs were paid. Whereupon he presented a petition praying the Supreme Court for a *habeas corpus* to inquire into the cause and legality of his imprisonment. The result was the opinion and decree just examined, the unanimous opinion of that high tribunal that the Constitution of the United States has vested in Congress the exclusive power to regulate the entire postal system of the country, to designate what shall be carried in the mail, and to determine what shall be excluded; and that Congress has, in the exercise of that power, excluded from transportation in the mail circulars concerning lotteries.

This is intentionally repeated, to impress more forcibly and indelibly the policy and the concurrent opinion of the Congress and the judiciary.

On the 13th November, 1879, the Postmaster-General of the United States, D. M. Key, issued an order to the postmaster at New Orleans touching money orders and registered letters addressed " to M. A. Dauphin, engaged in conducting a scheme or device for obtaining money through the mails by means of fraudulent pretenses," etc. (which the Postmaster-General particularly described), forbade the postmaster at New Orleans to pay any postal money order drawn to the order of said Dauphin, etc., "and directed him to inform the remitter of said postal money order that the sum of said money order will be returned to him under the regulations of the department." He further instructed the postmaster at New Orleans "to return all registered letters directed to said Dauphin," etc., "to the postmasters at the office where they were originally mailed, with the word 'fraudulent' plainly written or stamped upon the outside of such letters." This order, the Postmaster-General wrote, was made "upon satisfactory evidence before him that the said Dauphin was so engaged."

M. A. Dauphin brought suit against Postmaster-General Key to enjoin the execution of this order. The decree of the court of original jurisdiction was (must have been) adverse to Dauphin, and the injunction was refused. Dauphin appealed the case to the Supreme Court of the United States. But the court of original jurisdiction had already sustained Key's order. It was valid and binding in law, in the hands of the postmasters who were bound to obey and enforce it; the Postmaster-General satisfied from evidence that the order was necessary, its immediate execution was about to be pressed. "What could be done to arrest the prompt, immediate execution of the order, so injurious, perhaps fatal, to the lottery represented by Dauphin?" Let the following order of Postmaster-General Key show what was actually done: —

POST OFFICE DEPARTMENT, WASHINGTON, D. C.,
Feb. 27, 1880.

SIR, — This party (M. A. Dauphin, Prest. of the La. S. Lottery Co.) having brought suit against me, to enjoin the performance of this order, and having appealed the same to the Supreme Court of the United States, and having this day presented the certificate of the Governor and state officers of the State of Louisiana that he has complied with all the legal requirements of that State, and other evidence; and "not being satisfied" from the evidence submitted to me that the said M. A. Dauphin is engaged in conducting a scheme or device for obtaining money through the mails by means of false and fraudulent pretenses and representations and promises, I do hereby authorize and direct the suspension of said order of November, 1879, so far as relates to said Dauphin, until the case shall have been heard and determined by the Supreme Court of the United States.

D. M. KEY, *Postmaster-General.*

To Postmaster New Orleans, La.,
and Postmaster New York, N. Y.

It is plain that the Postmaster-General had consented to a mere " suspension of said order of November, 1879: " a temporary suspension of that order until the case under appeal should have been heard and determined by the tribunal of last resort. The order of November, 1879, was not revoked or canceled. It was simply provided that, during the pendency of the appeal, the execution of that previous order should be suspended. Now we learn that the appeal was dismissed in vacation by the appellant's counsel, with the consent of the solicitor-general. This put an end to the suspension, and restored the binding effect of that previous order, as Postmaster-General Gresham justly maintains.

The notion " that Congress had not power to pass a law prohibiting the transmission through the ' mail,' and refusing its facilities for distributing matter deemed injurious to the public morals," corrupting publications and articles, and circulars concerning lotteries, institutions which are supposed to have a demoralizing influence upon the people, — because that would abridge the liberty of the press, deserves no further refutation.

When the fathers proclaimed in the Constitution of the United States that no senator or representative, in either house of Congress, shall be questioned in any other place for any speech or debate he may have made in Congress,[1] it was under the perfect conviction that the freedom, the most absolute freedom of discussion is necessary to expose error or delinquency, and to bring the truth into full light. And it was to secure this freedom of discussion that the first amendment to the Constitution was made, containing the clause respecting the liberty of speech and of the press: "Congress shall make no law abridging the freedom of speech or of the press."

Truth does good. On questions of a general and public nature, there is no means of discovering what is truth and what is error or imposture, but a full examination of the questions, with all their evidence and under all their aspects. Truth cannot gain by suppressing and restraining the production of facts and arguments. "If power be given to the government to say what opinions shall be published and what shall not be published, the whole knowledge, talent, and intellect of the country is under the absolute guidance and control of its political rulers." To decide what opinions shall be permitted and what prohibited is to choose opinions for the people. "The absolute power of suppressing opinions, if it could be exercised, would amount to a despotism far more perfect than any which has yet existed."[2] If general happiness and national prosperity be connected with the general diffusion of knowledge, and if knowledge be the result of freedom of inquiry, then it is truly said freedom of in-

[1] Constitution, Art. 1, Sect. 6.
[2] 6 Westminster Review, p. 290.

quiry is at least one of the main sources of national prosperity. Energy of intellect increases as the field of its exertion is extended; full and free discussion leads to public information and sound judgment. "Men are never," says Macaulay, "so likely to settle a question rightly as when they discuss it freely. A government can interfere in discussion only by making it less free than it would otherwise be."

The framers of the Constitution were wise, patriotic, and experienced; familiar with and properly appreciating the principles of public liberty existing in England, and which they brought to America, leaving all that was objectionable. They were great reformers.

Among the objections against the Constitution, it was contended that it provided no express protection of freedom of speech and of the press from the government about to be created, — a protection which English history painfully proved to be indispensable to general knowledge, to purity of government, and to true liberty. The atrocious cases of libel tried before the judicial tribunals of England, revolting to justice and humanity, showed the wisdom and necessity of the proposed amendment: and the promptitude and zeal with which it was supported evinced the good faith, patriotism, and regard for their posterity characteristic of the fathers.

The liberty of the press is the liberty of printing as well as the liberty of publishing. It consists in the right to publish freely the truth and sentiments on all subjects, with good motives and for justifiable ends. To publish is to make public, to announce, to disclose, to promulgate, to put forth or issue to the public. The press conveys the same thought to ten thousand minds at the same time: and the mighty power of public opinion, embodied in a free press, checks and controls human governments. "It is," says M. Thiers, "the privilege by means of which he who vainly lifts his voice against the corruptions or prejudices of his own time may leave his counsel upon record as a legacy to impartial posterity."

It was with full knowledge and a just appreciation of the liberty of the press that the power was vested in Congress " to establish post-offices and post-roads."

We have seen that the power possessed by Congress . embraces the regulation of the entire postal system of the country, — the carriage of the mail, its safe and speedy transport, the prompt delivery of its contents, and the designation of what shall be carried and what shall be excluded ; that Congress, in excluding various articles from the mail, did not intend to interfere with the freedom of the press or with any other rights of the people, by the act of March 3, 1873, but to refuse the facilities of the mail for the distribution of matter deemed injurious to the public morals. It meant, by the act, that the mail should not be used to transport such corrupting publications and articles (as those mentioned in the act), and that any one who attempted to use it for that purpose should be punished ; that the same inhibition has been extended to circulars of lotteries which are supposed to have a demoralizing influence upon the people ; and that the Supreme Court of the United States have emphatically declared, " Of the constitutionality of the act we have no doubt."

The liberty of the press consists in the right to publish with impunity truth, with good motives, for justifiable ends. It is the constitutional principle in our country that " every citizen may freely speak, write, and publish his sentiments, being responsible for the 'abuse' of that right, and that no law can rightfully be passed by Congress to abridge the freedom of the press."

To suppose that Congress is bound by this constitutional principle to aid in the transportation, distribution,

20

and circulation of immoral, corrupting publications and articles, contrary to its own judgment and the policy of enlightened States of the Union, through the national post-offices and post-roads and mail, for the purposes of a lottery system, a system of gambling, of delusion, and deception, of a general excitement for gain and of popular spoliation, — for instance, to entice citizens of New York State, bound by her law prohibiting lotteries, and to seduce them, in violation of her law, within her own territory, into gambling lottery contracts and business; and now to threaten to harass the officers, Postmaster-General of the United States and others, with suit for a proper exercise of their duty under the constitutional laws of Congress! Such is the claim and such the position of the Louisiana Lottery.

It is not necessary to notice at any extended length the pretended impossibility of enforcing the regulations of Congress as to what shall constitute mail matter, and, of course, what shall not, consistently with the fourth amendment of the Constitution of the United States, which proclaims, "The right of the people to be secure in their papers against unreasonable searches and seizures of papers shall not be violated; and no warrant shall be issued but upon probable cause, supported by oath or affirmation, describing the place to be searched, and the persons or things to be seized."

Undoubtedly, letters, and sealed packages subject to letter postage in the mail, are as fully guarded from inspection as if they were retained by the parties forwarding them in their own domiciles. The guaranty against unreasonable searches and seizures of papers extends to papers wherever they may be. But whilst regulations excluding matter from the mail cannot be enforced in a way which would require or permit an examination into letters, or sealed packages subject to letter postage, without warrant, issued upon oath or affirmation, in the search for prohibited matter, they may be enforced upon competent evidence of their violation obtained in other ways, as stated already in the extract from the decision of the Supreme Court.

Nor is it necessary to inquire how, by what evidence, what abracadabra, Postmaster-General Key or Postmaster General Howe became convinced that there was nothing "fraudulent" in the Louisiana Lottery business. If fraudulent means false, deceptive, misleading, delusive, it is impossible to find a word more strongly and truly descriptive of the character of the Louisiana State Lottery.

THE GOVERNMENT OF THE REPUBLICAN PARTY IN LOUISIANA.

[Extract from notes of a speech delivered by Mr. Hunt, in 1876, when the Hon. Francis T. Nichols was the Democratic candidate for Governor of the State against Mr. Stephen B. Packard, Republican.]

THE government of Louisiana is truly called the Kellogg government. It is a government of usurpation and tyranny. It was created by judicial fraud, and enforced by military despotism. It has been, and still is, upheld by the will of the President alone.

In its origin, it trampled upon the principle of popular representation, and substituted a barbarous horde of needy and greedy carpet-bag adventurers, and ignorant negroes, their deluded and unhappy dupes, in the place of the constitutional representatives of the State. The legislature thus composed was a band of oppressors and spoliators, who loaded the people with taxes to enrich themselves, their governor and his followers, and impoverished and ruined the owners of property.

It is known by acts hostile to liberty and free government, and injurious to the interests and the welfare of the people. A judiciary to uphold and support the acts of the legislature was of course established. Judges were selected for their supposed subserviency to the will of the executive and the behests of their party. With few, very few exceptions, they have been deemed corrupt and ignorant, and are justly held in public odium and contempt. The citizens of Louisiana have no confidence in the integrity, learning, and judgment of the existing judicial tribunals of their unhappy State. The executive department of the Kellogg dynasty is akin to the legislative and judiciary departments, and is well adapted to the purposes of tyranny and spoliation.

Its officers have been charged with breaches of public trust, false assessments of taxable property, and corrupt bargains with taxpayers, with defalcations and embezzlements. The governor himself, once poor, has become rich by gainful speculations, by means of legislative action. He has pardoned a large number of convicted felons, in contempt of law, justice, public opinion, and the peace and good order of society.

One act, for which, however, he has only been left responsible to public opinion, is the slaughter, under his authority, of a large number of our fellow-citizens on the 14th of September, 1874, — citizens whose sole objects and intentions on the occasion were to take possession of arms belonging to them, which they had imported legally, and which they had been obstructed unlawfully in obtaining.

He has several times deserted his office, left the State, and gone to Washington to poison by calumnies and false reports the mind and heart of the President against the people over whom he rules ; to procure troops to be sent to Louisiana to overawe the good citizens, white and colored, of the State ; to effect a rupture, if possible, between those citizens, allied together to choose honest and well-qualified public officers at the coming election ; and to continue, by means of the presence of a large armed force, a rule foreign and hostile to the State, — a rule of greed and corruption, of spoliation and wasteful expenditure for party and selfish purposes.

The means used to give a semblance of popular action to these outrages, grievances, oppressions, wrongs, and abuses were false registration acts and a pretended and miscalled returning board. They were inventions of a time when the noblest citizens of Louisiana were proscribed and disfranchised, and they descended as a legacy to Kellogg.

The registration frauds are familiar to you by the exposure made by a conservative committee of our citizens and the daily publications and comments of a well-informed and spirited press. The other abuse is the infamous returning board.

This board, under the stimulating encouragement and protection of the military power, notwithstanding it had no returns before it, officially announced the election of Kellogg to the gubernatorial chair. I know that there are many persons who fear that the board will again make a false report, equally unfounded, and in favor of Packard. But it is a false fear. The day for suffering such a fraud to be perpetrated has passed away. Every eye is fixed upon the election, every heart is determined on honesty in its conduct; and audacious as those in the service of our tyrants are, they will not dare again to trample upon the rights of a free, outraged, and offended people.

Supported by the full sense of right, by the Constitution and laws of their country, and by the sympathy and countenance of every lover of American liberty, they will maintain their liberties. The people are aroused and vigilant. Let them be calm and prudent, but determined not to be intimidated or cheated.

The presence of armed men, if that foul wrong should be effected, and the glitter of arms should inspire no fear in the breast of the patriot. In the last event, if unavoidable, it is better to die freemen than to live slaves. But the people of Louisiana will not be reduced to such an extremity. They are in a large majority, and, if undaunted, they will enjoy a peaceful and noble triumph. Louisiana will rise from her prostration, and stand, redeemed, regenerated, and disinthralled, with a pure, constitutional American government, — a State, the herald of liberty and prosperity.

When, at the instance of Packard, Casey, Judge Durell, and other officers of the United States resident here, Louisiana was converted by General Grant into a satrapy, and the ambitious and cunning but timid Kellogg was made its ruler, two assemblies claimed to be severally the legislature of Louisiana, — the McEnery legislature and the Kellogg legislature. Each of them elected a citizen to be a member of the Senate of the United States.

The claims of the two applicants for membership were severally considered, and both, after examination and due consideration, were rejected by the Senate, the constitutional and exclusive judges of the claims. Let us assume that their judgment was correct. Neither legislature was recognized as a constitutional and lawful body, whose presentment of a senator was entitled to acceptance. The facts reported by the committee of investigation showed that there was no republican state government in Louisiana.

The guaranty clause of the Constitution of the United States required the United States to secure to every State in the Union a republican form of government, but the government of the United States failed in its duty, and General Grant has held Louisiana from that day to this. Louisiana ceased to be an equal in the Senate of States of the Union, in the Senate of the United States, — a Senate of equals. Her people stand degraded and wronged as a people of a sovereign State.

The active politicians and party speakers of many of the States deny this statement.

Let us go early into the senate chamber at Washington. The roll is called. Massachusetts' two senators answer, and so of other States, until Louisiana is called. No two names then strike the ear. She has not her equal representation, her full right as a sovereign State, in the Senate, to which the Constitution entitles her; and why? She has been deprived of it by military tyranny, and Congress has failed to do her justice.

The patriotic senators of the North, the East, and the West should not fail to keep this fact in view. The wrong done to Louisiana is a blow to our constitutional system of government. What to-day is done against one State may be to-morrow done against another, unless the population of a great State should successfully resist the act of despotism. The danger to liberty is patent, and calls for the sympathy and coöperation of every patriot to overcome it.

Fellow-citizens of Louisiana! you are engaged in a great cause, — the assertion and restoration of your rights as a sovereign people, and the work of reform in your own State, by the election of honest, capable, and worthy men to the offices of the State.

I congratulate you upon your choice of a leader. General Nichols is known to us all. He is a well-educated, sensible, plain man, in every way worthy of confidence and support. He is honest, pure, and disinterested: not connected with rings or cliques: perfectly free to do right, and conscientiously bent on a faithful discharge of his duties. He is also a brave man, not to be deterred by any exhibition of military force or any sounding proclamation from addressing you without disturbance of temper and mind. Give your full vote to him, and those joined with him on the state ticket. His pledge of equal justice to every citizen, white or colored, will be fully redeemed.

COUNTING THE ELECTORAL VOTE.

[At the request of a great many of Mr. Hunt's friends, he wrote his views upon the powers of Congress, under the Constitution, in relation to the electoral votes of Louisiana, Florida, and South Carolina, in 1876.]

IT is a well-established historical fact that the creation of the Electoral Commission was an act passed by a conspiracy of the two great political parties or factions of the country to subvert the Constitution, and substitute in its stead, for the electoral count, a body of men which each of them believed would be devoted to itself, and would, therefore, make a fraudulent account for its favorite. It was a gambling game, which each believed it was safely playing with loaded dice against its adversary.

The conspiracy grew out of the demoralization of the times, a demoralization brought about chiefly by the state of feeling between the two great sections of the country towards each other long before the war, and leading to it, and, notwithstanding reunion and apparent harmony, still existing: by the corrupting nature and influences of the war; and by the following administration of the government under a successful military leader in a spirit of favoritism to his followers and relatives.

The act creating the Electoral Commission is the greatest wrong that has been done in civilized times to the cause of free government and popular liberty. An act of the legislature was made to subvert a certain portion of the Constitution: and the result of the subversion has been the defrauding the majority of a free people of their right to choose their chief magistrate, and substituting for an eminent citizen, elected by a majority of a quarter of a million of votes to the office, an obscure partisan of General Grant, — a man wholly unknown to fame, civil and military.

The wrong and the disgrace of this act, let it be fairly understood, are national, for it was passed by the representatives of the people in the two houses of Congress, and approved by President Grant, and has been submitted to by the people.

The great misfortune and injury of the act are the shock it has given to republican government, and the temptation it holds out to bad, ambitious men to make further invasions and inroads upon the Constitution and to destroy our free system of government. It remains for the people to bear in mind what has taken place, and to be careful with respect to those to whom they will give their confidence as their representatives in the future.

Men too easily overlook wrong-doing; and even the learned and experienced suffer themselves to be betrayed into submission by the success of iniquitous schemes. We have an instance of this kind of submission in a pamphlet which is now before us.

Judge Campbell, of this State, formerly of the Supreme Court of the United States, after writing a learned and able letter to the Hon. Thomas F. Bayard, a senator from Delaware, "on the powers of Congress over the returns for the electors," approving in the clearest and strongest terms the provisions of the Constitution on the subject, - having read " a synopsis of the report of the joint committee of the Senate and House of Representatives of the Congress of the United States relative to the subject he had considered," — pronounces his acceptance of it in the following strain : " It is a measure of high and magnanimous statesmanship, which manifests that

'Great men still live among us, — heads to plan,
And tongues that utter wisdom.'"

Let the errors, the manifest and dangerous errors of the learned, put sensible, plain men on their guard, and teach them to trust to their own honest and sound minds for guidance. Dare to be wise. Think for yourself. This is the patriot's motto.

The act creating the commission was passed in the fear that the assertion and maintenance of the vote of the majority for a President would break up the peace of the country, and lead immediately to an internecine war, which would probably end in the destruction of the Union and the overthrow of our American system of government. The fear was irrational and wholly unworthy of the citizens of our country as patriots and lovers of liberty. The vote of the majority was not the vote of a section of the country, but the full and fairly expressed choice of the whole nation. The people of America had not so degenerated from the manly virtues of their ancestors, courage and devotion to liberty, as to allow a military leader and his followers to destroy the republic, and upon its ruins to erect a fraudulent and tyrannical dominion over them. Had the choice of the people happily fallen upon one of the noble and high-spirited sons of the republic, — such as a Jackson, a Clay, a Webster, or a Calhoun, — their right of choice would have been asserted and respected, or, if in the madness of faction denied and opposed by arms, would have been honorably maintained and triumphantly established. And if, in this latter event, blood had been shed, copiously shed, as that of our fathers was in their revolutionary struggle against the greatest power of the earth, the sacrifice upon the altar of liberty would have been holy and pleasing in the sight of God and man.

The duty to count includes the duty to canvass the electoral votes; that is, to weigh and determine any objections made against particular certificates and votes, and to pronounce judgment. It is a deliberative and judicial duty, the duty of the two houses.

To inaugurate a President simply on the proclamation of the president of the Senate is a usurpation which the people will resist. If the two houses disagree, and if, upon the count, the fact appears that no person has the constitutional majority of votes, the function of the Senate, *pro hac vice*, ends; the duty of electing the President devolves, *ipso facto*, upon the House, and the duty of electing the Vice-President upon the Senate. The House is not to wait for the action of the Senate. It is the representative of the whole people of the United States, and is required "immediately" to choose the President.

.   .   .   .

Government is essential to man's happiness and existence. It must have power to protect the community against internal violence and disorders, and against dangers from abroad. This power, unless wisely limited and guarded, will be used by those who administer and control it for their own advantage and aggrandizement at the expense and to the oppression of the rest of the community. The evil and dangerous effect and tendency of this power and control may be seen even under our own government, and especially in the patronage and power of the President of the United States.

The large sums of money to be collected and disbursed by the government; the host of officers, agents, and others employed for its administration : the honors, emoluments, and other advantages it confers; the stations, salaries, patronage, and influence attending it, — all these lead to the formation of parties, a governing and a governed portion of the people, with the tendency to abuse of power by

the former. Mr. Webster, in speaking of this subject,
declared that the power and patronage of the President
had become dangerous to liberty, and that if ever he who
was the head of the nation became the mere head of a
party, that party would, by the power and patronage which
it grasped, maintain that power and any policy in direct
resistance to the will of a majority of the people, unless
that majority became overwhelming in numbers, or excited
only short of civil revolution.   Mr. Calhoun concurred in
this opinion, and pronounced the patronage in the hands
of the President too great for the magistrate of a free
people, greater than that of the autocrat of Russia, and
predicted that when the number of office-holders should
reach one hundred thousand the people might almost as
well surrender their liberty; the contest would be too
unequal.   Since the expression of these opinions the executive patronage has increased.   President Grant has, it
is said, designated the Republican party as his party, and
the number of office-holders has already exceeded one
hundred thousand.

On whom, then, does the duty devolve of ascertaining
and determining the election ?   It must be on the Senate
and House of Representatives, before whom the certificates
are opened and the votes are placed to be counted.

The Constitution is express: if there be no choice of
these high officers by the electors, the House of Representatives shall choose immediately by ballot the President,
and the Senate shall choose the Vice-President.   The duty
to act immediately upon the contingency implies the duty
to ascertain whether the contingency has arisen, — that
is, the fact whether any candidate has obtained the constitutional majority of the electoral votes; and this must be
done by the houses who supervise and see the result themselves.   When the fact is ascertained, neither house can
control the other.   The House cannot interfere with

the election of a Vice-President by the Senate, and, on the other hand, the Senate cannot control and direct the House not to elect a President. The command of the Constitution is peremptory, — "The House shall choose immediately by ballot;" and there is, under the Constitution, no other tribunal for the purpose.

To suppose that the Constitution required the Senate, composed of the senators of every State in the Union, and the House, composed of the representatives of all the people of the United States, to attend for the mere idle purpose of looking on and seeing electoral votes counted is childish; and to contend that the houses have no authority or power to examine into and determine the truth and validity of the certificates and votes, and so to count, ascertain, and determine the result, and to act thereon, is unreasonable and unconstitutional.

But the attempt is now made to establish a doctrine which, if approved, will maintain and give effect to fraud, and lead to the overthrow of American government.

It is said "that the certificates transmitted by electors of a State, appointed in the manner its legislature directs, are conclusive evidence of the votes of the State, and that the votes must be counted as true and binding on the people of the entire nation, however false and fraudulent."

It is impossible that the framers of the Constitution intended to sanction such a principle. No argument is necessary on the subject.

True votes, constitutional and honest, should be counted. Unconstitutional, false, and fraudulent votes must be rejected. The power and duty to count the true votes only necessarily includes the right and duty to reject false votes. Honest certificates, made in due legal form by the proper state authorities, are undoubtedly conclusive; but certificates, no matter how formally and solemnly executed, are absolutely void when proved to be tainted with fraud, corruption, and immorality.

Our entire system of governments, national and state, rests upon the people their virtue and intelligence. The ends aimed at by all the Constitutions are truth, liberty, and justice.

In 1865 a joint rule of Congress was adopted, and has since been followed. It was framed by a joint committee appointed to report " a mode for examining the votes for President and Vice-President of the United States."

It has been briefly and correctly stated : " Not a single presidential vote has been counted, from 1793 to 1872, both inclusive, in which Congress did not assume, by express and formal words, or by action, or by both together, that it possessed the undoubted power and duty ' to examine' the electoral votes." No electoral vote has ever been counted against the objection of either house. The famous twenty-second joint rule, " that no vote objected to by either house should be counted," only expressed what had been embraced in previous orders, or the action of the houses, and was the practical construction by them of their constitutional power in this respect.

.   .   .   .

The press has laid before the people of the country, in numerous essays and communications, a full and clear statement and review of the procedure or usual practice of counting the electoral votes for President. It has always been under the direction of the two houses of Congress. In 1789, when General Washington was first elected President, there was no Vice-President, and the framers of the Constitution made a special provision for the election necessary to the inauguration of the new government. But at the next election, in 1793, the houses named tellers, one for the Senate and one for the House, who presented a list of the votes, which was read to the two houses, and the result was declared.

In 1797, John Adams, the Vice-President, declaring the result of the election, said: "By the report of the tellers appointed by the two houses, there are," etc., and proceeded, "In obedience to the Constitution and law of the United States, and to the command of both houses of Congress, expressed in their resolution, I declare," etc. In 1877 an objection was first made to receive an electoral vote in the case of Indiana, and the houses at once withdrew to consider it.

In counting the electoral votes, the houses, though in joint session, are distinct bodies. The votes of the several States are offered in distinct regular order. Those not objected to are received as genuine and true, openly announced, and severally entered and put upon the list as parts of the count. Those challenged and objected to are set apart for consideration and for final action until all the votes not objected to are entered upon the list. If a person has, out of the votes not objected to, the number of votes required by the Constitution for an election, he shall be the President, and no further notice or decision upon the challenged votes is necessary. If no person shall receive the requisite number of votes, and the two houses differ as to the validity of the votes objected to, each house must act for itself, and the duty of each is to decide for itself. The Constitution is express: if no person shall receive the requisite number of votes, the House of Representatives shall choose immediately by ballot the President; and, in a like contingency, the Senate shall choose a Vice-President.

This duty cannot be performed without ascertaining that no person has received the requisite majority: it depends upon the state of the electoral vote. The duty is urgent.

The Constitution has not provided for a notification to the House that there has been no election for President by the electors. It leaves the House sole judge of the happening of the contingency calling for its action. As one of the counters for the electoral vote, the House must know whether that vote has resulted in a choice. The House is therefore left to act upon its own knowledge, and is directed, in the contingency of which it is itself to be the judge, to proceed to elect the President. The Senate cannot interfere and forbid the House to elect. The duty, the entire business of the election, is confided and confined to the House, to men chosen directly by the people. The Senate has nothing to do with it.

. . . .

Mr. Morton has said: " The effect of this section is to determine which set [of electoral returns] is to be counted; and if the two houses do not agree, neither set is to be counted." And again : " The vote goes out; the State has no vote ; because unless there is some tribunal to settle which vote shall be counted you cannot count both, and therefore you cannot count either. You must have some tribunal to settle that difficulty, and what tribunal is safer than the two houses of Congress ? " And again : " I do not accept the suggestion that the Vice-President of the United States has anything more to do in the business of counting the votes for President and Vice-President than that specific duty which is prescribed for and enjoined upon him by the Constitution. That duty is, in the presence of the Senate and House of Representatives to open the certificates. There being no other duty assigned to him, I infer, naturally, that he is to do nothing more. . . . There can be, under the Constitution, no tribunal to decide on that [two sets of returns] or any other question arising in the course of counting the votes. The duty is imposed upon the two houses of Congress. They alone can perform it."

Senator Christiancy argued that even without a joint
21

rule or Mr. Morton's bill, it was a reasonable conclusion that if two sets of electoral returns were presented, and the two houses could not agree upon the reception of one of the two, "there is nothing to turn the scale in favor of either. . . . Could the vote be counted? Certainly not." It being urged that it was a serious matter to deprive a State of its vote, Mr. Morton replied : "There are two sets [of returns]. The Senate resolves in favor of one set, the House resolves in favor of the other set. There is a disagreement. The Senator from Ohio [Mr. Thurman] said that it was the intention that the State should have a vote, and so say I. The intention is that the State shall have a vote, but if the thing is in that condition that Congress cannot determine which is the correct vote, it will be the misfortune of the State if the vote is lost. That is all you can say about it."

The vote in the Senate upon this measure shows that the Republican party has approved and adopted the true constitutional rule and principle which has uniformly prevailed from the organization of the government. that it is the right and the duty of the two houses to examine the electoral votes and determine the result. The appointment of a special committee by the Senate now in session, and the appointment of a special separate committee by the House to investigate the charges of fraud against the recent return of the electoral votes in Louisiana, and the request and quasi-appointment of a party committee of inquiry by President Grant. avowedly for the same purpose, and his communication by message to each house of Congress of their report, are further instances of practical construction by the executive, as well as by Congress. of the duty of each house to determine for itself what electoral votes are valid and shall be counted.

The mode of procedure in this matter is clearly pointed out by the Constitution and law.

The Senate and House of Representatives will assemble in the hall of the House at a time appointed, and the president of the Senate will be their presiding officer. Tellers will be appointed on the part of the Senate, and tellers on the part of the House. The certificates of the electoral votes shall then be opened and handed to them, to be acted upon in the alphabetical order of the States. The tellers will read them in the presence and hearing of the two houses, and make a list of the votes as they appear ; and, the votes having been counted, the result will be delivered to the president of the Senate, who shall thereupon announce the state of the vote, and the names of the persons, if any, elected. If, upon the reading of any certificate by the tellers, a question shall arise in regard to counting the votes therein certified, the presiding officer shall state the same ; whereupon the Senate shall withdraw, and the question shall be submitted to it for its decision. And the Speaker of the House shall, in like manner, submit the question to the House of Representatives for its decision. When the two houses have voted they shall immediately reassemble, and the presiding officer shall announce the decision of the question.

If persons have, out of the votes counted, the number of votes required by the Constitution for an election, they shall be, respectively, the President and Vice-President. If no person receive the requisite number of votes for President, the House of Representatives shall choose immediately, by ballot, the President, and, in a like contingency, the Senate shall choose a Vice-President.

. . . .

TRIBUTE TO MR. TULANE.

[Mr. Paul Tulane, a prominent and benevolent citizen of Louisiana, donated about one million dollars to the University of that State. At the opening of the law school Professor Hunt paid the following tribute to Mr. Tulane.]

GENTLEMEN, — Welcome! welcome to this hall of science, this school of profitable knowledge to the industrious and reflecting student! A short delay in the opening of the college has been occasioned by the resignation of Professor Eustis, and by the duty of the Faculty to supply the vacancy properly. That duty has just been happily performed, and the usual course of lectures is commenced under auspicious circumstances by a complete Faculty.

Since the last season of the college a great change has taken place in the fortune and administration of the University of Louisiana, and in the destination of the University to promote public education in the State. Mr. Paul Tulane, a wealthy and public-spirited citizen, formerly a merchant of this city, has beneficently donated about one million dollars for fostering, maintaining, and developing the University of Louisiana, and of so expanding it as to create it a great " University of the City of New Orleans." And it is further announced by his honorable and trustworthy friends that he will increase his noble gift twofold more.

Moved by this generous and philanthropic act in favor of public education in this State, the legislature of the State has passed an act to receive the donation as made, and, in accordance with the views of the donor, to change the administration of the University, substituting a body of intelligent, well-known citizens of high character in the city of New Orleans as a permanent board of administrators for the late board, as legally constituted, and empowering the new board to fill in the future the vacancies that may occur in their body. The board thus made is purely of an honorary character, and will discharge its duties disinterestedly and with a single view to the public good.

And the legislature of the State, properly appreciating the noble act of Mr. Tulane for the instruction of his fellow-men, has fitly incorporated his name with that of the University which he has sustained, and contributed to enlarge and increase in fame and usefulness. I have thought it my duty to communicate this information to you, gentlemen, as students of the law college, a department of the Tulane University of Louisiana. And, gentlemen, I cannot conclude these preliminary remarks without expressing my conviction that our University is destined to become, under the government of its public-spirited, able, and learned President, and its enlightened and liberal board of administrators, what its generous patron expressly desires it to be, — a great university in the city of New Orleans and an honor to the State of Louisiana, imparting the manifold and various blessings of liberal and useful knowledge to her sons and to their worthy brethren, the youth of her surrounding sister States.

ADDRESS TO MEDICAL STUDENTS.

[Remarks made by President Hunt to graduating medical students of the University of Louisiana.]

GENTLEMEN, — I congratulate you upon the completion of your collegiate studies, and hail you as doctors of medicine. You are about to enter upon the practice of a profession that commands the admiration, the respect and gratitude of all men, civilized and barbarous.

The Greek mythologists deified Æsculapius ; and their scholars tell us that Pluto, incensed at his withholding those he claimed as his subjects, induced Jupiter to strike him dead with thunder. Under the benign influence of the religion of our day, you, gentlemen, sons of Æsculapius, free from fear of angry deities, are left at liberty to practice your mission with the blessings of God and man. Yours is indeed a noble profession ; it is essential to the well-being and happiness of society.

Health is the first blessing of life. It stimulates to action, gives strength to labor, and crowns industry with success and joy. It is the source of our sweetest affections and the charm of our brief existence.

It is impossible to free the condition of man from death. But disease does no good to the individual or to society. It is attended with pain and anguish of body and mind, with great uneasiness and anxiety to the relatives of the sick. It paralyzes productive industry, and is an unmixed evil ; for which, however, Providence has furnished man, by his intellectual faculties, the means of alleviation or cure.

It is then that the physician is sought for aid. Having studied the structure of man, and the derangements and diseases which assail it, having studied also his intellectual structure, his passions, motives of action, and habits, he eradicates disease, assuages pain in the suffering body, and ministers to the mind diseased.

Here, gentlemen, I would impress upon you a full sense of the charge that you have assumed, and of its influence and service to the cause of morality and religion. It is to minister to the ailments, sufferings, and afflictions, corporeal and mental, of your brother man; to raise him from the bed of sickness, and restore him to health, strength, and usefulness; to minister to his mind diseased; to calm his passions, and regulate and direct his affections; to soothe his wounded spirit; to lift him from despondency, grief, despair; to cheer, to animate and impel him to the exercise of his reason and all his powers and energies. A seasonable word, says an eminent and wise son of Massachusetts, unobtrusively uttered by a serious and enlightened man, who stands at the bedside, clothed by the imagination of the patient, if not in reality, with the power of health, of life and death, will often sink deep into the heart, and prove a safeguard of morals and character.

Truly, gentlemen, this is an inspiring and noble undertaking. For this you have fitted yourselves by scientific labor and moral training. The occasion and the exercises of the day do not admit of my expatiating on the field here opened for the exercise of the intellect and the cardinal virtues of the heart. It only remains for me to express the wish and trust that your efforts to be useful and to minister relief may meet with due success, and be crowned with the blessings of Providence and the love and honor of your fellow-men.

SPEECH FOR BELL AND EVERETT.

[The following description of a Bell and Everett political meeting, held in Philadelphia on August 15, 1860, is taken from the "Philadelphia Enquirer" of that date.]

THE BELL AND EVERETT CAMPAIGN.

SERENADE TO HON. RANDELL HUNT OF LOUISIANA.

ENTHUSIASM AND EXCITEMENT.

THE citizens of Philadelphia, under the lead of many personal and political friends of Hon. Randell Hunt of Louisiana, tendered him a public serenade last evening at the Continental. The entire affair, which was more immediately under the auspices of the Minute Men of Philadelphia, passed off in the most pleasant and creditable manner.

THE MINUTE MEN.

As early as seven o'clock the scene presented at the club-room at the northeast corner of Tenth and Chestnut streets afforded a gratifying indication of the enthusiasm with which the Minute Men had entered into the spirit of the affair. It is described by those who were fortunate enough to be present to have been a "perfect jam." The stairs, sidewalks, and street were crowded, thus rendering access to the hall an utter impossibility.

At eight o'clock, the Club, accompanied by Beck's full brass band, marched through a number of our most popular thoroughfares.

SCENE AT THE CONTINENTAL.

At half past nine o'clock, as they arrived in front of the Continental, the scene presented from the balcony exceeded in interest anything we have ever been privileged to behold, from the same standpoints, either in the political or in the Japanese line. The streets, from curb to curb, were literally packed with a dense immobile mass of humanity, while the right of way, as far as the passenger railway cars were concerned, was for the nonce totally ignored.

Cheers and shouts for the Union candidate rent the air, while the ringing of innumerable bells added emblematical significance to the popular tumult. As the head of the procession reached Ninth Street, a number of Southern belles, guests of the hotel, stood upon the balcony and waved their handkerchiefs in expression of their " sentiments," and general adherence to the tenor of the inscriptions, mottoes, etc., upon the transparencies. As some of these were unusually expressive and extremely well worded, we have jotted down a few : —

" The Minute Men of '76 and '56."

" Beware! a base counterfeit! The Continental issue of 1856."

" Query — Are Abe's rails used on the underground railroad ? "

" Rails are a good institution, but we do not intend to ride on them to the White House."

" Sambo can't ring this bell ! "

" Uncle Sam says Abe can't be elected because he keeps colored company."

At the head of the procession was a large bell, which was rung incessantly until the commencement of Mr. Hunt's speech, and at those appropriate points where the " applause came in."

One of the largest and most beautiful transparencies in the line was one representing the American patriot in the time of '76, leaving his ploughshare to hasten to the field of battle. Two medallion portraits of the respective Union candidates were also exhibited, eliciting general commendation for their faithfulness and artistic coloring. We cannot avoid mentioning a pictorial representation of Old Abe standing on the shores of the Ohio, with a firebrand in his hand, and about to throw a stone or two at Kentucky.

At one point, previous to the commencement of the speaking, some individual, whose excited feelings were perfectly natural under the circumstances, proposed three cheers for Bell, which were given with stentorian energy. Cheers were also proposed for Stephen A. Douglas, but a low muttering was the only response. About half past nine o'clock, Judge King, of this city, stepped upon the balcony, and said : —

"Fellow-citizens, I introduce to you Mr. Hunt of Louisiana. [Cheers.] He is one of the electors at large for the State of Louisiana, and when you have heard him I think you will agree with me that the *no chance* of John Bell is an obsolete idea. [Cheers.]"

SPEECH OF THE HON. RANDELL HUNT.

FELLOW-CITIZENS, — I appear before you to-night at the request of the Executive Committee of the Union Constitutional party of Pennsylvania [cheers], a private citizen, unknown to more than two or three of this vast multitude that I see before me. It seems yet to have been sufficient to state to you that I appear before you an elector selected by the Union party of Louisiana, as a candidate for elector of President of the United States from Louisiana, to insure this heartfelt greeting. I thank you for it. In the name of the Union party of Louisiana,

I receive it as a token of the brotherly feeling that the Unionists of Pennsylvania feel for the Unionists of the South. [Cheers.]

I know, fellow-citizens, where I am. I am in the old State of Pennsylvania, — one of the glorious old thirteen, famous for her love of liberty, the Union, and the Constitution. [Cheers.] The keystone of the federal arch will support this Union, and by the aid of which this Union will stand, I trust, forever. [Cheers.] I am in the city of Philadelphia, — this beautiful city, with its magnificent private structures, with its splendid public edifices, abounding in brave men and beautiful women. [Cheers.] Dear, no doubt, to every Pennsylvanian, and equally dear to every true-hearted American, for this, that in her Hall of Independence, in the Congress of 1776, was passed the glorious resolution which declared these colonies no longer subject to the King of Great Britain, but free and independent States. [Cheers.]

Yesterday I went down to old Independence Hall to refresh my patriotism and kindle anew the fire of love of country, which has never yet left my heart; and as I walked around and beheld the old bell that proclaimed "liberty throughout the land and unto all the inhabitants thereof," and as I turned my face to the venerated statue of that man who above all mortals must deserve the reverence of the Sons of Liberty, George Washington [prolonged cheers], and as I looked around, fellow-citizens, as I beheld these ancient things connected with our revolutionary history, as the grand swelling sentiments of liberty filled my heart, I could not help exclaiming to myself, "Glorious Philadelphia! [Cheers, and cries of "Good!"] Glorious Pennsylvania!"

Born thousands of miles away from this spot, I yet feel that I have a part of the glory and fame of Washington. I know that I was born far from this spot, but is patriot-

ism connected with a single spot? No, fellow-citizens. It
consists in the love of the fame of the great men of our
country, and I tell you now my heart swells within me
up to my very lips as I say I am proud to address you
here this night as fellow-citizens of the United States.
[Cheers.]

I have nothing new to tell you : I have nothing, fellow-
citizens, to say to you with which you are not already
familiar, — that you have not already heard from your
favorite orators, or that you will not hereafter hear from
orators in better terms and in more glowing language
than I can possibly use ; yet, as I have been called upon
to address you, as I am an elector at large in the support
of the glorious Union ticket that has been presented to
the people of the United States, I felt that I would be
derelict to my duty if I did not come forward and say
something to you.

Fellow-citizens, we are almost upon the eve of a presidential election. Whenever this time comes round, whenever the lustrum in which we are to elect a President of
the United States occurs, there is always something,
some question of great importance, before the people.
But it appears to me that, from the origin of our government to the present day, there has never been any
question, any issues, more important than those that are
now presented to the public ; for they are not only issues
that affect the policy of the country, but they are issues
that affect the very existence of the government.

It is now, fellow-citizens, some seventy-two years, or
nearly seventy-two, since the Constitution of the United
States, under which we now live, went into operation.
During that period numerous elections have been held for
Presidents of the United States : most of these elections
have been made by the electors, and a few of them
have been made by the House of Representatives of the

Congress of the United States. All this has been done peaceably and calmly, — everything in good order, — our government efficient. Presidents have died, and Vice-Presidents have succeeded them. The laws have been enforced, — everything done without commotion, without popular tumult, without any undue excitement, without any relaxation of the law.

Now, before this Constitution went into operation, or rather, just as it was going into operation, it would be difficult for any man to describe the deplorable condition of our country. The State had the honor of regulating commerce for herself. The consequence was that a State like Pennsylvania, ripe for manufactures, anxious perhaps to encourage her domestic industry, might feel it her duty to lay an impost upon the importation of goods from abroad.

But if she did so, her neighboring State, not ready for manufactures, not yet prepared for their introduction, believing that it would be for her advantage to introduce goods without any duties whatever, could effectually countervail all the legislation of Pennsylvania. And why? Because the goods, when imported into any one State, could be carried immediately, free of duties, into another State. Thus it happened, I say, that at the time when the Constitution of the United States went into operation, the policy of one State was frustrated by the policy of another. Did one State attempt to encourage its domestic industry, it was checked by the legislation of another State. There was a commerce of Massachusetts, a commerce of Rhode Island, a commerce of Pennsylvania, but there was no commerce of the United States.

The consequence was that we were completely at the mercy of foreign nations, and especially at the mercy of our great trader, Great Britain, whom, though we had conquered in war and achieved our independence, we were yet subjected to by our commercial laws. Well, fellow-citizens, for the purpose of correcting this, for the purpose of making our commerce one, for the purpose of creating a national government for national purposes, leaving a local government for merely local purposes, the present Constitution of the United States was adopted; and what has been the consequence?

Immediately our country entered upon a career of prosperity such as the sun of Heaven had never before witnessed in the history of the world. Look at our condition then; look at it now! While we were a nation consisting of three or four millions of persons, what are we now? The census returns are not completed, but, beyond a doubt, our population will swell to thirty-two millions of people. Instead of a narrow strip along the border of the Atlantic Ocean, we have a vast extent of territory, extending from the Atlantic clear over to the Pacific Ocean. From the St. Lawrence to the Gulf of Mexico our territory extends.

Our States from thirteen have advanced to thirty-three. Thus, fellow-citizens, advancing in territory, thus advancing in population, we advance at the same time in the arts and in the sciences, in refinement and in literature. Liberty was preserved, — liberty of speech, liberty of conscience, liberty of action, liberty to speak, the highest liberty that man can enjoy under Heaven. [Cheers.]

All these liberties we have enjoyed. Look at our material progress! Look at our progress in agriculture; look at our progress in manufactures: look at our progress in commerce! Why, our agriculture is so varied that we produce almost everything that can be found upon the face of the earth. Look what our manufacturers have done! Aided by the proper encouragement of government, our home manufacturers have learned to imitate the foreign manufactures, and so work at home materials until they equal the manufactures from abroad.

Look at our commerce! See how it spread its wings
when the little restraints and bars of local legislation and of
state provisions were removed! Like an uncaged eagle
it flew abroad, to every portion of the earth. See the
sails of our commerce whiten every sea, and our government has been tried in peace and in war. In times of a
little local excitement there may have appeared some
little opposition to law, but where upon the face of God's
earth, in despotic Russia, in France, in more enlightened
and liberal England, where has the law been so constantly and so faithfully enforced as it has been in the
general government of the United States? I say, fellow-
citizens, nowhere! [Cheers.] And while this has been
done, while our commerce has increased, while the resources of our country have become infinite and unex-
haustible, what has been done for the glory and renown
of this free republic on earth? Where else is there a
leader of liberty throughout the enlightened world?
where the man who, when he hears the sound of liberty, does not turn his eyes instinctively to America?
[Cheers.]

I have said this government has been tested in peace
and in war. In peace she has executed the laws in spite
of the resistance of lawless men. In spite of the threats
of state authorities, the general government, calm and
unmoved, has gone on and executed the laws; it has protected the liberties of every man before me. I say it,
and I challenge denial that it has done all this without
infringing upon the liberty of a single individual.
[Cheers.] Who can point out a man who has been deprived of his liberty or property by the government of
the United States?

And if these are the operations of government in peace,
what have they been in war? Shall I refer to the War
of 1812? — for I pass by now at once our glorious Revolution.

[The speaker then referred in detail to the policy of the general government during the war with Mexico. He explained that the Constitutional Union party had had its origin in the desire of the good men of all sections of the country to put an end to the unceasing criminations and recriminations of the Northern and Southern States.]

We have formed a party that has carried Kentucky by nearly thirty thousand majority; we have formed a party that will carry Virginia as sure as to-morrow's sun will rise. Tennessee is with us, and North Carolina will be with us. They tell you Louisiana is unsound. I deny it. She is sound to the very core. She is true to the Union. She will vote for John Bell and Edward Everett. [Cheers.]

I tell you, gentlemen, the South will present almost a united front. [Cheers.] South Carolina will be misled by her politicians, it is possible that Georgia may go astray, but I venture to say that at least twelve out of the fifteen States will cast their electoral votes for John Bell and Edward Everett. [Cheers.]

I believe that you can do much. I believe that you can effect what you desire if you only go to work, and my hope is in this. You have not heretofore done your best; many of you have abstained from voting. Do your duty, and may God be with us and protect our country and our liberty. [Cheers.]

On the conclusion of this eloquent speech, Hon. H. Bucher Swoope, being loudly called for, came forward and briefly addressed the assemblage. He said that the hour was extremely late. He hoped he would have other opportunities during the campaign of addressing his friends. At present he would not detain them, and therefore proposed that the meeting should adjourn.

INDEX.

22

www.ingramcontent.com/pod-product-compliance
Lightning Source LLC
Chambersburg PA
CBHW021337110726
47900CB00005B/1508